CRESCENT

MARY JANE CAPPS

Copyright © 2017 by Mary Jane Capps

ISBN: 978-0-9992614-0-8

All rights reserved.

No part of this book may be reproduced in any form or by any electronic
or mechanical means, including information storage and retrieval
systems, without written permission from the author, except for the use
of brief quotations in a book review.

To Jake and Bronnie, for being who they are.

*P*eople lie when they tell you that time heals all wounds. As far as I can tell, the gash on my heart keeps widening.

The smell of freshly brewed coffee is calling to me from the café below, but I'm not going to get up. I'm too busy trying to get my dead grandmother to talk to me.

I lay colorful cards out before me, feeling as though I'm trying to crack some kind of code, and really, I am, as I run my thumb along each glossy surface—each secret symbol.

Judgment. The Fool. The Hermit. Death. The Tower. The Lovers. The Wheel of Fortune. The Moon . . . I set this one aside. *Justice. The Empress. The Hierophant* (like Father Brian). *The World. The Star. The High Priestess* (reminds me of GG). *The Hanged Man. The Devil. The Chariot. The Emperor. Temperance. The Magician. The Sun. Strength.*

Spades, hearts, diamonds, and clubs; staffs, cups, swords, and pentacles. I flit through these mindlessly and stop on the Nine of Swords. This one makes me uneasy. I saw my GG pull it many times, and it usually wasn't good. The card reeks of despair.

GG used to say, *"As long as you have a drop of magic in your blood and a beat of love in your chest, nothing can really kill you, not here in the Crescent City."*

I've got the love, but my magic must be broken, because I haven't been able to connect with her since she left her body. Everyone loses their grandma, but not everyone loses their best friend when she goes.

"Stella!" My mother's voice comes up through the vent in my bedroom floor.

I roll my eyes and continue to rummage through my "GG Treasure Trove," an old gray tackle box that lives inside a drawer in my vanity dresser. I stop to admire an old black-and-white photograph of my grandmother. She's wearing a lacy bridal gown, arm in arm with my long-dead grandpa on their wedding day—each of them young and beaming. I smile at the sight and shuffle through the rest of the pile. All the other photographs are of GG and a bunch of random men.

An open pack of stale Pall Mall cigarettes makes everything else in the drawer stink, and yet, I can't let go of them . . . can't let go of *her.* A shiny Zippo lighter mirrors the late morning sunlight streaming through my open window, causing the engraved words to glow: *"Darling Evie."*

A soft tune from a jazz trumpeter outside swims into my ears. The melody is sadder than usual. I flip open the Zippo lid for the thousandth time and spin the flint wheel to light a candle. No flame. It's finally run out of lighter fluid.

"Stella!" Time to apply some more charcoal eyeliner. There's no such thing as too much of it.

It's been two years since she died. Sometimes it feels like no time has passed. And sometimes, it feels like forever.

"Happy Birthday, GG," I murmur to my reflection, as if it could be her looking back at me. Same round face, dark hair . . . if I squint my eyes just right, I could almost pass for the young bride in the photo. "You promised we'd always be close. You *promised*." I keep my vision blurred, waiting, hoping.

"Stel-*la*!" I glance at my phone. 11:15. Lunch rush. "Fine." I sigh. I put the cards back in their box, wrap a lavender scarf loosely around them, pull my apron off my doorknob and tie it around my waist, then bound downstairs to the café.

Evie's Creole Café is one very positive tribute to my grandmother, although, come to think of it, I don't remember her cooking much.

Only a few of the recipes were Evie's own creations. Some were hybrids of hers and Mama's (beignets with Nutella, anyone? Mmm . . .), and some have been in our family for generations. My mother told me she'd

3

consider sharing the secret ingredient in our praline crumble pie with me on her deathbed.

I pull my hair into a loose ponytail, straighten my apron, and push open the door from the old servant's quarters to the kitchen.

"Two beignet plates and a Stack of Toast!" My best friend, Colette, calls out, making my mouth water.

"Stack of Toast" is café-speak for our super fluffy French toast drizzled in Mama's own concoction of local honey and maple syrup with a few added spices. One of my favorites.

"Gross, Stella." Colette laughs as I ladle the syrup concoction into a coffee mug and down it like it's water. *Mmm...*

"You just don't get my sophisticated palate."

Colette raises one eyebrow in disgust. She happens to be one of the most stunning girls around. The girl's got perfect mocha skin, with not a single strand of her long dark hair out of place. She only wears a little makeup. Okay, maybe she wears a normal amount. Colette has this classic elegance, a preppy beauty. She's like a Haitian American Audrey Hepburn.

I also have long dark hair, but it gets in my way constantly, and the jury's still out on my very round face. I was kind of hoping it was a babyish feature I would grow out of. Not yet. My skin is very white with a fair amount of freckles. I'm good with that, except that any blemish shows up like a neon sign.

"All right, let's MOVE, girls!" My dad claps—his huge

hands startling me. He's like an overgrown kid, and my mother is like a tiny blonde ballerina moving to the waltz of the stove. She jumps back from her skillet of frying beignets.

"My *Lord,* Ben, you can't do that right by my ear! I could start a grease fire!" she yells.

"Sorry, Moni." He kisses her on the forehead. He towers over Mama's petite frame, but her strength seems to add to her stature. My mama is the queen of this kingdom, the beignets her loyal subjects.

"It's all right," she says. "I know we don't have much time to clear out the lunch crowd before the Courteau event."

Colette and I look at each other and groan. We've obviously both forgotten about the dreaded party.

The Courteaus were celebrating the birthday of Lucille Courteau, mother and matriarch of the family. It's anyone's guess how old she's turning. She's very beautiful, although she's now a bit on the eerily smooth side a la Botox.

I pull myself together, remembering that not only is my mom stressed about the Courteau event, but she's also working to clear out the café by late afternoon so we can visit GG's grave before dark.

The cemeteries in New Orleans are notoriously dangerous at night. Getting mugged while visiting a deceased loved one is a real downer. Since today would have been GG's eighty-second birthday, we will leave a bouquet of orchids—her favorite flower. Maybe that's what really has my mother on edge? I suspect she's finding a little distraction in the business of the café.

"Stella, the linens! Where are they?"

Ummm . . . folded up in a corner of the kitchen, where they were when she told me to iron them this morning.

She rushes over to the pile, trying desperately to shake them out.

"Mama, I'm sorry, I totally spaced it. But they look fine. No one will notice the wrinkles." I grab one and start shaking it out with her.

"No one will notice? Have you met Lucille Courteau?" she asks sarcastically.

Lucille Courteau has been a good customer, but she's not the warmest person. All right, she gives me the creeps. My mom defended her once after they did charity work together. *"A little chilly, but it would be odd to marry into such a family. A lot of pressure."*

The word "chilly" is generous now. Lucille's been standoffish since I first met her, but in the last year or so, the woman's turned ice cold. It's like her snootiness has become a tumor that's taken over her whole body. Mama rips a cloth from my hand and furiously tries to wipe the creases smooth. It's just too freaking much for me to take.

"You're being crazy, Mama." I glare at her.

"Crazy?" Her voice rises to a high-pitch frequency that only dogs and I can hear.

"Yeah." I'm boldly sticking to this word. "Crazy.

Everything will be fine." I try to pull the wrinkled linen back from her. When GG was around, it was a struggle for my mom and me, but GG acted as a buffer between us. Now it's like a fight with no referee.

"Why don't I just take these? I can iron them quickly." Dad steps in, gently taking the linens from our hands. He attempts to fill in as mediator, but it never works. Not like it did with GG.

At a quarter past one, the restaurant is nearly empty. Colette brings checks to the remaining guests while I polish our antique silver candlesticks. Colette's mom, Dena, helps bus the tables before heading back to the kitchen to help my mother with the cooking.

The final customers leave. I make my way into the small entry room, past the overstuffed green couch where patrons squeeze together when they're waiting for a table. I hang a "Closed for Private Party" sign on the front door and gaze over the dining room to check any last-minute issues. Colette has topped the tables with the now smooth white cloths. My mother carefully places each setting.

Light from the large windows bathes the old brick walls in a golden glow. Our mismatched family china sparkles on shelves lining the main room. This place has been in my family for well over a hundred years. People ask me if it's weird, letting strangers in my house to eat every day. What they don't realize is that I never feel like it's just my family here. Long after closing time, my home feels crowded. Over a century of parties, weddings, receptions, deaths (even a duel, I believe), leaves a place coated in palpable energy. There has been more than one instance of a spooky occurrence, though my mom likes to pretend it's not so.

I begin placing white tapers into the candlesticks when the jingling of the bell over the door alerts me to company.

Jack Courteau. Lucille and Richard produced offspring: one scarily good-looking son to match nicely with their Mattel-style family.

Jack, something of a mystery, has grown up in only the finest of prep schools. Apparently, he begged his parents to let him leave the all-boys middle and high school behind and begin tenth grade with the rest of us. At least, that's the rumor. I know more than a few girls who can't wait to share oxygen with him, and even though I'd rather not admit it, I'm more than a little curious about him myself.

"My mom wanted me to bring these for the party . . . ." He holds an open box with tall copper candlesticks poking out. His voice trails off as he notices the freshly polished ones I'd set out. "Sorry"—he frowns —"my mom can be kind of . . . well." He ended on that, as if he'd just explained everything about her. And he kind of had.

"No worries," I say quickly, but he's obviously embarrassed.

"You want something to drink?"

"A cup of your chicory would be great. My name's

Jack by the way." He's a mixture of his parents—two pretty people and something else. Something different that I can't quite put my finger on.

"I know. I mean, I'm Stella. You've never dined here before, have you? Just the pick-up pastry orders?"

"Right. I've always wanted to eat here, but my mom insisted we celebrate special occasions at Rouge."

Rouge was an overpriced restaurant down the street that had fooled patrons for the last decade into believing their food was good because the portions were tiny and the atmosphere was pretentious. They had finally gone out of business last spring, so I guess the Courteaus are slumming it down at our place now.

I nod, attempt a smile, and head back to the kitchen for his cup. Colette's waiting right by the door.

"What'd he say?" she hisses. I pour his chicory, which is like coffee but more nutty and made from the root it's named after. Our chicory is ordered from a family in the neighborhood, whose more recent deliveryman is their not-so-bad-looking son, Dylan.

"I don't think he's as much of a creep as I expected, Col."

"He's GORGEOUS . . . I call dibs." Colette grins.

"You got it." I shrug. "You couldn't pay me to deal with that mother of his."

Colette takes the steaming mug of chicory from my hands and heads back out the parlor doors toward lover boy. I glance at the dining area where Mr. and Mrs. Courteau have been seated by Dena, who's taking a break from her famous molasses sauce to listen to Lucille Courteau. Lucille's listing her various "food allergies," the same ones she has already warned us at least three times about.

With white blonde hair, high cheekbones, and large green eyes, Lucille certainly doesn't need much in the way of accessories, and yet she never seems to leave her house without appearing as if she's emptied the contents of her jewelry box and draped herself in sparkly baubles, and a heavy dose of sweet olive perfume. Anywhere else, her display of finery would probably be viewed as vulgar. Not here. In New Orleans, there's really no such thing as "over the top."

Lucille's husband, Richard, looks exactly like a graying Ken doll with clear tan skin, large blue eyes, and a carved-on smile. It's nauseating.

During the rest of the meal, I bus the table, allowing Colette to take drinks and linger around Jack . . . who cannot take his eyes off her. I can't help but feel a tiny bit jealous. I realize now what that quality is that I couldn't put my finger on. It's kindness. He's smiling warmly at her, even trying to help her clean up. His mother grabs his wrist and warns him with a glare.

I've just cleared the last of the sweet bread pudding when Lucille gasps.

"What is it, dear?" Her husband, Richard, couldn't sound more bored.

"My—my charm! The fleur-de-lis! It's MISSING."

"Oh, Mom, are you sure?" Young Jack looks skeptical,

perhaps because his mother jingles like a cash register in her beads. I don't know how she keeps track of a thing she's wearing.

"Yes, I'm sure," she says, tightly gripping a golden bangle around her wrist. "It's always on this bracelet. I put it on when I left the house. One of the waitresses even admired it. Now it's gone." She stares at me.

I quickly begin to scour the room, looking under tablecloths, in chair cushions . . .

"What exactly did it look like, Mrs. Courteau?"

"It was a twenty-four-karat-gold fleur-de-lis . . . Sasha, is it?"

I'm surprised she even attempted to address me by name. "Stella."

"Whatever." She waves her hand. "It's trimmed in pearls that have been in our family for generations. Any decent jeweler would recognize their age and value, so it would be very suspicious to them if someone just showed up to sell—"

"Mom!" Jack scolds her as my face flushes. I can hear Evie cackling in my mind. *That trophy wife. She's just trash married into wealth. She doesn't want anyone to know she came from north of Saint Charles. How she got her hooks into that family, who knows? She's a tramp playing a queen.*

The memory of GG's insults lightens my mood enough to keep me from launching the rest of the pudding at Lucille's heavily decorated head. To avoid giving her any satisfaction of superiority, I pretend I don't understand what Lucille's insinuating.

"I'm sure it's here somewhere," I say. Colette, Mom, Dad, and I spend the next hour searching tirelessly. I begin to reconsider flinging the pudding when Colette distracts me with a whisper as we check the floor for the fifth time.

"Stella, I swear I didn't take it. I know I said it was pretty, but I would never—"

"Don't be ridiculous. Of course you didn't. It's got to be here somewhere. We just keep missing it."

How? That is a mystery. We'd checked the floor, the stairs, the powder room; upturned tables, candlesticks, and linens. Mrs. Courteau's husband and son triple-checked her jewelry—just to make sure she hadn't gone insane.

"Be assured, I'll be filing a complaint with the Chamber of Commerce, the Better Business Bureau, and, well, EVERYONE!" Lucille announces to no one in particular.

"Mom? Isn't this it?" I look up from my CSI-style search of a coffee cart to see Jack lean over his mother's place setting. He reaches into her bread pudding and pulls out something sparkling and gold.

"What? That's not possible." Lucille's shock can only be matched by my own.

She's right. It's not possible. I had personally gone over that table, fork to bowl to glass, at least half a dozen times.

The charm was gone. Now it's right before her. She looks back at me, bewildered.

"I guess we must have missed it," I say.

"Well," is all she manages.

As the Courteau family makes their way out, I notice Jack straggling behind.

"Thanks again, y'all were great. Sorry about my mom." He is addressing me, but his eyes are clearly fixed on Colette.

"What the hell was *that*?" asks my dad, staring at the place where the charm materialized.

"Yeah, what the hell *was* that?" I smile, looking at Colette and nodding toward the door.

My mom comes out of the kitchen, where she was cleaning up.

"Guess we just missed it," she says, a bit too dismissively. "Come on, let's go visit GG."

☾

Since I'm only sixteen, my dad had to purchase my personal gift for GG this year—a pack of Pall Mall cigarettes. I figure she'll appreciate them on the Other Side. My mother wouldn't normally approve, but she was brought up in this city and raised like the rest of us: Honor the dead, especially by gifting them with what they loved in life. Kind of like how the ancient Egyptians buried their dead with keepsakes and personal belongings to bring to the Other Side. We do the same.

Summer's not done pressing down yet. The daylight has taken a rosy turn, so we'll need to move quickly.

Mom, Dad, and I head down Washington and turn the corner into Ash Grove Cemetery. Gothic angels greet us at the entrance with family mausoleums looming behind. I shiver, but not because I'm cold. In New Orleans, we bury our dead above ground. We learned that lesson a long time ago—one of the many devastations of flooding was the uprooting of loved ones in the graveyards. I love Ash Grove; I love all the cemeteries, really. They're so full of energy, a bit like our dining room. The living come here to mourn and to celebrate lives well-, or not-so-well-, lived.

You can learn about a person just by a glance at their stone. Sometimes you can even guess how they died, based on the gifts left there.

John Pardeau, 1940–1975. Short life. Someone's left a fresh bottle of whiskey for him. I'll put money on liver failure.

Justine Baptiste, 1876–1966. A well-known madame of a brothel. She lived a long life. I wonder if she ever found love . . .

The foot of her grave is littered with flowers, costume jewelry, even a bit of money.

Seven-day candles beam around the graves like holy jars of fireflies. We must make quick time in our tight little group before the thugs that terrorize these sacred spaces come out to play.

We arrive at GG's grave. It's just her here in this small tomb. My grandfather had wanted to be cremated, so GG cast his ashes into the ocean near a favorite vacation spot of theirs. A lot of folks with similar interests or employment share tombs, but my grandmother gets her very own bed. My GG had insisted on a "proper New Orleans burial". The rest of us might get squished in there later. That's how it's done when you run out of room for the dead.

Golden-brown granite, her monument glistens in the fading light. The wings of a seraph are etched in the stone just above the words "Evangeline Louise Borleaux, beloved mother and grandmother."

I turn to see my mother, who appears to be glaring at something. It's the way her eyes squint when they're holding back tears. My father puts his arm around her, and I take her hand in mine. She gives it a small squeeze.

"Happy Birthday, Mama," she whispers, releasing herself from us to place her offering of flowers at the foot of GG's stone. My father pulls a seven-day candle from his deep jacket pocket. It's got the Virgin Mary on it. Mom strikes a match on the back of a book from our café and sets down the candle graced with the pious face of a woman revered by Catholics and Voodoo priestesses alike. My dad awkwardly pats the top of the stone, muttering something that I can't quite make out. I pull the cigarettes from my pocket, flip the pack upside down, and tap them against the base of my palm the way I saw GG do a thousand times. I rip off the plastic seal and set them next to the bouquet, all ready for my grandmother.

The sunlight's fading fast, so I press my fingers to my lips and gently tap her cold stone tomb. We make our way out of the cemetery. It's only now that I begin to hear the whispering . . .

"You may not begin life as a witch, but if you spend your life in the Crescent City, that is certainly who you'll be by the end."

A throaty chuckle always followed this favorite saying of my grandmother's, one that seriously irritated my straight-laced mother.

Voodoo, folk magic, angels, demons, specters and spirits, curses, hexes, and blessings . . . these are the strange and delicious ingredients in my gumbo town. But as I've been busy growing up, I've been watching my mom and GG wage their own supernatural battle.

I spent my childhood watching old black-and-white movies on my GG's lap. Mainly westerns, she had a thing for John Wayne. It's only in the last couple of years that I've begun to notice much of anything besides work at the café and life at home.

Like Dylan, for instance. He's helped his family run what is arguably the best coffeehouse around. He joins his grandad making the rounds and delivering their fresh-roasted beans to any decent restaurant in the Garden District, which has always included ours. Dylan got his license a couple of month's back, so sometimes it's just him. Lately, it seems like he goes out of his way to find me, to get me to help him with the delivery, but it could just be my imagination.

There's plenty that isn't just in my head. I've seen shadowy figures, heard the sounds of music that wasn't really playing, or faint laughter when no one was around. I've seen enough to be suspicious of—and to know—what was *really* going on with Lucille's missing charm this afternoon.

Now this whispering . . . I don't know how to explain it. It's dusky, throaty, and I can't quite make out the words. It sounds like someone's trying to choke them out. It gives me the creeps.

I look around, even though I know it's useless. Mourners are filing out of the cemetery—some silent, some chatty. No one's whispering. No, this is just meant for me, and it ain't coming from the living.

What is she telling me?

At least, I think it's a woman. The voice is so hoarse; it's difficult to tell. I'm not saying anything to my parents. My dad will blow me off, and my mom, well, she doesn't like the dead taking up too much time from the living. So I keep my mouth shut.

The whispering fades further and further into nothing as we leave the cemetery and head home. I'm thinking I'll need to stop by Mama Pearline's Mojo Parlor tomorrow to ask Mama Pearl about the voice. For now, I'll do my best to get some sleep.

I kiss my parents goodnight, climb the narrow creaking hallway to my bedroom, and tug twice on the old stiff door to make sure it's shut. I'm wiping off my eye makeup when I notice talc powder on my vanity dresser.

"Jasmine Mystique" it's called, though if I remember correctly, a more apt name of GG's go-to fragrance powder would be "Jasmine Suffocation." The combination of cigarette smoke and old age probably messed with her ability to smell because she used to load this stuff on in her later years. My mom must have found this and put it here to make me smile. She once made me vow to tell her if she ever became one of those old ladies who wore such heavy sickly sweet perfume that you couldn't stand to be in the same room as them. Neither of us had the heart to say anything to my grandmother.

I pick up the tin bottle and dare to take a whiff. Almost immediately, my nostrils are burning with the aroma of chemical jasmine and baby powder. It's strangely comforting, as if the smell of my grandmother can protect me from the cemetery whispers or any bumps in the night. I'm exhausted from this day and flop onto my bed into a deep sleep before I even turn out the light.

I wake up in a jolt, scarcely able to breathe. It's difficult to get air into your lungs when you've got a pair of hands gripping your neck. Everything's dark—what's going on? I try desperately to adjust my vision to see what's happening, who's there, as I rip their fingers away from my throat. There is no sound, save for my heart throbbing in my eardrums.

The strangling stops. I fumble for the lamp, pull the cord, and light bathes the room. Nobody's there.

Not a trace. I run to my mirror to get a look at my throat. I gasp. The movement of my vocal chords stings the inside of my neck—my neck that looks like it's streaked with fading finger marks.

VISITORS & VOODOO HOUSES

THE HIGH PRIESTESS

he slam of a locker door pounds in my ears. I press my fingertips to my temples.

"You okay?" asks Colette.

"Yeah, just a headache. I got crappy sleep last night."

I'm not exactly sure how to tell her about my dream. We've been super close since she and her mom moved here last fall, but there are certain things I hesitate to share. She is terrified of anything of an oogedy-boogedy nature. And I have my own strange relationships with things of the oogedy-boogedy vein, thanks to GG. The thought of my GG reminds me that I've packed a little something in my bag to offer some clarity. The first day of tenth grade is enough to deal with, even without freaky nightmares to herald it.

I reach into my junkyard of a purse, get stabbed by a

pencil, touch the bristle of a stray eyeliner brush, and then my fingertips find silk.

"Here we go," I announce, pulling the wrapped up tarot deck from my abused leather bag. I plop down on the linoleum floor, ignoring the chatter and scuffle of shoes surrounding me. I know Colette's saved me the locker beside hers, and I also know that she's working out my combination. For the life of me, I cannot freaking deal with my locker combo. It's like I'm missing the part of my brain that tells you, "Turn left to pass your first number, then stop on your second . . ." Thank God for Colette.

"Jesus, Stella, do you want *everyone* to think of you as the weird girl?" Colette hisses under her breath, watching me begin to shuffle the trusty tarot.

I lift my head, which feels like it weighs about fifty pounds atop my freshly wrung neck, to glance her way and sing, "Too late."

She just laughs because she knows it's true. One look at my face and most could tell that ship has sailed. I spent nearly thirty minutes on my eye makeup this morning and that was only because I woke up late. It's usually an hour. I like to treat my lids like I live in an Egyptian hieroglyph: lined in thick blackest-black liquid liner with generous coats of "volumizing" mascara so it looks like my lashes are fake. My mom is the only reason I don't have half-inch eyelash extensions. She says I don't need them—whatever that means. Of course I don't *need* them; I also don't need the dusting of iridescent glitter over my bright emerald powder eye shadow, but that didn't stop me from giving the tin of sparkles a few heavy shakes. I must admit that it complements my pale blue-green eyes quite nicely.

I don't wear makeup to hide something or to cover up (okay, yes, I cover up zits). Or because I think I'm ugly. I am aware of the fact that I'm somewhat pretty. I'm not saying I'm the most beautiful girl in New Orleans, or in my school, or even in the little nook that houses my locker and Colette's.

Okay, I'm kind of vain. But so is my mom, and my GG had a crazy case of vanity. It's an inherited trait.

I shuffle the cards once more, trying to focus on pulling the one that I need for today. I draw one and flip it over. A man dangles upside down, bound to a tree.

The Hanged Man.

The same cards can feel differently, depending on what's going on. This one has a few meanings. My first thought is that the man in the card should have seen it coming. Could it be telling me to trust my gut, perhaps?

GG always took a special interest in my dreams, an interest that frequently made my mom's eyes roll. I know I need to pay attention to what I dreamed last night. The question is how? I need another head on this. I'll have to find a way to talk with Colette soon.

Colette's left and come back again, clutching a bottle of tea and water from the vending machine.

"Here." She hands me the water. "You're probably dehydrated. Water will help your headache."

And it does. Colette's like a medicine woman: she's always got a stash of vitamins and herbal teas to detoxify. She's constantly drinking beverages that promise to "rejuvenate." I think my GG would have liked her. She probably would have made fun of her, but she would have liked her.

Colette and I part ways, not to meet again until lunch. I've got two periods before that: French and Geometry. I don't speak French well, but I love the language, and it's intertwined with everything in my city. Geometry is something I fumble my way through, and I'm relieved when it's time to eat.

We take our seats at our usual table, which is populated with a few other girls who also don't seem to fit into any particular clique. They're nice enough, and they've all let me experiment on them with some of my homemade cheek tints and lipsticks.

Last year I brought a batch that I had colored using crayons—an idea I got online. There was a traditional berry that looked gorgeous on Joanna, a very modest, shy girl who's surprisingly hilarious. I put a plum on Colette, who had no choice but to go along with it as my best friend. Besides, it looked great. So great that she still wears it on special occasions. Shelly was the brave one. She tried the shade colored with a crayon called Midnight Blue. It looked like a pen exploded in her mouth, and for some reason, she couldn't rub it off that day.

I'm taking my fork to some melon slices, letting my

fried catfish sandwich cool a bit, when I notice him staring at me. The man standing at the cafeteria entrance looks to be in his forties. He's wearing a T-shirt with some kind of logo on it and dark-washed jeans. His skin has the same kind of creamy brown tone as Colette's . . . wait, is he staring at her?

She notices my gaze and follows it, turning toward the entrance. Her blueberry muffin drops to the floor.

"Daddy?" Colette hasn't spoken much about her father, except to say that he had every problem a person could think of: a drinking problem, a gambling problem, a not-being-around problem, a lying problem, a commitment problem. Apparently, her mom threw him out years ago after he'd gone off on a drunken spree following another promise of sobriety. He'd spent everything her mother had been saving up from waiting tables. Colette said that sometimes he sent them a card for a holiday, but most of the time he forgot. She always seemed sad when I asked about him, so I stopped.

Colette slides off the bench and begins walking cautiously toward him. His arms stretch out, and she picks up the pace to a near run. Suddenly, he's scooped her up in his arms like he's holding a six-year-old, and she's going along with it, lifting her legs off the ground so he can spin around with her. Our table is shamelessly staring. Actually, the whole cafeteria is playing audience.

"What's up?" Shelly asks. "I thought her dad was a total deadbeat."

"Yeah, so did I." I can feel my lips pursing

involuntarily. Colette is too nice. Much too nice to a dad who, as far as I know, has all but abandoned her.

I watch as Col is ushered away by her father. She's completely forgotten her second muffin. Normally, big fat blueberries with that crumbly topping Colette's mom created especially for our café would meet their fate instantly in my mouth. I guess I've lost my appetite.

Where is she going with him?

"More for us." Shelly grabs it, offering some to the rest of our group. Joanna accepts. I say nothing, still staring off at the cafeteria entrance. I'm brought back to the present by Shelly's next question.

"So anyone have a class with the new god . . . I mean, guy?" she asks, pointing her remaining bit of muffin at a table across the way.

There sits Jack Courteau with the most popular people in school. Just his name would grant him automatic entrance to their inner circle, but it doesn't hurt that he looks like, well—Shelly's joke was right on —some kind of young Grecian god. I've been so distracted by my nightmare and subsequent tarot card that I hadn't thought about today being his first day at school with the common folk.

"No." I need more dirt on him. Shelly looks happy to see me dive into the topic.

"What about you two?"

"He sits next to me in Social Studies," Joanna chimes in. "We're in the back . . . so we can make out without interruption." She has such a dry expression, and seems so timid, that if you didn't know her you'd take everything she says seriously.

"Want to see the counselor about you and me trading classes?" I ask.

"You know," she continues, "he actually seems really nice. You'd think he'd be full of himself, but he seems pretty cool. A little awkward, but cool." She smirks, recognizing the irony in her criticism of someone else as "awkward."

I text Colette. "Where did you go?"

Her only reply is: "Lunch with my dad. If you see my mom, please don't say anything. Talk later."

My final period proves interesting as Jack Courteau is already seated in the back of the classroom when I walk in. Knowing that Mr. Menley, the English teacher, doesn't assign seats, I give in to curiosity and boldly make my way to the back, taking an empty desk right beside Jack.

I smile. He gives a small sweet smile back. I can feel the poison darts shooting from the glares of several other girls—girls who were just a few seconds too late and missed the golden seat where I've apparently staked my claim. No conversation between us, though. He spends most of the class texting, unnoticed by Mr. Menley, who's pretty sucked in to his own dramatic reading of "The Premature Burial" by Edgar Allan Poe. Such a grim story.

My GG used to read me Poe when I was a little girl. My mom was pretty pissed when she walked in on us dramatically reciting "The Raven," wearing black lace doilies over our heads. Something about it being "too dark for children."

As Mr. Menley reads on, I'm haunted by the story. So awful. Buried alive. Everyone thinks you're a corpse while you're desperately trying to escape. I place my hand around my throat, shivering.

The bell rings. I'm collecting my books, heading out the door toward my locker, when I feel a tap on my shoulder.

"Hey, it's Stella, right? I'm so bad with names." Jack Courteau stands there, looking sheepish. Any expression wears well on this boy's face. "I wanted to ask you about something. Mind if I walk you home?"

"Mind?" I murmur dreamily. *Oh god, is that drool at the corner of my mouth?*

"Great." He gives that small smile. "Meet you out front in a couple minutes."

Oh my god. Wait, didn't Colette show some interest in him? Oh, she won't mind. After all, it's not like I threw myself at the boy. I don't even know much of anything about him, except what I've seen in our restaurant. He's cute and polite. Yeah, that's riveting.

Ugh, and that mother of his.

Through my thoughts of the son and the Lady Courteau, I've made my way to my locker. Locked, of course, and I can't remember the combination. I feel my phone vibrate in my back pocket. It's a text from Colette.

"Sorry to take off. Everything's cool. Will call you later tonight. Oh, here's your combination."

And she texts it to me, step by step. I feel slightly irritated as she's texting the combination to me like I'm five, but hey, I'm the girl who can't figure the dang thing out and may be stealing her would-be boyfriend.

I feel a soup of guilt swirling in my stomach. Maybe I shouldn't walk with him?

Stop it, I tell myself. *You're not stealing anybody. They never went out. Besides, you've never had a boyfriend, like, a REAL boyfriend, and Colette has, so it's kind of your turn.* I comfort myself with this last thought as I begin to concentrate on the ticking dial.

Clink! It opens. I breathe a sigh of relief, put away the books I don't need to take with me, and grab the ones I do. Not much homework on the first day, so I'm only taking a few textbooks, which is good, since I'm also carrying a purse weighed down by a two-ton makeup bag.

Jack looks like a khakis advertisement. He's got a hand tucked into his pocket and the other casually grasping the strap of his red backpack over his shoulder.

"I'll carry your bag," he offers. I hand him my pack. He eyes my purse suspiciously. "That looks . . . pretty heavy. Should I . . . ?"

I shake my head, sparing him the embarrassment of having to wear my purse. I grin, pull out my makeup bag, and cram it into the backpack, thereby removing 90 percent of the weight from my bag. I think I hear him moan a little in discomfort.

"Sorry. Bet you didn't plan on carting an entire cosmetics counter, huh, Jack?" I give an apologetic smile.

He just shrugs. Well, I suppose what he seems to lack in sense of humor he makes up for in . . . well, look at him. But I know that looks only go so far. Never mind. He's gorgeous. I can be personality enough for the both of us.

We step through the crosswalk adjacent to the high school. It's still sweltering—early September doesn't feel like fall yet. Not here. I'm grateful to be carrying my lightened bag as I feel the sweat clinging to the hair on the back of my neck. I realize I've been awkwardly staring at Jack as he's heaving around two backpacks.

"So, Stella . . . " He says my name as if he's still slightly unsure that he has it right, as if he's expecting me to correct him.

"Yeah, Jack?" I encourage him. I'm running multiple scenarios through my head. Will he just ask me to hang out? Will he ask me on a full-blown date?

"I wanted to ask you about something."

"Yes?" I whisper. Oh my god, did I just whisper? He seems to not have noticed, thankfully.

"Is your friend Colette with anybody?" Well. That is that, then. The feeling I'm experiencing is hardly anything resembling heartache. The thing that really hurts is my pride. It's bruised. I'm also slightly offended. I'm pretty. I'm . . . cool, I think. In my way. I'm way more interesting than he is. GG might have called this "karma," for my eagerness to flirt with a guy my best friend has her eye on. My mom would call it "reaping what you sow." They'd both be right. Ah, well. Goodbye, beautiful blond khaki catalog boy.

"No, she's not." Then I decide to be a good friend. "You should ask her out."

"Really?" His whole face beams. "I don't know her that well. We've only talked a little . . . here and there in your restaurant . . . when my mom sends me out to pick up an order of those blueberry muffins. She seems . . . cool."

And his use of "cool" fills the word with an intense amount of gooeyness. He's in love with her. How much of an idiot can I be? How did I not see this?

I run through slides in my mind, recalling how quiet he always was. How she was the only person he would really talk to at the counter. Now that I think of it, he always stood aside, like he was thinking about what he wanted when I was ready to ring him up. Then I'd go to pour coffee or take an order and he'd be getting help from Colette. He waited for her to help him. Well, I can only hope that he didn't notice my swoon.

"She's really cool. I mean, she's my best friend. I know she doesn't work tonight. You should call her."

There. I have officially done the right thing. He'll have to get in line to talk with her, though. I want to know what the heck is going on with her dad. "Yeah, definitely call her," I reiterate. We've turned onto Jackson Street heading toward Chestnut. My neck still aches a little, and I remember my idea about stopping by Mama Pearl's to see if she had any thoughts on my dream.

"Jack? I actually need to stop somewhere. See you later?"

"Oh, sure. Thanks for . . . everything." There's that small smile.

"You got it." I roughly pat his back like a jock after a football game, effectively sealing our fate as platonic buddies. He hands me my backpack and it tugs heavily on my shoulder.

☾

Nestled in the midst of touristy money traps sits Mama Pearline's Mojo Parlor. Visitors flock there looking to get a little spooked, stopping in a weird store, gasping at some of the curios, and maybe even taking home a doll with pins in it for a funny gift, all the while completely unaware of how close to Voodoo they are truly getting. It doesn't make Pearl's shop any less authentic.

She and my GG used to play canasta together at the shop. They'd go through two packs of cigarettes and about ten cups of Taster's Choice instant coffee within just a couple of hours. Pearl never spoke much to me. GG said she didn't really know how to talk to little girls. She has no children of her own and never married.

I approach the door to Mama Pearline's, a dark wood set into a stone frame. The knob is smooth in my hand, and the door sticks like the ones at home. Once I get it open, I hear the *tink, tink* of little chimes, and my senses are flooded with my childhood. Afternoon sunlight filters through the cracks of the windows that manage to escape a blanket of heavy curtains.

"Be with you soon enough." A raspy voice sounds from the back. It seems almost like a warning, and I am suddenly aware of how very little I know about a woman I've been around my entire life.

The heady aroma of Nag Champa incense, candle wax, and cinnamon has replaced oxygen on this strange planet. Christmas lights are haphazardly draped along the walls and the tables that line them. Antique oil lamps on posts have been wired for electricity, standing guard throughout the store to protect the Old Ways.

And the candles . . .

Red, blue, green, orange, pink, white, glittery—black with red centers, white that bleeds rainbows—you name it. The shapes are just as unique as the colors. There are candles sculpted as men and women burning toward one another, ones encased in glass with pictures of the Virgin Mary, or Jesus, or some saint on them. Candles litter every spare surface.

A more educated eye would recognize the five different shrines I spot.

One, I know, is for prosperity. I see Kwan Yin and a bottle of Money Oil sitting by a green candle. Another is to honor the dead. It holds a couple of old photographs with a seven-day candle burning in between. The first is a very old picture of a couple standing stiffly in one of those photographs that are so recognizably from the 1800s. Pearline's grandparents, perhaps?

The next is a framed photo of a woman wearing cat-eye glasses. It's another black-and-white, but more recent than the first. The woman is pretty in an unusual sort of way. Dark hair is piled up on top of her head and light eyes sparkle behind the lenses of her glasses. Gracefully bowed lips are curved into a tilted smile.

I know that smile. "She was a good friend, that Evie." I jump a little, knocking into the tall dresser that holds my GG's altar. Her picture rattles. A white candle with an image of the Pietà slides a little, causing its flame to flicker.

"Yeah," I mumble. "It was her birthday yesterday."

"I know." Mama Pearline nods toward the altar at a little purple cupcake with a birthday candle stuck into it sitting beside the picture of GG.

"Oh," is all I can think to say. One of Mama Pearline's clients is getting up from a seat opposite her and grabbing her purse. Probably just finished up a palm reading.

Pearl turns her attention back to the lady. "Don't delay. Get to the doctor as soon as possible. It doesn't bode well if you ignore this." She speaks as casually as if she were suggesting the lady try a new hairstyle.

I remember how GG used to always tease Mama Pearline for her "crappy bedside manner."

"Pearl," she would say. *"You gotta break the bad news more gently. These are human beings, for Christ's sake. Be a*

little more cryptic when you start talking about what frightens them. Don't throw it all at them at once."

GG said she'd never tell someone they were going to die soon, even if the cards spelled it out clear as water. She said the future held many possibilities, including ones where the seemingly doomed survive. The cards only show what's ahead if you remain on the same path, so my grandmother would suggest people get something checked out, drive carefully—that kind of thing. And she was way more empathetic than old Pearl here.

The poor woman who has just received a reading trembles all the way out the door. I hear it shut and the jingle of the chimes. Now it's just Mama P and me

She's distracted. Maybe she's forgotten that I'm here because she's pulled out a little gunmetal lockbox and starts counting money. I give a little cough to remind her of my presence. "What time is it, Stella?" She doesn't look up from her cash.

I pull out my phone. "Four."

"Shoot. If I drink coffee after three, I'm up all night." She shoves the mug sitting on her desk aside. "Better fix us some green tea. Less caffeine." She goes right back to her counting.

I stand there uselessly for another minute, then walk behind her desk and pull back the beaded curtain. Mama Pearl keeps a tiny apartment in the back of her shop. The aroma of incense and wax from the front carries over to mingle with the smell of pine-scented floor cleaner and dog food. Her elderly miniature poodle, Bert, is fast asleep on a beanbag chair.

Where does she keep her tea? As I'm trying to remember, I notice a calendar hanging beside her little blue gas stove. The tiny numbered boxes are full of scribbled writing.

September 15: *If you lose your glasses, don't worry. You'll find them before Saturday.*

September 30: *Mercury in retrograde. Stall so you don't have to resign lease until 10/14.*

I begin flipping through the pages, fascinated. Some of the scribbling is sad, some humorous.

December 13: *Throw huge birthday party for Bert. It will be his last.*

December 31: *New Year's Party at George's. Invest in some Spanx and a better brassiere.*

Each month has similar writings until I get to February. The twelfth is completely blacked out. Pearl's colored in the whole day with a dark Sharpie. Arrows are pointing to it from all directions and above the box she's printed the words *"LEAVE TOWN,"* which are underlined.

A prickle creeps up my spine as I stare at the date. February twelfth . . . What's with that day? I try to comfort myself with the thought that maybe she's just taking a fun day trip, but I know that's not true. "LEAVE TOWN" reads like, "Get the hell out of Dodge," not, "Bon Voyage."

I hear a slamming sound. Pearl must have finished counting and closed the cash box.

I scramble in an attempt to act like I've just been working on the tea. I don't know why, but I've never really felt comfortable around Pearl. I doubt she'd like me prying. I find the cupboard with the tea, and I'm instantly surprised. For a woman who drinks nasty, cheap instant coffee, she sure doesn't skimp on her leafy brews. Darjeeling, chai, ah . . . there's the jasmine green tea balled up into delicate little pearls. I take a whiff. I love this stuff. So clean tasting.

I fill her kettle with water and set it back on the stove, then rummage through the cabinets. I come across a chipped white teapot and some mismatched cups and saucers. While the water boils, I notice that the floor is wet in spots. She must have just mopped. That would explain the strong smell. I spot a bottle of Florida Water on the edge of the counter, next to a sliced lemon and some pine floor cleaner. I know that recipe. Lemon is known for its purifying qualities and Florida Water is popular in Voodoo, not just for magical cleansing, but also for "getting the job done." I remember when GG combined these it was because she needed to wash away some bad vibes.

I walk over to the back kitchen door on a gut feeling. As I suspected, coarse salt lines the base of it. I didn't notice it earlier, but I'm sure it's at the front door as well. She wants to keep some funk out of her life—in a bad way.

I turn to see her staring at me with a load of suspicion.

"I . . . thought I heard something." Why am I lying to her? Why can't I just ask her? GG would. But I'm not GG and I'm confident that Pearline wouldn't feel much like telling me, anyway. It's a bit hypocritical of her, I think to myself. She can peer into everyone's darkest secrets. I'm merely standing in her kitchen and I feel like I am trespassing.

Pearline keeps glaring at me, obviously not believing my story.

"How's the tea?" she asks.

"You know, I think it's about ready," I am relieved to reply.

The kettle whistles right on cue. Mama Pearl waddles over to the Formica kitchen table and sets her rather round frame into one of two metal chairs. I take this as a suggestion that I continue to prepare the tea myself. I obey, setting it to steep in the pot, gathering spoons and sweeteners, and laying them out before us. She adds about five cubes of sugar to her cup. I plop one in mine, watching it dissolve as we sit quietly. Finally, I speak.

"I had this dream," I begin, not addressing her by name, as I've never felt comfortable enough to call her Pearl, let alone Mama. What the hell is her last name, anyway?

She's spraying window cleaner on her rings. I'm not sure she's even listening.

"It was more like a nightmare." I clutch my throat. "I was being choked."

I notice her pause midpolish on that last word. "I was choked," I repeat. "Really hard. I couldn't see who was doing it, but when I woke up my neck hurt as if it had actually happened."

She glances quickly at me, then back to a ruby she's wiping.

"I've never, *ever* had any bad experiences with . . . ghosts . . . at our place. And GG, Evie, always said the energy was friendly at the café." I bring up my grandmother's name in an attempt to get this woman to care. I shut my mouth and watch her put her ruby ring back on, then pull off a silver bangle, which she begins to wipe methodically as well.

Without looking at me, she smirks and says, "Maybe you strangled yourself in your sleep. You shouldn't be so careless."

Why the hell did GG hang out with this woman? No wonder she never seemed to have any other friends. Only someone as tough as my grandmother could tolerate this hag. I can't help but glare at her. I don't care if she puts some hex on me.

Okay, I care a little, so I soften my squint. I measure my words.

"I know, I think we both know, when something is . . . otherworldly. *Haunted*," I hiss.

She sets down her bracelet and handkerchief, pushes the bottle of window cleaner aside, clears her throat, and takes a large gulp of her tea. The smirk has washed off her face, replaced by a steadied expression.

"Look, Stella. If Evie were alive she'd back me up on what I'm about to say to you." She takes another large gulp, draining her cup. "Leave this one alone."

I open my mouth to protest but she stops me by holding up her palm.

"I mean it. I don't care what you've got to do. Burn sage in your room. Hang lavender above your bed. Put some Tiger's Eye under your mattress. Salt the doorways." She raises an eyebrow knowingly at me with that last sentence. "Protect yourself. Let your friend work out her own problems."

Pearl can see instantly by my expression that I have no idea what she's talking about, and she's obviously given away more than she'd planned on.

"What do you mean? Is it Colette? What's going to happen to Colette?"

She just shakes her head. "How do you think I've managed to survive in this town?" Her voice is a heavy whisper. "I stay *out* of it. I tell the people what they pay me to know and I keep it to myself."

She gets up out of her chair, a signal that our conversation has come to an end.

I begrudgingly rise, swirling in emotions. Confusion. Dread. More confusion. She rushes me out of the kitchen.

I walk toward the front door of the shop when she calls to me. "Stella, wait."

I turn hopefully. She must have changed her mind. She putters around her store, fishing something out of a display case, scooping powder out of a jar and into a plastic baggie. "Here, open your hands."

I hold out my palms, wondering . . . *Plop!* A large polished hunk of Tiger's Eye lands in one hand, and *plop!* a sack labeled, "Pearline's Banishing Powder," lands in the other.

"This should buy you some time. Why don't you plan a trip with your family?"

I ignore her suggestion and in a slightly exasperated tone tell her I only have a couple of bucks on me.

"Oh, consider them a gift." She plasters on a sugary, phony smile. I've never known her to be fake.

My eyes search her face. She notices and drops the act. "A gift for leaving this one, and me, the hell alone for a while, 'kay? Bye now!"

She's literally shoving me out the door and onto the street, where, judging by the near-setting sun, it's time for me to go home.

SECRETS & SAINTS

THE DEVIL

"*T*here you are!" my mom says as I step in the back door to the kitchen. "I need help! Colette and her mom both have Tuesdays off now, remember? Where were you?"

"Sorry. I was hanging out with some of the girls," I lie.

She nods. "How was school?"

"Fine." Glad that she hasn't asked for details on my whereabouts, I lug my backpack upstairs, toss the stone and powder into my GG drawer, and throw on my apron to go downstairs and help.

I'm distracted, focused more on what Pearl said than on the coffee I'm pouring.

I'm relieved when my mom lets me go to my room shortly after seven to finish my homework. I just have a little reading for Social Studies and a worksheet for Geometry.

I open the lid to the old turntable GG left me. Playing music helps to drown out some of the noise from the café. I select an album my dad got me last Christmas. He insisted that, without The Ramones, I would be lost. But apparently even they can't guide me through studying. Problems swirl on the page to the point where I can't reason through the questions.

I hear my phone beep. It's a text from Colette.

"CAN U TALK?"

"YES," I reply, happy to blow off Geometry until tomorrow night when, with any luck, my head will be a little clearer. It's not due for a couple of days anyway.

My phone rings on cue. "Okay, what the hell happened today?" I press before Col can even get out a "Hi."

"I had to wait to call you until my mom left for her book club. By the way, I told her I was with you. Cover for me, okay?"

"Fine," I agree, but I'm not sure I want to. "What did your dad want?" The way I say dad sounds like I'm using air quotes as I speak it. I can't help myself.

"He wants to be close, for real, and make up for everything. He's been sober for six months and is working a steady job. He's sorry. He really is." Colette sounds like an excited four-year-old. She doesn't even stop to breathe.

"Col, that's all great, but why can't your mom know you were with him?"

"She wouldn't understand. They have so much baggage between them. We just need some time for him to get on his feet and find a way to tell her so she'll really believe him."

"What about you? Don't you have a lot of 'baggage' with him, too? How do you know you can trust him?" I'm recalling Pearl's words: *Let your friend work out her own problems.*

"Look, Stella, I don't expect you to understand," she spits. "*You* have a dad that belongs on TV. Some of us have to *work* for good relationships with our fathers."

"Colette, I'm not trying to be mean. I just don't want you to get hurt. I'm looking out for you." Christ, I feel like I'm stealing lines from my mother.

Colette must agree because she responds by saying, "Stel, I already have a mom. Can't you just be my friend on this one?"

I concede. I don't trust her dad, but I don't exactly trust Pearl either. Besides, any shot I have of Colette listening to me will be trashed if I don't at least offer some understanding.

"You got it. Sorry."

"Thanks." Colette accepts my apology. "I just need a little time with him before we tell my mom."

"Where's your dad staying?" I ask, trying not to sound like a CIA agent.

45

"Just outside the neighborhood, in the French Quarter. He's living out of a suitcase at a motel. In exchange for residence, he works as a handyman for them. You know, painting walls, fixing leaky faucets—that sort of thing. We're going to start meeting up for lunch a couple of days a week. He can sign me out of school during lunch period and it's easier for us to hang out then. If it's later in the day, I need to come up with too many excuses."

Steady job, huh? I still need to talk to her about the dream, but the timing doesn't feel right.

"Well, you may be pretty busy after school soon anyways." I change the direction of our chat.

Colette groans. "Great. Another wedding reception?"

The café hosts small wedding receptions from time to time—Colette and I hate them. The families of the brides and grooms are often crazy high-maintenance and often totally hammered.

"No, it's not about work." I pause for effect. "It's about Jack."

"What do you mean?" Our previous conversation is forgotten as we proceed to dissect my walk with Jack today—leaving out the part where I kind of thought he was asking me out. I let Colette know to expect a call from him and she's giddy by the time we get off the phone.

Me, not so much. I'm wrapped up with questions about her father, questions about my nightmare, and questions about Pearline.

"What happens on February twelfth?" I ask aloud to

no one in particular. Maybe the stars, because I pull out my tarot deck and begin shuffling. A card jumps out of the pack and into my lap. GG told me to always pay special attention to the ones that acted like that. I reach down to pick up the card and flip it over. A building in flames, splitting at the top. Tenants flee—someone leaps from the window. I feel dizzy as I look upon the words of the card.

The Tower. This does not bode well. I put the card back in the deck and shuffle it a few times as if to dissolve the message altogether. Wrapping the silk scarf around the deck and placing them out of sight helps too.

I open my window to let the night breeze in. It's nine and the café is closed. I can hear the faint trills of some zydeco music playing in the distance. The sound is coated with the sweet fragrance of the climbing roses beneath my window. I can reach down and just barely graze their petals.

The moon is high and she's nearly full.

"Approaching motherhood," GG liked to say. She talked about the moon like some talk about holy leaders. Each phase weaves a different spell, and each works better with different kinds of magic. She used to say the moon represented all women, playing out our lives before us in her cycles. She is a young woman full of excitement and energy as the growing crescent.

She is the nurturing mother—giving, generous, and bold—when she is full. She's the wise old grandmother, teaching, guarding, and letting go as she wanes into darkness.

It's a Harvest Moon now, full of promise. But promising what, exactly?

A soft knock at the door speaks for my own mother.

"Come in."

She holds out my rosary, with beads of agate and rose quartz, laced between her fingers.

"I had it restrung for you and they polished it, too. Isn't it pretty?"

When my mom was growing up, her ultimate rebellion was to become a Catholic after a friend introduced her to the Church. She told me that she brought GG a few times—after all, there are a lot of Catholic roots in Voodoo, alongside Haitian and Native American traditions. I think my mom secretly hoped she could convert my grandmother. It didn't pan out, obviously.

Although, in the last few years before my GG's death, she asked to attend church with the rest of us for Christmas Eve mass and Easter Sunday. She was a fan of Jesus Christ, but her and my mom's beliefs about the Man and his life were very different. GG saw him more as a spiritual leader, whereas my mom, of course, sees Him as God.

Me? I don't know. I love it all. I loved GG, I love the Church, and I guess I'm figuring out my own path.

"Thanks, I missed it." I really had. I usually keep it in my bag. I'll be holding it tonight as I sleep, after I light a candle to petition Saint Michael the Archangel for protection, salt my doorway and window, and tuck that hunk of Tiger's Eye beneath my pillow. Whatever will help me not get strangled in my sleep sounds great.

My mom places the rosary in my hands and kisses me goodnight. I do exactly as I planned: creep down the side steps to pour sea salt into a cup, then sprinkle it along my windowsill and the entrance to my room. I won't burn sage because the smell will bring my mother back with questions. I light a candle, hold the Tiger's Eye out my window to be charged by the waxing moon's energy, and whisper a prayer for safety on my rosary before climbing into bed. Sleep comes peacefully. I am certain my protection has worked . . .

I am sitting at my vanity. I've got a hairbrush in one hand, midway through my hair. There's snow in my lap. Wait, no. My mind adjusts to reality.

I set down the brush and feel my fist tightly clenched around something. I unfold my other hand to find GG's tin of powder perfume. I've dumped a good amount of it onto myself.

"What the—" I stand and slap the fragrant dust off me, coughing in a cloud of white fog. I'm somewhere between irritated and alarmed. I have never sleepwalked. At least, no one ever told me I did.

With powdered poufs still clinging to my clothing, I decide to crawl back into bed and forget about it until morning.

I feel long fingers encircling my throat. A pair of icy blue eyes stare back at me. I try to push the face, the body, away but I am weak. I feel my own body slip into submission on the earthen floor, noticing the brick structure of a wall as my cheek slams on the cold dirt. I turn my head, and it feels like it's coming loose. The fingers are relentless. It's as if they're getting stronger. Or maybe I'm getting weaker. I can't seem to focus. The wall, the ceiling beams, an oil lamp . . . and those eyes. I wheeze, feeling blood pour from my mouth. It stains the gold threads, the threads that brush my lips, my face in their movement. Her curls act like a mop as she violently shakes her whole body while destroying mine.

I take a quick glance in the mirror as I walk out the door to school. Nope, skull still there. The ribbon choker I'm wearing stings as it rubs against my skin, but I don't know how to explain the claw marks around my neck. Faint purple fingerprints above my collarbone help me to feel less crazy about what is happening. Or crazier, I haven't decided yet. It seems that I sabotaged my own protection during my little sleepwalk party, because in the morning light, I saw the Tiger's Eye and rosary on the floor by my wastebasket, and the salt brushed off the sill and away from the door. What am I going to do? Tie myself to my bed?

My stomach folds over onto itself. I've never experienced anything close to this. I've only heard of this kind of stuff from my GG. And I've got to say, those stories never ended well.

I don't care what Mama Pearline said; I am stopping

by her place later. I need something stronger than a stone.

Colette notices that something is wrong almost immediately. It could be the dark circles under my eyes that tip her off, or perhaps the fact that all I bothered to put on my face was a few dabs of mascara. I'm too exhausted to bother with eyeliner, and that is saying quite a lot. I tell her that I'll explain things later. Then she annoyingly clucks her tongue at me when I ask her for help with my unfinished homework. I don't bite her head off since she may be the only reason I pass Geometry this year.

At lunch, Colette leaves *again* to meet her dad and I'm left with a thousand questions from Shelly and Joanna.

"Why is she leaving with him?"

"Are you sure she's not dating an older guy?"

By the time school is out, I'm exhausted. Thank God the café closes early today so Col and I can hang out like normal teenagers for once. I have to talk with her about what is happening.

She walks me through the ordeal of opening my locker again and together we stroll down the steps in front of the school—right smack into Jack Courteau.

"Hi," he says awkwardly.

"Hi," Colette coos. I step out of the conversation and pretend to be really interested in something on my phone.

"Stella?"

A low voice from behind startles me into dropping my cell.

"Sorry, I didn't know you scared so easy." It's Dylan from Crescent City Roaster. The amusement in his voice is unmistakable.

"Well, maybe you shouldn't sneak up on people," I tease, attempting to joke my way out of explaining my shaky nerves.

Dylan raises his thick dark brows and grins. "My granddad wanted me to give you this . . . we forgot a pound of French Roast in the last delivery. Here you go." He pulls a paper bag full of coffee beans from his backpack. The aroma is so pungent I can smell it before he even hands it to me.

"Thank you." I take the sack and tuck it into my own bag.

He leans down and picks up my temporarily forgotten phone.

"You might need this." He passes it to me and I realize that part of the heady coffee fragrance comes from Dylan. It's got to be in his pores, working alongside that roaster, cooking coffee beans day in and day out.

I take another whiff. The scent is blended with something else . . . shaving cream. God, he smells good.

"Your nose stuffed up?" he asks.

"No," I reply, confused. Then I realize that I've probably been loudly inhaling like a maniac. "Maybe."

He thinks for a moment. "This'll clear you up." Dylan reaches back into his bag. "It's a sample. If your mom likes it, she can put it on her next order." He hands me a tiny paper bag, enough to hold a couple tablespoons of beans.

I unfurl the bent top, peeking into the sack. Beans nearly black as night look like solid lumps of ink and send a chocolaty, spicy aroma up like a puff of thick smoke.

"Wow." I feel my eyes grow big.

"Strong, huh?" He smiles.

"It smells amazing," I gush. I'm talking about the coffee and maybe a little about Dylan as well. "What's it called?"

"Black Magic." Did he just wink at me? Who winks under the age of sixty? Definitely not high school boys.

I feel wobbly in my knees. Ugh, Stella, do *not* overthink this. He probably just got something in his eye. I straighten my thoughts out in my mind. You don't need to misread signals from *two* guys in a twenty-four-hour period, do you?

"So"—he takes what seems like forever—"that should be right up your alley."

"Huh?" I'm not following. Colette, like the multitasker she is, has been eavesdropping while exchanging puppy eyes with the young Courteau, so she translates.

"Black *magic*, Stel? Because, ya know?" My heart thumps. Of course. Anyone who knows my family also knows that my GG was a folk magic practitioner, a tarot reader, and a witch. A damn fine one, I think. I still credit one of her Mojo bags for stopping the relentless teasing from a couple of girls back in fourth grade. I'm not afraid of magic. Okay, maybe some aspects, but I'm not ashamed of my ancestry. And yet, somehow, I feel exposed right now with people speaking freely about it on the school steps. Yeah, I know Dylan, but I've only interacted with him more recently because he started helping deliver coffee, and Jack—I hardly know him.

"Oh, that." I try to sound dismissive, like Dylan wasn't pulling a curtain back and baring something that's been screaming to come out.

"Yeah, *that*." Again a wink. And a look in his eyes like he knows all of my secrets, even ones I haven't told myself.

"Well, thanks. I'll share it with my mom. I'm sure she'll want to order some." I think I've successfully brought the conversation back to coffee.

A guy from my French class calls to Dylan, and with a nod and a grin, he strides off.

"Are y'all going out?" Jack asks innocently. What an idiot. Cute, but a fool.

"What!" I snort.

"I mean, not *going* out, but, a 'thing?'" Boarding school has done him no favors. This boy is painfully awkward.

"Was it our sensual coffee smelling that tipped you off?" I quip, hoping to deflect by making him feel uncomfortable.

"Y'all do put off a flirty vibe, Stella. It was definitely there." Damn you, Colette. The rescuer.

I narrow my eyes at her. There's only so much I can think about right now and very little that I wish to discuss in front of Jack Courteau.

"You ready?" I raise my brows in obvious annoyance.

"Yeah." She strings out the word.

"Great!" I link my arm in hers, practically dragging her away from Loverboy.

"I'll call you later!" Jack says with a wave.

"Calm down, Stel." She's pulling to save her arm in my grip. "We were just joking. What's up with you today?"

"I'm just feeling a little off," I grumble. I need to talk to her. I also need her to hear me.

The air is heavy with humidity, but a breeze promises of fall. The Garden District is still coated in honeysuckle clinging to wrought iron gates, holding onto summer for dear life. It'll be light out for a few more hours, so I suggest we stop by my house, grab a thermos of coffee and a few day-old muffins, and head to Coliseum Square Park.

I try to resist eating one of the pastries as we meander into the park. I'll wait until we get settled underneath Colette's favorite magnolia tree, stuff her full of sweets, and get down to the matter at hand.

We flop beneath the wide branches and I contort to find just the right spot where a root isn't digging into my back. I pull a pair of paper cups from my backpack and Colette begins to pour the coffee. It's cold.

"Iced . . . good call." It's still way too hot for a steaming cup, so I'm glad that Col had the vision to pull a pitcher of iced coffee from the fridge, instead of from the hot carafe that my parents down throughout the day, no matter the weather.

"Of course," Colette replies in an easy way. I never really had a best friend before, unless you count GG, but she was my grandmother. Colette has been my first actual best friend. It's not that I'm antisocial . . . I like the girls we sit with at lunch. It's just that I always spent so much time with GG or at the café instead of with peers. While other girls were going to the mall, I was sorting bits of flannel for mojo bags—GG sold these pouches in her friend's store, or used them for herself. She filled them with herbs, stones, powders . . . sometimes a message on folded-up paper. I even once saw her put a tiny ballerina in one. She said it was for someone's dance competition, to be pinned on the inside of her tutu. The bags were for things like that: luck, or love, or finding a job, or breaking a hex. That last one always irked my mother.

"The idea that any person, other than the Devil himself, could 'jinx' you . . . " she'd sniff.

Then I'd spend the rest of my time at mass with my mother as she attempted to purge me of GG's influence. I guess I wouldn't even have gotten to know Colette if it weren't for her and her mom working at the café.

A sparkle of sunlight bounces off of a long car parked on the curb nearby—a green Jaguar. I recognize it. I'm not a car person, but it's pretty unforgettable.

Lucille Courteau. It's got to be her in the driver's seat waiting . . . for what? My first thought is that she's come to inspect Colette.

"Ugh. Who does she think she is?" I ask.

"What?" Colette looks up from texting. Jack, I assume.

"Look." I nod my head in Mrs. Courteau's direction.

Col scans the line of cars. "Is that—"

"Yup." I answer.

"Do you think—"

"That she's spying on us? Don't you?" I have a bad habit of interrupting and finishing Colette's sentences.

"That seems kind of paranoid." She smiles.

"You know, I really hate when you treat me like I'm insane," I reply. I take a large gulp of my drink. I need to relax. Maybe long hours at the café aren't the only reason I haven't had a lot of super close friends.

Now Colette's gaze is locked on the car. The headlights flash twice, like a signal.

It must be meant for the white sedan, because the car abruptly jerks into a parallel park across the street. A man wearing a dark jacket and what looks like a Saints cap steps out. Cars passing block him from view, and I can only see him in short skipping frames now. He crosses the street, making his way to the passenger side. Colette and I are transfixed, no subtlety to our staring.

He's carrying a messenger bag, and he's pulling what looks like a large manila envelope from it. Mrs. Courteau leans forward, grasping it through the open window.

"Weird," I murmur, feeling as though we are suddenly in a movie.

"I guess," responds Colette. "Although it looks like she wasn't here to watch us. Guess we're not that big of a deal, after all." She laughs and shakes her head.

"Hey, I was just looking out for you, Col. I still think this is strange. Why is she exchanging . . . "

Mrs. Courteau hands over what looks like a stack of bills to the man.

" . . . money for some envelope from a guy in a park? Maybe she *is* spying on you. Maybe she's hired him to—"

"Do you hear yourself, Crazy?" she scolds me.

"Okay, okay." But even though I know it sounds nuts, there is something about Lucille Courteau—something that leaves me feeling awfully uneasy. Still, I need to stop talking about this. I have to save some credibility for more pressing issues.

We watch the mystery gentleman leave and Mrs. Courteau soon after. I'm pretty sure she never sees us.

"Let's talk about ghosts!" I blurt the word out. Credibility—gone. Oh well.

Colette groans.

"Seriously, Colette, let's talk." She hears the urgency in my voice and watches my face patiently. "I know that I've been acting like a freak. Well, more than usual." I follow up before she can add a smartass remark. "I had this dream, Col, more real than any of the others."

Her silence is heavy, and it seems as if everything around us just turned down the volume.

Colette hasn't always been so skittish about the supernatural. She actually loves my stories about GG, about palm readings and potions. She just doesn't like when it gets too real for her taste.

I've periodically had dreams that, well, were more like prophesies. Usually little stuff, like seeing my mom wear a yellow dress before she brought it home from a shop, or dreaming about a customer breaking a dish and then seeing one shatter the following evening—small moments and meaningless exchanges. A little while after Colette and her mother moved here, I had a dream about Rita, her maternal grandmother who had moved with them. Colette and I had just been getting closer as friends, and Nana Rita and I had met only a few times, but I had to share my vision about her with Col.

It felt very real at the time, very present. Nana Rita fast asleep. A coffin being set into a wall high above the ground: A New Orleans burial. A quiet procession, nothing like the wild affair my GG insisted upon. GG's featured a bunch of old witches from all over the country, some of the local hoodoo and Voodoo practitioners, readers, the owner of her favorite deli, regular customers of hers—they all came out to dance, sing, pound on the casket, and irritate my mother.

No, this was solemn and quiet. The kind of funeral

my mom would like to have held. Colette and her mom in simple church clothes, crying softly. I saw the dogwood trees blooming, so I knew it was May. Colette wore a green jade necklace I didn't recognize. I had to warn her. Even if Rita was dying of old age, I felt pretty sure that Colette and I were going to be very close. I was also sure that I was going to have a hard time keeping things from her.

So I told her, "*Colette, I had this dream . . .*"

She just looked a little uneasy at the time and shrugged it off. Later that week, she paled when she opened a gift from Nana Rita at her birthday party: a string of lovely green jade beads. I said nothing, and just tried to stay within reach over the next several days. When Rita died in her sleep the following evening, I brought over food from the café. My mom took care of their housework while they planned the funeral, and Colette and I spoke of everything but my vision.

So here, now, her discomfort is swirling in the breeze around us as I bring it all up for her again.

I take a breath and continue. "It's like before, but it feels . . . different. I'm freaked out, Colette." My voice is shaking. I am really blowing this cool thing. Are my eyes watering? *Jesus, Stella.*

"All right, all right, what did you dream?" And that's what makes Colette a good friend. No teasing now, no brush-off due to her fears. She can see how scared I am. So I give her the details. A few times I watch her eyes begin to widen, and then quickly draw back to normal. I fill her in on most of what happened at Mama Pearline's, except for Pearl's suggestion that I stay away from Colette. I see no reason to terrify her when I don't really have any useful information. But I feel compelled to keep her safe, to warn her in some way.

"I just think we should be careful," I say.

"Oh, so not hold séances in graveyards like I usually do on Friday nights?" She's sarcastic now because I'm no longer shaking. And she's kind of right to be so.

"Maybe chill out on making up dirty limericks from the names on the tombs," I retort.

"Maybe you should lay low on the grave robbery for a little while," she pitches back.

"The ceremonial blood drinking is probably not ideal." Now I'm smiling.

Colette's chuckles. "Gross." Then her expression becomes very calm. "Look, I get that you're scared. And you know that I think it's neat that you study tarot cards, crystals, and those kinds of things. It's just that there's a side to all this that"—Colette usually knows just the right words to use—"scares the hell out of me. I want to help; I just don't know what to do. I really don't know how much I *want* to know. Are you sure this wasn't just a very realistic nightmare?"

I pause, then pull some hair away from the side of my neck, showing her the very faded but slightly visible marks from where a set of fingers had somehow gripped it only hours before.

She's turning olive. Poor Colette. She never asked for

this. Poor me, too. I can't let myself go. GG always seemed to be steady and solid in her dealings with the supernatural, and I never knew anyone who had a better relationship with the dead than she did. It's what makes this even more frustrating. The one woman who seemed to straddle the fence between the living and the dead can't, or *won't*, help out her living granddaughter now, when I need her so badly.

Colette tries to help me piece together a plan. "Why don't you really dump that Banishing Powder around your room tonight—go crazy with it?"

I agree. "I still have some Four Thieves Vinegar I can wash my window with."

"You want me to stay over tonight, Stel?" I consider this, but I still don't know what kind of danger she may be in, and I don't want to trap her in the lion's den.

I remember that it sometimes helps to politely ask an unwanted entity to please leave, although I'm not sure how well a strangling ghost responds to good manners. I also remember that I didn't used to be such a baby. Of course, with GG around it was pretty easy to be brave. Maybe if I just relax and stop taking this whole thing so seriously it'll just resolve itself. Maybe it's just some beastie passing through town. Maybe it's got nothing to do with Colette or me. Maybe Mama Pearl is crazy. Okay, I *know* she's crazy. But nuts as she is, I'm finding it difficult to buy my own press here. Still, I attempt to sell it to Colette, she pretends to believe it, and we part ways. She's grabbing coffee with Jack, and

I'm going home to attempt my homework and then pass out.

I'm exhausted. So much for clarity with Geometry. I guess I'll just do it before class. I muddle my way through the rest of my work, wash my face, which doesn't take nearly as long as it normally does since this morning I was too tired to decorate my skin the way I like. Even with the shortened routine, I barely make it to bed before crashing on top of my sheets.

Heavy, quiet, restful sleep. I wake up before my phone alarm goes off and feel like me again—energized. I am full of relief as I gaze into my mirror. No bad dreams. No creepy marks. Just pure sweet slumber. I indulge, taking my time. One of the great things about living above a café means having access to great coffee pretty much whenever, and if he gets a chance before the customers start filing in, my dad brings me a cup.

This day, it's iced, since the heat is still coming on strong this September morning. He knows I drink it like this until autumn officially hits. He also knows I take it black, like my mom does. He smiles as he rests the dewy glass on my vanity, having found a bare spot amidst the junkyard. Then he makes a face as I take a huge swig of the strong stuff. He takes his coffee café-au-lait style— loaded with milk. I love that style as much as the next person, but when a girl's waking up, this is just right to get her started.

"Thanks, Pop." He kisses the top of my head and goes back downstairs.

I pull out my eyeliner brushes, blush brush, lash curler, and lash comb. Tugging at several different drawers, I retrieve one of my homemade concoctions of eye powder (a radioactive green color), a coal black liner powder, a paste rouge in the prettiest shade of apricot, a lip balm tinted in a similar shade to the rouge, and a very goopy still-too-sticky-for-my-liking super-glitter gloss. I haven't yet perfected how to make a gloss with all that sparkle to hold that doesn't have the consistency of molasses. It looks great on, though. I still buy my mascara from the drugstore. A girl can't do better than Maybelline Great Lash in black.

I begin decking out my face in its usual finery. I sweep the vivid green to my brow bone, use the liner brush with the coal color to create a serious cat's eye, rub a small amount of the blush onto the apples of my cheeks, then pucker my lips. I apply the apricot balm, then the sticky gloss, and finally, for good measure, I use the blush brush to dust my face in a gold shimmer powder. I feel like an autumnal Egyptian fairy rock star. That seems about right.

Brushing my hair, I opt to let it hang straight as usual. I pull on a cotton tank top in a rich shade of purple, toss my pajama pants in the hamper, and tug on a pair of frayed dark blue jeans. I slip into my socks and starry sneakers, then grab my backpack to go downstairs.

I'm pulling out freshly baked cranberry orange muffins and cinnamon coffee cake for the display case, laying them on the hodgepodge of white ceramic platters, when I get that creepy feeling like I'm being watched.

I turn to see my mom glowering at me, her arms folded like a straitjacket around her tiny torso. Every part of her is petite. I am not so dainty—more awkward. Clunky. I think that my hands and feet are just a tad too large for my medium frame, which is slender, but not tiny. I'm also about a foot taller than she is. I take after my dad this way.

Still glowering.

"What?" I finally ask, annoyed that my mother is intruding on my blissful morning with her funky vibes.

"You gonna take more today?"

"I was going to bag up some coffee cake for me and Col, why?"

She sighs, crazy irritating, then nods toward the pastries.

I ignore the heavy breath and plunk two thick slices into a paper sack—*one, two.*

"We have granola bars in our personal pantry. Those pieces of coffee cake sell for two fifty each. That's five dollars you're eating right there."

"So?" We do this all the time. What is her problem? "Mama, don't you help yourself to whatever you happen to be cooking up?"

"But I'm baking. I'm *working.*"

"And I'm not? School's not work? I'm not working here tonight? I just checked the log . . . TWO birthday parties, one with twenty guests. Who's going to have to keep them happy?"

Her face relaxes a bit, but I can see she doesn't want to back down.

"Mama, if you had your way, I would *never* have any fun. Thank God for Dad." I know this hurts her, and that's why I say it. And that's also why I regret it almost instantly. "Mama . . . "

"Just take your cake." She turns on her heels and heads back to the kitchen. I'll talk to her later. Now I've got to go.

GENTLEMEN & THIN VEILS

STRENGTH

I step out the door, where I know Colette will be walking up to meet me. Fridays are a late start day for us, with a free period first, so we usually hang out beforehand and walk to school together.

And there she is . . . with Jack. Gross. Really? This is the deal now? He's like a fairy-tale character that's been enchanted by a love potion, the way he follows her. I have never attempted a love spell. GG made a big deal about never performing one on a specific man.

"Too messy," she'd cluck. *"Love's already a wreck—then you wanna try and steer that sinking ship?"*

Colette offers a barely apologetic smile. "I told Jack about Friday hangouts and he wanted to tag along."

"I do hope that's all right," the southern prince drawls out in fine formality. What book did this boy step out of?

"Yeah, totally." I try to sound agreeable, but irritation and a bit of guilt is swirling around in my head from the quarrel with my mom.

"Oh, I thought we could *all* kind of, you know, *hang out*." She's looking past me, behind me, so I turn to be greeted by a wide grin.

Dylan.

"I *do* hope that's all right," he coos in an exaggerated accent, tilting his head and lifting an invisible cap. His smile spreads to Jack, obviously to let him know he's just kidding around.

I am amazed by this boy. I've never known a guy to be so at ease with himself.

I shoot Colette a look, hoping it goes undetected by the rest.

"Sure," I reply to Dylan, working hard to appear unfazed, "Want some coffee cake? I brought an extra slice."

"Don't mind if I do." I turn to quickly stick my tongue out at Colette. She knows that sweet pastry should have been hers. That's what you get, Col.

Dylan reaches his entire forearm into the bag, clutches a hunk of cake, and finishes it off in two bites. I can't help but notice how large his hands are: long wide fingers, scraped and slightly callused palms. It's pretty pleasing to note that compared to his, my hands look almost angelic.

Colette takes charge. "All right, we've got about forty minutes until class, so what do y'all want to do?

"Wait." I'm curious. "I know Jack's got a free period, but you, too, Dylan?"

"Woodshop." We all know what that means. Mr. Blathe, the Shop/PE teacher, is about a million years old and really doesn't give a crap what anyone does. The other gym coach, Ms. Lee, has a reputation for being rigid as hell. Luckily, I am very proactive in my hatred of all things athletic, so I had the foresight to put in a request at the end of last year for both Colette and me to be put into Mr. Blathe's sessions this year. My once-maligned gym class is now a perfect opportunity to stroll, chat, and talk a few freshman girls into being my cosmetic guinea pigs.

"We could go to the park," I suggest, hoping Colette uses this as a segue into asking Jack what his mom was up to yesterday. She misses the opportunity—I suspect intentionally.

We end up just taking a longer way to school. It's feeling a tiny bit cooler this morning and the full shade of the trees keeps it comfortable. Jack and Colette begin to lag behind. I slow down, too, until I'm practically at a stop. They seem like they're deep in conversation.

"No, my dad is hardly ever around . . ." I hear Jack admit.

This is awkward. It's like I'm trying to eavesdrop, but I'm not. I'm just not sure what to do with myself and . . . the other one. I guess I'll just have to deal with it.

I walk a little faster and catch up with Dylan. "I like your makeup," he says.

I tilt my face slightly toward his so he can see my eyes rolling to the heavens. *Real original.* Boys have teased me about my "Halloween look" since the seventh grade when GG helped me convince my mom to let me "experiment with color" ... and wear it to school.

"No, really," he protests. "I'm serious. I mean, I like how you look without makeup, too. Like, early in the morning, when I'm delivering something, and you just woke up, and your hair's all—"

"I get it," I interject. I'm not into thinking about what I must look like when I've been the one who greeted him at the door for a dawn delivery.

He's grinning as he continues. "It's just that I like how you are who you are. You just do what you like and don't seem to care too much about what you look like to other people."

I shoot him a glare.

"That came out wrong. What I mean is ... what I mean is that you are pretty comfortable with yourself. And that's cool."

I can't help turning up the corners of my lips. All right, Dylan. So far, so good.

"I just wish you could teach me how to be cool and confident like—like you are," he stammers. "I'm always so afraid that other people will think I'm weird, or gross, or smell funny ..."

"Stop it, ass." Now he's messing with me.

He stops his stammering and breaks into another smile. "Fine. But I was serious about you."

The way he says this makes me feel kind of swoony. I hear Colette loudly clear her throat and I realize that I've slowed way down again, to the point of blocking the two ambling lovers.

To avoid unnecessary gushing I busy myself with my phone the rest of the way to school. No need to stir further flirtation between Dylan and me.

By the time lunch rolls around, I'm starving. For some reason that cake didn't go very far. As I make my way over to our table, Colette's already seated along with the other girls.

I can hear her explaining, "Yeah, my dad's being really cool. He has work today, so he's just stopping by for a few minutes."

Shelly and Joanna nod politely, but as I approach, I can see that they're distracted. Sitting on the other side of Colette, hands locked in hers, is Mr. Jack Courteau.

Dreamy gaze? Check. Startlingly blue eyes? Check, check. He may actually be a little too . . . I don't know. *Too* pretty. If he were a female, we might have to hate him.

I rattle my tray obnoxiously to bring the girls back to Earth.

The ladies seated at the cool table are shooting mental flamethrowers in Colette's direction, but she doesn't seem to notice. The guys of said cool table actually look relieved, probably due to the fact that such hefty competition is now out of the running.

"Hey, Stel," Colette greets me as Shelly and Joanna break from their trance and scoot down to make room.

"Pretty." Joanna admires my eye color.

"Thanks. It's a newer creation. I finally did it." I can feel my face lighting up. "I finally blended just the right combination of blue mica and green mica to create the perfect shade of Electric Moss. That's what I'm calling it." I'm a little breathless. I tend to get that way about eye shadow. The girls are used to it by now.

"Oh," Colette speaks up. "There's my dad. Y'all want to meet him?"

Yes. Yes, I do. I want an opportunity to let him know what a creep I think he is and that he needs to leave Colette alone before he gets her hopes up, or gets her in trouble, or—wait, he's coming over here.

Colette gestures for him to come closer to our table, then turns to me with a pleading look. I know that look. Colette's my best friend, and no matter what I may think of her father, she just needs me to be cool right now. Plus, I am aware that she's introducing her newly involved father and brand-new boyfriend to each other, so that's got to be weird for her. Yup, I'll be a good friend.

I adjust myself in my seat a little, as if I'm preparing to pose for a photo.

"Hi, Daddy." There she is, like a little girl again. "I want you to meet my friends."

Her father wears a slightly unnatural smile, like a mediocre salesman.

I plaster on my own fake grin and jump to help Colette. "It's nice to finally meet you, Mr. . . . . " I can't help throwing in the "finally," but I realize that I don't know his last name. Colette took her mom's maiden name: Degruy.

"Davidson," he chimes in. "But my first name is Lawrence—Larry. Please, call me Larry." That disingenuous smile flashes again, revealing teeth so white I can almost hear the *ping!* sound, the one they use in cartoons when something is sparkly clean.

"Okay, Larry," I say. "I'm—"

"Estella. Miss Estella Fortunat. Of course. Colette's told me all about you."

All? I don't like the idea of this man knowing much of anything about me.

"Great. You can call me Stella." See? I'm being perfectly nice.

Colette looks relieved. She continues with the introductions. "And here are some of my other friends, Joanna and Shelly."

Both girls offer a friendly wave.

"And . . ."

I resist the urge to drumroll on the plastic tabletop.

"This is Jack. Jack Courteau."

"Sir." Jack reaches out and gives a firm handshake. This is one area where he is not awkward at all: etiquette. Prep schools know how to crank out well-mannered young men.

"Please, just Larry."

"Well, it's so nice to meet you." Jack is uber polite and I kind of love him for it—as a friend—for being the opposite of what I would expect from a Courteau. He's not snobbish in the least toward Colette's run-down dad. He's very respectful. Obviously, I don't care about Larry's feelings, but it's nice for Col.

"Listen, would you kids like to grab some pizza after school? My treat." Larry appears to have gotten his parenting know-how from watching old reruns. Pathetic. He pats his pocket. Must have just gotten paid.

Thank God for the café. "Oh, bummer, I've got work tonight." I attempt to sound regretful, but it comes out erring on the cheery side.

"Yeah, Dad, I've been scheduled for tonight, too." Colette's regret is sincere. "But Monday after school would be perfect. You're off, aren't you, Stella?"

Damn you, Colette. "Yep." Shelly and Joanna have snuck off to the other end of the cafeteria, dumping out their trays of food into the trash. No doubt avoiding being coerced into having an awkward pizza dinner.

"Great," Larry says, turning to young Courteau. "How 'bout you, Jack?"

"I'd love to." He sounds sincere. God love him. Colette's beaming.

"Well, I've gotta get back to work," Larry says. "I just wanted to drop in and meet y'all. See you Monday!" He gives Colette a quick hug, then waves goodbye to the rest of us.

"Thank you." Colette's still smiling at her boyfriend.

"I'm looking forward to it." Really, Jack? Really? You are so weird. And I dream about dead folks.

"Yeah, Col, you got it," I say. I'm feeling guilty for the

second time today. After all, doesn't Colette work for my parents? She has to deal with my family's crazy all of the time.

"It'll be fun," I add. Colette eyes me suspiciously but says nothing.

☾

Birthday parties at the café can be chaotic. Thankfully, my mom doesn't force us to sing "Happy Birthday" to celebrating patrons.

"You don't know them, why should you?" is her perfectly reasonable take. She just has us bring over a piece of cake with a candle stuck in the middle to the guest of honor, and then we let their friends croon away for them.

I grab my mother before the place gets packed.

"Mama, I'm sorry. I don't know why I . . . " She holds up her hand to stop me.

"I'm sorry, too, Stella. I was stressed and taking it out on you. But would you jot down when you take something and ease up a little bit?"

That seems fair. "Sure." She turns back to stirring her caramel sauce, just as I lean in to give her a hug.

"Oh." She gives me a pat, one hand still stirring.

Why is it like this with us? We're always just a little out of sync.

In walks my dad, sweeping me up into a big bear squeeze.

"Time to get to work, girl!" he yells. My father never needs a reason to hug me.

I can feel my mom watching us and I wonder what she's thinking. Why can't she be like this? GG used to be playful with me, too. Not super cuddly, but I felt excited just being around her. She radiated fun and adventure, and if you stayed close, you got to be in on the action.

My dad takes a spoon to taste my mom's sauce and she predictably slaps his hand away, laughing. Their routine is full of love. I know my mom loves me, too. She's always there, always doing the right thing. Sometimes I wish she would just do the fun thing.

The night moves pretty seamlessly. It's a packed house, no question, but when it's this busy, work moves fast. There's no time to think.

I'm cleaning up the table of the largest birthday party, saying goodbye to the last customers when I notice it.

A small crimson coffee mug and saucer with a bold onyx trim.

GG's favorite coffee cup. It's sitting on the table, a third full of coffee. I'm furious. This mug stays on display in a place of honor near the entrance alongside photos of my grandmother and her pale blue hat with netting. It's practically a sacred relic.

I leave what I'm doing, seize the cup and saucer, and march into the kitchen.

"Who gave this to a customer?" My cheeks are burning. I'm met with puzzled looks all around.

Colette's mom, Dena, walks up and puts her hand gently on my arm. It's then that I realize I'm shaking.

"Why don't I take that, sweetie?" She holds out her hands in offering. I guess she's scared I'll drop them.

"Who?" I ask again, this time more confused than upset.

Colette shakes her head, bewildered. My dad's been sitting at his desk near the back of the kitchen, working on the schedule,, but he's been focused on me since I stormed in.

Mom comes out of the bathroom and sees us frozen in the kitchen. "What's going on?"

Dena moves toward my mom in one large stride. She's a tall, slender woman, her hair pulled back tightly, with strong cheekbones and wide-set eyes. She's filling the room with a calm energy; I'm sure she doesn't want my mom to freak out.

"Monique, it seems that a customer was drinking out of Evie's cup."

"Oh?" Mom raises an eyebrow and that's it. Maybe Dena was being mellow for me and not my mom?

"Mama! Someone *drank* out of GG's cup!" How is she not getting this?

"I heard, Stella. They probably just didn't realize it was a display piece and brought it to their table."

This makes no sense, but before I can protest, something distracts me. A scent fills my nostrils. The distinct scent of crappy instant coffee.

My mom takes the cup and saucer from me and

heads to the sink to wash them. That's our cue to get back to work. Everyone's quiet, startled by my outburst, no doubt. We finish cleaning in silence. What just happened?

Colette and Dena say goodnight, then walk out the back door and down the block to their apartment. New Orleans has earned a reputation for crime, but Magazine Street is always pretty populated and safer in pairs or groups. That being said, I'm pretty sure Dena packs a pistol in her purse.

Mom heads upstairs to bed but Dad catches me before following. "Stella, what happened earlier? I understand being bothered, but it seemed a little . . . extreme."

"I don't know. I don't know why that made me so angry."

My dad just nods, kisses the top of my forehead, and says, "We all miss her. Night, pumpkin." He goes up to bed while I pause in the stairwell.

I do miss her, of course. But is it that? Or is it that for a moment I didn't miss her? For a moment I felt her here, observing. Observing, but offering no answers. And all I want are answers. A good night's sleep hasn't removed the very strong sense of fear from my heart. I turn off the hall light, climb the creaking steps to my bedroom, and wonder how a café guest could be drinking Taster's Choice when it's not on our menu.

Sleep is restless, taking me in and out of hazy dreams and my darkened bedroom. The sounds of the street usually lull me, but tonight it seems like there are more ambulances than usual. A soft rain pulls me into slumber a few hours before dawn.

I'm walking . . . being led through a small wrought iron gate. It looks like every old garden gate in the South except for the detailed scrollwork at the top, forming the letter "C." I'm surrounded by a ring of magnolia trees and stone walls in the background. A large fountain graces the center of the garden where water pours from the mouth of a lion. I sit on a small bench overlooking the fountain. Someone sits beside me. A man. He's fuzzy. It's all fuzzy. I inhale the rich rose fragrance. I listen to the gurgling of the water, watching the sunlight splashing off it, scanning this dream garden . . . wait. I blink my eyes and squint, trying to see through the blur.

Standing, I step closer to the fountain and rest my hand on the lion's head. The cool stone mane offers support as I feel my knees begin to wobble. The deep green grass in this place breaks in one spot, just across the way. It's topped with a large stone block with a black hole in it . . . I'm squinting more to try and get a clearer look, but it's not even necessary. I know an open grave when I see one . . .

I jerk awake just as the sun's coming up. Before another thought enters my mind, I climb out of bed, grab my purse off the vanity, unwrap my tarot deck from its scarf, do a quick shuffle, and pull a card.

A woman rests her hand on a large yellow lion.

Strength.

I haven't pulled this card in some time. I guess I'm going to need it.

Even though sleep was a joke, I take time with my makeup because, well, I've got the time. My dad's a no-show with the coffee today. I'm sure he's busy helping my mom refill the pastry case that got cleared out last night.

I go down to get a cup, and there they are, pulling out loaves of pumpkin bread. The smell of cinnamon floats around the kitchen like an invitation for the weather to cool.

Halloween is a popular time of year in New Orleans. Tourists love to play Voodoo. GG said it was usually harmless, like getting a mojo bag for luck, or a banishing wash to keep the bill collectors away. But sometimes people could get in over their head. My GG didn't have a storefront like Mama Pearline, so when people came to her for a reading, or the occasional magical assist, it was because they were either a savvy local or the rare out-of-town sucker who had brought some funky energy upon themselves by meddling with power they did not understand. Tourists in a magical mess didn't know how lucky they were when someone handed them Miss Evie's number. She could undo just about anything.

Although tarot was her specialty, I know she did, on occasion, receive payment for services involving the breaking of certain charms and hexes. Such services were more often required two times a year: during Mardi Gras and during Halloween. Halloween is also the time when the veil between the living and the dead is said to be at its thinnest.

Growing up, I can remember her and my mom both wanting to take a stand around this day. October 31, or All Hallows' Eve, was all GG's. Sure, my parents would take me trick-or-treating. The café was ghoulishly decked out and it was the only time my mother would get a little witchy (she has this black conical hat with a heavy lace veil that rocks). After I got home and picked through my loot, I always loved to creep up to my grandmother's room and see what was brewing.

As a little girl, I loved having a prophetic grandmother. She was older and wiser and knew what the hell she was doing. She even had Mama Pearl join in. On Halloween, my grandmother would pull out pictures of all the men she had loved (and there were a lot) and nestle them all together on her altar. To her credit though, my grandfather had the largest photograph, in the finest frame, in the center of them all.

Mama Pearl would show up with an enormous album of deceased cats that she had tolerated. GG also included a small photo of her parents that normally hung above her bed next to a crucifix, a portrait of the Virgin Mary, an enlarged copy of the "Empress" tarot card, and a charcoal sketch of Marie Laveau, the legendary Voodoo Queen of New Orleans. It drove my mom bonkers that the Holy Virgin and her Son had to keep company with such a shady cast of characters.

GG insisted that this was the time for the clearest

divination because you could get the strongest guidance from the spirits as long as you asked nicely. She would pull out all the stops: tea leaves for reading, her most expensive Victorian collector's edition tarot deck, her finest attire, which Mom liked to say made her look like the madame of a brothel (plunging necklines and heavy fringe should probably be avoided once you've reached your seventies), and a crystal ball that she insisted had been given to her by a Romani Gypsy lover. I'm pretty sure she was pulling my leg about the backstory on that ball because after she died I found a little box in her closet filled with love letters from old suitors. On the front of the box was pictured the very same "crystal ball" with a sticker from the Bargain Bin proclaiming it, "Gen-U-ine Glass—only $4.99!"

Still, I do think GG actually drew some prophetic goodness from it. Of course, she could do some solid readings from a plain old deck of playing cards, so I'm fairly confident that the secret to divination lies more in the reader than in the tools they use.

GG told me I had the intuition. She encouraged me to pay attention to signs and symbols that popped up. Her gift was so extraordinary, though. *No* amount of practice could give me such abilities, not that I had the time or opportunity anyway. And to be honest, I always liked playing with makeup and just sitting at GG's feet. There's a lot of enjoyment in knowing a good witch, but it's lonely being the one having to piece the puzzle of the Fates together. At least that's how it feels to me lately.

After I had watched my GG and Mama Pearl cackle and coo over the departed and stuff themselves with pumpkin pie—they always left a slice outside on her tiny balcony as an offering to ghostly visitors—my mom would whisk me off to bed. Although I would protest, GG actually seemed to support her on this one. God knows what the hell they were doing late into the night, but even my wild grandmother must have thought it was too intense for a child. Besides, my mom did have a legitimate excuse: All Saints' Day mass. That's right, my GG may have ruled over October 31, but the morning after was all my mother's. I was actually okay with that. I like church. I don't always go and my mom only pushes attendance on particular holidays, in which case my dad will join us as well. He likes to debate with Father Matthew, who's good-natured and playful, like my pop.

I'm a fan of Father Brian. He has never pushed me to be just like my mom and has never given me grief about the tarot cards he knows I like to work with right alongside my rosary. In this town, there are lots of Catholics who practice forms of mysticism that would be frowned upon by believers of their faith in other parts of the country, and there are plenty of witches who identify with aspects of Christianity that might irritate the rest of the Pagan community.

Ah well. This is New Orleans and New Orleans really doesn't give a crap about what anyone else thinks of her. School moves in its monotonous way. Students fall into its trapping rhythm. School and work; work and school.

Something is forcing me to break this lonely pattern, though. It's climbing into my bed and stealing me away from what is safe and easy.

I'm going back to Mama Pearline's. I need more answers and I know Colette's not going to be able to give them to me. I've got a dead grandmother whose spirit appears to be MIA. So I'm left with the loony old lady on Chestnut Street. Thursday will leave me plenty of time to visit with her.

My sleep has offered no more dreams, but endless turns of wakefulness. It's October 4—a full moon is approaching on Saturday. I'm hoping that Pearline will have something in mind for a waxing-moon ritual that will offer up some information.

School's out and I breeze past Colette and Jack with a, "See you later," but Dylan the tagalong stops me.

"Tomorrow morning, then?" he asks.

"Sure." Is this Friday morning hangout a regular thing now? It's not that I mind Dylan. Hardly. I just don't know what to do with this. Normally, I would be daydreaming and doodling in my homework and mixing up saucy concoctions of deep red lipstick. These days I feel too haunted to allow myself to feel much about anything else.

I move quickly to the shop. I'm fairly certain that she

doesn't close until seven, but I don't want to take chances. I'm going to corner this witch.

I approach the storefront as someone else is leaving —a shaky little brunette woman. Poor girl. I bet Mama was her usual comforting self.

"Just avoid all red trucks for the next few months!" A raspy voice calls out through the open door.

The small woman nods jerkily and walks away.

I reach out to grab the closing door, when I feel it pulling shut.

"Hello?"

"We're closed."

"The hours on the window say otherwise."

"They're wrong."

Slam.

Rats and curses. I guess I'll have to do a little research in GG's books. She had tons, most of which my mom got rid of, but I managed to rescue a couple: *Dr. Moses's Hoodoo Compendium* and *An Encyclopedia of Stones and Herbs*. I'll have to see if there's something I can dig up in there.

The internet has so much information on folk magic and Voodoo, but it's not at all discerning and often overwhelming. I always preferred "Google Evie" instead. Now "Google Evie" is gone, Mama Pearl sucks, and I'm left with no other options.

To the books I go.

ELVIS & GRAVEYARD DIRT

THE EMPRESS

I find my mom in the back of the kitchen sorting through index cards.

"Hi, Stella." She doesn't look up, but she knows it's me.

"Hey, Mama."

"I'm putting together the fall pastries. I'm thinking of adding apple turnovers."

I hadn't asked her what she was doing . . . did she think I had? Or was she just attempting conversation? "Sounds good." I really just want to get to reading. "Listen, Mama, I've got some stuff I need to—"

"So, how's Dylan?"

"What? What do you mean?"

"His mom came by with a new coffee—Black Magic. Haven't tried it yet. Anyway, she said that Dylan has been walking you to school lately." My mom's attempt at sounding casual is beginning to fail her.

"Just *one* time last Friday . . . and tomorrow," I concede.

"Are you two an item?"

I can't help but laugh. "Who says 'item?' No!"

"Well, I'd like to talk with Dylan."

"What? Why? You already know him. Plus, you know his mom, and Dad's fished with his grandpa, hasn't he?"

"But I don't really know Dylan. He's only recently started making deliveries. Do you know him well?"

"He's just a friend. It's not a big deal."

"Have him come in tomorrow so I can talk with your 'friend' for a bit."

I roll my eyes. "There won't be time, Mama. Colette wants to stop at the bookstore to pick up a cookbook for her mom. That could take a while."

Maybe it's the magic in me, or maybe it's some mother-daughter link, but I swear I can see my mom's eyes narrowing with suspicion through the back of her head.

"Call Dena if you want," I add. Col did mention that her mom had ordered an out-of-print book on Creole dishes. She's a very good cook in her own right, but I suppose it's always good to keep learning.

"No need. I'll just call Angie Reed and tell her to send Dylan over a few minutes earlier so we can get to know each other better."

Ugh. I want to smack the smirk off her face. I know

it's there. I also know if I continue to protest I'll draw more questions regarding my whereabouts these days and I can't afford that.

"Fine. Can I go now?"

"You may."

Christ. I trudge to my room, texting Colette on the way.

Me: MY MOM IS MAKING DYLAN COME EARLY TOMORROW SO THEY CAN TALK. I DIDN'T EVEN SET THIS HANGOUT THING UP. WHY DO I HAVE TO DEAL WITH THIS?

Colette: AW THAT'S AWKWARD . . . I GUESS WE COULD CANCEL IF YOU WANT.

Why do I feel like she's trying to call my bluff? I can hear my mom's voice ringing up the stairs. "Hi, Angie, it's Monique. How are you? No, I haven't tried the coffee yet, but I did want to ask you about something . . . "

Great.

Too late, I text her, in a mix of embarrassment and annoyance. I tell Col I'll meet them tomorrow in front of our place, and then start looking through my books.

There's really not much to find: Selenite works like a vacuum sort of stone, sucking the weird vibes out of an item or even the aches from a person. Lavender produces peace and comfort and is great for tucking under your pillow. Cinnamon and chili powder will produce results fast; a little hematite will aid in protection, blahdy-blah blah.

Where's the good stuff? I'm looking for heavy-hitting information. GG and Mama Pearl used to cook up some insane concoctions. I remember smelling them from Mama Pearl's kitchen and occasionally from our own when my mother wasn't home. Mojo bags that were amplified with some interesting additions. Balms and potions of a sort—sometimes stuff you'd wash your kitchen with or items you'd gargle with. Whatever it was, it always smelled disgusting. Animal parts? Occasionally. No puppies or kittens, more like frogs and chickens. I recall them talking about using these potions for major protection—fighting off serious hexes and the like. Sometimes they'd tie bones together to make amulets. This kind of work definitely held a macabre fascination for me, but I didn't see much of it, and I never heard too much about it either. Probably another thing that they thought was inappropriate for a young girl, especially one with a devoutly Catholic mother. So be it. Except that now I'm blindly combing books, looking for charms that probably aren't even in print because they just pass from witch to witch by word of mouth.

Wait. It looks like the good Reverend of Voodoo is on to something. He's got a listing in Charms, Amulets, and Gris-gris Bags. It's called "Charm for Dire Situations." Okay, I'm feeling pretty dire.

A handful of graveyard dirt

1 blue candle

Devil-Be-Gone Powder

Tooth

I do not have any of those items, except for maybe the blue candle. I could probably get the powder at Mama Pearline's, and if she won't let me in, I can get it from another shop in town. *Tooth?* What sort of tooth? I'll go back to that one. *Graveyard dirt?* Okay, I've never collected it, but I know GG has because she gave me strict instructions about how to retrieve it properly. The dirt is the riskiest item because you don't want a bunch of pissed-off spirits that feel as if you've disturbed their resting place on your hands. A practitioner must take extra care.

"First," GG said, *"when you get to the gate of the cemetery, you need to make an offering of silver coins. Dimes will work. If you get an unwelcome feeling, walk away right then. If you feel okay, proceed. Once inside, you can ask permission to retrieve a bit of earth. It's nice to ask this of a specific person. Just stop at a headstone and ask by name. Leave some more coins by their grave. Again, if you get that unwanted feeling, just walk away without taking anything. You'll know if it's all right."*

I've never done this. I've never used graveyard dirt. It's typically reserved for the hardcore stuff, used by the experienced witch. My practice goes no further than lighting the occasional candle and putting together a couple of mojo bags when I was helping out GG. To say that I'm in over my head might be an understatement.

I begin to question these measures. Is this stuff really necessary? I mean, I haven't been strangled in a little while. So I saw a grave. So what? People have nightmares about zombies, but that doesn't mean they retreat to the mountains with a machine gun. Sometimes, a dream is just a dream.

I close my books and begin to distract myself with makeup. I pull out jars of mineral powder and a couple of tubes of craft glitter. Nope, that won't work. The craft glitter is too chunky.

My vanity houses five drawers: one just for GG, one full of miscellaneous crap, and the large center and two remaining ones devoted to all things cosmetic.

I reach into the lower right drawer, pushing aside stacks of small canisters containing rainbows of eye and cheek shades. I wiggle my fingers around until I grasp what feels like a thick pencil, as well as a long vial half full of iridescent white powder. If you could bottle fairy dust, it would probably look a lot like this. I twist the lid off a midnight-blue powder, dump a little on a small tray, and begin adding the white . . . and adding . . . and adding. Oops. I've made that gross powder blue eye shadow that only worked in 1980s music videos, and maybe not even then. Time to add more blue. Looks like I'm running kind of low. I buy a bunch of the mineral colors and lip bases online and keep a list of what I need to stock up on. I'm due to make a pretty big purchase soon.

It needs something more. I pull measuring spoons out of a Ziploc baggie from the center drawer and heap up half a teaspoon full of that mossy green I'd made, swirling it into the mix. Nice. It's producing a deep teal. I add in a pinch, just a tiny pinch, of a very pale yellow and stir it in to form a gorgeous aqua. Triumphant, I begin to pack it into an empty jar. I tug the lid off a Sharpie with my teeth and write on an adhesive label "Mermaid," then stick it to the outside of the little tub. I'll try it on for school tomorrow. I wonder if Dylan will like it?

It's nice to spend some time like this, being girly and dreaming about boys. Feels normal. I'm even beginning to feel a little sheepish about my recent freak-outs. Maybe I'm reading too much into everything. Maybe I *did* grab my own neck when I was sleeping. Who cares what kind of coffee I thought I smelled? I could be looking for pieces to fit together a certain way, when really there's no puzzle. Maybe I just miss GG. And maybe I'm a little pissed off that she hasn't bothered to pay me a visit. Not once. Not a face in my dreams, not a chill down my back—nada. I thought she was the Witchiest Witch in New Orleans. Maybe I don't see her because I'm not witchy enough. I'm trying to ignore the ugly little thought that likes to worm around in my brain from time to time.

Perhaps she hasn't connected with you because it was all bullshit.

I barely turn up the volume but the voice comes in quite clearly.

Perhaps the whole thing was a lie she told herself. You've had some insightful dreams in your life, so what? A lot of people think all this stuff is just hocus-pocus nonsense people tell themselves to feel comforted. Maybe they're right. Maybe they were just lies my grandmother told herself, told me, and told the tourists.

I've had this thought a few times in the two years since GG passed. I've never been able to find peace by jumping into the arms of Catholicism, either, because I see how my mom and my GG held the same degree of passion for different beliefs. When I have this struggle, this doubt, I start to think it's all drummed up out of passion, out of the need to be a part of something bigger.

GG lit candles and talked to nonexistent ears. Mom lights candles and prays to saints, who are just a bunch of dead humans rotting in the ground.

I didn't really question magic before she died. I drank it all in like a warm mug of coffee on a cold day. All magic. The magic of God, Jesus, Saints; the magic of burning a little sage bundle to clear out bad energy or counting Hail Marys on a rosary. Shit, just the magic of uttering a prayer and believing that somewhere between my wild-eyed GG and tight-lipped mother was something powerful that cared about me. Being with GG made it easy to believe. Some people are just like that. You don't have to believe very much because you're more than covered by their faith.

My mom's the same way, except her God didn't seem quite as fun. I mean, I like Him okay, it's just that GG was like the cool girl throwing a party you were dying to get invited to and Mom was like the geek trying too hard to get you to come over by enticing you with her badminton net or ping pong table. Now that GG's dead, sometimes it feels like the party's over. I can't help but wonder if all the weird stuff happening to me has been my own desperate attempt to bring it back.

"Where are you, GG? I miss you." I can feel my face crumpling and twisting into a gruesome expression. Oh no. Tears pour down my face too quickly to even attempt to slow down. They flow along the side of my nose and merge with my snot to form a salty river on my lips. It's hard for me to breathe. I finally just let go and boohoo.

"Where *are* you?" I gurgle out, a little louder than I mean to.

In an attempt to drown out my sobs and sadness, I pull open my little cabinet doors and slide out my turntable. I begin flipping through some of my grandmother's old records.

Neil Diamond's Greatest Hits. I smile a little. So cheesy, plus she was kind of in love with him.

I pass over a few records of zydeco music. It's like a crazy jazz-meets-bluegrass-meets-polka kind of sound— very Louisiana.

Elvis Presley catches my attention. That's where I'll start. I let his crooning cradle me while I continue crying.

Wiiise men saaaayyyy, only foooools rush iiin . . .

What the hell is going on with me? It's like she just died all over again. Yeesh.

I open my GG drawer and pull out the little box that holds some of her letters from admirers. I gently tug the burgundy ribbon that binds the stack of notes. The cloth gives way easily, and suddenly I am lost, journeying through stories, prying into her life. GG wouldn't care. She told me all about the wealthy banker from New Orleans who drew her away from her small world in the town of King, Louisiana when she was just sixteen. The one her parents told her she was much too young for. He was exciting. Her father insisted she not see him anymore, so off they ran. Daddy was right. Shortly after their courthouse wedding, the beatings started. I don't think my GG put up with a lot, ever, and even in a time when some women took "till death" at its word, even if it meant at the hands of an insane spouse, she got an annulment. She always said that her marriage to him didn't deserve a divorce. It just deserved to be labeled a mistake. But she kept some notes from this guy.

"My beautiful Evie, Our love has blossomed in the springtime."

Blech! She should have known he was a creep. She showed me this stack of letters a few years back, and told me about the men who wrote them. I asked her why she kept ones from the banker. She said that he loved her once, in those letters, and it reminded her of why she was willing to give up everything.

"Everything?" I asked.

"Everything," she'd answered. Her father got sick after she ran away, and when her marriage ended, she went back to King to see him on his deathbed. They sat and talked, cried and forgave. But her mother was not interested. She parked herself in the kitchen, refusing to speak to her daughter the entire visit. When I asked GG about her mama, asked if things changed between them, she said, "No, they didn't change. They were always that way between us, at the root of it. When she officially shut me out, she was just being honest."

I think it was around this time that my grandmother started investigating her gifts. Her intuition had always made others uneasy, but now she lived in New Orleans, a city that encouraged the strange—she was home. Her skills grew; her powers grew. I don't think she ever attempted to contact her mom from the other side. I guess in our family one can hold a grudge for a hefty amount of time. Letter after letter . . . my grandmother lived one hundred lives in her eighty years, before her heart gave out. Even in her old age, she had dated. Mom rolled her eyes whenever one of these gentlemen would come to call, and preferred to ignore them. GG's second husband, my grandfather, passed of cancer when my mother was a little girl. I think he made a big impact on my mom. *"He was a lot like your dad, Stella. Warm. Safe. Stable."*

I always thought it was weird that these qualities attracted her to my father. Sure, warm would make my list, too, but stable and safe? It sounds like she was in the market for a high school principal instead of a husband. My dad is funny, and outgoing, and probably the only reason my parents have any friends at all.

The record is starting over, and while I'm done with Elvis, I'm not done grieving. I poke through the rest of her music collection, picking up a sappy one I vaguely recall.

Dixie Romance: A Collection of Southern Love Ballads

I plunk it down upon the player, rest the needle, and violin music comes scratching through. A lot of the singers on the album have that nasal tone that was so popular in the 1920s. Others lean in with a folksy drawl, while others have a more proper Savannah lilt. Most songs are about courting and have lyrics like "Will you be true?" and "Let's marry in the old chapel"—corny but beautiful in their own way.

The scratch gets a little thicker, as if the needle was set on this one part . . .

We loved each other then, Lorena
Far more than we ever dared to tell
And what we might have been, Lorena
Had but our loving prospered well

The song stirs something within me, the way a smell triggers a distinct memory. Only no memory is coming into focus. Did GG used to play this? I'm sure she did. Probably played it on repeat when she and Mama Pearl holed themselves up in her room, playing canasta and trying to hide the smell of cigarettes by stuffing a towel under the door and blowing the smoke out the bedroom window. The melody has a haunting quality, like ghostly notes floating through the air. The song ends. I start it over. I sing along like I know the words. I do know the words. Some of them, at least.

Through the veil of sound, my mother's voice breaks in.

"Stella. Stella!" It gets louder. "What are you doing?" I turn to see her standing in my doorway, sniffing the air like a bloodhound.

"What is that smell? Were you *smoking?*"

"No! You know I don't smoke!" I don't. Never have. The one bummer about my grandmother was how badly she used to stink, although sometimes I get nostalgic for that mix of tobacco and heavy perfume.

"It smells like cigarettes. What are you listening to? What is that?" Her eyes fall on the pile of letters.

"Nothing. Just some of GG's stuff. Music and notes and stuff."

The room does smell funny, kind of like, well, shit. Kind of like jasmine and tobacco. I think my mom can see that I've been crying because she backs off.

"I miss her, too, Stella."

Does she? I remember what was so familiar in the chorus of the song, in the sound of my mom yelling up the stairs, probably even the reason why I think I'm smelling smoke. I have heard this tune before. My GG played it right before she and my mom got in the biggest fight I can recall—just a few weeks before GG's death.

My GG was in her room, blowing smoke out the window and putting together some mojo bags for attracting money. I sat at her feet and handed her the green muslin pouches one at a time while she stuffed them with various trinkets and herbs. There was music playing in the background, an old ballad.

And what we might have been, Lorena . . .

I leaned my head against her knees while she twirled my hair in between stuffing bags.

"Ya know what this song's about?" she'd asked. "It was popular during the Civil War. Confederate soldiers liked to sing it to their brides. It was a true story about a man who was denied the hand of a woman because her parents didn't approve. It's about loving someone so much, and yet not being able to be with them."

"It's about loss—being pushed aside and rejected for better prospects." My mom answered, her tone hushed but still audible across the music. She stood in the doorway like she stands in mine now; only in place of suspicion she wore a pained expression.

My GG jammed her cigarette butt into a small crystal dish on the table by the armchair, waving the smoke away.

"Don't bother, Mom."

"I didn't know you remembered this song, Moni."

"I remember plenty about it. Stella, go downstairs and help me fill some tarts."

"Mama, I wanna stay here!"

"Stella, just do it. Okay?"

"Moni, let her stay with me. Can't Ben help you?" GG asked.

"Yeah, Mama. Can't Dad do it?"

My mom glared at GG. "Stella, I need you to get out of here."

My dad overheard her as he was walking down the hall, and he must have caught her tone, because he promptly led me downstairs.

"It's not about you, sweetie." He tried to comfort me. "It's about their own crazy."

"What do you mean?"

"Aw, you know—"

Yelling broke his words. "You're stifling her, Moni! She needs room to explore. She can't breathe like this." GG's voice shook.

"Yes, Ma, you know *all* about that! Horrible, pesky families just weighing a girl down."

"That's not what I—"

"That's ALWAYS what you mean, Ma!" The door slammed and my mother flew down the stairs.

"I'm going out. I'll be back." She grabbed her purse by the front door and off she went.

My mother silently stepped in the door late that evening. The next morning, she woke me up to tell me that GG wasn't feeling well and that she was taking her to the doctor. When I got back from school, I went to GG's room to check in on her. She looked as if she had consumed an aging potion. Is it possible for a person to lose fifteen pounds over the span of twenty-four hours? I could have sworn GG had. She lied and told me she was fine. I didn't believe her, but I also didn't want to stress her out further by fighting about it. My mom had already done enough damage.

Over the next couple of weeks, she made a few more visits to the doctor. A home-care nurse came by regularly, along with a handful of GG's friends. My mother slept with her every night and always tried to coax her into taking a variety of medications. By then, I knew my grandma's heart was giving out.

So that was it. GG would have me pull cards and tell her what I thought they meant. Sometimes, when she had a bit more energy, she'd offer to brush my hair. I was happy to let her. I soaked up her attention, always. I wish I'd done something more. My mom hardly cried at her mother's funeral; she shed the kind of tears that could easily be put away with the dab of a tissue. Not me. A bucket couldn't have collected all my drops.

"Yes, I miss her," Mom repeats, then turns and leaves without saying goodnight.

I close the door behind her, annoyed that she's interrupted yet another opportunity to connect with my grandmother. Maybe I'm feeling something else, too.

My window sticks. I have to knock it with the side of my fist before I can crank it open. Layers of paint spanning nearly a century do that. I had knocked the needle off the record when my mom broke in and now I just want peace. But the outside brings more distraction. Maybe distraction is as close as I'm going to get to peace right now. Traffic can be lulling, like the sea.

The moon's belly is full. I like her well fed like this. A

content mother watching over her brood below. I hold my hands out to Her, palms up.

"GG, please. I need you now. Please. Help me. Guide me. I'm lost."

Sometimes the simple prayers are the best. My mom wouldn't like this, my petitioning GG like she's some kind of saint, but I don't recall any experience of having in-depth discussions with the Heavenly Father in the flesh. Besides, she's *my* saint.

I wait for something, some kind of sign, but there's nothing. The only answer to my plea is the sound of sirens, the laughter of a crowd walking out of a nightclub, and the trill of a trumpet player who frequents the corner. Plenty of other people have plenty of their own prayers tonight, and I'm not so sure that God, or my grandmother for that matter, have room in their ears for mine.

I think about the girl and her lion on the face of the *Strength* card. I set a pen and notepad by my bed, determined to write down my thoughts the minute I wake so I don't lose anything important through my already clouded vision. I salt my doorway and windowsill, make the sign of the cross, and place crystals under my pillow for protection.

But tonight I'm taking another precaution.

"Bingo!" I smile as the very Evie-ish word escapes my lips. I notice an old headband in the drawer I'd pulled the notebook from. It's wrapped in a deep scarlet ribbon. I pick the glue off one end, unravel it, and then rip it off the other side. I snip both ends at an angle with a pair of scissors to keep them from fraying, then grip one side tightly as I lay down on my bed, letting the rest trail off onto my pillow. I remember hearing somewhere that shamans like to hold onto ribbon or string when they go on a vision quest. The idea is that the string tethers you to this reality, so you can feel safe to explore vast dimensions of spirit and know that you'll find your way home in time for dinner.

I slip into sleep feeling a bit more ready. If GG won't help, I'll take matters into my own hands.

It's dark, nothing but black for what feels like hours.

In a flash, I zoom in like a camera onto the setting. It's the same small garden, only now the tomb is sealed where there used to be a gaping hole. I am immediately struck by two things: the fact that my vision is so much clearer than it was the last time I was in the garden and the strong floral aroma. It's so out of place as I watch golden leaves falling to the ground. I can't see blooming flowers anywhere, and yet the smell nearly burns my nostrils. It's got an artificial quality to it, though. As I consider all this, I can feel warm fingers wrapping around my hand. Sitting beside me is a boy—more like a man—in his powder blue uniform. He's wearing a cap with a symbol. He's a Confederate soldier. My mind swirls with questions but my mouth never opens. It seems I'm just along for the ride. The young soldier removes his cap.

"It's beautiful," he remarks, looking down at my lap.

I follow his gaze. With my free hand, I'm holding the tip of a pen against a sketchpad. I feel the corners of my mouth turn up and set aside my drawing. He wraps his arms around me so tightly it's almost painful. His lips press to mine and I accept. His kiss tastes of tobacco.

"Happy birthday, Miss Beatrice."

A second of black and my eyes are fluttering open again.

I'm sitting up in bed, feet planted on the cold floor. The scent is as strong as ever and I know exactly what it is: GG's dusting powder. This time it's not dumped all over me but scattered a bit across the sketchpad on my bedside table. I'm holding the bottle in my left hand and, in my right, my pen.

I tug on the chain to the wall sconce and squint. The powder almost looks like snow that's fallen across the picture. It's not the most artistic sketch—drawing has never been my strong suit, unless it's a cat eye with liquid liner—but I can tell what it's supposed to be. It's a gate with a finial on top in a very specific shape. A fleur-de-lis.

The fleur-de-lis is an old French design. It is an interpretative pattern of a lily. It's as much a part of New Orleans as crawfish étouffée, Mardi Gras, or Voodoo. The symbol can be found everywhere. Lord knows how many front doors and gates in this city bear it.

My drawing doesn't really offer any helpful clues, but I'm not totally disheartened. I can take a hint. I tighten the lid on the bottle of dusting powder. The front of the tin tube has a smattering of pink, purple, and blue flowers on the label and reads, "Jasmine Mystique."

I turn it over in my hands. A bit of scotch tape holds a tiny scrap of paper to the underside. GG's handwriting is scrawled along it, forming little letters. "Vision Powder." There we go. She must have blessed and magically charmed this dime store musk for assistance with divination. I had seen her apply a bit to her wrists and collar, but I had never asked, and she had never told me about it. I smile. Maybe GG is listening after all.

I'm so distracted with this thought that I almost forget that my mom has conspired to destroy me.

SHAMELESS GHOSTS & AWKWARD MEETINGS

THE LOVERS

*D*ylan is already sitting in the parlor that acts as a small lobby of the café. He couldn't look calmer as he sips from one of our mugs.

"I really do like this coffee, Dylan. Black Magic, is it?" My mom's chatting away like they are a couple of girlfriends out for lunch.

I want to vomit on her. "Yes. Thanks, Mrs. Fortunat. I actually helped develop this roast. Can you tell how it starts off with a little bit of sweetness and then finishes with a smoky flavor?"

Now I want to barf on Dylan, too.

"You're really doing a great job," Mom says. "Your dad would be proud."

I have yet to reveal myself. I'm perched on the landing, just out of view.

"So you and my Stella are becoming good friends?"

My Stella? "I hope so." I almost tip over.

"Stella, sweetie, why don't you join us?" Dammit. How does she know? I try to play it off.

"What? Oh, hey, Dylan. I didn't know you were here." Pathetic. "Morning, Mom." I lay down the "M's," hoping she picks up on my irritation.

"Morning, sweetie." She's acting like she didn't notice, but I know better.

Dylan turns to look at me with a smirk. "You knew I was here."

"What? No, I didn't."

"Yes, you did." His grin deepens and my mom snorts. Why can't I fling fireballs at people? One for each.

I clear my throat, ignoring Dylan. "I'm going to grab some coffee."

They continue their pow-wow while I saunter to the fridge for ice-cold coffee. To my horror there is none—just the steaming-hot type. I decide it's fitting since it's actually a little chilly. I felt an unexpected breeze blow in my window while I was getting ready. It's unusual for Louisiana to get that way before the end of October.

I pour the Black Magic blend, trying a sip before I add cream and sugar. Sweet with a smoky finish. It is pretty delectable. I just add a splash of cream to my large to-go cup.

"Well." I burst into their chat. "We don't want to keep Colette and Jack waiting."

I have a difficult time looking at Dylan on the walk to

school. Colette whispers something to Jack, prying away her hand that has appeared glued to his and instead takes my arm, letting the boys pass. We cut through the park. The exotic scent of sweet olive blossoms contrast with the crispness in the air.

"So how was your chaperoned date?" She giggles.

"The only date was the one between my mom and Dylan." I make a gagging sound. "They were so cozy together."

"There's nothing wrong with a guy who's nice to your mother. My mom *loves* Jack." She gets that swoony look as she says this.

"And you? Do you *love* Jack?"

"I might . . . " A smile creeps across her lips. Colette was never one to dive into anything. "He's so sweet, right?"

We look ahead to see Jack's arms up, as if moving with an invisible dance partner on the sidewalk. Dylan's hands are in his pockets as he stops to watch.

"So, like this, Dylan. It's more formal, of course, but it's fairly simple. Luckily, I can practice it with Colette now. Back at my old school they would just pair me with smaller boys." I can barely stifle hysterical laughter, and Colette can't help but giggle. Dylan keeps listening to him talk with an expression of deep concentration. A moment later, Colette catches back up with her boyfriend, distracting him from his solo dance, and Dylan slows down to walk beside me.

I think I count at least six fleurs-de-lis on the gates of the stately old homes we pass.

"My mom . . . " I begin, already regretting it. "She thinks she's really funny or something. She's always asking weird questions." I hope this covers any awkward residual left over from their conversation.

"I actually think she's pretty cool. I like her."

Now I just feel silly . . . and sound like a brat complaining about my mother.

We approach the steps to school. Just as Colette and I are about to head off in the opposite direction of Dylan and Jack, he says something else.

"And Stella, I don't mind answering questions. Especially not when it's about you."

I look everywhere, other than Colette's gaze, as we head to our lockers. She clears her throat loudly and I am forced to glance her way.

"Well, well." Colette crosses her arms in satisfaction. "Looks like your mother was right to meet with him. He's pretty intense, isn't he?"

"He's . . . something." Dylan is his own brand of magic. But if I go there, I just might lose myself and I can't afford that. Not when I feel like I'm sacrificing chunks of my mind to the dead and their undead grievances.

I have been dreading pizza Monday with Colette's dad,

Lame Larry, and now it's finally here. I try not to roll my eyes as he flaps his mouth about the café.

"I'll have to drop in. I hear your desserts are legendary," he says between bites of pepperoni pizza.

"Come by anytime," I manage. "We'll hook you up."

"Dad? Maybe we should just bring you something to go, you know?" Colette widens her honey-colored eyes.

"Oh, right," Larry sets his overcooked crust down and wipes his hands with a paper napkin, his narrow face looking longer than usual.

How could he forget? Wasn't it his idea to keep quiet?

"Listen, guys, I don't want to put you in a weird position. It's just that Colette seems to think we should wait a little while to tell her mother about me. Maybe closer to the holidays, when I can really show her that I've had solid work—that I'm here to stay." He puts his arm around Colette's shoulder and squeezes. "And I want to respect Colette's wishes. Whatever I need to do to put things right between us."

Colette gives him a pat. Her wishes, huh? He stares down at the table. Is that guilt I see?

"Why don't I get some more garlic knots?" Jack volunteers, leaving the table to go talk with a server.

Larry clears his throat as he watches Jack stride off. "He seems nice."

"Oh, Daddy, he's great. I mean, he's so sweet to me. I've never met anyone like him."

Neither have I. Young Courteau really is a throwback

from a different era. He's taking his time . . . I wonder if intentionally?

"Stella, what do you think of Jack?" Oh, no. You don't get to do that, Larry. You don't get to drop in and play investigative dad like you have some right to be protective.

"I think he's kind of a weirdo."

Colette's horrified expression is almost cartoonish.

"But in a good way. I just don't know many boys who seem more comfortable with grown-ups than people their own age. And he has this weird way of speaking— kind of like he's from the 1920s."

Larry chuckles.

Colette's shoulders droop in relief. I've done my friend duty. I'm just trying to be myself. It's pretty much the same thing I said to Colette's mom when she asked about Jack Courteau.

"But I do think he's the real deal." I tie it up with a bow. And it's true. I do. I think he's good for Colette, too.

"I agree." Larry gives me a wink that suggests we're chummier than I feel we are.

Colette pats him again. Man, I envy her heart. She's so . . . forgiving. Everyone in the world would do well to have a friend like her.

Along with our garlic knots comes another delivery: a massive fudge sundae. Our server sets down a few small plates so we can dish it out.

"Dessert's my treat," says Jack. "Happy one-month anniversary, Colette."

Barf.

Halloween's just around the corner, and with it, an opportunity to hopefully get more clarity from my dreams and spectral grandmother. She's got to know something, right? I know she set me up with that Vision Powder.

I invite Colette to stay with me Halloween night. We'll dress in fun costumes, give goody bags to café guests, and hand out candy to trick-or-treaters like we always do. Only this time, I need her help. My visions have gotten the best of me. It's time.

I go to bed with my ribbon and a dab—just a dab—of the powder between my eyes, where they say the Third Eye chakra is—a point of intuition. The dreams float in and out of focus. Some nights I'm in Beatrice's house, others I'm in the garden with the soldier boy. In one dream we seem to be walking the grounds surrounding the manor. They're far reaching and perfectly manicured. Beatrice's small cottage plantings are a bit wilder, a little less refined.

I've gathered that I'm Miss Beatrice, yes. I've also gathered that the gate I doodled after my last dream is the smaller wrought iron gate to our private little garden.

My arm links in his as we stroll. The words are muted but I can pick up occasional lines.

Across the grass, I see a stately brick home, but I don't go inside. I go back to my own place. As our walk is coming to an end, he leads me outside a very large gate, much grander than the one in the small garden. We walk along the cobblestones for a short time until we round a corner and stop at a charming narrow townhouse. In the tidy courtyard, we walk past a gardener who tilts his large sun hat at us.

The boy leads me to the front door, kisses my hand, and says, "My dear, I have a duty to uphold; a family to think of. But you'll never want for anything. I will personally see to it —not a thing on Earth or heaven."

"What about hell?" I can feel that same small smile tugging at my lips.

He starts for a second. "You'll never want for anything," he repeats, and then he lets go of my hand.

A servant is at the ready, opening my door, removing my shawl and bonnet. I pay attention to my hands as I remove a pair of delicate lace gloves. There's no ring on my finger. No surprise there, based on what I just heard. I notice something else . . .

"Miss Beatrice, I've got some of those little cakes you like. Baked 'em up this morning." She's a short woman and her skin has the deep glow of molasses. I remember my hands again. They're like molasses, too.

I wake from the last in this week's string of dreams. Okay, a young black woman named Beatrice. And a boyfriend? Or suitor, I guess. Except, I'm pretty sure that he just broke up with me . . . her. And, I think she was sort of okay with it. I mean, she joked with him and smiled. At least, I think she was joking. And what was up with the, "You'll never want for anything" remark?

I'm full of questions, but it isn't lost on me that by inviting only little dreams, thereby getting only little answers, I've been able to avoid the violent nightmares.

My dad's the history guy, so I'll take a chance on the living with this one. I find him rereading a Zane Gray novel in the overstuffed armchair in my parents' bedroom.

"Dad? Do you have a second?"

"Always." He finishes what must be the sentence he was in the middle of, then tucks a scrap of paper in place, and lays the book down.

"So . . . " How do I begin? "Obviously black people were enslaved in Louisiana, right?"

"Yes."

"I mean, of course. I knew that," I say, more for myself than him. "And I know that there were some free black people here, right? Around the same time?"

Dad nods patiently. "Were they treated the same as whites? Would it have been all right for an interracial couple to be together in New Orleans?"

His bushy eyebrows close in on each other. "There were more free blacks here than in a lot of the South because of our French-Haitian population. Those people typically were not sold into slavery, so the laws did not apply to them. And they did have some rights. Some. They could own property, run businesses . . . some had their own paid servants or even their own slaves, but they still weren't on par with white people. They couldn't vote."

"Neither could women." I can't resist getting that in, even though it's got nothing to do with our discussion.

"Right." My dad smiles. "Even the men couldn't hold public office. They faced their own struggles—"

"But what about relationships?"

He looks confused by my question. "Oh, well, yeah. There were interracial relationships, sure. Plenty. Not marriages. Not official, legal ones, anyway. You know." He's got that look that he gets when he's offering up interesting trivia. "Some of the wealthier white men of New Orleans had a special setup. There were these grand gatherings. You know how we have Mardi Gras balls here?"

Duh. I might stab someone to get into one. Wear a killer gown, crazy makeup . . . wait, *come back, Stella.*

"Well, they had these balls. They called them quadroon balls. Young women of color would be invited as the debutantes—the guests of honor, so to speak. Well-brought-up, mixed-race ladies of society. The gentlemen in attendance were wealthy Creole white guys who were perhaps looking for a placée—sort of like a bride."

"A bride?"

"Well"—he looks uncomfortable—"brides, or, you know, women they would 'look after.'"

"Gross. Like prostitutes?"

He nearly spits out his coffee. "They wouldn't have

called it that. The arrangements were referred to as left-handed marriages. But yes, it was creepy."

"Look after . . . as in buy stuff for?"

"Why are you so interested in this?"

"Just curious. I heard something about it somewhere."

My dad can appreciate pure curiosity. "It is unusual. They mostly happened in New Orleans, these formal events. And yes, if there wasn't to be a wedding, the man would probably furnish a house for the girl, buy her clothes, keep her bank account full, etc."

"So, a sugar-daddy-type thing?" It does feel awkward to have this conversation with my dad, no matter how cool he is. He's still my dad.

"Right-o." It's clear he doesn't want to get into any more details, history buff or no. That's okay, I get the picture.

"Colette, I think I've got it! Nope. Damn." She's already at my locker, working the combination for me. All she does is snicker. She finishes smoothing back her long brown curls with a thin green headband, adjusts her crisp white button-down blouse, and applies a coat of clear lip gloss. Clear lip gloss—so boring.

"You're a dear." I blow her an exaggerated kiss.

"You know it."

"So it was cool hanging out with your dad on Monday," I lie.

She smiles. "That's the third time this week you've said that. Do you really mean it or are you just kissing my ass?"

Damn, Col.

"I don't know." I did *not* mean to say that. It just fell out of my mouth. "I'm being supportive, okay?"

"I know you are."

"All right." I'm eager to switch subjects. "Hall-O-Weeeen!" I say the "Weeee" part like I'm a five-year-old on a high-flying swing.

"You know I left my night open after eight."

"Perfect. It's Thursday so the café will close at five. I can't believe I don't have a costume yet!"

A boy in my fifth period walks past us. I must be loud in the halls because he gasps, "WAIT! That's not a costume?"

I roll my amethyst-glitter-lined eyes. "Douche."

I add a few more crystals to the corner of my lids as I continue my discussion with Colette —just for spite.

"Anyway, I figured we could talk about what we're wearing. So I thought we'd—wait, what do you have before eight? Evie's closes at four that day."

Guilt is evident in her puppy dog eyes. "Jack invited me over for dinner. He wants to properly introduce me to his parents . . . and then we're going to hand out candy to trick-or-treaters. But I'll be over right at eight. I promise."

My face must be revealing my disappointment.

Feeling like a loser, I try to play it off. "So dinner with Lucille? That does sound like a scary Halloween."

"I know. Jack says she's actually very sweet once you get to know her."

"It's a good thing your boyfriend's so sweet because he's a lunatic."

We giggle as we walk to class. I spot Dylan on our way. He's wearing a dark blue T-shirt with the Crescent City Roaster logo on the back and running his fingers through his dark hair—scribbling what looks to be some last-minute notes in his homework. He glances up to see me looking. I muster up a little courage and offer a smile. He returns something weak and watered down.

"Did you see that?" I ask Colette as we head to Social Studies, a class we share. "He practically gave me a dirty look. What the hell?"

"He didn't give you a dirty look. As for, 'What the hell,' you haven't spoken to him since last Friday."

"So? We've hardly spoken at all until recently."

"Stella, he met with your mother. He's been meeting you to walk to school. You act like he's not there, or at least like he doesn't matter."

"I do not!" But my heart drops as I think about her words. She might actually be right—I just didn't expect this. And Dylan is just so . . . so . . . intense. He means some kind of business and I don't have a clue what to do about that.

"Colette, I do like him." I'm surprising myself with these words.

"I know you do. But *I* know you."

"It kind of seems like he does, too."

"Yeah, but who wants to feel blown off?" She glances down at her phone as Ms. Lerner tells the class to turn them off.

"It's Jack." She's now glowing. "He likes my costume idea."

"Which is?" Class has begun, but we're in the back where if you whisper, you can pretty much talk through the whole thing. I think Ms. Lerner's hearing ain't what it used to be.

"A medieval princess and a knight in shining armor." She grins, seeing my look of disgust. "What do you want to be?"

I think about it for a minute. I was planning on asking Colette to dress up as a Greek goddess with me. I already have the white sheets for togas and some sandals. I thought we could be Aphrodite, goddess of love and beauty, and Hera, queen of the gods. I was even going to let her pick.

Now? I don't feel too queenly and I definitely don't have a grasp on the whole love thing. All I can think of is Medusa, a good old-fashioned Greek monster with a beautiful face and snakes for hair. I throw it out to Colette.

"Isn't she the one who could turn men to stone with a look?"

"That's the one. Seems appropriate, doesn't it?"

Colette starts to protest, but she knows I'm in a funk and there's really no point in trying to talk me out of it.

I don't want to think about it. I don't want to think about these absurd dreams, or the ridiculous boy who has an effect on me, but they won't stop haunting me. I just need to focus on Halloween plans. That'll wipe 'em away.

Colette and I plot out the night: we'll hand out candy to any straggling trick-or-treaters, gorge ourselves on the remaining café treats from the day, then watch something spooky, and I'll do a tarot reading for her. She likes to humor me on special occasions like Halloween. I'll keep the reading light and fluffy because I plan to hit her with the real favor I need afterward. Maybe, between the two of us, at my haunted house, we can piece this puzzle together.

I know it's a long shot, this idea of Colette doing this with me, but I can't afford to think that way. I've got to make this happen.

WOBBLY KNEES & ALL HALLOWS' EVE

THE MAGICIAN

*I*t's a perfect Halloween morning, one where the sky is bluer than any summer day. The leaves put on their prettiest dresses before they dance and die. I'm getting dressed up myself, sweeping black liquid liner along an eyelid and pull it out into a large spiral that almost looks like something on a Grecian vase. After I finish each eye, I apply a deep red to my lips with a paintbrush. A little vanilla powder thickens it and masks the taste of beets—they're what give it that raspberry jam color.

I've got my toga on and I've borrowed a golden cuff bracelet from my mom. I'm shameless with the gold powder—it's going from the top of my forehead, across my shoulders, down to my tippy toes.

I pull the snake wig I purchased yesterday from my

bag. Little mean-eyed beasties are swirled in an acrylic pile, tongues out, ready to strike.

The perfect crown for a perfect weirdo. I walk downstairs and find Alice and The Mad Hatter. Impressive, Mom and Dad.

My mom looks startled. "I thought you were going to be a Greek goddess?"

"Plans change. Let's get to work." Colette's carting out the to-go orders for all the patrons who've counted on us for their Halloween party success. Dena and I work the front counter, shelling out café au lait and bags of pumpkin pralines, hunks of pumpkin bread, squares of pumpkin pecan bars . . . I'm pretty much over squash.

"I met with Jack last week. I'm sure Colette told you." Dena fills me in as I'm setting up a box of brownies for a church trunk-or-treat order.

"No, she didn't." Apparently there's a lot in Colette's life I'm not clued in on anymore.

"Well, I did. I think he's nice. And I think you were right—he's unusually polite."

"Isn't he?" It comes out sounding like I'm suspicious. I feel bad. "I mean, it's a little unusual but he is nice. Really nice."

There. Now I'm back in Destiny's good graces.

"Can I have a sample of a pumpkin praline and a sip of each of those coffees before I make a purchase?"

I roll my eyes to the heavens and turn to see what kind of a jerk I'm going to have to deal with.

Dylan is leaning on the counter, wearing that grin. I can't help but grin back. Damn.

"Got a minute, Stella?"

I'm about to tell him no, I do not, but I don't get the chance.

"Sure she does." Dena's motioning for Colette to come behind the counter and help. "I've got you covered, Stella."

"Thanks." Dylan walks behind the counter and sets two large bags of beans in the lower cabinets like he's an employee himself. "Let's go out back." It's more of a statement than a suggestion.

I don't say anything, but follow him like I'm a guest in his house. We pass my dad, who's on the phone taking orders, and my mom, who's pulling ghost-shaped sugar cookies out of the oven. They both offer a friendly wave as if it's perfectly natural for Dylan to be here with me.

In the last minute I take charge and cut in front of him, turning the doorknob and gesturing for him to go outside like it was my idea in the first place. He laughs, and leans against the short brick wall that borders the tiny patio. Just beyond is the small back parking lot and stretch of alley. My father planted a line of evergreen trees in a strip of dirt surrounding the outside of the brick border to offer a little privacy when we're out here, but that's not all too often.

"You know we aren't in a competition, right, Stella?" Dylan says straight-faced.

"What?"

"You know, 'the one who cares the least wins.'" I'm dumbfounded as to how to respond. Where did he learn this kind of honesty? I thought I was pretty forthright, but this?

My knees wobble. All I can do is repeat my question.

"What?"

"Because if that's the deal, if you need that contest, then you'll get the prize. Hands down."

I'm suddenly consumed by a lightheaded feeling, mixed with a twinge in my chest.

"I care." What? What is coming out of my mouth?

"Good. I'm glad, because I wasn't sure." The next thing I know, he's kissing me.

I've kissed a few boys. Joey Hertschmann last year, who was my boyfriend for about two days. Neil Lance at Homecoming, which was less about romance and more about not knowing how to say goodbye at the door. Cody Blagg in kindergarten behind the slides . . . some long-dead military man in my dreams.

This, with Dylan, is something entirely different. It's that coffee-and-shaving-cream smell—the sensory overload. It's in my nose, on my lips. Somehow it's taking up residence in my entire being.

I pull away, as if to make sure I can keep myself contained, seal up this feeling somehow, but it's too late.

"Scared?" Dylan's mouth is smeared with an unmistakable beet stain. Our faces are inches away. I can still smell him.

"Of you? Nah. Maybe of your face right now." I find

myself licking my thumb like my mom used to and wiping my lipstick from his lips.

He doesn't flinch. He just smiles, that smile that seems like he's been reading a diary I haven't been keeping.

"Shouldn't I be more scared of you right now?" His eyes rest just above my face. I completely forgot that I'm wearing a giant snake wig.

Dena pops her head through the door. "Sorry, sweetie, but I need you to come back here."

"Be right there."

"Look, Stella, I'm not the kind of guy who's willing to see past your oddness."

His words cut through me. I'm speechless.

"No, I mean, I'm not just willing to see past it."

"Yeah, I heard you say that already."

"Will you just give me a minute? What I mean to say is that I don't think your strangeness is something that should be ignored. It's one of the things that I really like about you. It's something special." He adjusts a stray snake on my wig.

No one has ever referred to what is usually considered a character flaw as "special," not in the nice way, at least. I've had plenty of unsolicited advice: "Wow, that's an interesting color. Have you considered something more natural?" or "Is that a tarot deck? Huh." or "Are you that Goth girl who sells brownies?"

I don't feel safe to let on my surprise, though. Not yet.

"I'm sorry I've been distant and weird. It's just that I have a lot going on," I admit.

"Stella! We need you!" This time it's my mom.

Dylan nods. "Clearly."

"Sorry."

"I've got time. I want to stick around and see what happens." He winks and heads down the narrow alley between our building and a dress shop, on his way back, I imagine, to his coffee roaster.

I have no idea what to do with any of that. I'm actually grateful for the work. It allows my thoughts and feelings to simmer and cook, so I don't have to try and make sense of them while they're still in their raw stage.

Jack shows up in chainmail wielding a foam sword.

"Nice, Mr. Courteau." I'm not so annoyed with the pair of them now. Apparently, I have enough going on in my own life.

Colette pulls off her apron and twirls in a velvety emerald green dress.

"Look at you two," I'm actually taking a picture of them with my phone.

"So, Stella, we'll get together at eight?"

"Yup. See you later!" I pull out my tarot deck and unfold the little card table that's usually stowed beneath my bed. There's a Vincent Price movie marathon on TV, which I fully intend on settling down to. My parents are going out on their rarest of rare dates to a friend's costume party, so I'm in charge. Since I'm more of a homebody anyway, I don't think they thought twice about it. When you've been working at a restaurant since childhood, you carry an air of boring responsibility. Sometimes I notice the energy in the house more when I'm by myself—a flit of a shadow here or there, the muffled sound of music, unusual smells . . . it's never really scary. It's actually strangely comforting.

It's a night for divination, so I prep my cards, scattering them across the table to break up any residual energy. Before heading downstairs to watch Vincent, I decide to do a little reading for myself. I've been waiting on this because I've wanted to exhaust all my options. I've been pulling cards out one at a time to gain a better understanding of them. I've been—wait, who am I trying to fool? I've been scared. I've been afraid of what even a simple three-card spread might show me, afraid of what Mama Pearline has been trying to shut out of her shop.

I fix myself some coffee and leftover pumpkin bread, still fairly full after the barbecue my dad cooked up at the end of our workday. Turning on the TV, I'm greeted by an old black-and-white film—not the Vincent Price marathon, that's not for another hour.

A wide-eyed native shrieks in horror as a mob of the undead slide upon him. The camera pans over to a medicine man chanting with a rattle. He's got a dead chicken at his feet. I snort and hit the info button on my remote.

Zombie Voodoo 2: Revenge of the Undead. Ah, old Voodoo movies. So corny, slightly racist, but often funny.

I've seen a few of these with my grandmother. She liked to correct the discrepancies.

"No self-respecting root worker would do that!" or *"Enough with all the dead animals, already!"*

She did divulge that animal sacrifice has certainly played its part in Haitian Voodoo history, but that its practice has been almost entirely wiped out in modern America.

"You know I would never hurt an animal, Stella. Not one I wouldn't eat and not myself! Now, every once in a while, a situation might call for something more extreme. But! If a practitioner has to get their hands on a bit of blood, they have a reliable butcher for that. No need for senseless killing. Just take from one that's already becoming Sunday supper."

My stomach used to turn at the thought of using animal blood for anything. I stumbled across a plastic carton full of dark red liquid in my GG's bedroom mini fridge on occasion. It always bore a sticky label: Poultry. Chicken blood. Gross. No way would my mother have let her keep that shit in our main refrigerator. It was with things like these that my mom and I could see eye to eye. I'll be keeping animal blood out of my future, thank you.

The bedazzled and feather-coated fellow in this film does not share my sentiments. He is gutting that poor fowl and rubbing its innards on everything within reach. Miraculously, it slows the zombies to a dead stop. Then the man yells some garbled nonsense and the monsters begin to drop, but not before one of them bites him in the neck a la vampire. The root worker growls and twists in agony, possibly because he is turning into a zombie himself, or possibly because he had signed the contract to star in the third installment. The camera moves away from him as he rolls screaming on the ground and pans out to show the full moon hanging above the tribal village.

And . . . scene. Credits roll. What? "So, a shaman-turned-zombie-turned-vampire with possibly a hint of werewolf—cause of that full moon business," I say out loud to myself, now feeling pretty comfy in my snake wig.

The doorbell rings. A few younger trick-or-treaters are waiting with their parents standing behind them. It's funny how people almost seem surprised that we live here, especially if they're regulars.

"Cool, the sign's working." I smile at the kids. We posted a sign that says "Trick-Or-Treaters Welcome."

Even the shops that don't house their employees usually keep their doors open for this day. It's big in New Orleans.

"So a ninja, a cowboy, and . . . "

"A butterfly rainbow princess."

"Oh, neat." I plunk big handfuls into their pillowcases and wave goodbye.

I stay posted there for a while as I spot a cluster of young ghouls and suspiciously older masked beasties running along the street. Our neighborhood boasts some large homes and businesses like us that are generous with the full-sized candy bars, so you can collect a pretty good haul.

A beaten-up pickup pulls to the curb. I recognize the face in a flash.

The driver is Dylan. Sitting shotgun is his little brother, Arthur. Arthur's got a sweet face. He looks younger than he actually is. I've seen him join Dylan on a couple of deliveries. I think he's about twelve, but I have a feeling he's frequently mistaken for an eight-year-old.

"Hey, we're studying you in school. Medusa, right?" Arthur points at my headdress.

"How'd you guess?"

"The snakes on your head look like the pictures I've seen of her." I guess Arthur doesn't share his brother's humor. "We're on our way to a party at my cousin's house, but Dylan wanted to stop and see you first."

He does, however, share his brother's forthrightness. But he isn't smiling. I don't think he's trying to embarrass his brother; he's just stating a fact. Dylan, of course, doesn't look the least bit insecure about it.

"Right. What he said." Dylan leans into the steering wheel and smiles at me.

"Cool. Where are your costumes?" Both Dylan and Arthur produce dark beards with elastic bands.

"Seriously? That's the best you could do?"

Arthur shrugs and Dylan says, "All right, so you and Colette are hanging out tonight, huh?"

"That's right."

"Okay, my grandpa's kind of sick right now, so I'm pretty much going to be working constantly outside of school this week."

"Until he gets better," Arthur adds.

"Right."

"I'm sorry he's not feeling well. What's—"

"Trick-or-treat!" The mob of older hoodlums has approached me, bags at the ready.

Dylan gives me a wave and they drive away. Irritated, I skimp a little on their candy, then head inside to wrap myself in the arms of Mr. Vincent Price.

I don't realize I've actually dozed off until I hear a knock at the back door.

Colette takes one glance at my lopsided wig and the candy wrappers stuck to my toga and says, "Wow, this is going to be one crazy night."

I'm kind of counting on it.

"You know you can always rely on me to bring the party, Col. How was dinner with Jack and company?"

"Jack was Jack. Sweet, considerate . . . but his mom?" She shakes her head.

"Mm-hmm. Tell me." I knew she'd be awful. I'm intrigued and maybe a bit into gloating.

"Everything felt like I was in an interview—only I don't know what for."

"Why, Mrs. Jack Courteau, of course."

Colette laughs. "Nope. That would have at least been weirdly flattering. No way. It was more like . . . sizing me up as a person."

"An interview for the position of person?"

Colette grins. "Yeah, kind of. And Jack's dad . . . "

"What about him?"

"Nothing. Quiet and . . . bored, I guess. He kept leaving the room. I could tell it bothered Lucille."

"Oh, so you're on a first name basis with her?"

"Only when she's not around."

"What did Jack say?"

"He was pretty much oblivious. He did jump in a few times, like when Lucille acted as if my mom's job at the café was a hobby."

I gasp. *Bitch.*

"But she knew, Stel. She knows my mom's a single parent and she figured out that we live in that little apartment." Colette didn't look ashamed as she said it, just proud and protective.

I can't help but hug her. She's used to my random acts of emotion and continues.

"Jack defended my mom, saying that what she does is important and that the café has doubled its business with her being there."

That's kind of a stretch, but Dena is a huge asset to the café. She's a great cook and a total workhorse.

"I've just never felt so small, you know? Lucille made me feel like I had no business being there . . . or anywhere for that matter. It pisses me off."

It pisses me off, too.

"You know what?" Colette's cheeks are now flushed.

We've made our way past Vincent and are heading

toward my room. It's time for deep discussion. No room for zombie werewolves here.

"What?" I ask.

"The thing that made me feel so crazy was how subtle her stabs were. I kept asking myself if I was just being paranoid. I wondered if I was making it all up in my head. I thought maybe she really was interested in my family background."

"She's not." I just know this statement is the truth. So does Colette. "You don't think—"

"Nope." Colette cuts me off, reading my mind. "It wasn't a race thing. I really didn't get that vibe."

I smile at an inappropriate moment, pleased at hearing Colette use the word vibe.

"No, it's about the money," Colette says. "It's all about the money with her. And why should she care? She's got more than anyone I know."

More than anyone I know, too.

"Look." I want to comfort my friend, and okay, I'm feeling a bit opportunistic. "This is exactly the kind of thing a simple three-card spread can be good for. Help get you through all the muck and offer a way to proceed. And then . . . " I don't want to push my luck.

"And then, what?"

"I thought maybe you could do one for me?" She raises her brows to the sky. "Just three cards. I can't read for myself very well. I get all mixed up. I'm too emotionally involved. That's why I usually just pull one card at a time. It's a little simpler that way."

"Stella, I don't think—"

"Look, you don't have to know anything about the tarot. I still don't know much. It's only been the last six months or so since I started really working with my grandma's old deck . . . when I have the time."

"That's right, you're a busy woman. What with back alley kissing."

Of course I'd told Colette all about it. "You make it sound so trashy! It wasn't! It was . . . " Heavenly is the first word that comes to mind, but I'm sure as hell not going to use that. "It wasn't trashy," I repeat.

"Oh my god! You're really bent out of shape. Is this boy bringing out your sensitive nature?"

"Shut up." I smile, trying to milk the wounded friend thing a bit. That way, she'll be more likely to get on board with my little adventure. Manipulative but it's for a worthy cause—my sanity.

I hand Colette a pack of matches and ask her to light a few candles while I scatter my cards on the table— taking a cue, once again, from GG. She also wasn't afraid to let people touch her cards. In fact she asked them to, saying that by touching her cards they put their personal energy into the reading.

"All right, Col, set 'em up."

She sits across from me at the rickety card table and begins to shuffle. The cards are larger than playing cards, so the shuffling is a bit awkward.

"Okay, now set the deck down and let me cut it."

She plops it down and patiently waits for me to

finish. Then she places the cards on top of each other again. "Now what?"

"Hmmm . . . how do we want to do this?"

I know I should keep this simple while I've got her in the mood.

"How about you just lay down the top three cards face up, in order?"

She does so, laying them before me.

One: Recent past.

Two: Current circumstances.

Three: Near future.

It's not as heady as the classic Celtic cross spread, nor is it as in-depth as the gypsy-carnival style, but it's easy and straightforward. It's about as much as I really feel like I can get a handle on right now.

There they are: *The Hermit. The Hanged Man. Five of Pentacles.*

Well, that's great. No real surprise, although the Five of Pentacles is pretty ominous. Hermit? Yeah, I've been pretty reclusive my whole life, definitely lately. Hanged Man? I've definitely felt stuck, not sure where to proceed. Hanged Man also suggests looking at things from a fresh perspective, which would be why he's hanging upside down by his feet. Five of Pentacles? Two beggars trudging through the bitter cold—alone, shut out from the warm castle beside them. It's a bitter journey.

I do not like this at all. Colette points at the cards one by one. "The hermit makes sense, I have no idea what the hanging man means, and the third one looks lonely."

Lonely. "I think so, too." I don't want to get into it any more than that with her. It's hard to look at the last card and not see us in those figures, cloaks pulled around our necks, fighting the icy chill, searching for . . . what?

I clear my throat. "Well, your turn!"

"Wait, what do you mean? What do the cards say?"

"Oh, you know, I'm a recluse who needs to explore life from a new point of view, blahdy-blah-blah."

She's not buying it, but Colette knows that when I don't want to talk, I won't.

"Here." I scoop up the cards and begin to shuffle. I'm beginning to worry about what her cards might say. "Cut it."

She obliges and I fan the deck out, pulling three cards from different places, as if that may bring better news.

The Hierophant. The Moon. Five of Swords.

The Hierophant is a priest, which represents everything from spiritual leadership and wisdom to dogmatic tradition. I don't need to consult the booklet that comes with the deck, or even my larger tome. I know this is about Mama Pearl. It's about her insight with Colette.

The Moon. It shows us what hides in the shadows; it's the revealer of secrets. Sometimes that's about a welcome enlightenment, and sometimes, well, it's all about deception.

I purse my lips. If I can't say something nice about Larry, I'll try not to say anything at all.

The Five of Swords. Two men stand in the distance, one with his head down, while a third is in the foreground, smirking and collecting fallen weapons. This card can be viewed many ways, like all the cards, but my gut says it's about being bullied, ripped off. Ah, Mama Pearline's foreshadowing.

Goddammit. I have to help my friend, but I can't very well do that if I scare the crap out of her.

I keep it as vague as possible. "Can you think of anyone who's been recently guiding you? Maybe a spiritual leader?"

"You know my mom and I only go to church on holidays."

"Well, any kind of wise person—"

"Oh! My dad! I mean, he just came back into my life, he's totally been there for me ..."

"Maybe." What else can I say? She's actually showing enthusiasm. If I play it cool enough, I can help her through the back door.

"Just be aware of things being hidden . . . like Jack having a secret wife in Idaho," I joke, trying to keep the mood light. "Make sure your locker is securely locked—that kind of stuff. I'm still trying to understand all this, so that's just my basic interpretation. Listen to your gut."

Having polished off my hazy description with a foggy cliché, I can see her listening, nodding at what I'm saying. She's actually taking this to heart. Maybe she's feeling receptive.

Okay, Stella, play it cool. Play your cards right. "So I've been having some really interesting dreams. Not scary at all. Just interesting."

She stops nodding. I can't read her expression. "And I've discovered something weird." I get up and take a few steps toward my vanity, taking out the bottle of dusting powder. "See this?"

"Uh-huh."

"Well, I found out something neat about it." I show her the label and explain how GG's potion has given me clarity in my visions. I also stress how safe I've been. "Nothing freaky, just like being in a book. Except that it's not really in order. It's like picking up a novel and reading different chapters at a time."

"Okay?"

"I'm just trying to figure out what's going on. I miss my grandmother."

"I know you do."

"I dab on just a tiny bit. That's all I do, just a half a pinch on my forehead." I point to my Third Eye chakra between my eyebrows. "But since the veil is thinner, I thought tonight could be perfect. And since you have a different perspective, I just thought maybe you could . . . "

"You want me to go on some freaky trance with you?"

"Well, yeah. Pretty much."

"Okay."

"Really?"

"Weren't you hurt in these dreams?"

"Not . . . seriously. We'll take all the precautions—crystals, holy water, you name it."

"I trust you, Stel."

"Really?"

"Look, I knew that sooner or later you were going to want to get into this with me and it's Halloween. Plus, I feel a little bad about you being alone watching terrible movies."

I'm about to defend the "terrible movies" when I remember that I should shut up and be grateful.

"Well, all right then." We agree first to head downstairs where we polish off some pumpkin pie in the fridge and gorge on the rest of the candy. My parents duck in before midnight, wish us goodnight, and go straight to their room. They're not usually night owls. Colette pulls out a blend of chamomile tea she keeps in her bag, along with some vitamins that she insists I take to detoxify.

"You have your way of 'cleansing,' I have mine. You need to take care of yourself." She presses two massive capsules into my hand.

Not wanting to push my luck with her, I force myself to take them and fix a pot of the tea to help us relax. It's after two when we finally go back upstairs.

I prepare my room and offer her a ribbon I scrounged up in anticipation of this. I take my own red cloth and dab the tiniest amount of powder possible on Colette's forehead. My hands are shaking. I can't hide it.

"Should I be scared?" she asks.

"I've got your back." That's all I know to say. And I do. I would never let anything happen to her. I'll make sure she's safe. I just hope she doesn't wind up hating me for whatever we find.

Sleep comes quickly, despite my anxiety.

I'm back in my little house, moving quickly. I take in everything in jagged sweeps: The dainty parlor furniture, the magnolia blossoms in a vase on the front hall table. I note a swinging door to my left. A push shows me it leads to the kitchen. I'm holding my rustling skirts as I sprint upstairs. I haven't explored the house like this before. Even though it's fast, it's purposeful. Down a narrow hall. Powder room. Study. A simple but elegant room that is so plain it must be used for overnight guests. The door is ajar to the room at the end of the hall. I push through to find a wide vanity across from me. My eyes close in on one item: a small silver box that rests atop a stack of folded paper. In one long step I seize it. My vision becomes flooded with tears. I'm blinded. I clutch the box in my arms and pick up the ribbon-bound pile that reminds me of GG's. It's difficult to see the words in the water.

"My darling Beatrice . . . " It's a strange sensation. My own mind wants to slow down, take some time to read these, but the girl I'm dreaming through doesn't seem to be in a leisurely mood. I keep scanning, allowing a few sentences to pop off of the page.

"He does have my eyes but he has your sweet face. He'll never want for anything."

There are those words again, those words that make me so uneasy.

142

"*She will never know, she can never know. You will always be my darling Bea. The child is a symbol of our love.*"

I toss the letters in the air and they scatter like giant furious snowflakes. I can see what Beatrice is pissed about.

I'm out the bedroom door in an instant, when something stops me. The sound of the front door closing. I wait breathlessly, for what I don't know. Only she does, this girl I'm trapped inside. I hear footsteps gliding down the hall. I'm just listening, waiting. She's probably past the kitchen. She's moved beyond the parlor. I'm down the stairs—it's as if I've got wings. I see the blurred back of a woman, her shape muddied by my soaked eyeballs. It's got to be the cellar door. She's got it open. I reach out both of my arms and push her through it.

Her body thuds down along the wooden steps. She's grabbing for a railing and trying to get up. I move so swiftly it takes my own breath away. One more good push and she's down on the earthen floor. The tears have been pouring all this time. Now they're clearing. The flood is drying away to reveal the landscape. My movements are strong and steady.

"Cora, please! Please, Cora! It's over between us. I swear to you!"

The cellar is dark, but we are offered light by the open door at the top of the stairs and two small windows in the dank room.

One more sweep, just breathing it all in. The lamp on a side dresser. Canned goods lining shelves. My hands wrap around her neck. The fingers are almost a ghostly white against her nut-brown skin. Her eyes. I've seen them before in a mirror. Beatrice.

"Cora!"

I squeeze tighter, shrieking wordlessly. Now the tears are back. Whose hands are these? Who am I? I can't stop. My hands just keep gripping tighter and tighter, like wringing out a washcloth. Her neck becomes almost limp.

"Stella!"

Now the eyes are even more familiar.

"Colette?" I can't stop. Then, in the wild spin, I see one thing that offers me control: a red ribbon tied to my wrist trailing off into reality. I must use it.

I focus my eyes on the ribbon. My hands begin to loosen their grip. I grab hold of the fabric like it's pulling me to shore from drowning at sea. Both hands are free, beginning to be back in my control. I put one in front of the other and tug. The ribbon stretches much farther than it does in reality, but I keep going until my eyes flap open.

"Col? Colette?" I sit up in a shot. She's beside me in my large bed, wide awake herself.

"Colette, are you okay? I'm sorry. I'm so sorry!" I repeat these words, unable to move past them. Colette sits up, turns on my bedside lamp, and looks in the mirror above my vanity.

Her neck is bruised and scratched. She takes hold of my hands, flips them over, and stares at my palm, inspecting my fingernails.

"Your nails are all still bitten down to the nubs," she says.

"Bad habit." It's the only thing I can say besides apologizing for the thousandth time.

She's quiet for a minute, or for several, I don't know.

"I'm so sorry," I hear myself mumble.

"Stella, it wasn't you."

"But I knew there was a risk."

"Stella . . . " She touches her neck, wincing in pain, and then speaks more softly. "Your nails couldn't have scraped me like that."

"Colette, I'm so sorry." I don't know any other words. Now the tears roll down my cheeks, one out of each eye, like great fat raindrops.

I start sobbing.

"Knock it off." She speaks even more quietly now. Something in her whisper twists in my gut. A level of unease shuts down my tears like some kind of survival instinct. "Stella, I have to think. I need your help."

"Okay. I think I have some antiseptic in my vanity—"

"No." She takes a deep breath, closes her eyes, and opens them again, fixing them on mine. "There's some stuff I need to tell you."

I wait. "I've seen some of this before—Cora's face." A chill runs through me like a bolt of lightning. It's terrifyingly real, as if her marks weren't real enough. But somehow her knowing the name offers proof.

My fear mixes with a strange sense of relief. I'm not alone in this crazy. But what have I done to my best friend?

"You didn't do anything," she says, as if she's heard

my fear. "Okay, you kind of did. None of this stuff really happened until I met you. At least, nothing that I gave much attention to." She's speaking in the lowest hush.

I'm hanging on to her every word. "I never told you this. I didn't want to say it. I didn't want to make it real."

I nod. I know the feeling. But I still don't know what she's saying, exactly.

"Look, remember when I freaked out after my grandma gave me that necklace before she died?"

I bob my head more vigorously. "You thought it was because of the dream you told me about. That was part of it but . . . " She leans forward, so close to my face. I don't move an inch.

"Stella, I saw the same thing—in my own dreams—days before you told me. There have been some little coincidences here and there, but that one was too much. I couldn't believe that we were dreaming the same thing. I didn't want to. That's why I never talked about it."

My mind was spinning out of control. "I'm not like you. I didn't have a witch grandmother to blame it on. I'm not saying I'm a witch." She shakes her head back and forth, then holds her hands up as if to block something.

I find a few more words. "GG used to say we're all gifted with abilities."

"Will you shut up about your GG for once? I'm *not* saying I'm a witch!" Her words grow louder as she cups her jugular in pain. "See, this is why I can't talk to you about this shit!"

I don't think I've ever heard Colette swear. She pulls herself back together quickly. "I'm so sorry." They're her words now. "I know how much she meant to you. I didn't mean it like that."

"I understand. I know it's kind of weird how obsessed I am with my grandmother."

This strikes us both as funny for some reason. It is weird. I throw my head back laughing. Colette raises her fingers to her lips to protect her grin. It is ridiculous, this hurting like hell. Everyone has a grandmother and everyone will lose her at some point.

"I don't know what my deal is," I admit.

"I do. You think you're alone without her." My sobbing is back. My injured friend comforts me. She pulls my hair back into a loose braid like my mama used to when I was little, when I'd still let her mother me.

"I've seen Cora before," she repeats. "It was really fuzzy, but those eyes are pretty hard to forget." She stares straight ahead.

I follow her gaze, pretty sure that we'll be looking at a ghost on the other side of my room. There's nothing. Just my ratty net filled with rattier stuffed animals tacked to the faded pink wallpaper.

I glance at her, afraid that if I say anything now I might break the spell that is weaving between us.

"Stella"—she's still staring into nothing—"there's something else. Those letters . . . the ones written to Beatrice. . . ."

"Yeah? That's the strangled girl's name." I've been

dying to fill her in on the details I've gleaned from my sleep—the sketchy kept-lady scenario, the strange balls, and the Confederate lover. I'm ready to say it all but she's not asking questions. She wants to give me answers.

"I recognized those, too." She turns only her eyes toward me. "Not from dreams, though." I wait, keeping my mouth shut. "I saw them in my daddy's desk drawer. In his room at the inn. I *saw* them." She stresses it like I'm going to argue with her. I'm not.

She turns to face me. "I went to his desk to get a pen. He had stepped out to make a call. There was this big envelope that I felt I had to open. I don't know why."

I know exactly what she's talking about. I've wanted a detective on Larry since I met him.

"But I didn't want to be the detective, Stella."

"Stop that. Are you in my head?"

"What?" Colette looked puzzled.

"I didn't say that thought out loud. You responded to something I didn't say."

"Oh. Maybe I just knew you were going to say it. Probably intuition."

Maybe you're a witch. "There was this big envelope," she continues, busy with her recollection. "I opened it quickly. There were these old letters in plastic sheets. I saw the name Beatrice in the same old-fashioned handwriting and a date—1864. Then I heard my dad coming back down the hall, so I put it all away before he saw anything."

I'm trying to ignore the goose prickles growing over my skin.

"That was it." She shrugs.

"So you didn't ask your dad about the letters?"

"No."

"That's good." I've never trusted him and it's pretty clear she's starting to see why, but I'm not interested in causing my friend more pain than she's already in. "Let's look at your neck." I turn on my bright overhead light. The scratches don't appear as vivid as they did minutes ago. "Does it hurt?"

Colette walks over to the mirror and examines the damage. "Not as bad as it did. It hurt like hell when I woke up."

I'm completely confused as to how the bruising could have nearly healed after only twenty minutes.

It's after three in the morning. Now's my chance to fill Colette in on the more recent details of my dreams.

She listens carefully, not interjecting. At no point do I bring up her finding the letters in her father's desk. We'll talk about that another time.

"Stella, I've got a weird theory," Colette says, tracing around the bruises on her neck. They look even lighter. "Your neck was messed up for a couple of days, right?"

I nod. It seems we're thinking the same thing. "Do you think the reason my throat started feeling better within minutes was because we're talking about it? Maybe . . ."

"Someone's been trying to get our attention?"

"Exactly."

"Hellish way to get someone's attention."

"Hellish way to die."

I can't argue with that. "It's got to be Beatrice."

Colette nods in agreement. I'm still trying to play it cool and not come across as too ecstatic that we're being haunted and talking about ghosts. After this, we're truly best friends.

"But why us?" I ask, trying not to seem too curious.

"Come on, Stella. Aren't you always talking about hearing music in the café when it's closed or the sounds of people in the halls when nobody's there? You're the one who keeps tarot cards in your purse."

"But that's completely different than this. This is not a normal spirit encounter."

Colette can't argue with that.

"Besides, Col, what about you? This whole Beatrice thing? You got involved for a reason."

"Probably because I'm hanging out with a crazy witch girl. Probably because I'm dusting myself in creepy powder and taking ribbons with me to bed to keep me tethered to the Earth." She rolls her eyes unnecessarily, I think. Her statement was eye roll enough.

"Oh no you don't. You just admitted to me that you've had premonitions," I countered. "Okay, maybe they ramped up after meeting me, but that could just be some coming-of-age stuff. Lots of people with abilities grow into them in their teenage years. This is not just about me."

She looks to the floor. "Okay. My grandma has mentioned that we've had some Voodoo practitioners—maybe a medium or two in the very beginnings of our family—but—"

"But nothing! You couldn't be bothered to tell me that? After everything I've shared with you? You never thought I would find that interesting?" My voice is getting a little too loud for after midnight. Colette raises a finger to her lips to remind me.

"Stella, my great-great-great-grandparents came over on a boat from Haiti. It didn't mean anything to me. Everybody there practiced a version of Voodoo. It was their spiritual practice. Then they blended it with Catholicism and American folk magic and voila! You have your modern day Louisiana Voodoo." She speaks like an anthropologist describing a civilization she's observed, not like a girl reaching back into her lineage for truth. That's fine. We'll get there.

"Colette!" I don't like her withholding what I consider to be pretty freaking relevant information. I also don't like the little history lesson, as if she didn't know I'd heard it a hundred times from my GG. "Have you considered the possibility that Beatrice is an ancestor of yours?"

"It's because I'm black, isn't it?" Colette smirks.

"Yup. That's it."

"That would be highly unlikely. I don't think I've ever heard that name from my grandmother, although . . . " She holds up a hand to stop me from arguing. "I will look into it. I think we have records somewhere."

I'm satisfied, for now.

"Stella, this is a lot for me to handle. You're way more comfortable with this kind of thing."

"Being choked by demonic southern belles? Hardly."

"You know what I mean."

"Yeah, I do."

"So now that this bag has been opened, how do we protect ourselves?" she asks.

I pull out some scrap leather from my GG drawer and lay it on top of my vanity, then take out my Tiger's Eye and lay it dead center. Then I rip a bit of sage leaves and crumble them on top, adding a pinch of salt from a jar I use to sprinkle the openings to my bedroom. I'm not 100 percent on what I'm doing here, but I know these are tools for protection and purity, so they can't hurt, right? Besides, Colette's watching me carefully and in complete seriousness. She thinks I know what the hell I'm doing. Poor misguided girl. If I act like I have a handle on things, maybe she'll feel safer. And if she believes I'm confident in what steps to take, maybe she'll believe in the magic, too. Maybe that's how this whole thing works —magic and God and religion. Believing in someone else who believes, until it becomes real for you.

I wrap the stone up with a shoelace and hand it to Colette in a matter-of-fact manner. She smiles. It's so refreshing, seeing my friend smile over charms and commiserate with me over ghostly encounters.

"Col, I can't promise anything, except that we'll be together in this. I promise I will look out for you to the best of my ability. I actually have a weird feeling, like maybe this whole strangling thing will calm down. If Beatrice needed to get our attention, she got it."

"Fully," Colette agrees.

"You hear that, Bea? You got it, sister. We want to help. Just, please, if you could avoid the whole physical pain and danger thing, we'd be grateful." I sound more casual than I feel about this one, but I'm really trying to keep fear out of my tone now that Colette appears to be more on board than off. I'd like to keep it that way.

Amazingly, Colette begins closing her eyes for longer and longer stretches of time, drifting off into sleep. What the hell is this girl made of?

As for me, I lay awake trying to form a basic plan. I've got mass with my mother tomorrow morning for All Saint's Day. I've got a later start on Fridays, and she's already called into school to have me excused from my second period. Mom takes school seriously, but Jesus trumps education.

After school, I'll make another stop at Mama Pearl's. I need to stock up on supplies. There are plenty of other magical shops in New Orleans, but so many are overpriced. Mama P. has the best selection, and she's the closest to my house. When you don't have a vehicle or time to take the streetcar everywhere, you've got to make do. I eventually drift off myself. By morning, Colette's neck is completely free of any sign of injury. My mom invites her to church, but she politely declines. She was raised Protestant, so even if she did attend services regularly, the whole sit-kneel-stand situation at a Catholic mass is not really her bag. That's cool. I can appreciate that. But I actually love the ritual. I don't like to let on to my mom how much I look forward to it sometimes. I don't want her to ever get the false impression that in her battle with my GG for my soul, she won out, because it's not true. My soul's still very much up for grabs.

If I even have one.

INVITATIONS & ILLUMINATIONS

THE SUN

*T*he beauty of St. Dominic's Catholic Church absorbs me. Cathedrals like these could convert even the most resistant nonbeliever with their majestic architecture and delicate artwork.

The smell of incense is reminiscent of Mama Pearl's shop, as are the trove of lit candles. But instead of burning in a wild cluster as they are at Pearl's, these candles are arranged row upon row like a fiery little choir. I don't understand the Latin that's spoken, but I do understand the energy. It's searching and peaceful.

I survey the room and the faces aglow with light from the arched stained glass. They all sing, kneel, and repeat after the priest when they're supposed to. They bow their heads in prayer, but do they pray? I bow my head, too, but I'm stealing peeks at the crowd. Times like this create a feeling of loneliness. Like everyone is onto something that you somehow missed out on. It reminds me of a busy day in Biology when the whole class seems to have learned a volume of information. You try to catch up, but no matter what, you still fall behind. Of course, I happen to hate Biology. I don't hate God. Not at all. I just don't know what to do with Him. Her. It. Them.

The service comes to an end. My mom goes straight for the confession booth. I light a candle for GG and another for Miss Beatrice, then saunter toward an open confessional that Father Brian went into moments before.

"Bless me, Father, for I have sinned," I recite. "It has been . . . many days since my last confession. Probably just a couple of hours for my mother, but she lives by a higher standard."

I hear a quiet chuckle. He knows who I am, though he'll keep it a secret because that's how confession works.

"Father, can I talk with you another time in person? I need more than a confession. Well, I probably need the whole package, but I'd really appreciate the counsel."

Through the slits in the window he smiles and nods. "Of course, my child."

"So how do we do this, Father? Are you available later this week or . . . "

"You know, I don't have my calendar with me. And I don't take my smartphone into the booth."

"Oh. Right."

"But you can call the church office tomorrow and

they'll patch you through to my secretary to set an appointment."

"Appointment?" It sounds so official, like an expectation for me to bring something important to say. Truth is, I don't know exactly what I want to talk about.

"Does that sound all right?"

"Yes, thank you, Father." I guess I leave now. The door sticks as I try to open it. Suddenly it pops with a bang. I feel my face heat. Anyone looking? Yeah, the lines of folks that have formed to make a legitimate confession are staring.

"Bless you, my child." The priest's words follow me out.

"You, too!" *You, too?* What the hell is my problem?

I'm so distracted by my lameness that I almost don't see Lucille Courteau. She's standing between two marble columns as if she's trying to be inconspicuous. Hmm. Her husband's face is blank. He's looking down at the floor like he's being . . . is she scolding him?

I duck behind a tomb of some saint my mom probably talks with regularly so I can try to hear their voices clearly without being seen.

"Richard, I'm doing what I can to take care of it, but you are cut off. Completely."

"It's not just me! It's you, too!" He sounds like a teenage boy arguing with his mother.

"I'm doing my job as the matriarch of this family!" Lucille hisses.

"That's what this is? Your 'work?'" He snorts. Bold,

Richard. I've never heard someone get feisty with this woman. Whenever I see her, be it church or the café or just walking around the neighborhood, she's usually got several pairs of lips glued to her ass.

There's silence after his remark. It's so uncomfortable that I feel compelled to take a quick peek around the stone block. Yep, Richard is still standing.

"I'm taking care of this family," Lucille repeats herself. "I'm taking care of our boy."

Richard says nothing in response to this. I would love to see their faces, but I don't think I can pull off another peek.

"Stella, there you are! I just texted you." Dad looks worn out from religion. His collar is unbuttoned to relieve the pressure.

My mom appears behind him. "Ah ha! I saw someone else go into the booth, so I knew you were finished making confession"—she's speaking about it rather loudly and proudly—"what are you doing back here?"

"Oh, just checking out Saint . . . " I glance around the stone for a plaque or something.

"Dominic? As in Saint Dominic's Cathedral?" Is my mom trying to suppress a laugh?

My dad takes down another button and grins.

"Yeah, Saint Dominic." I move out in the open now but the Courteaus are gone.

"Right." My mom stares.

"Ah, it's Stella, isn't it?" Another voice cuts through.

I turn to face Lucille. How did she get behind me? Does she know I was listening? I don't even know what she was talking about, so it doesn't really count, does it? Wait, why is she talking to me?

"Hi, Mrs. Courteau."

"How are you?"

Really? We're doing this? Okay. "I'm doing well."

Richard stands beside her, smiling at me like we're old pals. "Hey there, Stella."

"Hi."

"Monique, Ben, beautiful mass, wasn't it?"

My father murmurs something and nods. My mom agrees. "It really was. So lovely." All right, then. I've had enough fake for the day, so I'll just . . .

"Oh, Stella. I almost forgot," Lucille says. "I wanted to ask you something."

Sure, Lucille. You almost forgot cause you stop to chat with me after church never. "Oh. Sure."

"I usually send these out, but I thought I'd see you today. I gave Colette hers the other night at dinner. My boy, Jack, had mentioned that you girls are best friends, so of course we'd want to include you. Colette's such a sweet girl."

I don't think anybody would believe Lucille meant that last remark.

"Anyway . . . " She reaches into a large designer handbag. What she pulls out actually makes me gasp, which must horrify my mother. It's a golden envelope with the shape of a mask stamped into a wax seal.

I know what this is. There are many opportunities for revelry during Mardi Gras, many of which completely gross me out and are best left to drunken tourists and the locals who will rob them. There are large public balls, or dragoons, that one may attend for a fee. Then there are the private balls. Some of these are held by organizations or krewes. The Courteau ball is the best of the best—legendary. You have to know somebody to get an invite to this event. I guess being the bestie of a Courteau girlfriend means knowing somebody.

I ignore the chill of Lucille's unusually long, perfectly manicured fingers as she places the silken gold into my chipped sparkly polished grip. Do I open it in front of her?

"I do hope you can make it." She gives my arm an unnatural pat, not clarifying what "it" is since it's obvious, then walks away with Richard in tow. No Jack to be seen today. I don't think too much about Jack's absence as I'm pretty sure that I just became Cinderella. Okay, at least Cinderella's BFF.

I wait for the Courteaus to be far way and completely out of earshot before I start letting out a squeal. My mom shoots in softer squeals herself.

"Open it up, Stella!" I carefully pry it apart like an artifact I'd like to keep intact. My pinky is still too big to slip under the flap of the envelope. My dad offers up his pocketknife. I'm creating a delicate incision. This is like open-heart surgery. It's as if I might negate the whole thing if I mess with the contents of the invitation.

I've got the top open. I wipe my right hand on my plain black skirt, one of my few mom-approved articles of clothing for church: "*The Lord died for us, Stella. Perhaps you could make your own sacrifice and forego ripped jeans today?*"

The vellum topped paper slides out easily, accompanied by a parade of gold-and-purple glitter confetti. It looks like a wedding invitation, except for the embossed pale purple and gold masks that match the one stamped in wax. Upon closer inspection, I note that there's a letter C in between them. Tiny gold fleur-de-lis line the top and bottom of the card. It's printed in black ink calligraphy and reads:

You and a guest are cordially invited to attend The Courteau Family Grand Mardi Gras Ball on Friday, February the Twelfth.

Dinner will be served at 6 o' clock in the evening—Dancing will begin at 7 o' clock.

Marquis Ballroom – 612 Fourth Street Please RSVP by December the Twelfth.

That may sound like a lot of time to plan for an event, but I actually don't feel like Lucille is being too anal-retentive on this one. Mardi Gras is *crazy*. A ball with as elegant of a reputation as this one must require an enormous amount of effort. I'd text her an RSVP right now if it wouldn't be the tackiest thing in the world.

"Stella, there are only a few boutiques worth going to. They're very exclusive, but this is an exclusive event." My mom eagerly offered to drive me to school the next morning. Now I know why.

She draws in a breath. "And masks. The shops carry them . . . . we can always order one. Did Lucille say anything about a theme? I didn't catch that. Now there's a certain way to eat—I'll show you how to use all the silverware. And dancing. So much to plan!"

I'm still getting in my first gulps of coffee, but I'm excited, too. We usually don't get psyched about the same things. She's never been a huge fan of my dramatic makeovers on her. The woman just can't hang with a cat eye. But this? This is nice, this shared happiness.

"Would you like to be my plus one, Mama?" I ask, partly joking.

"Don't be insane, Stella. I'm just excited for you. It would be silly for me to be your guest when you have a perfectly respectable date." She sounds like she's reflecting out loud.

It takes me a second to process what she means when she says "respectable date." Dylan. Of course. My heart spins like a funnel cloud within my chest. He would be my date, right? But I still feel so weird asking him. We haven't really been on any official dates yet. Walking to school and making out behind my parent's café hardly counts. I've never actually been on an honest-to-goodness date.

I can see my mom trying to read my expression, so I hold up my phone and bury my face in it. Thank God the school is only seconds away. I quickly say goodbye, then make my way inside, where I stop at the office to get my pass. I'm a bit bummed that I won't see Colette until PE and I have no classes with Dylan.

I sulk through the first half of the morning and finally start to feel better when PE comes around. Gym clothes seem completely unnecessary since I have no plans to break anything resembling a sweat. I'm reluctantly yanking them on when Colette comes walking around the corner. I attack her with a hug and squeal.

"I see you received your invitation." Colette's smile spreads across her face.

"Why didn't you tell me?"

"Because I thought it would be funnier for you to get the good news from your *most favorite* person," she teases.

"Isn't it the prettiest thing you've ever seen?"

"Actually, I didn't get one since I'm Jack's guest. He gave me all the details at dinner. By the way, he's home sick. Want to come with me to check in on him? You can see their house."

Sold. "Yes. But I have to talk with you about some stuff." I look around and notice a couple girls have gotten suspiciously quiet. I don't trust that our conversation isn't private, so I'll wait until we get into the gym.

As we're walking laps around the polished wood floor, occasionally picking up the pace for appearance's sake, I take the opportunity to hash out what to do about Dylan and the ball.

"Just ask him," Colette says.

"But what about the fact that no one's ever asked me out on a date? And the fact that it's a ball? Isn't this a time to keep things old school?"

"Fine. Ask him to ask you."

"You're no help," I say, gasping for air. "So are we bringing your man chicken soup or something?"

"No, I just wanted to see how he was feeling."

"Is your dad coming to take you to lunch today?"

"No, he's got a really busy work week."

"Cool. I mean, just that it's good he has work and that we can hang out at lunch . . ."

"I knew what you meant."

We spend lunch distracted, while Joanna and Shelly dissect a show they're sucked into. Colette and I both know we have to get our hands on those Beatrice letters. We know we have to figure out what her dad's doing with them. We also know we've got to buy some bitchin' ball gowns. My brain is almost coming undone from all the different threads tugging in varying directions. After lunch, I spy Dylan waiting by my locker. *Thump-thump. Thump-thump.*

"Hey, Dylan." God, I sound awkward saying his name.

"Hello, Stella." He sounds as natural as ever as he reaches out and takes my book. "What's your combination?"

Colette giggles and lists it off to him. Let's face it; she knows it better than me. He nods at her as if there is nothing weird about this and proceeds to spin the dial on my lock. I lean against the metal feeling blissful. There's something so perfectly normal about this moment in the crazy of my life, something so right about watching this boy hoist my textbooks into a little shelf and straighten up all the wrinkled haphazard papers with a smile.

He props the plastic jar full of eye shadow and lip-gloss canisters behind a binder and wipes the smudges on my purple framed mirror with the back of his sleeve.

"I have a ton of work at the roaster this week," Dylan says. "My grandpa's still taking some time off, so I'm going to be super busy."

"Well, maybe I can stop by and pick up some orders for you. I don't mind helping out."

He reaches out and grabs my hand. His is warm and slightly rough.

I try to focus while my heart's pounding. "I didn't get to really talk to you the other night. Does your grandpa have that cold that's going around?"

He frowns. "I don't think so. He's just not himself. The night before I saw you at the café he completely forgot where he was and flipped out on my mom. She's taking him to the doc tomorrow. He probably just needs an adjustment on his meds. He's been on so many different heart and blood pressure medications ever since last year; it's probably just messing with his head." Dylan pauses for a moment appearing lost in thought. "He was fine yesterday—totally himself, laughing, telling jokes—but my mom wanted us to keep an eye on him."

"Since last year?" I ask.

"Yeah, he had a mild heart attack."

"That sucks. I'm sorry."

He shrugs. "He's fine. Like I said, it was mild. If anything, the drugs he takes are more damaging than the actual heart attack, so I hope they figure that part out. My mom hates it, too. And Pops hates it most of all."

I feel like he's giving me credit for knowing way more about him than I actually do.

"Oh. Well, let me know how he's doing today. Text me or something."

"I will." He squeezes my hand tightly and then releases it. I wish he could just keep holding on.

Instead, he turns and heads toward his next class.

Colette and I meet back by our lockers after school, then proceed to the Courteau house. I'm sure I've passed by it a thousand times. It's on the other end of the park in a part of the neighborhood the Garden District is famous for: grand, stately, southern mansions.

We live in a beautiful old row house ourselves, courtesy of my late grandfather—my mother's daddy. It was her family home, and it was really all that remained, no other wealth involved. He had grown up in it, as had his father before him, as had my mother, as had I. My grandfather had used the lower level as a high-end shoe store, but after he got sick, hospital bills started piling up and GG sold the business. It still exists down the block under a different name. My mom had no use for shoe sales anyway. Baking was always her passion.

Our street is a blend of businesses and private residences, while others are just lined with historic homes, many of which, like the Courteaus, are occupied by some of New Orleans wealthiest and oldest families.

Colette and I walk in silence, letting the chatter in our heads occupy the space. The leaves have turned and are starting to lay a blanket on the sidewalks, waiting to be pushed out by a leaf blower; the scent in the air has shifted into that crisp fall smell. It's mingling with smoke from burning wood. It's a comfort this time of year when the city dies; it'll lay entombed, waiting to be born again come February while the plants stir beneath the earth and Mardi Gras bangs on in.

My feet hit cobblestone, then pavement, and then grass as we cut through the park.

It's easy to imagine that every one of these homes has been featured in a magazine spread. They are, I think, what most people fantasize about when they picture a New Orleans mansion. They're southern and traditional, laced up with Parisian style. Large gates are wrapped in vines; formal columns stand like stone soldiers. These estates have kept audience to battles and blood, parties and floods, unmoved and still holding strong. They are New Orleans. It's as if everything else that has occurred acts like a passerby, a tourist.

My own home has the same permanence, but the café is so accessible, whereas these mansions . . . not so much. Intimidating is one word that could describe them. Ominous is another.

Courteau Manor stands in the background, away from the riff-raff of the street. It is white with black shutters, has tall, narrow windows and a ruby-red front door. Between the house and us is a large wrought iron gate topped with a curled C.

"Nice touch," I remark. "That's not over the top at all."

Colette walks over to a black paneled box on the side of one of the brick columns supporting the gate. This is perhaps why I don't remember seeing this house. It's because you can't see it—not from the road at least. A high brick wall lines the property. You have to be walking along and gawking through the fence.

"Colette, I can't see the guard tower." I shield my eyes from the sun and pretend to try to scan the grounds from outside the gate. Colette doesn't seem amused.

"Go easy on Jack when we see him. He's sick, all right?" She flips open the lid of the box and begins punching the buttons.

"You've got the code? Score."

"Yeah, and I'm not telling you."

"Whatever." I hear the buzz and click of the bolt opening. I push open the gate like I live there.

We walk up the long path toward the front door. There's a separate four-car garage on one side of the house with a driveway that stretches out to another side gate.

When we approach the front porch, I notice a glass-and-iron lantern hanging above our heads. The door bears an impressive brass knocker. I note the electric buzzer on the side. Colette reaches for the doorbell, but I can't resist lifting that brass ring and pounding it against the lion's mouth. I knock it a few times too many, then ... we wait.

The door opens to reveal Jack, who clearly made a wise choice in missing school today. He sneezes into his sleeve before he can speak. His nose is reddish and raw, his eyes puffy. He's still pretty, in spite of it.

"Hi." Colette steps in to give him a hug and lean in for a kiss. Jack embraces her, but turns his mouth at the last minute.

"I don't want you to get what I have." He kisses her cheek instead. I'm still standing outside, like a vampire awaiting her invitation to be able to cross the threshold. I certainly look the part.

"Oh, hello, Stella. I'm glad you could come." I think he really means it.

"Don't you have a maid who answers doors?" I ask. It sounds so much ruder than I mean it to.

"Stella!" Colette admonishes.

"I'm sorry, I didn't mean for that to come out the way it did. It's just that I figured—"

"You figured that this house required some assistance in the upkeep. And you'd be right. My mom has been on a streak of releasing the help recently. No one's quite up to her standards." He grins, and then removes his smile quickly, as if he feels a little guilty. I don't know if it's guilt over his mom firing people for likely ridiculous reasons, or if it's for making that kind of remark about his mother. Maybe a bit of both? A young southern gentleman's life must hold many complications.

"Anyway, come on in." I step onto a marble floor. If I found the front entrance intimidating, it was only because I didn't realize it was meant to prepare me for the inside. The chandelier hanging above me is three times the size of the lantern on the porch. It's like something from an opera house. The house feels like a museum . . . or a mausoleum. Same difference.

I follow Colette and Jack from the front hall, past a study, a sitting room that I doubt anyone actually sits in, into a larger space on the left. One side of the room is lined in bookcases. It's clear this was just a library before the invention of television. Now it's a media room of all sorts: books, tablets built into the walls, speakers, an obnoxiously sized TV.

"You ladies want something to drink or eat?" Jack offers, walking toward a pair of French doors.

"You should be resting." Colette leads him over to the couch and poofs up a pillow, propping it behind him.

"We're here to look after you, remember? Do you need anything?"

"No, thank you. I'm just glad you're here. But help yourself to whatever you'd like."

I take him up on this and open one of the glass double doors, leaving doctor and patient behind. The kitchen is vast and sparklingly spotless like the rest of the house. I spot a high-end stainless steel coffeepot and look in the cupboard above for coffee. There's a bag marked *Crescent City Roasters*. It's a Colombian blend—always reliably strong. It takes me a few minutes to get past all the buttons and figure out how to grind, but the kitchen and family room fill with a cozy smell that is undeniable, even in this cold castle.

"All right, I'm stuffed up and even I can smell that," Jack says from the other room. "Stella, would you mind pouring me a cup?"

"Sure, you want one too, Colette?"

"Yes, thanks." She's rubbing Jack's forehead and having too much fun playing nursemaid.

I go back to lurking in the kitchen. Everything in this room looks contemporary, whereas the rest of the house is stocked with antiques, making most of the place look like one of those immaculately maintained historic homes they let you take tours of.

Another large pair of French doors captures my interest. I walk over to look through the glass panes. Even as the plants are dying, the garden is beautiful. It looks royal with manicured shrubs marching in a row toward a stone fountain that's been shut off for the winter. There are high metal arches covered in curling vines that are probably coated in blossoms come spring. The fountain is in the center of a wide brick courtyard flanked by benches. At the start of the row of shrubs, several round tables sit circled by pillowed chairs on the first tier of the patio. I'm sure the lawn stretches far past all this, but the evergreen bushes block most of it.

This is a beautiful place for entertaining. I can imagine the grand parties that must have been held here, graced by belles of southern sophistication and gentlemen who kissed their hands. There are times I'm sure I should have lived in another era, except for my glitter eye shadow obsession. Voodoo, however, would have been more welcome.

In the old days, free Haitian immigrants and slaves, maybe the occasional eccentric white aunt, were the people who mostly practiced Voodoo. It was the sort of thing those in high society snubbed until they needed it. There's something in this place I can feel, a sort of magic that's remained in spite of the years that have worked to polish it away. I hear a buzz that must mean the contraption has brewed coffee. I pull out a container of half and half from the fridge, grab an ivory colored ceramic mug, then begin to pour the hot liquid over the kitchen sink. The window above it offers a side view along the hedges surrounding the patio. I can see large oaks and willows dotting the property. Further off it looks like magnolia trees form some sort of wall.

Curiosity eats at me. I take my mug of heaven and head outdoors for a better look. The air is getting cold. It's always a gamble this time of year. Today Old Man Winter is placing his bets.

Steam rises from my drink, which I begin to sip. It's smooth and rich. Dylan and his grandpa always make an excellent roast, but some credit must be given to that insane brewing device. I'm in love with this cup of coffee. Each sip is like a little push as I make my way down the steps from the first porch tier, along the corridor lined in boxed hedges, around the dry stone fountain, and along a smooth dirt path that leads away from it. Now I'm passing the trees, which are larger than I thought they were, the kind of size that only comes with age and care. There's a huge oak surrounded by freshly dug holes for planting. I stop and look around to try and get my bearings. I'm almost upon it now— the circle of magnolia trees that have been trained around the wrought iron. I can see the back gate to the property from here—it's just as obnoxious as the front. But right now I'm busy; my coffee and I are exploring something . . . .

I move alongside the bushes. There's a break in the green with its own smaller gate, a keyhole at the center of it. I don't even need to push it to know it's locked. Everything I'm looking for is trapped within. I look up at the old gate to see a topper that takes my breath away. In a city full of traditions, imagery, and symbols, I could pick this specific fleur-de-lis out of them all.

I hear Colette call, but I'm too intrigued to move from this spot.

"Stella! What happened? I thought you were getting coffee . . . ." Colette's voice trails off. I don't turn to look at her, not just yet. I'm afraid that if I move I could break the spell and ruin everything. This gate is just about to tell me its secrets.

"Is that the—is that what I think it is?"

I smile. Finally, something in the world outside of our dreams reaches out. The gate is as familiar as a friend.

"Stella, what is it doing here?" She's asking me like I put it there. And then it hits me. Colette's already dealing with the fact that her father's probably got something shady going on and it involves someone who's been haunting us. Now, in her boyfriend's backyard, she's confronted with yet another image from her crazy visions with no explanation attached. This ghost is screwing with her life.

"I have no clue," I reply, still staring. I'm holding onto the bars tightly, as if it's all going to pick up and fly away.

It's my garden. I see the bench, the same urns, and large marble blocks between them. There's no doubt about it—it's my garden. Untouched. The only difference is that it's the only place in this perfect plot of land that's overgrown and neglected. The magnolia trees seem unfamiliar, too. I don't remember them.

"Why does it look like that? It was so pretty in my mind . . . why is it here?"

"I don't know." We both stand and stare for what feels like an extraordinarily long period of time. It must be long enough because the coughing Mr. Courteau eventually joins us.

"Is everything all right?" Jack asks. "I don't mean to interrupt." So polite, as if he's barging in on us in the powder room—not in his own backyard.

"Oh, sorry, Jack. I promised you coffee, didn't I?" I'm still fixated on what's before me.

"Do you like the garden? It's been on the grounds for generations. My mom's been doing a lot of the pruning and planting—she's got a green thumb, I guess you would say."

It's difficult for me to imagine the ever-plastic Lucille doing something so wholesome and organic and, well, dirty as gardening. The image makes me smile.

"But she doesn't do much with this one."

Colette remains silent, but I take the opportunity. "Why not?"

"I think it feels odd to her. It feels odd to me. What I mean is that it's not a normal garden."

I wait.

"It's got sort of a mini graveyard in there. Well, just a few buried, really, but still." He takes our lack of response as shock, I think. "It's not uncommon with these older estates, you know. A lot of families buried their dead on the property." He pauses. "But this is kind of different. What I mean is, some of the graves aren't of ancestors."

"Who is she?" I ask, pointing to the smaller one a couple of yards away from the others before I realize what I've just said. Colette draws her breath in.

"She was a servant, I think." Amazingly, Jack doesn't seem to notice that I'm aware of the gender of the corpse in his garden.

"Must have been some servant. To get in on the garden graveyard, I mean."

I know Colette wants to hit me and shut me up. I can feel it. She thinks I'm going way too far. But she does nothing and says nothing, just waits for Jack's response.

"Strange, isn't it? But sometimes servants were like family to the homeowners. Maybe she took care of the children or something."

I'm holding tightly onto myself now.

"Huh," Colette finally makes a sound. "Jack, I just remembered that I have a ton of homework. Will you be all right?"

"Yes. I feel better already now that you've come by." He gives her a hug and pecks her on the cheek. Her face is traced in fear.

"Come on, Stella. I know you've got a lot to do, too, and I could use your help." She grabs me by the hand and practically flies us out the front door.

"Whoa. Hi, Stella. What's the rush, ladies?" Dena asks as Colette and I practically fly through the door of their apartment.

"I have a history project due. I've got to do some family tree research." Colette lies more coolly than I would have expected. "Stella's helping."

"Oh. Well, we can go back a few generations. My side or your father's?"

Colette flinches at the mention of her dad. She's pretty close to her mom; it must feel weird to keep such a huge secret from her. Well, we're both keeping way too many secrets now.

"You have both?" Colette asks.

"I believe I have a little of each. In the old family bible, there were some slaves on your father's side and a bit of info on them. On my side were free Haitians." She walks over to a bookcase and squats down, pulling out a huge book that's got a cracked spine. Holy Bible. She sets it down on their coffee table. It's old, beat up, and beautiful. My own mother would treasure this sort of thing. I'm pretty certain that my grandmother got nothing of the kind from her own family.

Dena lifts the cover and opens it. There, tucked in the binding, are what appear to be some brown papers and some newer white computer printouts. She unfolds the old papers first.

"Here is a birth certificate for your great-great-grandfather, John DeGruy, and a marriage certificate for him and his wife, Elisabeth. And here's a diploma for your dad's great-grandfather who was a slave but then attended school after the Civil War. It was a huge deal for the family, obviously."

The certificate is made out to George Watson. "And his wife?" Colette asks. "Let's see . . . " Dena opens the newer papers. They show a print from work done online. "Louisa. Louisa Rutherford."

"Oh." I don't think Dena catches the relief in Colette's voice, but I sure as hell do. It's taking a good amount of energy to keep from laughing. I feel for her, I do, but the idea that she might be related to her boyfriend is pretty damn funny to me.

"So, that's what we've got from that time period?" Colette asks. "The Civil War, I mean? You said George Watson was a freed slave."

Dena is quietly flipping pages over, scanning each

one. She goes back to the massive bible and turns it over, checking behind the back cover. Then she walks back to the bookcase and pulls out a shirt box from the bottom shelf, the same spot where the Good Book was. She lifts it up and pulls out what looks like a lace christening cap for a baby and then frowns.

"What is it, Mama?"

"Oh, I'm not sure who this cap belonged to—maybe your grandmother?" She stares at the empty box she took it from. "I thought we had more documents, that's all. More family information, historical records, letters or something . . ."

Letters?

"We might have lost them in the move. That's a shame. Hopefully this will help with your project, honey."

"Definitely, Mom. It's a huge help." Dena heads back into the kitchen to work on dinner, which smells insanely good.

"You're staying for dinner, right, Stella?"

"Absolutely."

Colette speaks softly after she feels safely out of earshot from her mom. "Thank God. Not a Beatrice in sight."

I giggle. "What about the missing stuff? Your mom mentioned letters."

"She said *maybe* letters. Or maybe wedding licenses, or birth certificates, or . . ."

I'm doubled over laughing.

"You brat!" She hits me with a pillow from her couch. "You want Beatrice to be related to me. You want Jack to be my cousin. You think that's just too freaking hilarious."

I breathe. "No, I don't really. Not *really*." My smile is suggesting otherwise, but I swear I'm a decent friend. Honest. "The idea was just too much and you were so freaked out when we left the Courteaus . . . I couldn't help it."

"But we're not related. Elisabeth and Louisa were the names, Stella. And there *are* other black people in New Orleans."

I hold my hands up. "Fair enough. I will continue to support your romantic relationship with the young Courteau."

Colette smiles. It's nice to have a friend who can take a joke. Then her smile falls.

"We still need to figure out what the deal is with those letters, though."

She doesn't mention her dad when she says this. My heart stings for her. She's had way too many crappy questions come up in the last few days.

"Yup, we do. Any ideas?"

She drops her voice lower, just to be safe. "I'm working tomorrow, then my mom and I are hanging out the next day. I have a test the day after that in English— I've got to study— "

"No, you don't. I don't believe you've ever needed to study for a test."

Colette repeats herself. "I've got to study, then let's see . . . I can try to get over to my dad's to look at the letters."

"You mean to take the letters. We've got to see them."

"Yeah, right. I can try on Saturday."

"You're okay with sneaking them out?"

"Yes, I want to know more and I don't think asking is going to give me answers."

I agree wholeheartedly. "Are we going to talk about the garden?"

"No. No. I don't know what that's about; I just need to take time."

"I totally get that. Totally." The truth is, the curiosity is murdering me. But I need my best friend, so I'm going to do my best impersonation of a patient person. "I totally get that." I repeat the words again as if to cast a kind of spell on myself.

The week goes by more quickly than I expected it to. Dylan is swamped with work, like he said he would be, but every morning he passes my locker and squeezes my hand as if to let me know he's waiting for me, just as he promised. I'm grateful. This boy has some sort of magic that I can't get a handle on, though I can't seem to get a handle on much these days. I want to take my time with Dylan—it's important to me.

Thankfully, he seems to be on the same page.

I've got an insane test in Biology on Friday, and unlike Colette, I really do have to study to get a decent grade. I have a little room to do this between work and school because I'm sleeping better this week—thank God. Col and I agreed to chill out on the prophetic dreaming, at least as much as we have power. Basically, I'm laying off the Vision Powder, and we've both been asking the spirits to give us a little vacation. I think they've obliged. It's nice when ghosts are accommodating.

On Saturday, I send Colette a text to let her know I'll be off at three and ready to meet up as soon as she's able.

Three comes and goes with no word from Colette. I text her again.

Colette: SORRY. I HAD TO WAIT FOR MY DAD TO MAKE A PHONE CALL. IT TOOK WAY LONGER THAN I THOUGHT. HE WANTED TO HANG OUT AND TALK.

Me: NO WORRIES. WHEN WILL YOU BE HERE?

Colette: IN A WHILE. HE'S DROPPING ME OFF AT THE PARK THEN I'LL WALK OVER SO MY MOM WON'T SEE. SHE'S STILL THERE, RIGHT?

Me: YEAH. DID YOU GET THEM?

I hesitate to type anything else, since it sounds like she's in the car with her dad and who knows what he might see.

Colette: YES.

The café is pretty tidy. I'm wiping down the tables while Dena is back in the kitchen cleaning and prepping for tomorrow afternoon.

"Stella!" she calls through the swinging doors. "Colette just texted me. She's finishing up homework and then heading over."

"She texted me, too."

Dena pushes the little doors aside and begins straightening up the pastry case. "Between you and me, I'm worried about Colette."

"Oh?"

"I'm concerned she's overloaded." She's spraying the glass front with window cleaner and then wiping it with a cloth.

"Yeah?"

"All this extra work this year. I told her she was taking on too much by adding extra-credit projects to her load, but you know how she is."

"I do."

"How does she seem to you? She's so busy between this boy and all her studies. We used to talk all the time, but now it never seems to be the right time."

I feel crappy lying to Dena. I also feel bad that Colette's lying to her own mother. Colette used to tell her everything. I know she'd probably love to talk to her mom about what's been going on, just like I'd give anything to share it with GG. But GG's dead and Dena's very much alive. I do my best to reassure her.

"She seems all right to me—just busier than usual. I'm sure she wants to talk to you."

The bell hanging from the front door jingles. I

assume it's a customer who doesn't know we're closed, but it's Colette, who's clearly out of breath.

"Hey, sweetie. I saved you a croissant," Dena says.

"Thanks, Mom. I'll eat it later. I've got to go to the bathroom." She clutches her side, looks at me knowingly, and then moves to go upstairs.

"Baby, why don't you use the one down here? It's quicker."

"Well, you know, it's public. I'd rather use this one," she calls back down to her mom.

Dena seems to accept this. I give a final wipe to a table.

"I'm going to go get a shirt that I wanted to give to Col," I say, trying to sound as convincing as possible. It is true. I really do have a shirt that I think would look fantastic on her. That counts, right?

Colette's in my room removing a manila envelope from her jacket. She sets the envelope down on my vanity. "We have to be really, really careful with them."

I nod and gesture for her to take a seat, then grab a stool from the foot of my bed. The pages are antique brown with beautiful handwriting—identical to the ones in my dream. The scribble is so fancy and full of flourish that it takes some time for us to decipher the words.

My dear Miss Beatrice,

I am so pleased that your mother granted permission for our courtship and I hope this idea pleases you as well. I believe that our meeting at the Uptown Quadroon Ball was absolutely fortuitous. If you agree, I would like to call on you every week—perhaps Mondays and Wednesdays? I would also like to take you out on Saturday evenings. It would delight me to have you to lunch, take you to parties, and introduce you to my friends. There are many things for us to discuss regarding your future, as well. I hope this note reaches you in good spirits. I shall call on you tomorrow at one o' clock.

Ever Yours, Mr. Jonathon Courteau

Our gasps are like something you'd hear during the showing of a scary movie. We both suspected. Hell, I was pretty dang certain after seeing the garden, but still.

"Are you going to tell—" I begin.

"No. Not until we know exactly what's going on," Colette says.

"I think that's wise." I reread the letter, this time out loud. "Gross," I murmur, fascinated.

"Yes, truly gross," agrees Colette.

"I mean, you can just read between the lines on this one. He's such a cheeseball. And what's with her mother granting permission?"

"Money, security, it was a different world then. What's weird is that he didn't ask her father. I'm guessing dad was out of the picture."

"You're probably right. Wait, these look like the letters you saw before our shared vision, right?" It's a silly question. Like there are two different sets of Civil War

185

era letters to a woman named Beatrice that have appeared in our lives. I just love feeling less insane.

She humors me and answers yes as if I hadn't just asked her the most ridiculous thing.

"Where do you think the envelopes are?" I ask.

Colette shrugs.

"Right." I turn the paper over. There's nothing on the back. The next letter is dated June 12, 1862. Two months after the first letter.

My dearest Beatrice,

I hope you know that my thoughts will be with you every day while I am away at war. This will all hopefully end soon so that we can get back to the wonderful life that we have created. I've spoken to my father, who has promised to look after you while I am gone. Will you kindly do the same for him? I worry about his health, as he allows concerns of money to overwhelm and sometimes consume him. He obviously trusts you; I've never seen him trust anyone else with the safekeeping of our wealth. I hope one day you will let me in on the secret the two of you share. I imagine that we'll share many of our own secrets in the years to come. Please keep me in your prayers, darling one.

Ever yours,

Jonathon

"Well, that's interesting. Of course money was involved." I shake my head.

"Wasn't it always? Wasn't she an escort? A prostitute-type of escort, not like an escort to the ball? Not like Dylan." She grins, delighted at the opportunity to bring him up to me. I ignore her, too engrossed.

"Yeah, but this is weird. How was she in charge of their wealth? Why would his dad put her in control? Why didn't Jonathon know much about that? He's talking about a 'secret the two of them share.'"

"It's definitely strange. But I don't think she was in charge of anything. That's not what he says. He says she's trusted with the 'safekeeping of their wealth.'" Colette points at the sentence on the page.

"So, like a guard?"

"I don't know. I guess."

"Why would a young girl be a guard of some old guy's riches?"

"Why are we debating this?" Colette says. "Let's keep reading."

"Oh. Yeah." Now she's the impatient one. Rightfully so.

I hear the front doorbell ring. A few moments later, my mother's call reaches up the stairs

"Stel-la!" Weird. When people come to see me, they usually come by the back door, since that's really the entrance to our house.

Colette's wondering the same thing I am. "Maybe you got a package. Maybe a ball gown from your fairy godmother." I actually get excited upon hearing this, until I realize that it's not likely.

"You thought about it, didn't you, Stel?"

"Shut up. What are we going to do with these?" I look down at the letters.

"Stel-la!"

"Coming, Mama!"

"Can you keep them safe? It's probably better that they stay here anyways."

"Totally." I ease them back into the envelope for safekeeping and slide them into my GG drawer beneath all her treasures.

Colette follows me downstairs. There in the parlor, in what I suppose is becoming his seat on the sofa, is Dylan. My mother is beside him. I really wish they weren't so chummy.

"I've got to clean up in the kitchen. Colette, would you mind giving me a hand?" my mom says.

Colette takes the hint. "Sure." She and my mom move behind the counter and exit through the swinging double doors.

I sit beside Dylan, keeping a couple of feet between us, as if we might start passionately kissing if I don't set some sort of boundary. Dylan smiles at the gesture.

"I thought you had work," I say.

"I do, but I have something to take care of first." He reaches for something tucked beside him on the couch. I hear a crinkling sound. He holds out a rose lying within a clear plastic container. It's a long-stemmed flower surrounded by baby's breath—the kind you can pick up from the grocery store—only this one seems different.

It's a deep shade of lavender, almost silvery. I think they call them Sterling Roses. It's special. This rose is for me.

Dylan's hand shakes slightly as he offers it to me. I seize it, maybe a little too enthusiastically. Whatever rare case of nervousness Dylan may have had relaxes into a laugh.

"I hear you're going to a ball without an escort. I'd like to take you. May I?"

"You may." That rose smells really good. And then there's that coffee aftershave-y smell to go along with it. Why does a meeting with Dylan always seem to overwhelm my olfactory senses?

"Great. Thank you." He leans over to give me a kiss on the cheek. I can see my mom and Col peeking from the kitchen out of the corner of my eye. He must know they're watching, too. "So we'll discuss the details after Christmas then, a little closer to the event? I just wanted to lock you in before anyone else tried asking."

That smile. "Sounds good." My voice is unnaturally high—maybe a few decibels too loud. I have no idea what to do in this situation. "I'll go put this in some water."

Women in old movies are always rushing to put bouquets in water. That seems practical.

"Okay. Well, I better head back to work. See you at school?"

"Yep, see ya." I remain seated on the couch after he's walked out the door. "Enjoy the show, ladies?"

Colette and my mom burst through the door,

giggling like they're both about eleven years old. This whole ball situation is bringing out a playfulness I'm not used to seeing in my mom. It's sometimes fun but mostly annoying. She and Colette are holding hands, prancing around me in a circle. This is the fun part.

"We can go shopping for a gown soon, and pick out corsages, and—"

I cut my mom off. "I was going to do that anyway."

"I know, honey, but now you have a date." This is the not-so-fun part, the part where I can just picture my mom trying to dress me up like the normal little doll of a daughter she never had.

The café smells of pie almost 24/7. I never tire of it. It's nearly Thanksgiving. Dylan is in overdrive at the roaster, while the rest of us are flurried with orders for holiday desserts. My mom likes to offer up the classic autumn treats, but sometimes she'll add a twist, like in addition to pumpkin, she'll throw in a pumpkin chocolate mousse pie. Dena loves to experiment with classic flavors. She seems to inspire my mother to play more in the kitchen. Fine with me. I could eat pie all day.

Colette and Dena are joining us for our Thanksgiving feast—the café is closed that afternoon. Pies take over our entire lives the Wednesday before the holiday. We stop seating customers earlier than usual so we can all focus on taking orders. I'm sent to take the delivery van out to drop off some of the larger orders for big events. I love doing this. When you don't have wheels and your family only has one normal car that they're not about to let you take off in, driving the delivery van is fun. Plus, it smells like freshly baked pastry. Bonus.

I'm tempted to stop by Crescent City Roaster. After I make one of my deliveries, I give in to temptation.

"Stella, so nice to see you." Dylan's mother is a tall woman with long dark hair she keeps in a neat ponytail. "I'm really glad that Dylan gets to go to a ball with such a sweet girl."

I can't avoid the deep blush I feel seeping into my cheeks at her mention of "Dylan" and "date," especially since she's his mom.

"Yeah, it'll be fun. Can I help?" I feel like I should offer. She's shoveling beans into paper sacks. I notice her stop and lean into the doorway toward a flight of stairs. I've seen the actual roaster, but I've never gone upstairs. They live in their shop, just like we do.

"Dad? Do you need something?" she calls.

I hear footsteps. Dylan's grandfather is holding tightly to the banister as he makes his way down. He's long, like his daughter and grandson. We've spoken briefly a few times, when he would make the occasional delivery instead of his daughter, but it was long ago.

His eyes meet mine. "It's Stella, right?"

"Yeah. Good memory." I could kick myself—a thousand times. Why do I say stupid shit?

I stand there, desperate. Dylan's mom leans over and squeezes my arm gently.

"Sometimes he'll remember names of people I went to grade school with. It's uncanny."

I love her.

"It's true." He smiles like Dylan. "Angie, I just came down to check on the temperature settings. You know how temperamental these machines can be."

"Thanks, Dad. I've got it taken care of."

His face drops.

"On second thought, I haven't checked them in a while. Why don't you take a look?"

He brightens, and with a nod to Dylan's mother and me, he walks to the back roasting room.

"Sorry," I blurt out. "I didn't mean to say that about his memory. I just mean, Dylan mentioned . . . "

Why can't I take my foot out of my mouth?

"Stella, it's okay, relax." She pats me and smiles.

"It's not a taboo subject. My dad is just having a hard time. Sometimes he's lucid and very aware. Other times, he just doesn't know exactly what's going on."

"Angie! What's going on here?" Grandpa calls.

"Excuse me. What is it, Dad?" She follows his voice to the back room.

"This one's set way too high! You'll burn the beans! Who did this?" I hear him yell.

"I don't know, Dad."

There's a long pause.

"Oh dear. Did *I* do that? Did I just do that?"

"It's okay, Dad. It's no big deal. Look, we'll turn it down. This is a pretty dark roast anyway. It was only like that for a few moments. You just came back here."

"I just came back here?"

"It's okay, Dad. It's all right. Come here."

Angie appears, holding him by the arm at the staircase. "Excuse us for a minute, Stella."

"Sure." They start to move up the stairs.

"Have a good night," I call.

"You, too, sweetie."

My eyes are soaked leaving Crescent City Roaster. My heart aches for Dylan's mom and her dad. But it aches the most for Dylan. This is worse than watching your grandmother grow sick for a little while, then die peacefully. To watch someone you admire lose their sense of reality . . .

I shake my head, as if to shake the images out of it, then make a mental note to light a candle in prayer for Dylan's grandfather tonight.

On the way home from my last delivery, I whisper my own request to GG to please look after the Reed family. Exhausted from the day, I throw myself onto my bed and manage to pull on a pajama shirt before falling fast asleep.

The Macy's Thanksgiving Day Parade is well underway, blaring from the small kitchen television. My mom's been up since dark o'clock rolling out the last of the pies, and judging by the contents of our personal fridge, prepping a lot of side dishes for the feast, even though my Dad and I told her we'd take care of the dinner, since she basically hadn't left the oven in a week. She's shuffling around in the kitchen when I stumble in still half asleep.

"I see you couldn't help yourself." I smile, pouring a piping hot cup of coffee.

"What?" She's too busy to comprehend my small talk. I nod toward the refrigerator.

"Oh, right. I had some extra time."

"Liar. Let me help." I lean over and grab a spare rolling pin out of the drawer.

"Stella, thanks, but I really need to focus."

"I can help."

"Just set the table, okay?" A job that's unnecessary for the next five hours.

I sigh and take my drink out to the family room to watch the parade on the big television, hoping Colette and her mom will arrive soon. I had promised Colette that I would wait for her to read the rest of the letters. It wasn't that difficult to keep my word, since I was so distracted with work and Dylan's situation. In the midst of my thoughts, I realize that I forgot to light a candle for the Reeds, so I head back to the kitchen to grab one of the little white tea lights we keep in a spare drawer.

"Stella, sweetie, I've got it," Mom says, feverishly stirring a pecan mixture on the stove.

"I wasn't coming in to help or get in your way. I'm just grabbing something, okay? Geez." I turn on a foot out the side-swinging door to our den.

"Stella . . . "

I pretend not to hear her. I take a box of matches from above the fireplace, light the candle, and picture every statue of every angel from church surrounding Dylan's grandpa and the rest of his family. My dad comes through from the kitchen in his sweatshirt and jeans, getting ready to play his annual football game in the park with some of his old friends. It's a yearly ritual where they pretend they're sixteen and then spend the following week griping about the pain. He's passing the football back and forth from each hand grinning.

"See you in a couple of hours, sweetie."

"Okay, Dad." I take a sip of my coffee. "Have fun."

Colette and her mom finally arrive. To my annoyance, Dena is permitted in the hallowed kitchen to help my mother. Colette joins me on the couch. We make fun of the bad lip-synching while still admiring the dancing in the parade. Soon we are stuffing ourselves at the family table.

By evening, we're all painfully full. Colette turns to me as we lay sprawled across the couch.

"Hey, Stella, have you been working on any new glosses?"

"Lip glosses?"

"Uh-huh."

"I've been playing with some earth-toned lip stains. Wanna see?"

"Sure."

My energy's back. Colette's so pretty and she wears colors so well that I always get excited when she'll be my dress-up doll. She used to let me paint her face all the time, but ever since she broke out *one time* from a blush (one that I immediately stopped using, I might add), she's not always enthused about playing with makeup.

"We could go up to my room and try them. Want to?" I'm like a puppy about to go for a walk.

"Love to." I spring off the couch and hoist her up by her arm. She laughs and follows me up the stairs, leaving the rest of our families to digest and watch cheesy movies.

"So, I've got this pale pinkish color that would look absolutely angelic on you."

She begins to pull at the knobs on my vanity. I feel a bit vulnerable. "Oh, that's not the makeup drawer. That's my GG drawer."

"Sorry," she says, immediately drawing her hands back. "Will you get the letters out, then?"

"Oh, right. So you want to try the stain while we read over them?"

Colette smiles at me. "I was just using the makeup as an excuse, but if you really want, you can show me what you've got. I've been looking for a creamy pink shade."

I feel a bit silly but don't let it ruin the moment. I gently pull the letters from the drawer and grab some of the plain small toothpaste-style squeeze tubes from a jar on the edge of my vanity.

"Okay, I marked these, let's see . . . this one's kind of a brown-y pink, this one's a dark plum shade . . . you should try both the plum and the pale pink."

I hand them over to her. She sits on the chair in front of my vanity, while I pull up my little stool and begin reading.

DEAD ENDS & DEAD BEGINNINGS

THE FOOL

My dearest Beatrice,

It pains me to go for so long not hearing from you. The decision to propose marriage to Miss Cora Roland was a most difficult one. As I told you, I must consider the legacy of my family. Being the only child, I have an even stronger responsibility to uphold. I must also always consider you, my sweet Bea. I trust you know that this shall not interfere with our arrangement, so long as we both take care. Seeing you on my brief leave was the highlight of these long months. This war is so ugly, but the thought of your beauty gets me through each day. I heard our song being played on the banjo by one of the younger fellows, just a boy really, in our brigade. It made me ache to see you.

Ever yours,
Jonathon

"*O*MG. Seriously?" I really couldn't be more disgusted with this guy. "So he's marrying another woman, but he doesn't want it to interfere with their 'arrangement?' Classy."

"It's deplorable, definitely, but—"

"But what? Are you defending this douche?"

"Calm down. I didn't say he's an angel. But this girl, this Beatrice . . . if she goes along, she's just as guilty as he is. Wait a minute, what was that woman's name?"

I read it again. "Miss Cora Roland." We both speak at the same time. "Cora!"

"So Cora must have found out about them. That must be why she killed her."

"Mistress or not, she was virtually a kid, right? A teenager," Colette says this, processing the reality. "She didn't deserve this."

I shake my head. "She sure didn't deserve to die."

"Why is she telling us about this, though? It still doesn't make sense. What do the other letters say?"

"Let's see, it looks like there's four more." I gently thumb through the tops of the ragged papers. I pull the next one on top of the pile and clear my throat to begin reading. But no words come out.

"What is it, Stella?"

"Oh no." The page is severely water stained, to the point of being illegible, save for a word here or there. I turn to the next page. And the one following that. And the one following that.

"What is it? What's the matter?"

I hand her the stack of papers to see for herself.

"Goddammit." Seriously, Colette never used to swear.

"I knew this was going too smoothly. You know what this means, right?"

"Goddammit!" Colette moans. "I don't want to get choked in my sleep!"

For some reason, I have to resist laughing at this.

"Look, Col, I don't want you to either. I've been through it, too, and there's nothing to say it might not happen to either of us again. But you know we've got to find out. And maybe it'll be totally pain free. I mean, Beatrice knows she has our attention. And neither of us have had any physically violent dreams since the night we shared about it with each other, right?"

"True. But can't we take some sort of precaution?"

"Yes—yes." I repeat. What precaution? I take a deep breath. "Mama Pearline."

"I thought you said that lunatic barred you from the door."

"She did. But I made the mistake of letting that stop me. We'll go together. You walk in first and we'll force her to talk to us."

We devise a plan to bombard Mama P for information on Ghost Safety 101. As we talk, we each take turns looking over the ruined letters.

"Why did my dad have these when it's impossible to make any sense of them?"

There's no answer for this, so we make a plan to visit

the Mojo Parlor on Saturday after our shift is over. I encourage Colette to bag both shades of gloss before we go downstairs for seconds on everything.

The next morning I make a point to call the church office.

"Hi, I was calling to set up time to meet with Father Brian? I was supposed to call weeks ago, but stuff's been . . . oh, okay. This is Stella Fortunat. Wednesday would be great. Thanks."

Done.

I intend to use the rest of my holiday break from school to get some spookier questions answered, starting with tomorrow's little adventure to Mama Pearline's.

Colette and I get a chance to talk while setting the tables for the first of the Saturday morning customers. "So how was hanging out with your fella yesterday? How's he feeling?"

"Good. He's feeling much better. He took me for a walk around the grounds."

"Really?" All is quiet so we're careful about what we say. "How was that?"

"Familiar."

"You passed by the garden again?"

"That and, I don't know . . . "

I do. "The feeling of it?"

"And the look of it. I mean"—she lowers her voice —"there's just no denying it. It's uncanny. It was the weirdest feeling, like an intense déjà vu, just being there."

That's the kind of feeling I've always had when real life plays out one of my odd dreams.

"I get that."

"I know you do, Stel."

"Is it weird?" Now my voice matches her whisper. "Not talking to Jack about this?"

"Yes, but once we get all of this sorted out, I'll tell him. I don't even know what I would say at this point."

I nod. The ring of the bell over the door places us in position. Work has begun.

It's getting easier to come and go without too many questions since the increased business has kept my dad extremely occupied. My mother's so pumped to learn that I'm meeting with a priest that she's treating me like an adult.

Colette and I leave as quickly as we can without seeming suspicious. Anxiety builds as we pace the sidewalks. The early snap of cold seems like it's setting in to make itself at home this winter. I send a text to Dylan to say "Hi." I couldn't be more awkward with messaging him, especially considering his response.

Dylan: THINKING ABOUT YOU A LOT. WHEN MY GRANDPA GETS BETTER WE'LL HANG OUT.

On the outskirts of the Garden District, the edge of the neighborhood gets a little rougher, a little more worn. Things still have that beautiful, classical appearance, but the energy shifts a bit. I look at Colette, realizing we've been sneaking around a lot these days. If

I didn't have her, I think I'd be going nuts with all of these secrets.

Once we're a block away from the shop we go over our plan again: Colette goes in because Mama Pearl doesn't know her. I wait outside. Colette asks for help with purchasing items for protection against some violent spirits. She comes back out to check with me to see if I think they sound heavy-duty enough (okay, not that I totally know, but if Mama P just tries to sell her a smudge stick of sage, that clearly won't be enough) and if it comes down to it, I just might pop in while Colette distracts her and demand some more information.

We're set.

Colette cautiously peers into the window of the shop, then backs away quickly.

"What is it?" I ask.

"It's my dad."

"What?" I risk a look into the window, and sure enough, I see Larry sitting across from Mama P, getting what looks to be a reading.

"What do I do?" Colette asks.

"Check it out."

"How?"

An idea strikes me.

"Here." I take off my hooded jacket. "Put this on and tuck your hair into the hood."

"If my dad sees me, he'll recognize my face."

"Duh, already on it." I pull my sixties-style red-framed sunglasses out from the top pocket of my book bag. "Put these on. You would never wear these. Your dad won't recognize you if you avoid talking and stay toward the other side of the store."

She puts on the jacket, pulls the drawstrings tightly around her face, and slides on the sunglasses. She pulls a compact out from her purse. "Wow. You're right. I would never wear these."

"Well, they look awesome on you. Now you can finally be as cool as me."

She offers up a small grin. I stick to the all-brick side of the window, while she moves through the front door. I can't resist another quick peek. She's messing with her phone. Who's she texting? Come on, Col. Focus. The minutes drag as I wait carefully out of sight. I check to see if she sent me a text that I didn't notice. Nothing. I keep waiting. Did they catch on to her?

Finally, the front door opens. I slip into the side alley, just in case it's not Colette. It's not. It's Larry. I press my back against the tight alleyway, feeling safely out of sight. Thankfully, he doesn't see me as he pushes past, but I hear him.

"Stupid bitch. Goddamn useless crazy bitch."

I watch his back move down the block and then turn a corner. I wait. Something tells me to stay outside, even though I desperately want to get my hands on some good protection tools. In a rare moment of self-control, I choose to listen to that something and remain posted in the alleyway. It's been almost thirty minutes when I hear the bell of the shop door jingle. I peer around the corner to see the back of someone walking in. Right after that, another jingle. This time it's Colette.

Her disguise is dropped—hood down, glasses off. She's carrying a large paper sack.

"Let's walk down to that coffee shop on the corner," she says. "The artsy one."

I take the bag and together we walk. Colette is strangely silent. I know to let her talk in her own time. There's a strange mixture of smells coming up from the bag, but I can't see anything because a layer of tissue blocks the contents within.

We've been in Marlee's once or twice before. Its exposed brick walls are draped in eclectic local art. There's a small stage for the occasional musician or open-mic night celebrity . . . it's what I think a coffeehouse should be.

As we walk up to the counter, I notice with pride that they use Crescent City Roaster for their beans.

"Want me to get us some drinks while you get settled?" I offer.

Colette nods, takes the bag, and winds down the hall to one of the two back rooms in the coffee shop. I get a café au lait for myself, and a café mocha with extra whipped cream for my friend, who clearly needs it, then go hunting for Colette. She's in the darker of the two rooms. The space is filled with even more art and dark red pleather booths. I sit across from her and set our drinks down on the table. Colette takes a sip from her mug, then holds onto it for warmth.

"You were right," she says, bursting into tears.

"What? Why?" I've switched to her side of the booth and put my arm around her shoulder.

"My dad sucks. He's a liar and I'm an idiot. I'm so stupid." She gulps in breaths. "I thought he wanted to be my dad."

Do we have time to kill Larry in the middle of our little mystery?

"You're not stupid. What happened?"

She pulls her phone from her pocket and sets it down on the table.

"Listen." She goes to the voice memo section and presses play.

Larry: "I need something more specific than that, Ms. Pearl."

Pearl: "I'm afraid I can't tell you more. Spirit is not sharing."

Larry: "I don't have any more to pay you this week. I paid you what I had to tell me anything else. When I find the money . . . "

His voice drops and fades out.

Pearl: "I'll be with you in just a couple of minutes. Take your time, look around."

She was talking to Colette.

Pearl: "Look, I don't know if you're going to find that money, but I don't want it as payment, do you hear me? I don't want that on me. I don't want that energy."

Larry: "Look, I'm the only one who cared to pay attention. I'm the only one working on this. Somebody has stolen one of my only connections. They could take it from me. They could rob me!"

Pearl: "I think it would have to actually be yours to be considered robbery, correct?"

Larry: "It is mine. I promise I'll share it with her. Just tell me how to get to it. Please?"

Pearl: "Like I said, everything I can see stops at the hiding space. It's marked, protected by powers."

Mama Pearl doesn't seem to give a crap about who can hear her. It sounds like Larry is trying to shush her, but she seems to ignore him.

Pearl: "When something is cloaked like that, you have to know the magic to find it. It's the only way. You could tear down every wall, dig up every bit of earth in this city, but you won't find it." She laughs. "That'll be fifty dollars, please."

Larry: "What! I'm not paying you for that."

Pearl: "Yes, you are. You took up more of my time, and now you will pay for it."

Larry: "Fine."

I'd pay her too. No way would I want to owe that woman money.

Larry: "But I'm not coming back to you. I've got someone better. She'll help me."

Pearl: "She doesn't know what she's made of, and I wouldn't be too sure that she'll be rushing to help when she figures it out."

Larry: "Oh yes, she will. She's daddy's girl."

Pearl: "You're a fool. Get out of town and forget."

I hear the slide of a chair. Larry quietly mutters something . . . and that's it. The end of Larry and Pearl's conversation . . . but the recording doesn't stop there. After a pause Mama P. speaks up.

Pearl: "Get everything you needed?"

Colette: "What?"

Pearl: "You were recording, right? Was I loud enough for you?"

Colette: "Um . . . "

Pearl: "You want to buy something?"

Colette: "Yes, I need protection." Then the recording cuts off.

"And she just loaded me up." Colette gestures a hand toward the bag. I reach into my purse and pull out my wallet, not really knowing what else to do.

"Here." I shove a wad of tip money into her purse. She's been listening blankly throughout the recording and now fresh tears are spilling down her face, only this time in quiet. I sip my coffee, thinking.

"I'm so sorry, Col."

"Me, too."

"I don't get it."

"I don't either, but it's all shady, right? He was talking about me. About using me for something."

"This sucks so badly." I take another sip. "He thinks you know something you don't."

"I know. What's he talking about?"

I keep nursing my coffee, hoping it will give me super

brain powers. "He didn't know you took the letters. Did you catch that? He had no idea."

"No, he didn't. But he wants me to find something for him."

"Maybe he knows you're a witch." Once again, words come out of my mouth with no thought or planning from me. I clap my hand over my lips and stare wide eyed at Colette, waiting for her reaction.

She takes another sip. "Guess he does."

We burst out laughing. It's true. And it's a relief to say.

"Well, he knew before you did."

"What the hell is happening to me?" She's laughing through her tears. "What the hell is going on? It's you, Stella Fortunat." She points a finger as if to hex me herself. "Ever since I met *you.*"

We both quiet down. "I'm sorry. You should have stuck with the rest of our lunch table. You've always had these abilities, I'm sure. I've heard that when two intuitive women get together, they supposedly magnify the other's abilities."

She nods. "It's not your fault. It's definitely not your fault that my father is a lying sack of—" she stops when we notice someone coming in to wipe down the empty tables.

I shake my head. "We'll get to that. What did Mama Pearl say? What's in the bag?"

"She didn't say anything really. Nothing specific. She just started walking around the store, putting stuff in this bag. That woman is a loon."

"I know. Total freak show."

"Anyway"—Colette reaches into the sack to retrieve its contents—"these are some powders"—she pulls out colorful vials and sets them down—"and some herbs, incense . . . she just scooped a little out. Said it would cost way too much if I took the full jars she had of each."

"She's right. That stuff's expensive. I hope she didn't rip you off."

"She didn't. I saw the wad you put in my purse. That definitely covers half. Plus you got me coffee."

"Fair enough."

Colette pulls out a couple of labeled sandwich bags with crushed flowers and greens inside. "This is mugwort and thistle . . . I feel like a drug dealer." She laughs. "Oh, look at this."

A clinking sound precedes the small jar she fishes out next.

"Coffin nails."

Yup, I recognize those. Long nails used for a variety of purposes, from psychic protection to magical attacks.

"A pretty stone . . . I think she said it was hematite?" She presents me with a polished metallic rock. I nod in recognition.

"She said she wasn't interested in handing out recipes but that you should have some books."

"Yeah, I have a couple. Wait, she knew you were with me? You told her?"

"Nope, didn't tell her. She knew."

"Of course she did."

"Oh, and along with those coffin nails . . . ta-da!"

Colette pulls something in paper out from the bottom of the sack. She sets it down and begins to fold up the now empty bag.

"What is it?"

"Go ahead, open it up. Happy Birthday." I peel the tape from the paper and begin unraveling. Solid form starts to take shape in my hands. I realize what it is just before I remove the last sheet.

"Ah." A tiny coffin, shorter than a foot long. It looks like it was made for a doll. Of course I've seen them before. They're so recognizable, and so unforgettable.

"She really thinks we have some work ahead of us, doesn't she?"

"Stella, she kept saying to leave her out of it. That she was only doing this much because of Evie." Colette pauses, searching my eyes. "Stel, she kept saying, 'That's what she gets for ignoring me.' What did she mean?"

It's time.

HOLY MEETINGS & GRAVEYARD GREETINGS

THE CHARIOT

I take a breath. "Col, that day in Mama P's kitchen, she told me to stay away from you. She said it was too dangerous."

"Really?"

"I didn't tell you because things were going so well— your dad was back and you had Jack. I didn't want to freak you out."

Colette sighs. "Anything else I should know?"

I shake my head. "It's full disclosure now. If something comes up, I'll tell you first. I promise."

We both agree that it's best for her to not say a word to her father, since we still don't really know what he's up to. All we know is that he's incredibly shady and we've got a much better chance of finding out what is going on by playing dumb.

That evening, Col and I pulled out our arsenal of tools from the magic shop in my room.

"Okay, we know if you use the Vision Powder sparingly it aids in prophetic dreaming," I say. "But we've also established that too much of it seems to make the dream come to life."

Colette puts her hand to her throat. "True."

I begin reading from my folk magic reference manual. "All right, so mugwort is known for psychic protection, Van Van Oil for banishing evil . . . let's see . . . coffin nails . . . also useful in fashioning a witch's bottle, a capsule of items designed to protect the wearer from magical harm. A strong magical defense. Sounds useful . . . " I thumb through the pages. "There's a bunch of different uses for the small coffins. I guess that one will have to become more obvious."

"So what should we do tonight?"

"Let's salt the doorway and windowsill, keep Tiger's Eye and that new hematite stone under our pillows, tie those journey ribbons to our wrists, sprinkle on a touch of the powder . . . I can put some of that mugwort in a sachet and tuck it under the mattress, too. I'll also pull a tarot card and maybe it will give us an idea of what to look for."

I separate the Major Arcana from the Minor, thinking that the Major, with its straightforward titles like *Judgment* or *The Lovers*, may be simpler for Colette and me to decipher. I shuffle and pull the one at the top. *Death.*

"Oh no," Colette whispers.

"It's okay. The Death card usually doesn't mean actual death. It's a transformative card. It's about major change."

"So like the death of something and the birth of another?"

"Yeah, sort of. It's a shift. It could mean, well, anything."

Colette nods, appearing curious. We prepare the room, put crystals and herbs beneath the pillows and mattress, dust on a hint of the powder, and begin again.

I'm walking along the grass. I've got a parasol in my gloved hand. My other arm is occupied with the arm of a gentleman. It's Jonathon, but he's not in a soldier's uniform. He's wearing a gray suit, a little darker than his Confederate wear. We stand beside a tree.

"My father had these oaks planted just before the war. He felt that, no matter what, it would remind us of who we are, of our life here." He leans over and places a hand on my stomach. I let it lie there.

"The war is lost," I say, looking down at his hand.

"Some still aren't ready to face that, my darling, but yes, it is. It's over."

The sound of footsteps breaks in. A servant carries over a tray of two cold drinks. Jonathon hands me my glass. The sugary tea slips down my throat.

"Thank you, Mary."

"My pleasure, Miss Beatrice." She pauses for a moment, as

if wanting to hear the rest of our conversation. Then she slowly walks away.

"Yes, Beatrice, it's over, but we're not. My father seems to be beating back this fever, and our life is just beginning." He pats my stomach again. "He'll never want for anything."

"You are sure it's a he?" The servant returns, breathless. "It's company, sir. Miss Cora."

Jonathon kisses my gloved hand and then turns me toward a gate. It's the Courteau gate. But it looks smaller than the front one. It's the back gate. The servant girl lets me out. I move quickly toward my home. I'm at the front door. I touch my own hand to my stomach, looking down.

"I've got a good home waiting for you . . . " I murmur to my belly.

"What the *hell* was that?" Colette and I sit up from my bed at the same time. I turn the lamp on and realize we're being loud.

I put my finger to my lips. "Shhh."

"She was holding her stomach."

I nod.

"You saw it, too?"

I love this. "What's up with 'he'll never want for anything?' She's pregnant, isn't she?"

"I think so. It's like a ghostly soap opera."

"Totally."

I've got a date with Father Brian. My mom gives me the

keys to the delivery van since I told her I wanted to check on Dylan afterward. She doesn't like me walking the streets after dark.

By the time Father ushers me into his office, my stomach is churning. What am I doing here? Why did I set an appointment for Christ's sake? I take a seat in the chair nearest the door. He doesn't sit behind the desk; instead, he takes a seat in the chair across from me, giving me plenty of room to escape. It's a smallish mahogany-paneled room with a large window behind the desk chair. The window has stained glass set into it. The sunlight transforms the room, shifting colors and patterns.

"I feel like an idiot," I admit. "I'm sorry. I don't know what the hell I'm doing here. Oh, Jesus—I mean, God—I mean, gosh! I'm so sorry."

Father Brian laughs. "Wow, you're looking to offend the whole Holy Spirit today, aren't you?"

I exhale. "I feel like I'm wasting your time."

"I assure you, you're not. What would you like to talk about?"

"Do you think my GG's in hell? Because I don't."

He looks at me for a minute and then smiles. "Is that what you came here to ask? I get the feeling you're not really worried about that."

He's right. I'm more annoyed with the fact that my grandmother hasn't bothered to contact me. I'm pretty sure she can handle her own immortal soul just fine.

"And no, I don't think she is in hell, for the record." I

217

find this relieving. Huh, maybe I was a teensy bit concerned?

"Stella, we live in a city like nowhere on Earth. I know that there are members of my congregation that could fight pretty bitterly over their own beliefs with each other. There are the devout, and then there are the devout who read cards and tea leaves."

"What do you think about that, Father?"

"I think I love New Orleans." He sits back and grins. "What did you want to talk about, Stella? You brought up your grandmother. She only passed a couple of years ago, wasn't it? You must still miss her."

"She's nowhere to be found." I had really planned on avoiding tears, but here they come, stubborn and forceful. "She was always there for me, and now I need her. I really need her but she's nowhere."

He listens patiently.

"I don't even know what's real. I'm having weird dreams, Dylan's grandpa is losing his mind, and Colette's dad sucks. I don't know what's going on anymore."

"I'm sorry, Stella. I don't know who you're talking about. Colette? Dylan?"

"Colette's my best friend. Dylan's family owns Crescent City Roasters."

"Ah, yes. I know them. Great coffee. We keep their beans in the cafeteria. I actually have a pot ready to brew in my office." He looks toward the other wall where there's a small sink and black coffeepot. Praise the Lord.

"Would you like some?" he asks.

"Yes, thank you." The aroma of brewing coffee works like a mild tranquilizer to put me at ease.

"You were talking about dreams as well?" There's so much I want to talk with him about, but I've sworn to not tell anybody. Besides, I don't think he'd be super comfortable with the whole haunted visions topic. Or maybe he would. They still do exorcisms, right?

"Father, I don't mean to be rude, but I . . . is that Colombian coffee I smell?"

He nods.

"Awesome. Sorry, what I meant to say is that I don't wish to talk about the specifics. Not now. I just want to talk about my grandmother. Or God. Or something other than the crazy stuff going on in my life."

"I think it's ready. Let's have a cup." He takes two mugs from a cabinet above and pulls cream from a mini fridge. I normally take hot coffee as a café au lait, but I'm not about to get snotty and high-maintenance with my priest.

"Cream?"

"Yes, please. Just a splash. And a little sugar, please."

"You know, I was in seminary school when I first started coming to this cathedral. I'd been going to Saint Vincent's in the French Quarter. Your mother was already a fixture here. She had been, ever since she was little."

I know this. My mom told me she converted to Catholicism when she was old enough to take the bus alone.

"Yeah, this cathedral always stood out to her." Father Brian nods. "It can be like that for people. Like coming home."

"Well, I must be homeless." I'm not trying to be funny, but I can't help but smile when I say this.

"Would you like to know what I think?" He takes a long sip of his drink. "Mmm. I think you're an adventurer."

"A what?"

"Like an explorer, or a pioneer. Someone who's looking so hard to find a home, they may just wind up settling on a patch of land and building their own."

"You mean like starting my own religion?"

"No. I'm not talking about religion. I'm talking about a relationship with God. I'm talking about your personal relationship with God."

I sift this in my mind, taking in frequent gulps. Cheap-o coffeemaker or no, good coffee is good coffee.

"I don't know what that is. I'm not even sure about what my God is."

"And that's what makes you an explorer."

An explorer. I take another sip.

"Stella, I am a Catholic priest. I take the Catholic faith into my whole heart. Obviously, it is the way that I believe is the truest way to the Divine. To suggest anything else would be misleading."

"Thank you. I've always appreciated your honesty."

"It's all about honesty. If we can't be honest talking about our spirituality, then we really are wasting our time. But, Stella, just because this is ultimately the path I've set my course on doesn't mean it's right for you. You may discover another way to connect with your Creator. What I mean to say is, maybe you don't need to worry about which map to use. Just hold out your moral compass and keep sailing until you hit land."

I'm struck by this. I drink to the bottom of my cup as he glances down at his watch.

"I'm so sorry, Stella, but I do have another meeting."

"Oh. Of course, thank you for the coffee. And the thoughts."

"Would you like to continue these discussions? Say, every other Wednesday? I'll keep a fresh pot on hand."

"Thank you. Thank you, Father, I would." The thought of being buds with a priest weirds me out more than a little, but I really do like Father Brian. I find his company comforting. Plus, my mom will poop herself with delight.

"Great. I'll see you in a couple of weeks then."

"Okay. See you later, Father."

An explorer. The words follow me out of the church and into the delivery van. I almost pass the roaster as I drive, deep in thought. I had sent a text to Dylan earlier letting him know I'd be picking him up. The few parking spaces in the front are occupied, so I drive around to the back, park, and ring the doorbell. A few minutes pass before anyone comes.

It's Dylan. He's wearing a white apron, looking flustered.

"Hubba, hubba." Did I seriously just say that? Why don't people stop me? I stare in horror.

He bursts out laughing. "Really, Stella? That's what we're saying?" He takes my hand and leads me to the roasting room.

"Hubba, hubba. Hubba, hubba." He's repeating it in a sing-songy voice.

"Shut up. Do you need help with anything?"

"Yes. May I?" He leans in for a kiss. I lean in as well, but make it quick when I realize that his mother is standing a few feet away.

"Hi, Stella." She's unfazed. Does he kiss lots of girls here? Is this common procedure for her? I try to dismiss this.

"Hi. Can I help?"

"Yes, please. Dylan will show you. I'm dropping Arthur off at karate and coming right back. And then, my son"—she takes his jaw in her hand—"I want you to take a break. Take off for a half hour or so. Have fun."

Dylan gives a nod as she releases his chin.

"Good. I'll be up front."

"All right." He's pure business. "See all these beans? We just finished a huge batch."

I'm in paradise on Earth. I take a deep breath. "That's Black Magic, isn't it?"

"Yes." He beams at me and then refocuses. "Okay, see the big scale and the bins? Here, you take one of these bags." He pulls a paper sack from a pile and shakes it out. "Take this big scoop and pour beans into the bag until the scale hits one pound. Then stick this label on and write Black Magic in your coolest handwriting. Remember, you're now a reflection of our fine coffees. After that, fold these tabs at the top closed and you're done. Would you do that while I work on roasting the next batch?"

I eagerly begin. I'm such a dork with projects like this. They're always so much fun to me. Dylan and I mesh well since he's obviously the type of person that works hard when working instead of goofing around, which I respect.

Before long we're both finished. Dylan removes his apron, throws it on a hook, takes my hand, and says, "Let's get out of here. I'll drive."

We bolt down the hall.

"Back later, Mom!"

"Have fun!" She says it with a bit of desperation.

Dylan walks me over to his beat-up truck and opens the passenger door for me. He hops into the driver's side, and after a few tries, the engine is moaning alive.

"You want to just drive around?" he asks.

"Sounds perfect." So we drive around. The sun's dipped below the horizon and night has begun to creep up on all that is familiar. Lights flick on in the elaborate manors and gas torches burn in front of shops as we circle around.

"I have some good memories of my dad. Fishing, mostly. I think he was a really good dad." Dylan begins speaking and breaks open the quiet. It's kind of unnerving, this comfort he has with being so personal. Unnerving and beautiful.

"Oh yeah?" I say, not really sure how to respond.

"Yeah."

"My parents have told me about your dad. About what a sweet man they thought he was."

"Really?"

"Yep."

"Your parents have always been cool. I remember, after my dad died, your mom helped out at the roaster while my mom was busy . . . being sad, I guess. Planning a funeral."

"Burying her husband," I whisper.

"Right." I know my own grief with my grandmother. I can't imagine what it was like for Dylan to lose his father.

"Do you miss him? I'm sorry, that's a stupid question." I look down at my hands.

Dylan is messing with the radio. It doesn't seem to want to play.

"Damn radio is so moody." He shakes his head. "I'm lucky if I can get anything."

Something besides static finally comes on over the airwaves. It's a sports show, football, I think. We both listen for a moment and then he switches it off.

"I think so." Dylan startles me. I forgot that I had asked him a question. "I mean, it's a weird thing. I don't know what I miss, you know? But I know I'm missing something."

We circle around again, passing the park and the

graveyard where GG lies. I notice a bright flashlight behind the gates. That person would do well to get out of there. Not only is it closing soon, but also everyone knows that being in a New Orleans cemetery at night is a great way to get stabbed. I'm distracted by this thought for a moment, and then my mind returns.

"Dylan?"

"Yeah?"

"Are you close to your mom?"

"Sure, I am. But I was way closer to my grandpa. My brother's always kind of been the mama's boy. I mean, I love my mom, and I think we have a great relationship, but my grandpa, he's like . . ."

"Your best friend." I know the feeling.

"He was my best friend," Dylan agrees.

"Why do you keep saying that?"

"What?"

"Why do you keep saying 'was?' Like he's gone?"

"Because he's going, Stella. He's pretty much gone."

"That's not true. I saw him the other day. He remembered my name and everything."

"Yeah, I know what you're talking about. My mom told me about it. That was just before he forgot where he was and burned the beans, right?"

I say nothing.

"That day was the most clear he's been in a while." His voice breaks. "Stella, he was the sharpest guy I knew. And now . . . sometimes—sometimes he's like a little kid. It pisses me off. I get mad at him."

I've never seen Dylan cry. His tears squeak out, big and fat, marching like uniform soldiers down his nose. He stares straight ahead and then wipes his eyes on his sleeve. I love that he's not apologizing for this. I take my hand and gently rub up and down his back, pausing to sweep his hair on the sides of his ears, like my mother used to do with me.

As we sit in the cab of the truck, I feel like I could show Dylan every part of my soul. It's as if we've already shared all of our secrets. Is this what being with someone so genuine feels like? We've parked in front of the graveyard, and though I'd forgotten it, that blinding flashlight takes me briefly out of the moment. The person holding it has been standing not far from the entrance, and now they're leaving. I see a guard opening the gate for the person and then turning to close and lock it as they leave.

A large hood covers the visitor's head. They switch the light off. A gust of wind pulls off their covering. It's a woman. She quickly adjusts a light-colored beret and pulls the hood back up. Is it . . . ? My question is answered in an instant. I see the woman cross the street and climb quickly into a green Jaguar.

What is Lucille doing at Ash Grove Cemetery in the dark of night?

I guiltily leave this thought behind. Why am I so curious? Dylan is hurting and needs me. I focus on rubbing his back, being present for him, as his best friend, his hero, slowly loses his mind.

HIDE & SEEK

THE HERMIT

*D*ecember is taking over my life at the café. More pumpkin pie again, yes, but this time it's being overtaken with gingerbread cookies, Cajun cake, and red and green meringues as far as the eye can see. We're busier than ever, but my mom sets up time especially for us to go on what she seems to view as a crusade: the search for my ball gown.

We take the first day of my winter break from school to begin our venture. My mother has mapped out a few different boutiques. Colette and I set up a plan for her to check in with Mama Pearline to see if she'll be willing to divulge anything more about Larry: why he's visiting, what he's up to, that sort of thing. We know it's a serious long shot. Mediums, readers, and the like usually protect the confidentiality of their clients pretty fiercely. But we have to at least try. Colette hasn't visited her dad in weeks, not since her mom started to get more nervous about her overworking herself. Dena's beginning to feel at ease again, it seems.

I really wanted Colette to be the one gown shopping with me, but I can't burst my mom's bubble. I tell myself that Colette and I will go together another time to actually buy the dress. This mom trip will just be a preliminary hunt.

Mom takes the wheel to the Buick. I don't fight for the keys, since she knows exactly where she wants to go. I'm pretty much along for the ride. First stop is what appears to be a bridal shop a few blocks from the café. The window is filled with poufy tulle and decorative birdcages.

"Mom, really?" I couldn't be more apprehensive as we approach the place.

"Just give it a chance, Stella. They carry all sorts of dresses."

"It looks like a bridal shop."

My mom doesn't respond. Instead she opens the door for me and practically shoves me into the store.

A woman sweeps upon us from behind a small desk. "You must be the Fortunat ladies? Ten o'clock, right on time. My name is Barbara; I'll be helping you find your dress."

"You made a reservation?" I'm thrown. She has an entirely different plan than me, apparently.

"It's what you do," she says in a hushed tone.

"This way," says Miss Peppy. "I've chosen three gowns

based on what you told me about Stella's measurements and coloring. Are you excited for the ball, dear? I remember my first krewe event."

"Yeah, I'm excited. You've *chosen* gowns?"

"Of course. Here you are." She leads us into a small dressing area lined with mirrors. There are three dresses hanging on the wall in pale pink, lavender, and creamy white. First, she pulls the white dress down.

"Let's try this one first, shall we?" She stands there, waiting, until I realize that I'm supposed to get undressed. My mother begins unbuttoning my top and yanking down my pants. I feel like a department store mannequin. They lift my arms up and tug the tight fitting bodice down my torso. The full skirt skims around my legs. It's a lot of silk and a lot of rosettes swirled around the . . . is that a train?

"Lovely." My mother admires me. I stare at the uncomfortable girl in the glass.

"You know I'm not getting married, right, Mama?"

"Stella." My mom sighs. The store clerk smiles.

"White's not your style? What about this pink? Very romantic. Gorgeous with your dark hair."

Before I can say a word, it's off with the dress and on with the next. It's just the shade of one of my favorite lip glosses. It's actually quite pretty. It's not for me, though. I shake my head. It's the same process with the third dress.

"Let's try a plum. Do you have that shade?" asks my mom.

"Can you give us a minute?" I ask Barbara. She obliges.

"Certainly, take your time to talk it over."

"What is it now, Stella?"

"What is it? It's like I'm not even here. Who are you shopping for?"

"You wear that shade"—she points at the pink dress —"on your lips every week. I thought it would be pretty."

"It's just not my style."

"What *is* your style?"

I shrug. "I don't know. Something funkier."

"You know this is a ball, right, dear?" She's looking at me like I've just rolled out of a barn. I hate it.

"Don't be such a snob, Mom. I know it's a ball. I just want something . . . not lame."

I can tell this stings her a bit. She takes a breath.

"Okay, what are you thinking?"

"Well, I kind of thought that I could check out some of the shops with Colette."

"Oh. So it's not really about the dresses. It's about the company."

"No, Mama, that's not fair. It's just that Colette gets me, you know?"

"I guess I don't know."

I sigh. "Barbara?"

She instantly appears from behind a curtain. "Yes? Do you have a dress in mind?"

"Sure. Something in plum?"

"I've got two that will be stunning." She leaves the room to retrieve them.

"I think plum will look very pretty on you, sweetie."

I shrug again.

"Stella, you must have five shirts in shades of plum. I know you like that color."

God, she's driving me nuts.

Out come the dresses—one long and sleek, one strapless and full. I lift my arms up like a puppet. They take off what I'm wearing and proceed to pull the gowns onto me. I turn from side to side and inspect myself.

"They're just . . . I don't know. They're just . . ."

"What? I think they look spectacular." My mom's adjusting the second of the purple ones on me. "Both of them. You don't like either of them?"

"Not really."

"Well, what *would* you like, Stella?" Now my face feels hot. Barbara is standing back, watching. She's probably thinking I'm some spoiled brat who always gets fancy dresses and always complains about them. She doesn't know that I work my ass off. She doesn't know a thing about me.

I turn to see my mom, her arms folded across her chest. I've had enough.

"Why can't I have an opinion?"

"You're perfectly entitled to an opinion, Stella, but that's not what this is about. You had your mind made up before we even walked into this shop that you weren't going to like any of these dresses, no matter what they looked like."

I can see Barbara backing away. I don't know why I'm upset with her, too. She probably just wants to avoid yet another mother-daughter battle in her dress shop.

"That's not true!" Maybe it's a little true, but it's only because I don't feel like she hears me.

"Fine. I'll stop torturing you. Go with Colette." She takes out her phone and makes a call.

"What are you doing?"

"I'm canceling our second boutique appointment. Barbara, thank you for your trouble. I'm very sorry."

"Oh, it was no trouble. I hope you find what you're looking for, Miss Fortunat."

It's all we can hope, isn't it?

We make the drive home in the sort of stiff silence that's special to pissed-off mothers and daughters everywhere. I head to my room to mix up some colors and stew in my feelings a bit.

When I look down at my phone, I realize that Colette texted me an hour ago asking me to call her. So I do, ready to launch into a tirade about my mother and her ability to make me feel so crappy, but Colette starts the conversation off.

"Looks like there's another fun piece to this puzzle."

"All right, what you got?" I'm in.

"Well, I went into Mama Pearl's and she was definitely not into talking. In fact, she actually told me to stop at the door. She said it was way past time that you and I stayed the hell away from *all this*."

"All *what?* What does she know?"

"She won't say. But she did say, 'Protect yourself, child. Stay out and protect yourself,' while frantically cleaning the shop."

"Hmmm."

"I watched her throw away her appointment book, Stella."

"So? What does that . . . oh my god, did you—"

"I totally went through her garbage. I left, waited, doubled around back, and WENT THROUGH HER TRASH."

"You are such a badass. Seriously."

She continues. "I pulled out her appointment book from the past year. Guess she got a new one. Anyway, I saw my dad's name in there about five times. Then I saw something else."

"Colette, you're killing me."

"Lucille Courteau had a phone appointment written in every week for the past six months."

"What? I didn't know she goes to readers."

"Yeah. Neither did I. Neither does Jack, I think. I mean, he knows about your grandmother and he's never said a word. I'm sure that's why she just has phone appointments instead of going in person."

"My GG had clients who only wanted to call. People that were too embarrassed to be seen in a shop like that, or with a person like that."

"Right. But what does a woman like her need with a weekly appointment with a psychic?"

I remember what I saw at the cemetery with Dylan the other week and proceed to tell Colette about it.

"Okay, but Stella, I just want to make sure we're not jumping to conclusions here. Remember how weird you got about Mrs. Courteau picking up that envelope in the park? You know she told me later she thought she saw us but didn't stop to say hello because she was in a hurry picking up the invitations for the ball? Do you know how paranoid you can be?"

"Fine. But Col, she's sketchy. She's totally sketchy. You and I know it. Are we going to blow past the fact that her family's name is in part of our dreams, or that we saw the exact same garden from her backyard in our visions? The same one, Colette."

"I know. I just want to be careful."

"For what it's worth, I don't think your boyfriend is shady at all. He's a totally good guy. Obnoxiously good guy, perhaps."

"I just don't know what to make of any of this."

"Me, either." I take the opportunity to fill her in on my fight with my mom.

"Go easy on her, Stella."

"Seriously? Did you hear how crazy she was being?"

"I heard you, but still. You might want to invite her to join us on our shopping trip."

Ugh. I switch subjects, frustrated that my best friend is not siding with me in the way I'd hoped.

"Whatever. Can you get some time to hang out this week? Like, maybe spend the night after work on Saturday?"

"I think so. Like I told you, my mom's starting to relax a little."

"Great." I let her know that I plan to take an afternoon to help out Dylan, if I can get away from the craziness at the café. I also tell her that I plan to stop by Ash Grove to see if there's anything by the gate where Lucille was, for any clue at all. Colette is dubious but supportive since our dreams started showing up in real life, surrounding the Courteaus, no less.

☪

My slumber has stayed restful ever since Colette and I have been specific with our intent to seek out visions. No dumped out Vision Powder, no sleepwalking. I think Beatrice knows we're listening. I hope she gets that and doesn't change her mind, since I've enjoyed feeling like I have some say in the nature of our relationship, however small.

My mom and I have been speaking, but only as necessary. It's not too different from the way it usually is between us. I'm starting to feel that nasty guilt again, but I feel like I'm in way too deep for any apologies. Besides, I'm still kind of mad at her.

My dad's using the van to make some deliveries, and I don't feel like asking my mom for the car, so I put on my heaviest coat and layer on scarves and a knit hat before heading outside. First stop is the graveyard, while there's still light. The gates are set open. There are a few visitors scattered about. I look out over the rows of marble and concrete crypts to determine GG's location. I'll pay her a visit, too, if I have time. I'm still pissed at her, as well.

I scan the first rows of graves looking for the Courteau name. I know they had a few servants' graves, as well as Beatrice's grave, back at the manor. I seem to remember that one of the ornate mausoleums toward the back held many of their ancestors, leaving some room to spare for a few more generations. But that was in the way back, and I'm fairly certain that flashlight beam I saw the other night stayed close to the front. So here I am, grave hopping. Rosette, Gerard, Johnson . . . no Courteau here. Maybe her ancestors? She may hail from outside the neighborhood, but that doesn't mean she doesn't have roots here. What's her maiden name? No clue. I make a note to ask about this later.

I really don't know what I'm looking for. It's more about a feeling. I think it would be good for me to practice trusting my gut feelings more often. GG tried to. I think Father Brian would recommend the same, as well.

I pass a string of neglected, forgotten graves and then a line of more popular ones with fake flowers, trinkets, and statues surrounded by potted plants.

"What are you up to? Who were you visiting,

Lucille?" I murmur aloud. A breeze answers, picking out the fragrance and carrying it to me. It's distinctive, sliding beneath my nostrils, filling them with a puff of floral. Sweet olive. I know who wears that.

I immediately look around for Mrs. Courteau, but no one is near me. Then I think of her home covered in the plants she babies in her small green house.

That's when I see it. A couple of rows down, a white tomb bears an angel's face graced with a silver vase full of sweet olive branches. I dart toward it as if in flight, bobbing between some of the other graves. It's simple yet exquisite. When I look down to see who's buried here, it's the only acceptable answer to the question I didn't know was pressing on my brain.

Cora Roland
1845–1865

LOSSES & WINS

THE WHEEL OF FORTUNE

*O*f course. Who else would it be? I cannot wait to tell Colette. I have no idea what this means, but I know that if we can focus on the whole picture long enough, it will start to come into focus.

I hold out my phone to take a photo when something stops me. Fear. I take a second to remember that this is the grave of a murderer. A killer. The ghost who's been choking me nearly to death—or rather, the person who my Beatrice ghost has been showing me. I've been so intrigued with figuring out who Lucille was visiting, I almost forgot who's grave I was standing in front of.

Cora. Suddenly the beautiful angel's face, wings behind her haloed head, has a sinister feel. I put my phone back in my pocket, deciding it best to avoid any photographs, then back away slowly. I take quite a few steps before I feel comfortable completely turning my back to Miss Roland. I check behind my shoulder a few times on my way out of the cemetery. Once I'm safely out of the gate, I text Colette.

Me: GUESS WHO OUR LUCILLE'S BEEN VISITING?

Colette: WHO?

Me: MISS CORA ROLAND. WTF!

Colette: YOU'RE KIDDING. HOW DO YOU KNOW?

Me: FRESH SWEET OLIVE IN AN EXPENSIVE LOOKING VASE NEAR WHERE I SAW HER THE OTHER DAY.

Colette: ARE YOU SURE?

Me: I DON'T HAVE A PICTURE OF HER BUT COME ON, COL. CORA'S GRAVE IS HERE. AND LUCILLE WAS HERE. AND LUCILLE'S FAVORITE FLOWERS ARE LAID THERE!

Colette: I KNOW. IT'S JUST SO INSANE.

Me: I'M WITH YOU. LET'S SIT ON IT AND SEE WHAT BECOMES CLEAR THIS WEEKEND.

I make my way to Crescent City Roaster. Dylan is working on their "Christmas in the Crescent" blend, which I get to sample. It's crazy good, of course. A little nutty. I let Dylan know it'll go perfectly with our Cajun cake and text my dad to tell him about it. He requests an order, which I pass on to Dylan.

"You can bag up your own." He's got more softness to him. I'm certain it's the bond we forged in his truck the other night. I don't know if I should say anything about it, so I don't. I feel like he just needs my friendship and company right now, and that's what I offer. We work side by side, with an occasional check-in from his mom, who's working up front. His grandpa makes an appearance. Amazingly, he seems pretty clearheaded.

"He's looking good," I tell Dylan, observing Gramps heading to the front to help put bags in boxes for delivery.

"Yeah, he's doing better today. My mom's figured out some jobs he can do that are less stressful. It helps."

"How's she doing?"

"Oh, you know."

"I wasn't asking to be polite. I was asking because I wanted to know. You can tell me if you want."

Dylan kisses the top of my forehead. It sends a burning blush all the way down to my toes.

"She's off and on. I mean, she had her dad to lean on after my dad died. I was so little . . . and my dad's parents are cool but they live in Florida. She's not exactly close to them. I'm just trying to be there for her, but I think it weirds her out, you know? I'm her son."

I think I know. My mom didn't exactly include me in her personal grieving process.

"Just the fact that you're doing all this extra work is amazing. It's probably what's keeping her from going totally psycho." I wince at my last remark. "I'm sorry. I don't know why I said that."

"Don't be sorry for being honest. It's true. My mom would go bat-shit without some help. Thank you."

"For what?"

"For reminding me how I can help her in a way she's okay with."

I'm struck by him. I always think of Dylan as the honest one, the genuine person. I try to be upfront, but all the stuff I've been hiding lately has made me feel like a fraud. Now's definitely not the time to burden Dylan with my feelings, so I help him finish up more bags and make a plan to assist him in deliveries on Monday morning. The café is closed that day, anyway. The new blend I bring home from the roaster proves to be crazy popular with customers (and my parents), and it offers another excuse to pop in more often to bag up some more orders.

When Saturday approaches, it feels like it's been forever since I've hung out with Colette. She's picked up more shifts again since we've been on break, but the business has kept us from any real hanging out. I miss her, so I'm super excited when we get some time alone in my room. We spend a little time talking about boys while she humors me by letting me try three different lipsticks on her.

"These are totally different from glosses. I'm working on colors that will stay put, too. Isn't this red awesome? I think it's the perfect red—it's the one I tried on the girls at lunch last week. Remember? It looked pink-red on Shelly and orange-red on Joanna. Which was perfect. And on me it has almost this watermelon undertone. Anyways, it'll be great."

As predicted, it looks gorgeous on Col. She agrees, which delights me. I don't talk too much about the details of my conversation with Dylan in his truck that night. It was too sacred. I feel like I'd be betraying a confidence by sharing it, even if it is with my best friend. I just tell her that he and I are getting closer and that I'm worried about his family and his grandfather, which is absolutely true. Then she proceeds to tell me about the little bit of time she's been able to spend with Jack and how much she hates keeping stuff from him.

"As soon as we piece this together and figure out a way to clue him in, we will," I assure her.

She nods in agreement.

"Shall we?" I prep the room for prophetic dreaming and pull out a tarot card. *Death* again.

"Hmph." I look around the room. "Miss Beatrice? Can you hear me? Will you show us what we need to know to help you? Will you do it without hurting us, please?"

There's no answer. Colette shakes her head. This was not how she had planned on spending her sophomore year.

I set the Death card on my makeshift altar on top of my dresser and remember something I'd just read in one of GG's books. I pull that odd little plaster skull of hers from one of my drawers and place a top hat from one of my more formally dressed teddy bears on top of its bony head.

"Weird," says Colette. "I'm pretty sure I saw

something like that in Mama Pearline's. Only, he had something in his mouth—"

"A cigar? Yeah, I don't have one of those handy. Hey!" I pull my grandmother's pack of old cigarettes out and place the butt of one in the skull's mouth. "Hopefully this will do. He's a guardian of the dead, a sacred figure in New Orleans Voodoo."

Colette looks impressed with my knowledge, so I just play along.

"Let's get out the Vision Powder. We need to start being extra careful with how much we use. I don't have any idea how my GG made this stuff. The bottle is starting to feel really light."

"All right, just the tiniest blot on my forehead, okay?"

We grab our ribbons and crystals, then lay down to sleep.

I don't know if it's me being overeager, or if it's because we used even less Vision Powder than normal, but hours pass with nothing but restless sleep. In the middle of the night, I sit up to find Colette fast asleep. I feel more anxious than ever. I begin counting downward from a hundred. I do this once more, and at some point, I drift into a fuzzy rest.

I'm in a large room, a parlor. I recognize the chandelier in the foyer to the left. I'm in the Courteau mansion . . . My restlessness seems to be keeping my mind and body a little more connected to my dream. I make sure to look down and see what body I'm occupying. Blue silk dress, white hands . . . uh-oh. Is that a mirror above the table in the parlor? I go to it. Cora's lovely angelic face greets me.

"Beatrice, show me please. But let's take it easy, okay?" The lips move as I form the words. The head nods in reply to my question. Okay, Beatrice is still driving this train. Fair enough. I let her lead, pulling my body back to the parlor. I'm standing next to a long window. I see a dark woman in a red dress and shawl walking the path in front of the house. It's Beatrice. She's headed in the direction of her house. Jonathon passes her. They exchange a nod, but as she walks off, I can see him turn through the glass and stare her way.

"Cora, what are you looking at? Was that that Beatrice girl? You know, I had heard she was very ill last year, but it recently came to my attention that she may have been"—the voice drops to a whisper—"with child."

Gasps follow this remark. My stomach is twisting tightly. Tears sting my eyes. I turn to see who made it. There's a group of ladies seated, sipping iced tea and eating cake. I look to each of them, but recognize no one. Empty chatter fills my burning ears.

"Mr. Courteau is so thoughtful, inviting you here for my birthday like this."

A few of the young women giggle. I realize that we're all just barely out of our teen years, if that.

"Well, Miss Cora. The ring on your finger seems like quite a fine gift for your nineteen years!" one girl exclaims.

My hand pulls a fan from a small purse on my wrist and begins fluttering it against my face. I'm Beatrice's puppet, acting in some show only she understands.

"And that's not all. He had the most charming surprise commissioned for me."

"Whatever are you talking about?" another lady presses.

"Well, don't tell him I told you—he doesn't know I peeked —but there was such a lovely satin wrapped box on the desk in his study. I saw it when he was out of the room. He must have thought I didn't notice it, because after he went in there to get something, he hid it away." My lips turn in a smirk.

"Well, what was it?" I have a rapturous audience.

"The most beautiful music box you ever did see. Polished mahogany, and the song it played! That beautiful tune, that lover's tune." I pause for effect. "Lorena."

"Oh, such a sad and beautiful melody. Aren't you lucky to have such a romantic beau?"

Footsteps echo down the hall. "Hush!" I wave their voices down with my fan. In Jonathon walks, holding a small box. It's wrapped in silk. He hands it to me with a bow.

"For my beautiful bride-to-be." The girls giggle wildly.

Was Cora friends with these people? Seriously?

My hand tugs at the bow and gently lifts the lid. Reaching in, my fingers pull out a long black fountain pen.

"Do you like it? It's from a company in Virginia. They specialize in fine ladies' pens. I know how important correspondence is to you."

The girls stare at me. "This is my birthday present? This is my only present from you?"

"I beg your pardon, my dear? Yes, this is your present . . . is there something wrong?"

My hand reaches toward my throat. "No," I whisper. It's

like I'm being strangled, the way the word chokes out from within me. "I'm not feeling well. Forgive me."

The ladies all rise, as does Jonathon.

"Miss Cora, may I?"

"I'll see myself out."

I know what I'm going to do next. I'm going to commit murder.

"Wake up!" I yell to myself as I move down the cobblestone toward Beatrice's row house. "Wake up! I don't want to hurt anybody!"

"Colette! Can you hear me? Wake me up!"

"Stella! What's going on? Are you having a nightmare?"

Light fills the room, momentarily blinding me. My mom stands in my bedroom doorway appearing concerned.

"Hi, Mama. Yeah, I guess, so." My hand is under my pillow, holding the ribbon. I think to release it before pulling out my arm and sitting up. Colette's jerked awake beside me, cloth in her hand.

"Are you okay?" Mom walks over to me.

"Yeah, just a bad dream. Sorry I woke you."

"Go easy on the coffee late at night, sweetie. That can make you restless." She gently sweeps my hair out of my eyes and kisses my cheek. The gesture awakens the guilt within me.

"Hey, Mama?"

"Yes, Stella?" She's standing groggily in her nightgown.

"Want to go dress shopping with me and Colette soon? Maybe next week?"

She looks completely confounded by my question.

"Oh, Stel, it's okay. You and Colette go together. It's fine, sweetie, really. Go back to bed now, okay?"

"Night, Mama."

"Night, Mrs. Fortunat."

"Goodnight, girls." She shuts off the light and disappears out the door.

I turn to Colette in the darkness, then turn on my small lamp.

"I almost strangled you again."

"You really need to chill out." I admire Colette's capacity for humor at this hour.

"How do you not have bedhead? How do you always wake up looking like a photograph? What demon have you signed a contract with?"

Colette just stares, thinking.

"Col?"

"Shhh. I'm trying to remember before it leaves my mind. I was Beatrice and my mother was there. Her mother, I mean." She sits up. "I think it was her mother, anyway. Yes. Beatrice asked if 'he could take the baby.'"

"He? Who's he?"

"I'm not sure. Her brother?" Colette pauses. "Her mother said something like 'at least I can count on your brother.' She was so harsh." Her eyes well up. "I think she disowned her for shaming the family. She yelled at her about getting a silly music box instead of a wedding ring. What was that?"

"A music box? I can explain that one in a minute."

"I gave her my baby."

"She took the baby?"

"Yeah, I handed—she handed over her baby to her mother. His face looked just like Jonathon's. He had golden hair. He was beautiful." Colette's tears fall harder as she remembers. "I can't even imagine. Her own mother said she wasn't her daughter anymore; that at least the baby would never know he was a bastard and that she was out of the family. It was all so fast. She just walked out with the child."

"Then what?"

"Then someone woke me up." She raises her eyebrows at me.

"My bad for not wanting to kill my bestie in her sleep."

She laughs through her tears. "Stella, it felt so shitty." There she is, cursing again. Must be my own influence.

"Losing her baby?"

"No, it felt more like failure. Maybe in not getting engaged? Maybe in being a mistress?"

"What about the baby?"

"It's all screwed up in my head. Like the baby was always meant for her brother."

"Her own child?"

"I know, I know. But I don't think she was a bad person."

"That's relative. None of these people are particularly likable. They all lie to each other, they all hurt each other."

"True. But with the baby it was almost like she never saw him as hers to begin with. Like he would just automatically belong to someone else. That's how she handed him to her mom. Like she was giving back something she had borrowed."

"That's messed up."

"She lost everything."

"Yeah, but she chose to essentially be a prostitute, then remain his mistress."

"She was our age. Can you imagine? I think her mom encouraged her relationship with Jonathon."

"Oh, definitely. He mentioned getting her permission in the letter."

"Yes, so think about that. Her mother encouraged the whole thing, and then when her daughter got pregnant —which was almost a given—she tossed her out."

"That is wretched. You're right." Suddenly my own mom is looking pretty magical. "And you know what? I bet it wasn't even about the 'getting pregnant out of wedlock' line. It was because Beatrice failed to get the promise of marriage from him. She failed to marry into one of the wealthiest families in New Orleans."

"I bet you're right."

I fill her in on my own vision as she listens wide eyed. We go over the details of past dreams and consider theories that involve Lucille and her father. Not much of that is clear, except we're fairly certain that Larry is working alone. We don't know what Lucille knows, if she knows anything. We don't really know anything.

A realization falls into my lap like a hot coal, causing me to shriek and then quickly cover my mouth so as not to wake my parents again.

"What is it?" Colette's anxious about my reaction.

"Remember what we saw in the Courteau's garden?"

"The graves from our dreams? Yes, I do."

"No, the holes."

"The ones Lucille was digging for that garden?"

"In the middle of the winter?" I give her a look.

She tilts her head and, with a *slap!,* claps her own hand to her mouth.

"Yep. She was digging, all right. Digging for old treasure," I add.

"She *knows*." I'm so relieved that Colette's more and more willing to consider the wild possibilities with me. Maybe it's because they're beginning to stare us in the face as if they are facts in flesh.

"I think she does. I think so. Don't you?"

Colette looks bothered to agree. "Yes. That's entirely possible."

"Okay, but I don't think she has any clue about us, or what we know. Neither does Larry." I use her father's first name instead of calling him her dad, hoping that will lessen the hurt she's dealing with. Judging by her wincing whenever he comes up, I'm pretty sure it does nothing to help matters.

"Sorry," I apologize. "It's just, I want to be . . . "

"Open about it. Of course. I do, too. It's just really disappointing to think that my dad is trying to con me."

That's quite an understatement. I simply nod in response. Colette decides that she's going to try to get together with her dad after Christmas. She figures she'll have gone long enough without using the extra-school-work excuse and her mom won't question it. We know that she's going to have to be careful and creative about gleaning information from him. Who knows, maybe he'll tell her something outright. He told Mama Pearl he would. Colette considers that thought and gets a little too optimistic about Larry for my comfort. I knew he was a dirt bag; I know he is a dirt bag. Unfortunately, I'm sure whatever transpires from their conversations will set his dirt-baggy status safely into stone. I try to think more pleasant thoughts, thoughts of Christmas and Dylan and having an awesome coffee connection, before I fall into some decent sleep.

I love riding around with this boy, listening to his crappy radio, making deliveries. I usually volunteer to be the one to bring them in. I like checking out the different venues and meeting different folks. Some of them ask if I'm a new employee. I tell those who ask that I'm just helping out, that my family owns Evie's Café. Most are familiar. Some praise our little place, while others look at me suspiciously, clearly uncomfortable with the competition skulking around on their turf. No matter to me. It's all fun. We don't talk much, but I'm happy to just drive around.

Sometimes he wraps his fingers around mine. I so badly want to tell him what's going on, but I just don't feel like it's safe. I trust him; it's these crazy spirits and these loony living folks that I don't trust to be safe for him. So we laugh occasionally about a weird customer and talk a little about school, but mainly we just soak up each other's company.

I find myself looking forward to my next meeting with Father Brian. This time he's got a full pot of coffee waiting. We spend the next forty-five minutes talking about death and grief. I ask him why I still feel so shaken about losing GG. I feel like I don't have a right to it when Dylan lost his own father and is holding it together for his family now. He tells me about the varying ways people grieve.

"I meet with so many folks, Stella, around the most emotionally charged times in their life. Weddings, births, deaths. Christenings and communions to mark some sacred spaces in between. Some people are on their best behavior and some are at the worst. Some of the stiffest people I know have complete meltdowns. Others? Statues. Taking care of everyone around them, holding fast."

"Like my mom. She never really cried. Not once. How could she not cry?" I'm angry again, accusing her.

He continues his flow of thought, as if this whole time he was gearing up to respond to me.

"Holding fast, because if they don't, there's a very real fear that they will lose hold of everything, including their sanity. Some people don't let themselves go for fear of never coming out. And when you've got a family—a husband, a daughter to raise"—he gestures toward me —"a business to run—a person could feel that they have no choice but to rise in the morning, just like they always do."

I consider this.

"Stella, just because your mom rises doesn't mean she doesn't crumble in the quiet times. Everyone has to crumble a little bit."

"Like cookies."

"Yes, like cookies. That reminds me!" He pulls some hefty chocolate chip and walnut treats from a tin. "Cookie?" he offers.

"You are my very favorite priest."

A couple of days before Christmas Eve, Colette and I stop at a trendy boutique. The place is packed. Since it's not prom season, I can only imagine these girls are shopping for lavish Christmas parties or, even more likely I suspect, Mardi Gras balls of their very own. There's a wall lined in beautiful sequined and feathered masks. I see a shopkeeper pulling a hot pink one off the wall that is clearly meant to match the ruffled wild gown of a girl in the mirror. She then hands it to the girl, who holds it up to her face and is instantly transformed. Her smile shows that she knows it, too. New Orleans is like that. In all her traditions, she gives you permission to transform yourself. In some ways, she is like the moon herself. Steadfast yet ever-changing. Smiling down upon these maidens making magic in their dresses. This store is full of witches who don't even know what power they are crafting.

"Of course!" I throw my hands up.

"What?" asks Colette, slowly turning in a long ivory gown.

"Of course the first dress you try on looks incredible on you."

"It doesn't look too bridal?"

"Not with these accoutrements, my dear." A nearby saleswoman has already brought over accessories in anticipation. She's holding what looks to be a pile of cream-colored feathers that she unravels around Colette's neck.

"A boa?" Colette looks in the mirror.

"A boa?" I turn to the clerk.

"A boa," she says with a smile. "This is for a Mardi Gras ball, correct?"

"Well, yes. Specifically, the Courteau ball."

The woman raises an eyebrow. "You'll need this, too." She places a wide cuffed bracelet made of wire and crystals on Colette's arm. "And last but not least . . . " She hands her a short stick wrapped in ivory ribbon, bearing a crystal studded mask with feathers that match the boa.

"OMFG," I breathe.

The lady crosses her arms in pleasure. "OMFG is right, miss."

Even the more reserved Colette can't help but admire her finery. It's only brief, though, because she glances down at the tag on the bracelet, shakes her head, then looks down at the tag on the dress. It looks like she's about to collapse. She quickly begins to remove her accessories.

"Colette, don't. It's perfect for you."

"I'm sorry." Colette turns to the saleswoman. "This is far out of my price range. Do you have any dresses on sale?"

"Yes, but my dear—" The woman sweeps her arm toward Colette's gown, as if to say, "You can't be serious. This is the best you'll ever look."

"I'm sorry." Colette walks into a fitting room to remove the dress. The lady returns with a few more budget friendly pieces, and while a couple of them are pretty, none of them compare. Col's being so agreeable, acting as though she doesn't mind, but I mind for her. She insists I try some on with her, even though I'm in no mood since I'm personally depressed about her not walking out with that gorgeous creation.

"That green one is cute," she says. She's right. It's cute. But ordinary. And now I've seen what a killer dress can do. I aspire to conjure something close to that feeling for myself.

We leave empty handed, Colette saying that she'll probably go back next week and get the purple one if nothing else is on sale. I'm preoccupied. No, I'm obsessed. My friend looked blissful for the first time in a while when she threw on that gown. It was the whole picture with the boa and the crystals—the perfect fairy tale. Suddenly, I am determined to find a way to give that to her because a friend like Colette deserves a little fairy tale in the middle of a nightmare.

We sleep like the dead on Christmas Eve—probably because they didn't visit us. Colette had asked for a creepy-free Christmas. I obliged. Besides, being well rested allowed me to fully enjoy the look on Colette's face when she opened up a box containing a crystal mask, then one with a fluffy feather boa, and finally, the most beautiful satin gown. My mom, dad, Dena and I all gladly sacrificed our Christmas funds for the perfect gown and accessories. I'd never seen Colette so happy.

It was one of the merriest Christmases I can remember.

WARDROBE REVEALINGS & TAKING THE CAKE

THE EMPEROR

"*L*ook, I don't know if this will lead to anything, but would you call him and see? I already spoke to him about it. I hope that's cool," I say hesitantly.

It's New Year's Eve day. Colette's over at her dad's place, but I think she told her mom she would be with Jack. I've arrived to spend an hour helping Dylan out at the roaster. He's looking at the piece of paper I've just handed him. It's the number to my priest's office. I asked Father if the church had access to good affordable help for Dylan's grandpa. I told him they wanted to keep him living with them, if possible. He said that he had a few different contacts and to have Dylan call him. I'm feeling nervous. I've tried really hard to not be intrusive. I'm not sure how Dylan will feel about my talking about him, with some religious figure, no less.

A hug settles my concern. Dylan holds me in a deep embrace. I hear footsteps coming from the front room and pull myself away just before his mom walks in.

"Ah, coffee and romance," she sings when she walks in. I feel my cheeks turn scarlet. My relationship with Dylan is anything but traditional. We don't go on dates—we just hug, laugh, cry, and bag coffee. I don't really know what box to put "us" in, but it works for me, since I don't know what label to put on any part of my life right now.

Angie pats me on the shoulder, grabs a few finished sacks, and walks out. "I'm going to see if I can find something that'll work for Gramps before I tell her," Dylan lets me know. "I just don't want her to get all freaked about cost and stuff if she doesn't need to."

"Totally." A half hour later, I'm back at the café. We're closing early today, and closed tomorrow, so I hole up in my room and work on some blends with lavish ball makeup in mind for Col and me. I flip through a couple of magazines I picked to get an idea of what I want to wear, but nothing stands out. I decide to go back to the boutique where Col found her dress to see if anything new is on sale.

A berry gloss would look perfect with Colette's ivory fabric. Maybe some navy eye color smudged along her upper lids for definition? My phone beeps. I set down a pot of blue to see who it is. Colette wants me to call her.

"What's up? How was Larry?"

"Up to something."

Duh! But I don't say that. I wait for her to collect her thoughts.

"He's fishing, Stella. He started asking me all these questions about Jack, and then about the Courteau family. Things about their family history, how they made their money, how they make it now . . . and when I asked him why he wanted to know, he said he was just curious."

"What did you tell him?"

"Nothing. You know I've never asked Jack about it, and he doesn't talk about his money. I think it makes him uncomfortable. I think he just wants to blend in."

"Yeah, good luck with that, buddy."

She giggles. "I know. He has no idea how gorgeous and . . . different he is."

"Thank God. He'd be such an ass if he knew."

Colette laughs again. "I don't know if he could be an ass. Naïve, sure. But not an ass."

"Naïve? You see that, too?"

"Yeah—even more with his family. He does not see how mean his mother is, how disconnected his dad is. I just spent dinner with them and I was crawling out of my skin. I don't get how he's their son."

"So you really think he's got nothing up his sleeve." I'm stating it, just double-checking, really, because I think he's absolutely uninvolved in anything we're dealing with here.

"I really don't. You still agree, right?"

"Yes. I just wanted to check and make sure I wasn't crazy."

"Of course you're crazy. And he's my boyfriend, so I'm biased. But seriously, I only have good feelings about his soul."

"Do you hear yourself, witch?"

"Enough, you." She sighs.

"What?'"

"My dad. I'm trying to see how this could be innocent, but I can't talk myself into that."

"Yeah." I wait patiently.

"Stella?"

"Huh?"

"He asked about your grandmother. He asked if she was the real deal. And he said that I have my own New Orleans ancestors, that my grandmother told him that some of them might have been like your GG."

"What?" My thoughts go back to Beatrice. I'm wondering again what the heck her surname was.

"Stop it. I know what you're thinking. We already saw my family tree. She wasn't on it."

"But Col—"

"Please, Stel. Please. There's got to be so many possibilities."

"Sure. We'll figure out what's going on."

The desperation in her voice cuts me. She doesn't want me to say what she's already thinking. She doesn't want to consider the very real possibility that Beatrice's crap mother was so intent on disowning her that she even had a family tree put together without including her own daughter . . . as if she never existed.

I switch topics to dresses and the dance. It's so surreal and exhilarating, like some fantasy come to life. Colette suggests that the four of us—Dylan, Jack, she, and I—get together tonight.

"Jack invited us to his house, but I didn't know how you'd feel—"

"I'd love to." *A chance to look around some more?*

"Stella, you have to be composed. This is a New Year's Eve date."

"Oh, Jesus. Have you talked to Dylan?" Somehow, the word date makes me feel clammy all over. The ball is so far-off, but this? This is a couple of hours away.

"No, nerd. But since you're so weird about it, I'll ask Jack to call him with an invitation, okay?"

"Fine." Can you look forward to something and dread it at the same time? I think I'm proof that you can.

I brush on a sparkly white shadow blend that I named Snowflake, then add a thick stripe of black liquid eyeliner just above my top lashes. I've been so busy I haven't been able to enjoy playing with makeup like I normally do, so it's nice to get all dolled up.

My mom lets me take the delivery van since she and my dad are staying in to watch the ball drop on TV. Dylan, Jack, and Colette are already at the Manor. I feel a bit more awkward than I need to. I'm close to two of these people and fairly comfortable with the third.

Colette answers the door and then goes back to sharing a chair with Jack that's designed for one person. Dylan smiles at me. He sits up from his laying position on the couch to make room for me to sit.

"Hey there." He reaches out to gently hold my hand. I appreciate that he doesn't kiss me in front of Col and Jack. He must pick up on how uncomfortable I am in this social situation. The days when we were walking to school in the warm autumn air seem so long ago. We've all been going through changes. Well, except for Jack. He's just his ever-pretty, ever-polite self.

"Coffee, Stella?" he offers.

"Yes, thank you. I can get it myself."

"I'll get it." Dylan volunteers with a grin. "I know how to properly prepare a cup. You know it's that brew we just finished roasting?"

"The dark French Roast? Nice!" I start to relax. Dylan gives my hand a squeeze and walks into the kitchen.

"Where are your parents, Jack? New Year's Eve party?"

"No. They're actually out of town." I raise my eyebrows at Colette to imply a crapload. She shakes her head at me ever so slightly, her way of telling me to knock it off. I know she won't be spending the night. I know she hasn't spent the night with a boy yet, and she knows that I haven't either, so I guess I will refrain from bringing it up lest my BFF makes things super awkward for Dylan and me. Aside from chasing ghosts, murderers, and thieves, and lying about it in the process, we're actually a couple of fairly modest maidens.

Jack is more observant than I thought, because I believe he responds to my expression when he says, "They trust me."

"Well, yeah. You could sell sand to a camel, Jack. I don't mean that like you're a con," I clarify. "I mean that because you truly have the most honest face ever."

"Thanks."

"Where did they go?"

"Virginia. To visit my uncle—my dad's brother. Just for today and tomorrow."

"Oh, cool. What does your uncle do?" I try to sound casual, but I'm damned if I don't investigate a bit.

"Commercial real estate. He buys properties and rents them out to businesses."

So uncle is rich, too, it would seem. Not surprising.

"Jack, I've always wondered. What do your parents do?"

He laughs. "I wonder that myself, sometimes. My dad used to do a lot of investing. Like in different companies, stocks, things like that. I guess that's what he still does. He doesn't talk much about it."

"Is that what your grandpa did?"

"I think so."

"So your mom is a gardener?"

"Yes, she loves it. Not professionally or anything, but ever since she let go of the landscaping company, she's been out there a lot more."

"Didn't she get rid of your cook? And your housekeeper, too?"

"We still have someone come to clean a couple of times a month. But yeah, my mom really wants to try her hand at cooking, I guess." He wrinkles his nose and laughs.

I go for it. "Jack, this is going to sound incredibly rude, and it's none of my business"—I purposely avoid the look I know Colette is shooting my way—"but are your parents having money problems?"

"Stella! What's wrong with you?" Colette scolds me, but only to protect Jack's feelings. She wants to know as badly as I do.

Jack clears his throats and rubs Colette's back. "It's okay." He sits for a moment. "I never talk about this with anybody, Stella, so I hope I can count on your discretion."

"Absolutely."

"My parents never speak to me about money. Never. But contrary to what some may think of me, I'm not just some empty-headed stupid spoiled kid."

"I never thought you were."

He gives a half smile. "Thanks. It's been awkward making the transition in schools. That's when I started wondering things. About"—the word comes out uncomfortably for him—"money. My mom said that she thought it would be good for my character if I attended public school—this is after years of private school. I could hardly believe her. But she was determined, so I didn't fight it too much. I liked the idea of finally seeing girls in my school." He kisses Colette on the cheek. She's glued to this story.

He clears his throat again. "Then other stuff began to happen, like the staff firings. There's always some reason or another, but my parents have never gone this long without hiring new help. The only thing that she seems to continue to spare no expense on is this ball. She lives for these. All year it's what she looks forward to. I shouldn't be saying any of this. I don't even know if there's anything to it."

"Maybe it's nothing," I lie, more to ease his discomfort. He seems to appreciate the gesture.

"Maybe." He pauses. "And now they're taking this last-minute trip to visit my uncle before this lavish party. I just can't help but wonder . . . "

"Do you think they're asking for—"

"Dude, are those graves?" Dylan's voice breaks in from the kitchen. I thought he was taking a while. "Are those actual graves in your backyard?"

"Yes. Strange, right?"

"Yes. Who's buried in your backyard?"

Wouldn't we all like to know?

"It's a couple of servants from a long time ago—Civil War era. They're not marked with a lot of details. I don't completely know."

"You don't completely know whose corpses are parked behind your back patio?"

I think I'm in love with this boy.

"No." Jack smiles. "I suppose that I've just always been used to them."

It seems that we're dealing with a young man who is very accustomed to never asking questions. Dylan hands me a mug of coffee, looking at me in amazement over the situation. I would do just about anything to tell him what is happening, what is going on beneath the surface.

"You know what's funny?" Jack's face brightens. I get the feeling he's happy to be able to talk about his family's issues. It's as if he never knew that discussing it was an option.

"What?" Now Colette is pressing. There's my girl.

"I was looking for my tux for the ball this morning and I found something odd on the floor of my parent's closet. I'll show you." He disappears up the stairs and returns with a long rectangular box.

"Monopoly? Seems right." I joke.

"No." He turns the box. It's a Ouija board.

"Isn't that a Spirit Board? Like for contacting the dead?" Colette asks.

"Yes." Jack answers. He looks like a kid who went hunting for his Christmas presents. "I've never seen it before, but it was wide open, and there were a few things around. Candles, a bowl with some funny smelling stuff in it, some rocks . . . I have no idea what my mom would be doing with it."

"How do you know it wasn't your dad's?" Colette asks.

"Because that's the closet my mom uses for special-occasion clothes. He doesn't even know what's in there.

Besides, my dad would never. He doesn't believe in any of that stuff."

Dylan rubs his hands together. "Well, open it up. Let's play with it. Let's see who she's talking with."

"NO. Nope."

They all turn to look at me after my loud dissent.

"Really?" Colette looks surprised. After all, I'm usually the first one in the water when it comes to the mystical.

"My GG warned me of the dangers of amateurs playing with Spirit Boards. You don't know what kind of energy you could be inviting into your life. She told me horror stories about people whose lives were taken over by messed-up ghosts. Your mother really shouldn't be playing with that thing." I point to it, recoiling. I don't want to touch. I am officially creeped out by the methods and motives of Mrs. Courteau.

"Okay, sure, we won't touch it." Dylan puts his arm around me. I must look shaken. Jack just described a makeshift altar around the board. What the hell is this woman trying to pull?

Jack looks alarmed by my reaction. "What should we do with it, Stella?"

They all turn to me, again. Great, I've officially made myself the ghost expert in this crowd.

"Just put it back as you found it. Do you remember just how it was positioned?"

"I think so."

"Good. Put it like that . . . and Jack?"

"Yes?"

"It would be better if you didn't talk to your mom about it. About any of it."

"I have no problem with that." He nods, then goes upstairs with the board to put it away. I look at Colette. I can feel Dylan trying to read the both us. He must know it's a waste of time to ask me what's going on, so the three of us sit in awkward silence until Jack returns.

"Stella, may I ask you something? And once more, can I rely on everyone's discretion?" He's looking mainly at Dylan and me when he asks this. He trusts Colette completely.

"Yes. We won't tell anyone, Jack."

"There's something else that was in this dish of herbs. A piece of paper. I was honestly nervous to open it, isn't that funny?" He gives a quiet laugh. "Anyway, do you think this could be dangerous? Do you think my mother's in danger or something?" He hands me the note.

Colette and Dylan stand on either side of me, reading the swirled, elegant writing over my shoulders.

Dearest Cora, I'm asking for your guidance. Help me find the money we need, the money we deserve, the money that is rightfully ours. Blessed ancestor, I beseech you. I know you must know. Help me. Show yourself to me. So mote it be.

If I wasn't sure before, I know now that we are

dealing with a woman who is meddling in the supernatural with pretty much no practical knowledge of her own. Colette gasps behind me as she reads. I try on my best poker face, but Jack is honed in on Col.

"What is it?" he asks.

"Oh, I'm just surprised. I had no idea your mom was into this sort of thing." Colette pulls it off. Jack buys it.

"Me either. So, what should I do, Stella?"

I find myself repeating the words of a woman I'm very pissed at right now, a woman who I believe has a responsibility to be careful what she tells people.

"I think you should stay the hell out of it, Jack. I'm serious. Best to act like you saw nothing. I say we talk about this ball instead."

Jack appears more than happy to retreat back into denial. Dylan gives me a penetrating look that I try to ignore. My thoughts are filled with anger toward Mama Pearl. What is she telling Lucille and Larry? Why is she letting them get so out of hand? I know she's nuts, but she has an ethical responsibility.

Jack takes the paper back to where he found it and brings down his tuxedo at Colette's request. I work to shift myself into speaking about the event. My own excitement takes over fairly quickly. Mama Pearl later . . . right now we're talking corsages and dancing.

Jack fills us in on what to expect at an event such as this.

"I'm sure you all know something about how these balls work. There's a feast, the traditional king cake is served, and a king and queen of the ball are chosen beforehand. This year it's the president and vice-president of the Historical New Orleans Preservation Society. Besides us, everyone else who makes it on the list still has to purchase their ticket with a charitable contribution."

I knew that. Most krewes, which are like charitable clubs, are responsible for putting on these coveted Mardi Gras events. There are no boobs for beads at these affairs, especially not the famous Courteau ball. It is the epitome of elegant southern tradition. Of course, it still has the wild New Orleans underbelly. There'll be a jazz band, everyone wears a mask, and although everyone gets a piece of the king cake, we'll have the pleasure of being seated at the table of the high court, along with the king and queen. We'll get to participate in the Mardi Gras staple—looking for the charm in our piece of the cake. We always bake a huge amount of these cakes at the café with a fun twist: we place all kinds of charms, in addition to the little baby, within the treat. I grew up experiencing the excitement of my Mardi Gras predictions. I remember sitting around the dinner table with my dad, mom, and GG.

"*Stella, you got the bells? A wedding soon? Well, you are ten. I guess it's time.*" My dad would smile. Or, "*You got the baby rattle, Evie? Something you're not telling us?*" The cake held a power to me, a thrill of fun as a child. I consider that power once again.

"We'll bake the cakes," I insist to Jack. "Please, let us. It would be our honor."

"My mother was going to order them from your bakery anyway. She'll be happy to pay . . . " He realizes what he's just been discussing regarding his family's financial circumstance.

"Don't be ridiculous. It would be my mom's thrill to offer them as a gift." And I know that's true. She'd be delighted to offer them as a gift, especially since I received free tickets. "How many people? One hundred? Two hundred?"

"About one hundred fifty. Thank you so much. My mother will really appreciate it."

I'm not so sure she will.

CRACKING OPEN & POURING OUT

THE TOWER

I give Colette a small smile. She knows I've got something cooking.

Aside from my personal plotting, I'm so excited about the event. I was barely at school dances in years past, not just from being busy at the café, but because I thought they were awkward and awful. Homecoming this year didn't even come up on my radar and I have no use for prom. But a lavish, exclusive, and elegant New Orleans Mardi Gras ball? That's an entirely different matter. That's the stuff this sixteen-year-old girl's dreams are made of. Colette is the one who pulls me out of my spooky Cinderella fantasy.

"Stella, I'm getting really tired. What if we head back to your place? Is it cool if I spend the night?"

It throws me for a second, her wanting to leave her

own Prince Charming so early in the evening, but I'm sure she's got her reasons.

"Yeah. Of course it's okay if you stay. You can borrow some of my stuff to wear."

"I packed a bag just in case."

"Awesome. Boys, it's been real." Why do I say weird-sounding things? For as much as I make fun of Jack's social awkwardness, I'm just as guilty.

"Yeah, really, really, real." Dylan nods his head like I said something profound.

"Shut up."

"I'll walk you to your car." Dylan takes my hand, and Jack follows behind, arm in arm with Colette.

I'm still a little shy with all of us like this. Dylan knows it. He gives me a kiss on the cheek.

"Night, Miss Fortunat."

Once we're pulling out of the ostentatiously long driveway, I ask Colette what's up.

"What's *up*? Seriously, Stel? Did you not hear what my boyfriend just told us? We have to find out more. We have to protect him. You looked so freaked out about that Ouija board. I had the worst gut feeling. I felt sick. The whole time we were talking about the ball my mind was racing."

And here lies the fundamental difference between Colette and me. I can be distracted with glitter, gowns, and romantic notions. I feel sort of ashamed that I was honestly fascinated about the dance while my friend was considering all sorts of freaky possible scenarios involving yet another guy she cares about. She's right. It's what I've been trying to nail down about Lucille this whole time, this sickening, strange feeling I've had about her. And now we know she's up to no good.

"Right. So, what do we now know? Lucille is Cora's great-great-great-niece or whatever? What!"

Colette nods slowly.

I continue. "And she's got to be talking about the same thing your dad was talking to Mama Pearline about, the same thing that Jonathon mentioned in the letter. It's got be the same thing, right? Yes. I mean, how many freaking treasures can there be?" I'm laughing at the otherworldly feeling that's now surrounding me as I'm going over what just transpired at the Courteau house.

"Let's specifically ask for what we're looking for tonight," I suggest. "I think the clearer we are with Beatrice, the better."

Before the clock strikes twelve, Colette and I are all set up in my room, ready to talk to some spirits.

"Please, what does Cora know? Why do you want us involved? What can we do to help, and what can we do to keep safe? Please help us with clarity in vision. You do this, and we will do what we can to honor and help you, Miss Beatrice."

Now I'm sick, especially as I know we're getting the last clues . . . where will they lead? Colette has yet to acknowledge who Beatrice must be. I know she's thinking it. But one thing at a time, right?

We dab on Vision Powder. I close my eyes tightly, hold onto my ribbon, and sink into my bed like I'm being strapped into a rollercoaster.

The tea is scalding hot as it drips onto my shaking hands.

"Cora. What have you done?" Another slightly more plain blonde woman stares at me, questioning me from across the small table.

"Nothing. She had an acc-i-dent. She fell down the stairs." I feel myself looking at her, challenging her.

"Oh no, Cora. Cora." She moans.

"I found the servant out back. I told her to fetch a doctor, and I left," I say in a matter-of-fact tone.

"What did you say to Jonathon?"

"I didn't say anything. I saw his father walking around the property. I told him that I knew all about HER, that the engagement was off, and that if he did not want scandal brought upon his family, he would not ask any more questions."

"Surely he will—"

"No, he surely will not. He's ill, sister. Dying, I suspect. It's rare to even find him outside like that. It was lucky. Luck on my side." I give a laugh, and the woman stares at me while she pours her own cup.

"Cora. This isn't, you can't—"

"She's a WITCH, Susan. That crazy old man entrusted her with hiding part of the Courteau fortune. That whore was in charge of our money! And she was still bedding him . . . " I give out a cry that sounds like a small wounded animal.

"Whatever do you mean?"

"I mean that I heard Jonathon's father talking to her in his study one day. He asked her to keep the gold protected. He said that even though the war was over, he still didn't trust scavengers and carpetbaggers, and that he'd like to wait a little while longer before uncovering it."

"Gold?"

"Yes, he's crazy but no fool! He knew Confederate money would be useless. He never had any faith in the Confederacy. His only loyalties were money and the family name."

"How can you say she was a witch?"

"She was a Haitian and she roped my Jonathon into her arms. She was pretty enough, but she kept him in her clutches even while we were—" my voice breaks again. I can see that my audience is not convinced of my accusation.

"Everyone knew. She saw one of those Voodoo doctors regularly. She kept the strangest little garden out front of her house. She even had these symbols above her door. I knew she had kept him amused when they were younger. I knew that she still spoke frequently with his father, but even though she guarded the money, I still thought she was not much more than an elevated servant." I reach into my purse and pull out the sleek black pen Cora had recently received. "I loved him. I truly loved him. I just served the purpose of formality." I sit for a while. I feel this body barely breathing in and out. I note a rattling in her chest. I begin coughing and break into a round of heaving.

"Why don't you lie down, Cora? We'll talk about this later." Susan leans to take my arm as I notice how weak this *body feels. I look down to see a cradle beside the table holding a small baby.*

"Besides, I don't want to wake her. My little girl needs her rest," Cora's sister says in a hushed tone.

She takes me into a tiny room and helps me get into a dressing gown. As she helps me into bed, I take her hand.

"Susan?" I tighten my grip, but it seems to have no effect.

"Yes, Cora."

The words burn my lips. "She had his baby. I saw him before the brother took him. I saw him, and he looked just like—"

"Hush, sister. Just get some rest. You'll make yourself worse with this talk."

With that my eyes slam shut.

Images scramble from that small room to my own bed, to a sliver of moon. A voice carries though my ears.

"After a point, girls, it's all yours. My magic buried it. You'll have to do yours to bring it in the light. Or she may figure it out yet."

I shoot up, gasping for air, like I've literally been flung between worlds. Colette's in the same state.

"Stella!" she hisses.

"I know."

"What? What the . . . "

"I have no idea. So you were with Cora too?"

She nods. And then my flesh crawls.

"Colette."

"What?"

"Remember how we thought Beatrice was showing us Cora's perspective?"

"Yes."

"I don't think that's what's going on here. I think we're in Cora's head, or she's in ours, at least tonight. And last time."

"It felt like I was being pulled between worlds."

"Yes! Me, too."

"Did you hear that voice? I'm sure it was Beatrice."

I nod. "Speaking to us." We both shiver. Now it's getting even more personal, more real. It's feeling more out of control.

Colette taps her fingertips together. "I think someone is doing what we're doing. I think that's how we're getting in Cora's head. I'm not sure we were supposed to see that."

I think Colette may be right. "Who?"

"Who else?"

"So we're ruling out Larry?"

"I just didn't hear him say anything specific about her. Whereas Lucille—"

"Is practically her pen pal."

"Right." She can't help a smile.

"So, Col . . . shit."

"What?"

"It's entirely possible that she's seeing what we're seeing, too, if these worlds are blending. That Lucille, or whoever, is seeing—"

"That's if my theory is right. Which it might not be. I

don't know what ghosts are capable of showing me. Do you?"

This thought gives me some relief. Maybe no one else is in our heads, except for the one girl we're sort of okay with.

"Col? School starts back up on Monday."

"So?"

"So I'm thinking that you may want to get a bite to eat with your dad tomorrow. Just to see if you can figure out more without risking people getting into our heads. Sorry."

"I know. I need to. Will you come with me? I just need some support."

"Of course. We could go earlier. Neither of us has to work tomorrow."

Larry offers to meet at the same pizza place we ate at before. I try my best to be low-key. I'm not sure my tagging along is such a good idea. After all, what's he going to say in front of me? But Colette needs me, so I'm here.

"So Stella has lots of neat memories of her GG telling fortunes and stuff. Her grandmother was kind of a legend in this town, Daddy."

Oh, okay. She's going for it, then. I take a bite of steaming-hot pizza too early and almost burn my mouth out of my head. Instinctively, I spit it back out on my plate. Neither of them notices.

"I've heard about her. How interesting that must have been for you, Stella."

I'm throwing back ice water in a vain attempt to cool my tongue.

"Yeah." It's useless. The roof of my mouth is destroyed. I feel Colette nudge my side. "I learned a little from watching her, but she was the real deal."

"Oh, I bet you're real enough." Seriously, Larry? We're going there?

"Well, there are some frauds in this town, and then there are some truly talented folks. Take Mama Pearline from the Mojo Parlor, for instance."

He flinches ever so slightly.

"She's scary talented. Ever hear of her?"

"Hmm, I think so."

I stare at him, not knowing what to do next. I finally turn toward Colette, who's boring even more deeply into him with her eyes. Her father blows on his pizza, takes a bite, and chews for an unnecessary length of time. He looks from Colette to me, then back to Colette again, and permits himself a grin.

"Well, I'll be. I don't know how you know. Your fella onto something, sweetie?" he asks Col.

"Jack knows nothing."

He nods. "You know, your mother should have given you more credit. I knew you had something special. I knew it when you were a teeny tiny thing. You'd talk about things. I remember when you insisted"—he chuckles—"you insisted I take an umbrella out on a bright, hot, sunny day. I figured I'd humor you. An hour later, a storm blew in . . . out of nowhere. You must have been about four? Your grandmother said you had some folks in your family—your mom always thought it was nonsense, just chatter. She never listened to your grandma's stories about treasure, either. She never paid them any mind. But I did." He taps his temple with his first two fingers. "I knew there was something to you and those stories."

"Glad I could be useful to you," Colette murmurs so softly he doesn't hear her. He's happy to boast. I jump in before she gives away too much.

"Her grandmother talked about treasure?"

He looks at me. "She only mentioned it a couple of times. Dena asked her to stop spreading rumors about magic and gold. She thought Colette would be too impressionable. But that old lady believed it. She didn't advertise it, but I think she believed it. Asked her about it again when I came to try to win Colette's mother back a couple of years ago."

He throws his hands up as if to say that if it weren't for Dena, they'd all be one big happy family. I want to reach across the table and choke him myself, but I suppose I should leave that pleasure to Colette.

He must take my rage for surprise because he continues with, "Yup, paid Dena's mom a visit before y'all moved. Told her how I'd cut way back on stuff, and well, she always liked me."

"How did you find out details?" Colette's voice has a hollowness to it that sets me on edge.

"Piece by piece, baby. Your grandmother had all sorts

of old papers—mostly junk, but I was patient. We talked for hours and I borrowed a stack. You can find out a lot through a little online research and city hall records." He folds his arms across his chest and leans back in his seat. Then he leans forward conspiratorially. "Look, Colette, it's okay with me to give a small cut to your friend— if you can keep a secret." He winks at me. "And then we'll split the rest. After all, it is rightfully ours." Larry reaches out his soda to toast her.

Colette raises her glass and tosses her drink in his face. Before he can even react, she's heaved the pizza tray full of scalding deep dish off the table and into his lap.

"None of it's yours, you piece of shit!" She's knocking everything off the table. The entire restaurant has frozen. "You used me! That's all you came here for! You didn't want a relationship . . . you wanted money. I trusted you. You PIECE of SHIT!" She's sobbing. I try to pull her up as I see her about to collapse.

"Leave town," I seethe to her dad. "Leave now, or you will pay such a dear price. And yeah, I'm telling Dena. I'm pretty sure I can have you arrested for kidnapping, taking a minor out behind her mom's back with no custody and no parental consent. My uncle is the top attorney in this city."

I have no idea about the kidnapping thing, and I'm totally lying about the attorney relative. My mom's an only child, and my dad's brother runs a bed-and-breakfast in Maine. No cutthroat lawyers. But between his daughter going uncharacteristically ballistic and my own rage and threats, Larry looks spooked. I can see his wheels turning, though, like a sleazy salesman who hasn't quite grasped that he's not going to close this deal.

"No. We're done. Leave now," I repeat. A manager approaches. "You need to leave. I've called the police." He's not sure who to talk to as he says this.

"Couldn't agree more," I respond.

Colette's broken. It was bound to happen and here she is. I help her out of the restaurant, moving just behind her dad.

"Seriously," I call to Larry. "Dena, attorney, conspiracy to commit robbery . . . not to mention my GG trained me *specifically* in the art of jinxing and hexes." What does he know? I'm going for it all. "Leave now, or you will pay in so many, many ways . . . " For some reason, the last threat seems to spook him the most.

He begins to back away, taking one more look at Colette. "Baby, I—"

"Go now and we'll go easy on you." I've never heard such a frightening tone. I swear that her father almost runs away from her.

MOTHERS & DAUGHTERS

DEATH

olette doesn't want to talk. She gives me a small false smile the next day at school but spends every spare second pretending to be engrossed in her books. I don't blame her. Her dad's a lying, scamming ass, her boyfriend may be a distant relative, and everyone wants a treasure that I think belongs, at least in part, to Colette. But I'm pretty sure she doesn't even care about the treasure.

At lunch, I'm scarfing leftover gingerbread from the café when I spot someone standing in the entrance to the lunchroom. I double take to see Dena. She looks furious.

"Colette. Colette!"

"What? Oh." She catches sight of her mother. "What's she doing here?"

We give each other a knowing look. "You better go see what she wants."

Colette nods and takes her tray to the trash, then her mom quickly escorts her away from view.

"What is going on?" Joanna asks. Shelly leans closer.

I take a swig of my chocolate milk. "Well, it seems that her mom may have found out about her dad."

"Uh-oh."

I have a terrible feeling about what's waiting for me at home. The day's a little warmer than it's been recently. I take full advantage, slowly strolling my way back to the house. The café is closed, so I head in through the front door. No sign of my parents in the parlor. They must be in the kitchen or upstairs.

"Stella?" My father's voice calls to me. It's difficult to read his tone.

"Yeah, Dad?" Did that come out spazzy?

"Come into the kitchen, please."

Crap. I set my bag by the stairs, go behind the counter and through the swinging doors. Both my mother and father are seated at the wooden table on the other side of the kitchen near my dad's office. My father looks grave and my mother looks . . . betrayed?

"So, we've had a call from Dena . . . " my mom begins.

I pull out a chair and sit. And wait.

"Are we to understand that you've been lying to us and to Dena for the past four months? That you've been sneaking around with a strange man?"

I stare down at the table. "He's not really a stranger. He's Colette's father."

My mother cuts back in. "He may be her biological father, but that man is not her dad. He's a drunk, he's a scam artist—God knows what he was up to!"

God knows, and we do, too. "I was just trying to help—"

"*Help*? Who knows what could have happened to you? Or to her?"

My father speaks more calmly. "Our concern, sweetie, is that you were so comfortable with such a deception. It worries us."

"Comfortable? You think I was comfortable lying to y'all about this?" Now I'm angry. Maybe it's fueled by guilt because let's face it—my pants have been on fire this whole school year. But the fact is that I do hate lying to them, especially to my dad. Even to Dena. And now? I can't throw my best friend under the bus.

"Look, her father said he wanted a relationship with her. He said he would tell Dena when the time was right."

"But Stella, you've heard the stories about him. You should have known better. And you should have looked out for Colette," my mom says.

This sends me over the edge. All I've been doing is looking out! I stare at the table, feeling anger build.

"Mom, you don't get it."

"I get that you've been lying to us and there are consequences for that." She takes a breath. "We discussed it, and you will not be attending the Courteau ball."

I gasp, then lift my head to see if she's joking. She has to be joking.

"You have proven that you can't be trusted. We thought you were more responsible than this."

And it boils over. "Responsible? Are you freaking KIDDING me? ALL I EVER AM IS RESPONSIBLE! I NEVER get to do what I want to do! I have no life because I have a selfish MONSTER mother who works me in her restaurant like a goddamn slave. But what do you care? You don't care about anybody. You didn't even cry when your own mother died!"

"That's enough!" my dad yells. He never yells. "You need to go to your room now, Stella."

I race up the stairs and slam my door so hard I can hear the antique china cabinet rattle on the other side. I lock my door and throw myself onto my bed where I intend to cry my eyes out of their sockets.

"And where are you, GG? Where the hell are you?" I sit up and grab the photo of her, young and smiling. "Guess what? I'm screwed. It's all on me. My best friend is messed up, a dead witch wants me to solve some insane puzzle, I'm banned from the coolest thing that's ever happened to me, and you? Once again, you're NOWHERE."

Inspiration, or insanity, strikes me. I lunge for the bottle of Vision Powder, pull off the cap, and begin to dump it all over myself. I cough, then keep going, powdering my entire body.

"All right, GG, where are you now? I'm wide awake, I'm asking for you, I've doused myself in your prophetic baking soda or whatever, so—where are you?"

Once more, silence is the answer I receive. Then I close my eyes and images flash before me . . . my grandfather's face, as if in person, a birthday cake piled high with candles, a young blonde girl, and tarot card after tarot card . . . jazz music pipes in . . . and I open my eyes.

My room has become fuzzy. A soft glow fills it. I'm immediately drawn to the record player, where I methodically pull out an album and set it down to play.

"Lorena." The tune is rich and swelling, and I'm craving a smoke. I go to my vanity in search of those Pall Malls—where are they? Ah, here we go. I grab a small box of matches. It doesn't occur to me that I've never smoked, never wanted to, that it usually disgusts me. None of this crosses my mind as I jam the butt between my lips, strike the match, and puff until the flame takes, the way I've seen my grandmother do a thousand times.

I open my window and pull up my metal chair so that I can sit and smoke there. At first I cough wildly. The cigarette tastes wretched. I don't think it's just because I don't like them. I'm sure the fact it is about two years old has something to do with the matter. But still I keep taking drags. The room looks different. I'm pulling out my tarot cards, tugging at particular ones.

The Lovers. I'm taking a pen to paper, writing to a man. I don't even know to whom or about what, I just know that it's a love letter. There's a knock on the door. Somebody enters. That's funny; I thought I had locked it. The girl I just saw in my mind's eye stands there in a blue dress, staring at me. She can't be older than thirteen.

"Baby, are you off?" I'm asking her a question but still penning my letter.

"I think so. Are you sure you don't want to come?"

"Oh, honey, I've got a hot date!" I chuckle and look down at my watch. I guess it's my watch, except I don't wear a watch. I also am talking to a strange girl in my room, so whatever. "Oh shit! He'll be here in fifteen minutes!"

I move to my vanity and pull out tubes of lipstick until I get a deep red shade. I look up in the mirror to put it on. GG's face stares back at me. I'm too caught up in this world to be shocked, or to have any time to process this. Not unlike my dreams, I'm just along for the ride.

I turn to face the girl, puckering my lips. "How's it look?"

"A little dark," she replies, arms folded.

"Oh, Moni, you're so modest." I chuckle. "I'm starving, too. What about you? Are you going to eat with your girlfriends?"

"No, I fixed dinner. I called up to you. There's still some left. Cake, too."

"Oh, sweetie, you're the best. The BEST!"

"I thought we were eating together tonight."

"Why did you think that?"

"We talked about it yesterday."

"Oh!" I hit my hand to my forehead. "That must have been before Maurice asked me out! Sorry."

"Maurice? Our tailor?"

"Yes, I think he's sweet." I giggle.

"Sure. He's nice."

"Are you wearing that to the movies?" I survey her button-down top and long skirt. "I have something really fun—"

"No, thanks, Mama. I'm not going to the movies."

"Oh, Moni, you're not going to church on a Friday night, are you?"

"It's Thursday."

I chuckle again. "Oh, that's right. I think I've got a date with Bill tomorrow night. Don't tell Maurice!"

I look back to the mirror to apply another coat of the red stuff.

"You do have a date with Bill. You talked about wearing your blue dress. I pressed it for you. It's downstairs with the dinner and cake."

I turn back toward her. "Oh, baby, I'm so sorry about tonight. We'll get together to eat tomorrow night."

"You have a—"

"Right! That's right. Saturday, then. Oh, I have canasta with Pearl. Oh hell." I wave my arm. "We'll figure it out. Save me some of that delicious cake, okay? You're the best cook. I don't know where you got it. Must've been your daddy's side. I've only got those three recipes, and I can only make them from lots of practice. If it weren't for you"—I get up and *squeeze her, planting a scarlet kiss on her cheek—"we'd starve."*

"It's true. Have fun, Mama." She grabs a tissue and gently wipes off the remnants on her face.

My stale cigarette has burned down to the butt in the ashtray on the windowsill. The taste sits in my mouth. It must be the nicotine combined with all the coffee I've drunk that's sending my stomach into a wave.

I stand to reach out to her. "Mama."

Did I say "Mama" instead of "Moni?" Am I coming back? Am I regaining control?

Just as I begin to recognize this, the glow in the room is a little clearer. The record is turning on the end, silent and scratching. The air reeks like . . . GG. It's comforting and upsetting all at once. I look back in the mirror to see my face looking back at me. I'm wrapped in my GG's old kimono-style robe. I'm wearing a shade of lipstick that does not suit me at all. My thoughts are difficult to collect. There's something in my heart—pain. My mom was neglected. By GG. My GG. My beloved grandmother was a lousy mother. Anger and guilt fight for first place within me. I'm getting more than a little tired of these two emotions.

I hear the clinking of dishes through the vents. My parents must have just finished eating. They're voices sound muffled and then my father's gets just loud enough to hear.

"I'll go talk to her."

My mom says something; I can't make out what.

Shit. I look at my odd reflection, as if he might catch a trace of my GG there. Then I notice the dusting of Vision Powder on the crown of my head and lightly coating my arms. I quickly go to work, cracking open the screen on my window to flick the now-dead cigarette butt out onto the pavement. I light a bit of sage and a patchouli-scented candle, which reeks like hippies. It should help.

I run my brush through my dusted locks and rub the excess from my skin. I lose the kimono and am left in my standard blouse and jeans. The lipstick he won't question. I'm always experimenting with colors. I'm ready for the knock at the door.

"Stella? It's me." Right on cue.

"Come in."

My dad makes a face upon entering. "Jeez, what is that smell? It's like a filthy locker room and incense."

"Patchouli candle," we both say at once. I reflect his grin.

"Your grandmother loved to burn patchouli-scented stuff. She thought it was funny how much it drove me nuts. I swear, if someone touches you while wearing that oil—"

"It won't come off for weeks. I remember. GG gave me the extra-long hugs when she wore it." I smile at the memory and then feel it fade.

"Your GG loved you so much."

"I know."

"Your mom loves you so much."

I sigh. "I know."

"She didn't really mean what she said about banning you from the ball. We had briefly considered it, but that's it."

My heart jumps a thousand feet in the air. "Really?!"

"Oh, maybe I should have let her tell you that. Let her say it to you, okay?"

I nod, wanting to fly. But other things must take place first.

"What you said about her not crying . . ."

"It sucked."

"It really sucked. Your mom's relationship with Evie was . . ." He purses his lips.

"Complicated. It wasn't like mine, was it?"

He looks at me for a few moments. "All of you loved each other. You ladies just have so many layers . . . just when I thought I could figure something out between you three, it changed. You changed."

I smile at the thought. "Maiden, Mother, Crone."

"Is that a witchy reference? Never mind. I know it is. You know it was never about the magic, don't you? What kept them apart? What strains you two, even."

A voice comes up behind him. "It was what the magic represented."

My mom has stepped beside my dad, who takes his cue and walks away, leaving us alone. I see the barely teenaged girl in her blue dress, so small, so lost, standing in my doorway. The realization that my mother is so rigid is because nobody allowed her anything else consumes me. I begin to cry.

I cry for lost illusions of my precious GG. I cry as I feel my own magical maidenhood growing and the burden of responsibility with it. I cry because I never knew the truth. And I cry some more because now I do.

I let my mother hold me the way she used to, stroking my hair. Someone keeps apologizing. Is it me? Or is it her? The words "I'm sorry" pass back and forth like a canteen of cool water in the desert.

"She wasn't there. The Church was there, but she wasn't," I whisper.

My mom steps back a moment to look at me. "Stella, did she . . . I mean . . . ."

"Yeah, she wanted me to know. I think she needed me to know."

This is the stuff that makes my mom uncomfortable. That doesn't mean she doesn't believe in it.

"You didn't have anyone after Grandpa died, did you? I always had you, dad, and GG to look after me. I used to complain about not getting to know Grandpa." I'm ashamed at my own selfishness.

"Well, she was so much fun, your grandmother. But after Daddy died, everything changed. He was definitely the more parental of the two of them."

"You're making excuses for her, Mama? Why? She left you alone to go party with random guys."

"But I learned how to survive, Stella. Maybe a little

too well. It's why you didn't see me fall apart after her death."

"I'm so sorry, Mama. I know you loved her."

My mom just nods and cries. "I loved her with everything. But it's tough to love someone that you're not sure loves you back."

"But she did! I felt it. She was just . . . "

We speak simultaneously and laugh. "Nuts."

My mom throws her head back in a cackle.

"There's the witch," I murmur.

"You know, Stella, I don't fear magic. I see the magic in my own faith. I don't think I've done a very good job showing you, though. I've been so busy trying to be what I thought a mom was supposed to be. I've tried so hard to keep you close at the café with me and now—" She's gulping sobs.

This makes me screamingly uneasy seeing my mom like this, breaking down in this style. It's just not Monique. And then it strikes me that I've been wrong on several accounts on who the hell Monique is exactly . . . .

"And now you've missed out. You've missed out and you hate me for it." She cries.

So she does hear me. I wish she didn't as my mother shrinks into that little girl in my arms.

"Sometimes I do. But really, I love you all the time. Even when I've hated you, I still loved you. Father Brian says those two feelings are much closer than we think."

"Did you just quote a priest?"

"Don't get too excited. I'm not full-blown converting to anything."

"Oh, you've always misunderstood me, baby! I don't care if you become Catholic."

I raise my eyebrows at this lie.

"Well, I'm not opposed to it, but I need you to hear me now. All I want is for you to feel supported in a way that I wasn't. I was perfectly happy with my father, who was my best friend, and the sense of community I had at the church. But then when he died, I was so angry with my mom and how she dealt with it. She was blinded by her precious magic. I felt like I was second . . . " She doesn't finish, but I can imagine. A remnant of a former life. Evie's brief foray into normalcy.

"But Mama, you've never said anything about this, about her."

"Because she was my mother, Stella. You don't say things like that about your mother, not in my generation. Not to your daughter who worships her. She loved you so much. She really tried to make up for it by being such a fun grandmother for you. It scared the crap out of me."

"You were jealous."

"Yes." She laughs. "Your wild and wonderful personality is so much like hers and unlike my own. I was jealous because you could relate to her on a level that I never could. She was invited to a part of your spirit that I feared I had closed myself off from. Over the years, the more I tried to be the mother I thought you needed, the more I pushed you away. I just wanted what she had with you. But I realized that someone had to be the—"

"Grown-up," I say, finishing her sentence for her. "I know, Mama. I can only imagine how hard it must have been with GG's flighty spirit. You had to take the reins, otherwise you probably wouldn't have had clean clothes or a hot meal."

My mother stares at me as if looking into my soul. Our connection will never be the same. We are bound by common angers, sympathy, and pain.

"What I don't think you realize is that I haven't taken on all of GG's traits," I say.

She looks at me quizzically.

"Like integrity, loyalty, love for my family, giving . . . I'd like to think my scales are tipped more heavily to the Monique side."

She squeezes me into the tightest embrace I think she's physically capable of and covers my face with kisses and tears. After my head is sufficiently moistened, she draws back to look at me and says, "Keep some of that wild. I admire the hell out of it. You've got just the right amount of magic, Stella. Just the right dose."

And the deal is sealed. My mother and I have become fast friends.

She pulls me downstairs to have a cup of coffee, and begins to tell me about how she put the word out for a couple of new part-time employees.

"Colette's only working about fifteen hours a week now, and I'd like you to cut back, too. I'd still like your help with certain duties, but we can afford to take on some other employees—as long as we can trust them. At this point, we can't afford not to. Our business has tripled and I know it's taking a toll." She takes a sip from her oversized white mug. "Of course, with the strain has also come benefit. We've been able to put some cash away for savings, and some for rainy days."

"Rainy days?"

"Rainy days . . . and dresses." I see my grandmother in her as she stands and sweeps the curtain to the laundry room back with a dramatic flourish. Hanging from a pole is the most perfect gown that was ever created.

"I ordered it just for you after our fight in the dress shop. I took your measurements down from the lady who fitted you in the first dress shop and then I called Mrs. Clenor with some ideas."

Mrs. Clenor is a middle-aged seamstress who is a regular customer of ours. I finally understand why she's always talking about being overrun with business. Because she's phenomenal.

"Do you like it?"

I leap to put it on, throwing off my clothes and reaching my arms to the ceiling as my mother slides it down upon me. The back fastens with a million little hooks. I face the full-length mirror behind the laundry room door. A maiden shines back at me. She's draped in fabric made from mist and moonlight, bound in moth's wings. It shifts and shimmers with my movement. I'm a southern belle. I'm a goddess. I'm a witch. I'm a beautiful girl.

My mother pulls plastic covering off of another hanger. It appears to be a heavy cloak of some kind.

"I just picked this up from the dry cleaners. It was your GG's. She wore it to a ball with your grandfather."

I never knew this. I never knew much about my grandmother's life. I feel connected to the three of them in such a powerful way as my mother drapes the charcoal-colored velvet cloak around me and fastens it at my neck. It's a shade that is about ten times deeper than my silvery-gray gown. It seems as though it was meant just for this gown.

And then I lose it, bursting into tears. Jesus, this family is full of criers.

"It's the most wonderful thing anyone's ever done for me. It's—it's exquisite, Mama." I don't think I've ever used that fancy word before, but it's definitely appropriate now.

Dylan is going to freak out. My heart shoots to the ceiling. I haven't really allowed myself much room for dreaming about this boy, especially with his own family crisis and my dead relatives and abusive spirits. But now I'm a girl who's going to a ball.

The magic of this moment is more potent, more powerful than any other.

FAMILIES & FINDINGS

THE WORLD

After showing off my dress and cloak to my dad, I discuss details with my mom as she putters around in the kitchen. She says that Dena will be coming over later with Colette.

"Mom, I really am sorry about lying to you about Larry. It was just so weird."

She sighs, fixing three fresh cups of coffee for her, my dad, and me.

"I know. I overreacted. Everything just boiled over. But you have to understand that it's about safety . . . he's very untrustworthy, manipulative. He never seems to have good motives when he wants back into their lives, and the fact that he asked Colette to keep his presence a secret from her mom, well . . . " She throws up her hands.

"He sucks. I know. I never liked him. But Colette just wanted a father."

I see my own father nodding and sipping his coffee. My heart swells.

"I think he just wanted to use her, though." I step on out there with these words.

"Oh yes, he did. Dena told me an insane story. Apparently, Colette said he thought there was some sort of family treasure she could help him dig up. Her grandmother told some fairy tale and he actually took it seriously! Can you believe it?"

I just look at my mother, praying that she doesn't require an answer. She goes back to sipping from her mug.

"So of course Dena told Colette what nonsense it was. It would be funny if the circumstances weren't so awful, but they are. I know you were just trying to be a friend, and I respect the fact that you didn't throw her under the bus when we first confronted you with it. I just need to be able to trust you to be smart about these things, and to be safe."

My dad agrees. "Stel, you'll be seventeen next August. You'll be off on your own soon enough, and we know you're resourceful and clever—"

"And creative," my mom interjects. "All those things, but you are a young woman, and New Orleans is not the safest place in the world. Let's just say we'll sleep better if you don't talk to strangers, much less get in their cars, all right?"

I don't attempt to repeat the weak argument that

Larry wasn't a stranger because, of course, he was. He was a mystery to his own daughter for Christ's sake.

I can't keep lying to my parents. But I can't very well tell the full truth right now either. So I try to walk on the edge.

"I understand what y'all are saying. I totally agree."

My dad smiles, sure that this is the end of it. My mom knows it isn't. She watches me carefully as I speak. I watch my words with even more care.

"You know how GG had certain things to deal with in life that others couldn't understand? Well, I have that same thing." I stare mostly at my mother as I say this because she knows all too well about magic and how it can pull you in. "There are things that I may be 'called' to do, for lack of a better word. Things I must do. And I can't always talk in-depth about it."

My dad's usual grin wears off. As much as he teased his mother-in-law, he knew the seriousness that came with connecting with other worlds. I'm guessing he's been dreading this.

My mom? She looks perfectly calm. Like a woman who doesn't like to fly but fastens her seatbelt and gets in the upright position because she knows it's the only way she can get to where she's going in time.

"I can't always explain, but I promise to take precautions. For real. And I promise to tell you whatever you want to know when I can." I take a breath. "I'm saying all this because I really want to be honest with you. I hope you can appreciate where I'm coming from. I love you both."

My dad turns to my mom on this one. She takes my hands.

"I cannot stress enough how important it is to be careful, always. Especially with things beyond your comprehension." Her eyes widen in a way I've never seen. "Stella, never go where you aren't invited. Never."

My dad snorts. "What the hell, Moni? That's all you've got to say? Are you kidding me? We—"

"Ben, she's being honest. She's just being honest."

My dad simply nods. And that seems to be the end of it. We drink our coffees in silence until my father breaks it.

"So is what I hear true? Am I to understand that we're making twenty extra king cakes now?"

"Oh yeah, I volunteered you—us. I'll help," I reply.

"Hey," my dad says. "It's great advertisement. Lucille Courteau already called and insisted on paying."

"Of course we can't accept," my horrified mom says to my father.

"Relax, Monique. We struck a deal." He winks at me.

"Oh no, Ben. What did you say? Were you tacky? Are we going to be those tacky people?"

My father waves his arms. "No, no. She kept insisting, so I finally said, 'Mrs. Courteau, we'd be honored to make them our gift for the charity ball. If your emcee would like to make mention that the cakes are courtesy of Evie's Café, we would be thrilled.' She happily agreed."

I'm sure she did. How much blood is she selling to be able to pay for this event? I make no mention of this to my parents however.

"Way to go." I obnoxiously clap for my dad. "Great advertising!"

"Yes," Mom agrees. "We can say we're the official bakery of the Courteau ball, too. I'd better find some help—soon."

"Not to mention the charitable tax write-off." My dad is still so pleased with himself he can hardly stand it. Tax write-offs are like chocolate to him.

Dena and Colette arrive. After the initial awkwardness of how we last saw each other, Dena begins to tell my parents about a couple of people she knows that may be of at least temporary help in the café.

Col and I hang out in the kitchen with everyone. We're not about to take off for my room just yet, so we keep our conversation to the dance. I show her my dress; she jumps on me and screams. I go over makeup color schemes, and our moms offer to take us to get our hair done the afternoon of the event. I've never had my hair professionally done. School dances, when attended, didn't seem to warrant more than a set of hot rollers at home.

"Earlier that day, Col, I'm roping you into making some king cakes with us. We have so many orders in addition to the ball, it's going to be crazy," my mom announces. She's walking that line where she seems happiest, somewhere between a panic attack and a joyful celebration.

"I want to make the one for our table at the ball," I say. "We're seated at the head table as part of the royal court, so I think Col and I should make an extra-large embellished one to have on display."

This is all true. Yes, I have an ulterior motive for baking the cake myself, but Colette had mentioned that Jack told her how pleased his mom was about ours. Apparently, cakes in the past hadn't quite been up to her standards.

The ball is only a few weeks away and Lucille has put her son to work. It seems that his new job is running a million different errands for her. It's the kind of stuff she probably once had servants take on, but now Jack's the one to do her bidding.

Col and I see an opportunity to head upstairs so we take it. We commiserate; she fills me in on the details of her mom's discovery, their fight, and Dena's take on the whole fortune thing.

"I can't believe you brought that up to her," I say.

"I know it was crazy, but I had to see if she knew anything. I just went for it since everything else was out. Besides, my mom knew my dad wanted something."

"Totally. Did she call him? Did she go to his house?"

Colette looks down at her hands. "She tried to call,

but the number had been disconnected. She drove over to where he was staying, after demanding that I give her the address, but he'd checked out. Big surprise." She puts her hands to her face and through her fingers says, "It really was just bullshit. You were right. You were right."

I sit beside her and braid her hair, hoping to comfort her.

"I didn't want to be right. I wanted him to be cool."

"I know."

"You don't need him, you know?"

"Easy for you to say." She's saying this because she knows I'm a daddy's girl. I can't argue.

"You're right. It is. But that doesn't make it less true. You're so strong, Col. You're brilliant, you're beautiful—"

"I might be dating my cousin," she interjects.

I burst out laughing. I can't help it. It's just so ridiculous.

"I'm sorry. That really sucks." I'm still laughing, but I'm dead serious about this statement. "But truly, Col, it's so distant. It's nothing. Isn't the British Royal Family all a little inbred?"

"Stella, no one's talking about making babies here! No one's talking about a family! No one's talking about weddings!"

"But y'all are so sweet together." I sigh.

"Really? I thought we grossed you out."

"You do. But maybe I've been a bit jealous of you."

"Why? What about Dylan?"

"Dylan? I love Dylan." I startle myself with this remark. Colette leans in as if she's watching an intense scene in a movie. A train wreck, perhaps? "I mean—"

"You love Dylan!" Colette points an accusing finger at me.

"Spare me your curses, witch!" I push her hand away. "I just don't know what Dylan and I are. Or what we're supposed to be. It's my fault."

"Does he have a clue about what we're up to? I mean, you still haven't said anything, right?"

"Of course not. But he's not as clueless as Jack. That's not to say that Jack is dumb—"

Colette holds her hand up. "You don't have to explain. I know exactly what you mean. Dylan seems fairly insightful."

"He's so deep." I gush and Colette snickers. "Shut up. But seriously, he's asked me about Jack's house—he knows something's up. I just want to tell everyone everything, Colette. I'm tired of hiding."

"I know, me, too. I just don't know how any of this is going to work out."

"I have a feeling it will . . . somehow." I roll off of my bed and begin to shuffle my cards. I lay them on my vanity in the shape of a horseshoe and I pull one that's speaking to me.

Judgment. An angel blows her trumpet as naked folks rise up out of their coffins to meet her. As I look at the card, I think I have an inkling of how GG felt when she did readings and made predictions. It's natural and unsettling, this knowing.

"Colette? I think we need to find that treasure."

She gives me a look. She knows we have to.

"I think we've got to dig up Beatrice to do it."

POWERS & PEOPLE

THE HIEROPHANT

*M*ost everyone is all consumed with preparations for the ball. Not Colette and I. We have more dangerous matters seething in the backs of our minds—like grave digging. Colette was initially horrified at my suggestion to crack open a coffin.

"What do you want to do, consult her corpse?" Colette joked after her shock wore off. But when I told her that I knew, in a weird witchy third-eye kind of way that there was some reason we needed to get into that coffin, she became more receptive. It helps that she's as frantic to figure this out as I am.

Unfortunately, we're fresh out of Vision Powder and without a clue as to how to make it. It sucks to be without something that has offered so many answers. We figure it's worth taking a crack at Mama Pearl. If anyone would have the recipe, she would. We're so close to solving this puzzle. There's no giving up now.

We also don't have time to waste. Larry split town, and Lucille is doing some crazy crap with a Ouija board. She's got a plan, that we can be certain of, and it's probably a hell of a lot better than ours.

After my last dream with Beatrice's ominous goodbye and an infiltration from Cora, I really don't want to ask for help without a magical assist. Colette flat out says she's unwilling. So to Mama P's it is.

Colette and I take the streetcar. It's a very cold day. Neither of us knows if Pearline will even speak to us, but we're willing to exhaust every effort.

The shop's buzzing. Mama P is busy with several customers and more pour in as Colette and I enter. Mardi Gras begins in just a couple of weeks, which means the tourists will be paying her bills for the rest of the year. I note the shelves have been packed with love spell candles, Voodoo dolls, and ten different kinds of ready-made mojo bags, all waiting to be desperately consumed or offered up as an amusing anecdote. All of these tools would be powerful in the right hands, but most of the time that's not where they end up.

Col and I walk up and down the aisles, browsing and waiting. Colette leans over a glass case full of vintage tarot decks. I find myself looking at baskets of rough, unpolished crystals. A small sea grass basket holds what appears to be a pile of metal eyes. They're painted bright blue with heavy liner. They remind me of the glass circle from Greece that GG wore around her neck. She called it protection from the "Evil Eye" against gossip, hexes, and the like. Folk magic keeps all sorts of doors open. You could find a Shaman, a Christian mystic, a Wiccan, and a Voodoo priestess roaming the same aisles looking for the same thing.

I pick one of the metal eyes up and turn it over in my hand.

"Found what you were looking for?" A familiar voice cuts into my thoughts. Mama Pearl's arms are folded across her chest. She's tapping her foot ever so slightly. Apparently, she's finished with her other customers.

"I don't know." I eye her.

"Really, Miss Stella? That appointment book wasn't enough? Look, I'm standing by my decision to stay out of this, but—"

"You knew about that?"

"Of course I did. What, you thought I actually just threw that away in front of your friend with no rhyme or reason? Be serious."

I'd like to add here that Mama Pearline is wearing a mask decorated in rhinestone kittens and peacock feathers. For what it's worth.

"Getting ready for Mardi Gras already?" I can't help my smirk. She is so damn frustrating. If GG were here, I bet she'd make Mama P help me.

"Your grandmother couldn't *make* me do anything," she responds to what I haven't said aloud. "I will say that it's only because I was so fond of Evie that I'm willing to continually break my own rules here."

"Rules?"

"Come on, Stella. You know I never get involved in customers' affairs."

"But I'm not exactly a customer."

"I'm not talking about you. I'm talking about *them*. I never get involved, especially if it seems dangerous. I warned you."

"But we're willing to pay . . . a lot," Colette cuts in.

I try to read Colette's thoughts. Is she bluffing? With what cash? I've spent 90 percent of my tips on makeup, coffee, and snacks, as usual.

Mama Pearl's eyes narrow. "What are you so desperate to pay for?"

"Don't you know?" I ask. "Aren't you an amazingly gifted medium?"

"You should know better than anybody that it doesn't work like that. I'm not a mind reader. I get the information I'm supposed to get!"

"I saw your calendar! That was insane. It was as if you knew *everything*."

"Let's just say that my awareness was more 'elevated' during that time."

"What do you mean?" asks Colette.

"Never mind," Mama Pearl says. Colette gasps. I suspect that it's *her* awareness that's being elevated.

"You have Vision Powder, don't you?" Colette asks.

Mama Pearline looks a bit like a homerun slugger being charged with taking steroids.

"I don't know what you're talking about."

I shake my head. "Stop it. I know you know exactly what she's talking about."

Mama Pearl steps back a bit. She surveys the both of us as we sidle up to each other.

"Okay. I admit I did have Vision Powder."

"Did?" Colette asks.

"Did," she reiterates. "It was in a basket of items Evie had a friend deliver to me when she was ill. I hadn't gone through it until recently and there it was. No instructions, but I had an inkling."

"Did you use it with dreams?"

"God, no. That would be insane. Dreams are so wild. I would never combine—oh Lordy. *You* did, didn't you? You girls used it for—"

"How did you use it?"

"I dabbed a very small amount on my palms before readings and found that I had such clarity. I decided to use it in all my own readings. It was fabulous for a while."

"But you're out?"

She nods.

"Any thoughts on how to make it?"

"Not a clue, girls. I tried to duplicate it but it was impossible. There's much more to that stuff than its ingredients. It's magically charged. I never needed special tricks like Vision Powder to see what needed to be seen. Never. But it worked so well that I came to rely upon it. I lost my own sense of insight, my personal soul magic." She looks from one of us to the other. "Does that make any sense to you girls?"

We stare speechless.

Mama P rolls her eyes. "*Children.*" She walks back toward her desk.

"Wait! Mama Pearl, please," I call.

There's no room for my issues with her. I need her. She knows it, and I've got to be willing to work for it.

She turns around slowly. "I'm pretty certain you've never called me 'Mama,'" she laughs. "Come to think of it, I'm pretty certain you've never called me anything at all."

"That's because you kind of freak me out."

She smiles. "I always liked you, Stella. You have gumption, like Evie. But there's something else . . . " She sizes me up and appears to be lost in thought for a moment. I guess she's satisfied with that "something else" because she follows with, "All right, just a bit of help. But I can't talk about my clients."

She takes the metallic eye from my hand. "I will tell you that this Eye of Horus works wonders for bringing the truth to light. It will draw out what is just below the surface, so take care how you use it. That witch's bottle you bought?" She looks to Colette. "You're going to need it. And this."

She reaches into one of the bins full of crudely made

little Voodoo dolls and places it in my hand along with the eye.

"Wait, seriously? A poppet?"

She shrugs. "They're popular for a reason."

"Yeah, because of Hollywood. Should I mix up a brew of bones and chicken blood while I'm at it?"

"Stella," Colette murmurs.

Pearl turns and walks away. "Those are on me," she says.

"Thanks."

"But that's it. Our business is done." Her back is facing us as she speaks.

"Thanks." Colette and I say in unison as we make our way out of the store.

"And girls"—we turn to see Mama P looking at us with what appears to be a small grin—"I wouldn't be so quick to dismiss the chicken blood."

I don't disclose the details of my Evie encounter with Father Brian, but I do let him know that I have experienced a sort of awakening.

"I'm really glad to hear that your relationship with your mother is healing."

He's using a French press today with a Sumatra roast. I respect it.

"Yeah." I work on my coffee, not sure how to put

words to what I'm feeling. Disenchanted? Is that the word for this?

"You look troubled, Stella."

"It's just that I always knew how amazing my grandmother was." I take another sip, thinking. "This is going to sound so lame. Or weird. Maybe both."

He smiles. "What have you got?"

"It's like she's dying all over again. I feel like I'm grieving her again!" Tears run into my mouth. I accept Father Brian's offer of a tissue box and remove a generous clump. I try to soak up my tears, but my eyes keep up a slow, steady leak.

"You were saying?"

"I don't even know what to believe in. All this time I've had my mom pegged as the villain, but now she's looking more like the princess locked in the tower. And I'm so upside down about my GG." I hold a tissue up as if I'm stopping a nosebleed. "She was my idol."

That's the truest statement I could make about GG.

He pauses and then begins pouring a second cup. He's moving through the coffee more quickly than me, in a rare turn of events.

"If I may suggest, perhaps, that's exactly your problem."

"What?"

"Your grandmother was your idol but she was only human—just flesh and blood."

"She seemed like more."

"You loved and admired her. You had a very special

320

relationship. I don't think the tenderness, the 'magic,' has been compromised. I think you're coming into your own."

"What do you mean?"

"I mean that you're reaching a point in your life where you're searching for bigger answers. You've learned that as much as you cherish the people in your life, not one of them is infallible. Nobody is able to share all the secrets of the universe with you because we're all just human—Evie, your mom, dad, friends, and me—we're just like you."

I eye his collar and phonebook-sized bible, finding his last few words a little hard to believe. He must see this in my expression because he laughs.

"Have fun, Stella. The seeking of God is so much more joyful once you accept that everyone in the world is just a companion on your travels. I believe God provides us with the people we need in order to grow."

"GG used to say that we are the providers, we are the divinity." I toss this out, curious to see his reaction. He's unflappable. He doesn't seem upset by this statement.

"I understand what she's saying. Can we agree that we're all connected?"

I nod.

"Did Evie walk on water?"

"I thought she did, Father."

"You know, even Christ had expectations made of him. Wild expectations. And that was Jesus."

GG used to say that Jesus was one of the better witches, but I'm definitely not going to say that here.

"So I can't rely on people anymore?"

"Of course you can. You can rely more or less depending on your trust and connection with that person. I can rely on you to be on time to our meetings because you're good at that. But I'm not going to rely on you to memorize this tonight"—he points to the gigantic tome I was looking at earlier—"because that would be unrealistic. That's when you get into the messy business of people 'failing' other people. Very messy."

The light from the window has stretched across the desk, backlighting a garnet rosary hanging from the knob of a small lamp. It's glowing like a hot coal.

"You see, if your faith is in the Divine, if it's in something larger than any one person, then no one can truly let you down. Not in the real, major sense. No one has the power to fail you."

He refills my cup. "Your grandmother had her own setbacks in life . . . didn't her parents virtually disown her?"

I nod.

He shakes his head. "Can you imagine how difficult that must have been? And then your grandfather died."

"Everyone grieves in their own way." I recall an earlier conversation with my priest.

He points at me in recollection. "That's right. And your grandmother was right. We are blessed creatures as people. But Stella, looking to any person to be your source of perfect love is like trying to drive your car to the moon. It's a car, not a rocket ship. You will be disappointed if you expect it to do what it is not created to do."

I smile, imagining a convertible spinning me around constellations.

"But if you get a good car, one you really enjoy riding in, you can drive and drive, and see the moon rise and set, and see a million wonderful unexpected things." He takes another sip. "When you give people permission to be human, Stella, they will amaze you with their divinity."

These words are with me. They stick in the best sort of way.

"*D*ylan?"

"Yeah?"

"You have that toolbox, right?" I ask as I load raw coffee beans into the grinder during a shift. We'd been discussing details about my gown and his tux when thoughts of the dead crept back into my mind. Dylan's the only guy I can trust to keep my secret. "That old one of your grandpa's?"

"Yeah." He's half-listening as he's adjusting dials on the machine.

"You know how to use most of the tools, right?"

He stops for a moment, curious. "I know how to use all of them. Why?"

I clear my throat. "I'd like to borrow a maul and hammer."

"What? Why?" He looks wildly amused.

I don't exactly know. Colette did some research around our unburying issue, and as it turns out, Google gets pretty weird when you ask how to break into a tomb. When she came back to me with what she'd found, those were the two words she kept repeating.

"Do you know what a maul is?" he asks me.

I say nothing.

"Because I'm actually not certain. Is that a small axe? Are you asking to borrow an axe from me, Stella?"

"And a hammer."

"You have no plans to tell me what you need these for, do you?"

Silence.

"Just be careful, all right?" His humor has shifted to concern.

"I will. Thank you." I kiss his cheek, my lips burning. What he is to me I still cannot say, but he's something . . . special.

There's no way I can make it in the back door with these tools undetected, so I stash them in an alley grate just beside our house. If it rains, I'll move them.

My mom's in the kitchen sorting through bags on the table. I walk over and give her a hug. She looks surprised and that makes me a little sad, but I let myself off the hook. I'm human.

She's separating tiny trinkets by category. The traditional Mardi Gras king cake typically has a little plastic baby or a crown hidden inside it. Whoever finds it may be king or queen for the event, or they may win a prize, or they may just be happy at their omen of good fortune. Our family has always baked a variety of small items in our cakes—one of the reasons they've become so popular. There's always a baby, usually a crown, and then items of other meaning: Bells to signify a wedding, a dollar sign to foretell wealth, a little angel to bless the recipient. Some years we've thrown in tiny planes or boats to signify travel, or hearts to signify love. It's one of the witchier things my mother does. I love it. We always include a list with each cake purchased of the contents inside and their meaning. Customers dining in will order them and cheer as they discover their fortunes. We've even had a tiered one ordered for a wedding.

My mom pauses in her sifting. "Guess what arrived today?"

Before I can even venture, she picks up a box on the chair beside her and hands it to me. It's been mangled open. Someone was gleeful. I look in at a pile of tissue paper. Now I'm gleeful as I pull out a satiny gray fabric covering a small mask. Just where the mask meets the rod is a thin crescent moon that shimmers as brilliantly as my gown.

"Oh, Mama . . . "

"I know. It's fabulous. They made the moon out of some kind of synthetic I-don't-know-what. But I thought it was perfect."

"That's exactly what it is." I set it safely aside and give my mother another big hug.

"Col." I'm at my locker, blanking.

"Seriously? Stella, you're like a magical genius," she whispers these last two words. "How is it that you keep forgetting your locker combination?"

"No room left in my head, I guess."

"Yeah, I guess all the crazy drove it out."

I try to pay attention as she starts in on my lock, but the card I've just pulled mesmerizes me. It's the Three of Cups. Three maidens wearing flowery crowns are toasting their goblets. They're dressed up. It's a party.

"Maybe a ball?" I show the card to Col as a flying notebook attacks her.

"Oh god!" She hands it to me to put away, and then looks at what I'm looking at. "What are you saying?"

"I'm saying that I was thinking about how much time we have. It's not much. When are we going to do the 'thing?'"

We both look around, even though no one knows or even cares about what we're saying.

"This card I just pulled tells me we should think about doing it when everyone is distracted by a big party."

"We're not missing the ball!"

"Of course not! Don't be insane. But later that night . . . "

Colette looks the most frightened I've seen in some time.

"I looked at my calendar. It's the moon in First Quarter. It'll be a crescent, and it'll be in the process of waxing to full."

This is doing nothing for her. "It's the time GG loved to begin an adventurous project. It's the time of new beginnings, of all things being possible." I sound like I'm channeling my grandmother as I say this. I don't mind it.

"Fine. I'm in."

I give her a choking hug that she's tolerating in the high school halls. "You're my bestest friend ever, Col." And we move through the week leading up to the ball like this: consulting books, throwing out ideas, putting plans in place, and taking turns being scared shitless.

The day before the party we're all busy baking. I'm focused on a large regal-looking cake for the head table. It will look exactly like all the rest of our king cakes—a wide ring of a treat dusted in purple, green, and yellow sugar sprinkles—except I'm using a stencil to make crown shapes circling this one and adding purple sugar pearls as decorative trim. I'm crossing my fingers that the additional bauble I've placed inside will do the work I need it to.

"Hey, Stella, check out my bag." Colette shows me her creamy, feathery clutch. She lifts the flap to reveal an antique key inside. There's a "C" topped with a fleur-de-lis on the handle. I immediately know it's the one that goes to the old back gate that's just inside the modern one at Courteau Manor.

"I thought it would be easier than scaling the fence in

our gowns." No one can hear her muffled words over the bustle of baking and rushing last-minute orders.

"Awesome." Although there's a lump in my throat following the word. It's one thing to talk about it, but an entirely different feeling when it becomes reality. I try to project some courage as Colette studies me. I gesture for her to follow me as I begin loading cakes into our industrial oven.

"How'd you get it?"

She looks ashamed. "I totally stole it."

"Well, obviously."

"I really don't like that . . . at all. Especially the fact that I hid it from Jack."

"I know. We'll put it back, don't worry."

"I was over at his house yesterday—I've hardly seen him these last few weeks because of all the work his mom has him doing." She looks relieved at this. I'm guessing it's because sharing ancestors and swapping spit with the same person is making her uneasy.

"I'd noticed the key in the hall before. It was kept in a little frame. I asked Jack about it—he said it was the key to the old back gate—the original key. He said his family still had three copies, but they hung one as a creative homage to the manor, I guess."

"So . . . "

"So I took it while he was in the bathroom. I don't think they'll notice between this morning and tomorrow night. I hope not. Oh god, do you think they'll notice?"

"Calm down, criminal. You did good."

"You are a terrible influence."

"Thank you."

"Girls!" my mom calls. "I need you to load these into the van." She points to a pile of boxed-up cakes.

Colette and I take one at a time, carefully stacking them, grateful for the chance to talk more.

"Are we doing the right thing? Why are we doing this again?" Colette asks me.

"Because we'll be haunted until we die if we don't."

"But I don't need any treasure. Seriously. Lucille can have it."

"Obviously it's bigger than that. I think it's about justice."

"I do, too," she concedes.

"Do you ever think it's been about the money? Wait —" A thought crosses my mind. "What if it's Confederate money?"

"Then it would be virtually worthless, except as a collectible."

"No, it can't be. Jonathon's father wouldn't have protected it like that. And remember what Cora said to her sister? She said *gold*."

Colette looks unsure.

"What the hell. Beatrice wants us to find it, and apparently she's in charge." I throw my hands up.

Col can't really argue with this.

The hairspray is almost as suffocating as a pair of ghoulish hands in the small salon around the corner from Evie's Café. Colette is getting a variation on a French twist. I'm getting half-up, half-down cascading curls. We've just received pedicures, and soon we'll be treated to makeup application—using my products, of course. I told Colette I wouldn't be hurt if she used something else, but being the kind of person she is, she said she wouldn't dream of it. Except for the mascara and the lip gloss over the lipstick. I still haven't gotten the formula right on that.

As I eye the tackle box filled with pods of my color creations, I can't help but feel proud. The ladies working on us admire them, too, as I encourage them to try some out.

I'm in heaven.

A boy's voice breaks up the cackling of hens. I recognize it immediately.

"Where might I find Miss Fortunat?" Dylan bellows around the corner.

"Dylan!" I hiss. "You're not supposed to see me!"

"Why? Are we getting married today?" For some reason this remark sends my face into flames.

"No," I respond lamely. "It's just ... "

"Your hair?" Now he's looking at me in my curlers and glory. Fantastic.

"Maybe." I glare.

He presents me with a card. There's just the word 'Thanks' on the front.

"It's from my mom . . . and me and my grandpa," he says.

I open it up to see a short note.

Stella,

What a blessing your suggestion was. Father Brian placed us with an organization. I got to look through some profiles and choose a caregiver for my father. Mrs. Miller, the caregiver, has been here every day these last three days. Dad loves her. She's sweet, she plays cards with him, and she can get him to take his medicine . . . she's a good witch. Her rates are very reasonable. I'm finally able to know my dad is safe under our roof and I'm relieved to get back to business. Dylan will get a little more free time. I know he's been dying to spend some with you. How can I repay you? Free coffee for life. How does that sound?

Love, Angie

"Free coffee for life . . . " I murmur. I don't know if I'm more excited about this or the prospect of spending more time with the boy who's "dying" to see me.

"We're still charging for café orders. Y'all are some of our best customers. But your personal coffee will forever be on the house."

"It's a dream come true."

"I told her you'd say something like that. See you tonight, m'lady."

As he walks away, I realize that he must have read the card and okayed what his mother put in it. Every word.

I can't stop smiling, even as the stylist teases my roots to shreds.

Col and I have our gowns ready. My mom loans me a silvery beaded vintage bag of hers that goes nicely with my dress. Hair perfect, makeup divine . . . I pull one more card as we wait in my room.

The Moon.

I show it to Colette.

"See? It's a sign that tonight is the night." I open my window and breathe in the chilly, smoky night air. New Orleans is in her full bloom now. The French Quarter plays host to the dirtier, drunker side of Mardi Gras. I have no need to see some sorority girl's boobs being coughed up for beads . . . no, this is my Mardi Gras. We'll celebrate tonight. We'll dance, inhale the beauty, soak up all the power we can, and be merry; for soon enough we'll have our own penance to pay.

While many Catholics will be making their sacrifices for Lent, giving up meat, chocolate, social media, or dining out, my best friend and I may be giving up our lives. This thought crawls up my spine and lodges in my throat, making it difficult to speak for a moment.

I shake my head to erase the idea. The sliver of white moon offers her sideways graceful smile.

"Look, Colette." My voice comes streaming back as I point it out to her. "Our moon. The Maiden Moon."

I hold up the card beside it. The card shows a full moon with her face and a crescent cut into it. It's for all the moons, but tonight it's for this one.

"This card's about secrets. We're about to unearth some." How quickly my fears shift to a strange kind of excitement. Col has pulled up a stool to get a good look, and here we are, two mystics reading the sky.

"Stella?"

"Yeah?"

"Why do you think we've never gotten haunted by Jonathon or his father? What do you think happened to them?"

"I've wondered about this. We could probably look at records. But I almost like imagining better. You want to know what I've thought? I've thought that his father probably died not long after all that, right? Cora said he was sick. And Jonathon—"

"Probably moved on and married someone," Colette says matter-of-factly.

"That sounds right."

"And he probably had no idea that Beatrice was murdered, that her life had been ruined before that, or that he had driven another woman insane."

I giggle. It's so outrageous. "I don't really like any of these people much, how about you?"

"Nope," agrees Colette. "They're all villains, but . . . "

"But they're all victims, too."

"Yes. Because I think that Jonathon would have married Beatrice if his father had let him. I think he really loved her. And I think he even tried to love Cora."

"And yet just the maidens are talking to us."

Just the maidens. "Maidens usually keep deeper secrets, don't they?" She looks back to the moon. I consider this until I hear the doorbell ring.

We frantically get our things together, and then attempt to look relaxed as we descend the staircase.

ON WITH THE BALL & OFF COME THE MASKS

THE MOON

*O*ur handsome escorts wait, but they're not disappointed. Jaws drop all around. My mom and Dena hand us their boutonnieres to pin. Dylan graces my wrist with a rose corsage the same silvery color as the one he gave me before. Poses are struck; pictures are taken. This is miles beyond any school dance. This is my kind of heaven.

We're led outside to our chariots. Colette and I exchange knowing looks as Jack opens the door to Lucille's green Jaguar. She's back at the ballroom hall where my father is probably just leaving, having made the cake deliveries there. I had tried to not seem suspicious as I stressed how my special cake had to be clearly marked for Mrs. Courteau so she could cut it for the head table.

Dylan and I decide not to join Colette and Jack in Lucille's Jaguar. We opt for the truck instead. Dylan has been busy. The old truck is gleaming. Dented and rusty, but as clean as it'll ever be. As he helps me into the passenger seat, I look back to notice Jack taking Colette's hand and doing the same for her. At first my heart sinks a little—she's been so busy trying to protect him, and this situation between them could get so weird.

No, Stella. You'll deal with that later. Now? Now you're a Voodoo Cinderella. Now you enjoy the evening with your prince.

As if reading my thoughts, Dylan puts his arm around me and points out the window.

"Did you see the moon tonight? Look at that."

"I didn't know you noticed stuff like that."

"With a girl like you, I kind of have to, don't I?"

We're arriving half an hour early just so Jack can help with any last-minute details.

The grand ballroom's exterior is crumbling brick-and-marble columns. It's formal and southern and perfect. The sun has almost completely gone down, streaking a purple across the sky. It's as if Lucille Courteau phoned in a favor from the heavens as she comes out in a sequined gown in just the same shade as that purple.

She's beautiful, of course. She's smiling a little too wide as she moves toward the car. I can't help but feel a bit like Red Riding Hood trying to figure out if she's with her grandmother or whatever just ate her grandmother.

"Ladies! You look exquisite! Come, Jack will show you to your seats. I'm sorry, but I have to deal with an issue with our valet company. This is the last year we go with *them*, I promise you." And off she goes to terrify some young men in the parking lot.

I strain to hear, "Where is your manager? I told him the payment would be received in a bill AFTER the party. That's how we've always done it and there's never been a problem!"

"I'm sorry, Mrs. Courteau, but he asked for half to be received tonight. He said it was a new policy . . . " A man who must be the manager explains. Then I see him get on his cell to try to cut her a deal, no doubt.

Jack notices my eavesdropping. He looks down for a moment.

"I'm so sorry. I shouldn't have—"

"It's hard to ignore. I overheard one of those men say that the company owner is a friend with the company that's provided decorations. Apparently, they complained because they haven't received the rest of what they're owed yet. I guess word spread." He sighs.

Dylan and Colette stand awkwardly.

Jack pats Dylan on the back, ever willing to put others at ease. "But if anyone can negotiate a great party and figure it out, it's my mother."

"That's true." I nod, offering him a smile.

"Shall we?" Jack presents his arm to Colette, and Dylan in turn presents his to me. I take it and glide.

The large wooden doors are wide open and I'm

nearly blinded by the glitter. Once again, gaudy decadence is refined luxury in the Crescent City. The massive crystal chandeliers are lit and dripping with sparkling jewels of purple, green, and gold. On one side of the room is a platform with a band doing sound checks. Beside that is a table and microphone where a man I take to be the emcee of the evening sits. Flanking him and the stage are a wall of speakers and a truss full of dance lights being looked over by a tech. In the middle is the polished, gleaming dance floor.

The walls are covered in mirrors and draped in velvet. Several chefs are catering a buffet table. There's a carving station and a man preparing a gas burner and some skillets for some on-demand cooking, I guess. Next to that is the cake table, where I can see mine on a pedestal display from across the room. Daddy did good. Then there are about two dozen round tables with white linen tablecloths, gigantic arrangements of purple lilies, sparkly gold plume feathers, and greenery. The same can be found on the two tiers of long tables just behind the circular ones, which is obviously where the king and queen and the rest of the royal court will sit. And then there are the candles. Large white votive candles of varying sizes in pillars of tinted glass are everywhere. Seriously, the place is dripping in them. I half-expect to see a fireman on retainer.

But hey, the effect is exquisite.

I realize that my mouth has been agape while taking in the magic of the room. I'm relieved to find Dylan and

Colette in the same state. Jack has a smile that's out of control.

"What do you think?" He's not really asking, more like acknowledging our awe.

He shows us to where we'll be sitting. "The king and queen are in the center. Then to the king's right are my mom, Dylan, Stella, Colette, and myself." I remember how Jack said his father was away on business. I'd love to know what is so pressing that he'd miss his wife's reason for living.

"Wait, Jack, shouldn't you be by your mother?" I ask, possibly sounding a little like I'm pleading.

"I need to sit right by the end so I can run any needed messages to the emcee."

Or she really wants to keep an eye on me. I give a quick shake to bring myself back to the fun.

The crowd begins to pool in. Jack has to briefly excuse himself to take our things to coat check and make sure it's being run smoothly. We sit and people watch. The spectacle keeps us oohing, ahhing, and occasionally guffawing. Most of the guests look like they belong on the red carpet. Some . . . less so. But everyone is thrilled to be here. No one is too cool to be impressed and I love that. The excitement builds on itself into a crescendo as chatter mixes with instruments tuning. The main lights begin to lower. The sparkle and the candles make it look like a palace of lightning bugs and their wild guests.

Jack is back with us and a line begins for the feast. What a feast. Dylan is impressed with my gluttony as I heap on scoops of crawfish étouffée, request thick slices of the carving station roast, and wait on my custom order of sautéed shrimp and linguine.

"What?" I ask as I dump two ladles of gumbo into a bowl.

"I just like you, that's all."

"Well. I like you, too." And suddenly I wish two hundred people didn't surround us.

Colette and I try each other's plates and compare notes on food while Dylan gets trapped into listening to Mrs. Courteau explain why she had to have a certain kind of crystal bead that can only come from Italy.

"You have to be very clear with these decorators, or they'll just throw up any old thing. Honestly, if I didn't oversee every detail, they might grab beads from a five and dime."

I can see Dylan nodding out of the corner of my eye. I can't help but grin a little. Jack's grin is even wider. I can see he takes a similar sort of pride in the event as his mother, except for one difference. It's not all about him; it's about the shared enjoyment. Pretty big difference.

Up comes the emcee. He introduces himself as Louis March and beckons over a falsely modest Mrs. Courteau.

"The lady of the evening." He bows to her and kisses her hand, which she waves off in an affected laugh.

I suspect they do this exact thing every year.

We all stand as introductions are made, clapping until our hands hurt for the top charitable donors, the progress being made as a result of the ball, and of course, for the king and queen themselves, who enter from another set of doors as the band plays a royal march. Once they take their seats, Lucille rushes to the table, and we in turn all take our seats. The cake won't be cut until later in the evening, which works just fine for me. Our host plays a kind of court jester, telling jokes and sharing about the grand tradition of Mardi Gras and the Courteau balls. He lets us in on some New Orleans history, that of the Garden District in particular. It's clear that while the Courteaus typically foot a hefty chunk of the bill, they also seek charitable sponsorship, like our donated cakes.

Mr. March takes a moment to thank a few of these sponsors: Randolph's for providing the fabulous catering, The Marquis Ballroom for opening their space at an excellent rate, not to mention the numerous who have donated goodies for the gift bags that will be handed out to parting guests.

And with a gesture toward the band, the dance lights come on, the music swells, and the crowd with its revelers coat the wood floor. Some have masks fastened to their faces, others are holding them up as we are, and still others have already let down their guard. We had all removed them at dinner, of course, but now it's almost like the magic of this night requires some hiding, so back up they go. Dylan wore his charcoal gray mask when we first entered, but if there's anyone in our crowd who's not interested in pretenses, it's him. Plus, while I think it's elegant, he may or may not have felt like a douchebag wearing it.

Jack is still holding up his cream-colored one along with Colette—his mother may very well have insisted that he do his duty at this masquerade ball. Lucille loves facades. Her left arm never seems to tire as it keeps her mask in place. It's a sequined gold eyepiece that, with her dress, keeps her looking like an exotic bird.

And me?

It's a comfort, holding up this wand and protecting myself. I feel like the mystery somehow shelters me from what lies ahead. Plus it looks really cool.

Dylan can dance. Who knew? His grandpa taught him. Of course, Colette and Jack look like they've had lessons—actually, they did have a couple, courtesy of Mrs. Courteau.

As for me, let's just say I'm trying to follow Dylan's lead. The songs are fast-paced and he's so goddamned comfortable in his own skin, twirling me in circles and trying to teach me some steps.

At one point he sweeps me into a dip, causing me to drop my mask. I look into his eyes. I'm overcome by this boy.

Where the hell have I been? He's been right here. Right here and wonderful the whole time. The more I search his eyes, the more good I find. He hasn't asked me for shit. He's expected nothing from me, except that I am myself.

The music slows. He pulls me back up, looking to see

if public slow dancing is one of those things that freak me out.

Not with him, it's not.

"You let your mask down," he says with a smile.

I lean against his chest, sway, and let my vision soften on the candles lacing the room. The sparkles are draping us like stars in a night sky. I smell the wood floor wax, the sweat of the other dancers, the last bits of Creole spice from polished dishes . . . and coffee mingled with aftershave.

The last two are my favorite.

We sway like this through a few slow numbers, and even into a fast one. Out of the corner of my eye I see caterers make their way toward the cake table.

"Excuse me." I rush to my own creation to block a woman in a chef's jacket approaching it.

"I'm sorry, may I help you?" She appears startled by the girl who may have just thrown herself in front of a cake like she's shielding a baby from a bullet.

"Yes. This is my cake. From Evie's Café? I'll take care of cutting and serving this one."

"Stella!" Mrs. Courteau walks up. "That's what she's here for. You're my guest, not a servant! Please, don't."

"Oh, Mrs. Courteau." *Think, Stella.* "Didn't my dad mention it? As part of our sponsorship, I'm supposed to slice and serve the pieces of the main cake to the head table. For a fun promotion. You know, people get to see who baked it and all."

"Oh. Well, if that's what you wish. I'll have Mr. March

introduce you, and we'll make sure they spotlight you as you cut it."

"That won't be necess—"

But she's off. I turn to see Dylan watching me from the dance floor.

"What was that all about?"

"I need to cut the big cake. They're going to put a big fat spotlight on me. It'll be super embarrassing."

"Awesome."

I feel like I have to say something to someone who's fast becoming my other best friend.

"Dylan?"

"Yeah?" The music is getting softer, turning into a jazzy background as the sun's equivalent is switched on and shining upon the cake table.

"Ladies and gentlemen, it's everybody's favorite time! Would everyone please take their seats, and may I have Miss Stella Fortunat do the honors of cutting the first cake, please?"

"Crap. I'll tell you later." I plaster on a smile as I make my way through the crowd toward Mr. March. He hands me a long silver knife and a cake server. I stretch my grin as I look out on the sea of people to find Colette. The light in my face is so bright, there's no chance of spotting a friend.

"Please, take your seats." The guests move toward their places.

"Miss Fortunat is here representing Evie's Café."

I wait for the majority of the crowd to settle into their tables.

"Did you want to tell our guests more about the cakes, Miss Fortunat?"

"Sure." I clear my throat. He's holding the microphone to my lips as I'm awkwardly clutching servingware and a mask.

"Well, you're all familiar with the traditional king cake. Ours is something extra special. Of course, it's the classic cinnamon cake we all love, but at Evie's we include more than the baby. We space our surprises out so every person finds a fun treasure in their piece. Each one alternates yellow, purple, and green and has ten treats hiding inside. They're all specially marked to be sliced into ten pieces." I nod to the catering staff to make sure they follow, even though I'm certain my dad already went over this with them.

I continue. "At each table, your server will include a card listing the items and their meanings. So . . . " I lean in to begin cutting, noting the spot where I'd placed a toothpick during baking. Lucille's piece.

"*Laissez les bon temps rouler!*" I shout, slicing right in. The crowd cheers. I waste no time getting that slice onto a plate and sending it straight into the hands of Mrs. Courteau.

Let the good times roll, indeed.

The servers have begun cutting and serving cakes at each table. The band keeps a smooth and steady rhythm. I finish plating the rest of the large cake pieces, a light still on me as I set a slice in front of every person at the head table.

Well, here goes.

When Colette and I began preparing our supplies, there was no shortage of winging it. We fashioned a witch's goody bag that included everything we scored from Mama Pearline, but we tried to create it with specific intent. We placed all our magical tools to be "charged" in the light of the moon, and then I tossed old nails into the witch's bottle for protection, along with some unpolished hematite for strength, and a few silver dimes. I set the Empress card alongside them all to imbue them with the courage I've found from the women in my life, and the courage Colette and I now must carry. Colette crafted a couple of mojo bags for insight and, you guessed it, more protection, using tips from our books, the internet, and the better guide of the three—her own sense.

I expected her to giggle when I gripped the Eye of Horus in my hands and kissed it. She didn't. Nor did she seem amused when I held my palms open to let the eye soak up the moonlight and called out to the Maiden Moon to charge it. She didn't make a face when I dripped red candle wax on the back of it and marked a "T" for "Truth" (I did not mention to her that this was totally made up on my part—I never learned to read runes or other ancient symbols).

Colette was calm as still water as I rubbed olive oil and cayenne powder upon the metal eye and chanted.

"It works with a quickness, so mote it be."

I remember GG used to do this in urgent cases to give her magic a boost.

Time for cake.

Coffee's been poured and somehow I'm actually able to take some bites. I spot Colette staring dumbfounded at me, not touching her own plate. Dylan and Jack are both immersed in their dessert.

I see Colette's eyes shift. Do I dare look where she's looking? I lean forward to see Mrs. Courteau taking small bites. Jack finds a crown, Dylan a car, me the lips.

"Interesting. What does this one mean, Stella? I don't see it on the card." Lucille leans forward to look at me over Dylan. She holds the eye between her forefinger and thumb. Nothing weird so far.

"Oh, that's a neat one we had. It's very unique." The knot is back. It's swelling to softball size against my voice box as I try to think of what else to say.

"Is that right? So sorry, Dylan," she apologizes as he leans farther and farther back to let us talk.

"Oh no, it's fine. I need to excuse myself to the restroom." He pats me on the shoulder and catches me in his look for a moment before he goes.

I feel Colette staring. I glance over to see Jack chatting with Mr. March. Now I'm really locked in. But what if it does nothing? I seriously have no idea what I'm doing. What the hell am I doing sticking an eye in a cake?

An ice-cold glass bumps into my arm. I screech but

there's no drink. Just a hand. Long delicate fingers clenching around my arm.

"That's a funny trick, child. A funny trick."

I look at Mrs. Courteau. There's a shift—is it the lights? Her eyes flash and change. Her hair is washed in a lighter gold.

That eye worked.

Lucille's been up to no good.

I'm talking to Cora.

"Cora?" I whisper. She hears me just fine through the music.

"It's over for you. You're dead if you try to take from me." She squeezes my arm and inches her face closer. "I will kill twice more. I'll kill you both."

As if a spell has broken, I jerk my arm away.

Lucille's just eating her cake and looking at the eye.

"Well, it certainly is unusual."

I turn to see an open-mouthed Colette. Apparently, Mrs. Courteau is unaware that she just threatened murder. I rush to pull Colette aside.

"What the hell was that?" she asks.

"Did you see that?"

"I heard it, too."

"How could you? The music was so loud."

"I don't know. But she was perfectly clear." I guess our magic's more powerful than we predicted.

We're off to the ladies' room, but there's nowhere private to talk. So we reapply our lipstick and try to speak our way around it.

"I mean, what else can we do, Col? We have to go."

"Stella, I saw something."

There are ladies primping on either side of us, making it difficult to talk. We both look at our phones. Screw it, we'll text. Who cares if our parents see? At least it'll lead them to our murderer.

Colette: I THOUGHT I SAW HER PUT SOMETHING IN JACK'S COFFEE.

Me: LUCILLE?

Colette: YES. I THOUGHT SHE WAS PUTTING SUGAR IN IT BUT NOW . . .

Me: OMG. DO YOU THINK SHE'D KILL HIM?

Colette: NO.

Me: NO. RIGHT?

Colette: RIGHT BUT LET'S CHECK. I'LL DISTRACT HER. YOU SEE IF YOU CAN FIND SOMETHING IN HER PURSE.

Back at the table we get to work.

"Mrs. Courteau?"

"Yes, Stella?"

"Well, I don't mean to complain, but can we get someone to take care of the ladies' room? It's pretty bad."

"Oh no! Of course. Jack, can you find a maid?"

Jack looks like he might fall over into his coffee.

"Jack?" Dylan looks at him.

"I don't feel so good. I'm sorry. I'm just—I'm just so tired."

"There's nowhere private to go here. Take him to the car, please, Dylan. He can rest there. You can take the girls home later, can't you? I'll find someone to clean the powder room." She kisses Jack. "Feel better, sweetie. Maybe you're just exhausted."

It's the first time I've seen her do anything maternal. After they leave, I go to Col.

"I found these." She's holding a bottle of large white pills. "It says they're for insomnia?"

"Sleeping pills?" I open it up. The bottle looks almost full.

"Stella, I thought it was a sugar cube. I'm pretty sure she dropped one of these in."

"She would have dumped in the whole bottle if she were trying to kill him. That bitch just wants him to take a nap."

"She wants him out of the way."

"He'll be all right. But we have to go."

Dylan is back and all I can do is make lame excuses.

"Dylan, I'm sorry, but we have to leave. We have some stuff to do."

"What? What's wrong?"

I'm lifting my mask up without thinking and making my way to coat check for my cloak and Colette's coat. Dylan follows us. Colette looks at him.

"Jack is okay, right?"

"Yeah, he just seems a little groggy. He probably hasn't slept in forever. What do you need to do? I'll drive you."

"No!" I don't mean to shout, but we have to go.

"Dylan, I will tell you someday." If I can. If I'm still alive. "We really have to go. Thank you for everything."

I grab Colette's hand, kiss Dylan on the cheek, and we fly out the doors.

All of our supplies are stashed in the grate along with the hammer and axe. I'm grateful it's only a couple of blocks away. We pull our jeans on underneath our dresses, then unzip our gowns and pull dark shirts over our heads. I keep my cloak on. I'm going to be in a graveyard, so I think it's the dress code. The next thing I do when we get there is pull out the poppet.

"I grabbed this." Colette holds up a feather. Dark blue. It's from Mrs. Courteau's purse.

"Brilliant." I wrap the feather around the head of the faceless doll.

"Now it's her." Now what?

We've got to stall her. In a rush, I spy a patch of muddy dirt at the sidewalk in front. I jam the poppet into the earth. "And now she's stuck."

At least let's pray she is. Even just for a little.

STICK, STONES, TUNE & BONES

JUDGMENT

*T*he fog beckons. The nails clank together in my witch's bottle. So loud. Can everyone in the city hear that, or is it just me? My palms sweaty, I grip Col's hand as tightly as I can, as if she might leave. I can't do this alone. I'm not at all sure I could do this with an army. But Colette's not going anywhere. She's keeping pace as we foot through the streets. The slick pavement seems to slow our race, but not as much as this fog. It's as if it's alive, pushing us. Is that possible? Who knows? In the last six months I've realized that nothing should surprise in this town of carnival.

We reach the front gate to the Courteau Manor – but we need the back gate. Sweeping low, I clutch GG's cloak tighter to my throat. The dark velvet caresses my cheeks, like the night is making its presence known. We move past the manicured shrubbery, along the sidewalk and to the back. This gate is almost as large and looming as the front entrance.

A single "C" curls around the wrought iron, the imposing lock flanked by a pair of fleur-de-lis. My hand shakes uncontrollably as I open it to receive the key. I know this is mine to do. So does Colette. Wordlessly, and shaking more than me, she drops it into my palm. It hits heavily, like it might fall right through my flesh and bones. Well, we're a terrific pair. I guess this is one way to die—in the backyard cemetery of the bitchiest woman in town.

What am I doing? It's as if my limbs are moving completely independently from my mind as my hand suddenly lifts with sureness, a confidence that I can't conjure. It thrusts forward, key into lock, swift turn, like I've done it countless times—I guess I have, in my dreams. I gently push the gate open, the wrought iron creaking a warning. I lead the way.

The fog is weighed with something else besides ominous energy, besides the fear, besides our haunting dreams. It's laced with sweet olive and a pure hot rage. Lucille is on the move. We have to speed this up.

Colette and I dart between the sycamores, through the waterfall of weeping willow branches, toward the magnolias. It's a beautiful garden. A bit rough in parts now. Strangely, this doesn't feel like trespassing. It's hallowed ground for Colette. We come for many reasons, but the clearest one is to honor the dead.

"Here it is," whispers Colette. Her connection is

stronger than mine. It's her bloodline. Beside tombs of other servants lays a humble crypt, splashed in the generous moonlight. No date, only one word: "Beatrice."

Beatrice. It's time.

I kneel at the grave, reaching into the pocket in my cloak.

"May we visit with you, Miss Beatrice?" I murmur, as I plunk the silver coins into the thick dead grass around her headstone. Silence. I'm taking that as a yes. I pull my satchel off my shoulder and begin to cast the protective circle, lining the gravesite with salt. I don't think this will stop Lucille, but it's worth a shot.

Colette begins to empty the other contents of my bag. I can smell Lucille a bit more strongly now. I don't want to distract Colette, but it's driving me insane.

"Mrs. Courteau." I barely recognize my own voice.

"I know," answers Colette. Impressive little witch. Where's she been hiding?

Col pulls out the witch's bottle and a tiny flashlight. I drag out the axe and hammer. The ridiculousness of our present circumstances has us both cackling wildly in the cemetery. Laughing helps me to momentarily forget the morbid turn my life's been taking, like, you know, attempting to raise the dead, among other things.

"Forgive me." I take the first whack with the axe. Barely a chip. Ugh.

"Shit. This could take a while. I'll hold the axe while you hit it with this." I hand her the hammer.

Colette makes a sickened face, turning a tinge of

green in the moonlight. *Clink, clink, clink* against the small tomb. My insides flip up and down, up and down. Colette's pulled a note from out of my bag. She reads the words, hushed, like my mom sounds when she prays in church.

"Night and day, day into night. We ask you to join us, in your flesh, alight."

Nothing.

I can feel Colette looking at me, questioning, but I just wait and watch.

Patience pays well. Jagged lines have formed where we've made small cracks. The stone is splitting in the front. It's as if we are gods overseeing an earthquake on the planet below. The hard curtain crumbles open to reveal the star of the show. We reach in to heave out a very simple, boxy, and rather crudely fashioned coffin. I feel ice cold. What the hell are we doing? We've spent so much time with Beatrice that we've felt like we were close friends. But we don't know what this is. Not really.

What if some prankster or mischievous spirit has tricked us? GG told me stories about ghosts playing tricks, and that all too often, such tricks took a nasty turn. Or, much worse, what if we were facing something dark—something malicious? How did I trust so blindly? How could we be so naïve? And now it would all come crashing down on this night, in the Courteau's backyard, no less.

I wait. Colette impresses me with her guts as she kneels before the coffin, almost hugging it to get her fingers around the edge of the door. I can practically hear the spooky organ music playing.

As she creaks it open, I suck in as much air as humanly possible. I brace myself for a Hollywood moment—you know, where demons melt our faces off—but no such thing happens.

She pulls the casket lid all the way up, underestimating the weight of the door because as she lets it go, it hits the earth with a loud *CLOMP!*

Colette's not so bold anymore. She shrieks, jumps behind me, and grabs my hand. There's no course in high school, no heart-to-heart with a Voodoo queen that can prepare you for the sight of a hundred-plus-year-old corpse exposed in her coffin bed. Basically, bones wrapped in a simple wavy gown. Perhaps this was once the crisp white dress she wore when she was killed? Her arms crisscross over her chest like she is guarding her soul.

I feel like such an intruder. It's like we're sneaking into her chamber at night to watch her sleep.

It's okay, I remind myself. *She invited us here.*

Colette doesn't budge from her spot behind me. The combination of her fear and my guilt give me just enough courage to crouch beside Beatrice's bones and take a close inspection. To her right is a small cloth doll with braids and triangle eyes. A gift from her mother, perhaps? I guess she still slept with her toys, too. I smile to myself as this messed-up girl continues to endear herself to me. My gaze reaches downward to rest on her boots. Black, buttoned on the fronts. Bless this moon. Although it exposes us, it gives much-needed light to our search.

A click startles me. I turn, blinded for a moment. Colette has switched on the flashlight.

"Geez, warn a girl before you do that next time, okay?" I hiss.

"Next time?" Colette snickers. I can't fight my own grin. *Right*. Next time we unearth a dead girl.

I look back in the coffin. On the other side of her, gleaming in the white glow from the moon, I spy something shiny and metallic. I ask Colette to adjust her flashlight upon Beatrice's hand. I lean forward, prodding the object with my finger. It's a small round tin box. Colette shines the flashlight over me. I feel something on the outside of the tin. A keyhole. Strange . . . the lid comes off easily to reveal a velvet lining and a spool of wire thread. I know what this is. It's a music box. It must work with a key to twist and wind up the box.

I set the lid gently in my lap, cradling it with the tops of my knees. This could get . . . awkward.

I reach in and take the shiny box between my thumb and middle finger. Maybe I can shimmy it out? I give a gentle tug, only to be met with resistance. Plan B it is, then. I have avoided touching her skeleton up until this point, but it seems all my effort has been wasted.

"I mean no disrespect, Miss Beatrice. May I take your hand?" I slowly stretch out and clasp my free hand around her bony fingers. I gently lift them as I slide the tin down in a back-and-forth motion. Something gives way. Was that her thumb? Crap. I tug the box all the way out. As I hold it in my right hand, I reach down with my left in a vain attempt to reattach her runaway thumb. All I can do is lean it against her fingers and mutter a string of apologies punctuated by cursing. I pull the box close to my eyes. Colette stands behind me to shine light on it.

"What can you see?" she asks. I don't answer. I'm too busy studying the music box, admiring the beautiful simplicity of the thing. I open the lid and run my fingertips 'round the inside to feel a line of markings. An engraving? I tilt the top so the inside of it catches the yellow beam of the flashlight. Yes, there are words. Written in a flourished italicized font, they read:

> *"We loved each other then, Lorena,*
> *Far more than we ever dared to tell;*
> *And what we might have been, Lorena,*
> *Had but our loving prospered well."*

Lorena? Who's Lorena?

"I know this," Colette breathes. She'd been reading behind me.

I half-hear her as I'm dusting the cobwebs out of my mind, trying to get a better glimpse of something there, craning to hear the faint echo of a scratchy record. I guess GG was trying to show me more than her idea of a good time. I still want to hurl when I think of the taste of stale Pall Mall on my tongue. The music's faint in my mind, but I can hear some chords . . . da, da, dum, da . . . the old antebellum song about love torn apart.

I remember.

She once said that this was why Confederate soldiers claimed the loss of war—the song was so tragic, it saddened them to the point of taking away their will to fight. And that line, *"And what we might have been . . . "*

"Such a strange, sad thing to have engraved."

"She used to sing along while it played," says Colette softly.

I realize that she's been speaking while I've been lost in memory. I'm about to ask her to repeat herself, when it occurs to me that she isn't talking to me at all.

She's talking to Lucille.

I never heard her footsteps. I somehow missed her perfume. I had been so caught up. I'm too stricken to attack myself for being off my guard and getting my best friend and me killed.

Colette . . . what is she doing? She's still speaking. I have to grab her, have to run, but my feet feel weighted down, buried in the cemetery earth.

"So this is it. The music box. The token that broke you. How awful to find that out, how sad for you . . ."

Colette looks at Lucille with such sincerity, such sympathy. Is she really feeling sorry for this creature? Because I know she's not really talking to Lucille. She's talking to the meaner one, the monster inside of her.

My feet stay planted. I place the box in a pocket

within my cloak as I try to force my mind to think us out of this.

Cora *will* kill us. And she won't be very nice about it. Come on, Col, what's the phrase? Oh yeah. You can't negotiate with terrorists. I'm pretty sure that killer ghosts fall into this category.

What can I do? My mind is blocked. Images I'm not asking for are pushing their way in. The gift. The dream that Colette and I crossed paths in.

A shadow draws across Cora's face as she looks down, picking something up off a table and clutching it to her chest.

Her hands are covering it. I can't get a look, but I'm sure I already know.

She strides through the door and down to Beatrice's cellar in just a few steps.

"You!" Cora shrieks, her eyes aflame. "You . . . " She's pointing, gasping between sobs and screams. "You stole my life! You TOOK it!"

I'm magnifying the room in my mind, but it's so dark. There are only two petite oil lamps. Their glow is being sucked into spotlighting Cora's wild, twisted expression. But there's a mirror beside her.

I see the side of a white gown, the curve of a neck, and a trembling arm. There's Miss Beatrice. She's managed to get up after her fall down the stairs. I see Cora's hands as they cast the thing aside and get to work on Beatrice's neck. I recall my dreams with clarity I couldn't have when I was trapped in them. I stretch my vision to the tossed thing. The tin gleams so bright in this focused memory, so much shinier than what's tucked into my cloak.

Looking back, I begin to understand Colette's sorrow for Cora. Suddenly, I'm not seeing it all through Beatrice's lens as the victim of an evil murderer. Rather, I see this through the eyes of a broken-hearted woman who has lost everything in the war, including the love of her life. My heart wrenches.

Now my feet are becoming unglued from their spot. Time to do something. I reach into another pocket, searching the soft velvet to grab a little baggie. Thank God for the vial of Van Van Oil for banishing evil. It may buy us a small amount of time.

I pull out the stopper and fling it in Lucille's direction. I've never had good aim, so I'm relieved when it hits her in the chest, covering her dress. I'm also horrified because now there's no hope of stalling any other way. We've made it quite clear that we came to fight, and this spirit will be more pissed off than before.

She hisses and spits curses at us, shaking and convulsing. We cannot waste a second. I pull the music box from my garment. Lucille notices and is about to rip down the weak veil I've set up as a barricade. After all, the oil's best at holding back regular people. I don't know its effect on possessed ones.

"This has to be it," I tell myself, reaching into Colette's purse. This gate is original to the house, and this key—well, a Courteau would have a music box commissioned, wouldn't they? So they'd have the lock made to fit a key, perhaps, rather than the other way around.

It slips in easily. With quick flicking motions, I wind up the box.

The first *ping* brings me a rush of relief. "Da-dum, da-dum . . . " The melody chimes out, beautiful and clear in the middle of this horror film.

"It's the key!" I shout to Colette. "I mean, this song, 'Lorena!' Maybe we could sing?"

But she's already humming the tune. She focuses on me as if she doesn't notice that a demon is steps away, ready to rip off our heads. I desperately scan the land, looking, searching for some sign of the treasure while still trying to keep an eye on Lucille.

"I bet we need some words or lyrics—a chant, you know? Dammit, I can't remember!" My panic bubbles to frenzy. I'm past desperation.

Maybe the lines engraved inside the music box are all I need.

"More power if we both sing it, right?" Colette says shining the flashlight on the inside of the lid. The music box is beginning to slow. It may just have one more chorus, a handful of bars. We've got to make this count.

"We loved each other then, Lorena . . . "

Our voices shake as we begin to sing. But it's over. Lucille breaks free in one lashing motion. She knocks the box to the ground and wraps an icy jeweled hand around each of our throats.

Can I distract her by making the gold appear?

I frantically try to remember the rest of the words on the lid.

"Far more than we ever dared to tell . . . "

Colette's catching on, repeating the words a few syllables behind.

"And what we might have been, Lorena—" I gasp, my air being choked off. I reach for my witch's bottle, hoping that if I can touch the possessed Mrs. Courteau with it, I can weaken her grip. She's not fooling around, though.

"I'm SICK," she moans. "I'm sick of losing everything. I'm sick of time wasted. I'm SICK OF YOU!"

Lucille drops.

Did she pass out? Are we free?

A swirling mist-like gray dust rises from her in the shadowy form of a woman.

There's Cora.

Arms outstretched, she clings in a smoky way to my arms. Her face draws closer and closer to mine as I choke on the dust. Ice swirls inside my blood. My lungs seize— she's strangling me from the inside.

Bits of my mind, overwhelmed, burned, drift off and away. All that remains is one sentence:

"Had but our loving prospered well."

I open my mouth. I can hear the final chimes of the box, the delay between them getting longer. I can't push sound through my vocal chords. There's no room left.

Colette is passed out from being strangled, lying limp beside Lucille. Oh god, she's not . . . she can't be . . .

I mouth the words, "Had but our loving prospered well," as the last *ting* of the tin box rings. I slip into space, the music still ringing in my head. I'm exhausted in a way I didn't know I could be. I let the darkness win as I slide down into it.

Chicken blood. Goddamn chicken blood. Why is this available in the afterlife? Have I been so bad as to deserve this?

Well, I may have gotten my best friend killed, so . . . yeah. I may be spending a long time in some Voodoo purgatory with only the blood of feathered farm animals to drink, my bed in the Tower tarot card, in a perpetual state of burning.

"Stella. Stella!"

My bones rattle. I feel the blood coming back up my throat.

Who is this?

My mouth is slack jawed now; hands have pried it open, pouring a foul concoction down my throat. I feel a hand rubbing my neck downward—like when you're trying to force a dog to swallow a heartworm pill.

My eyes are slits as I try to make sense of what is happening before me . . . to me. I see a blurred face, a male? He lifts a jar of muddy red with God-knows-what sloshing inside. He presses it to my lips and pours the brew down my throat again.

"Stella!"

Who is this alchemist—more like mad scientist— yelling at me, forcing me to drink his awful potion? Must be the Magician. I usually like that card, but this one's abusive. Well, it is purgatory.

So, up in the Tower, being tortured by the Magician. If I could lift my head, I bet I would see nine swords floating above us. My least favorite card would be a must in this Spread of Doom. My cheek burns. Did the Magician just slap me? What the hell? I force my eyes open wider, ready to yell at him, when I realize that there aren't nine swords above me. Just a night sky.

No tower chamber. Just hard dirt beneath me.

My Magician? Dylan. Dylan? Dylan!

I sit up with a whoosh—too fast. A bit of the potion comes back up my throat. Metallic chicken blood aftertaste. Fantastic.

"Dylan!" I realize I've been saying his name in my head.

"Stella," he breathes with a sigh of relief. He's holding me. I'm okay with this. But where's . . . what's? I look around. Dawn is about to break over the horizon. The sky covering the cemetery has gone from midnight blue to a more vivid sapphire in color. My head is pounding. My eyes fall on Colette.

"She's cool," he reassures me. "Unconscious, but I could see her breathing."

My gaze slides to Lucille.

"Also unconscious," he says with less enthusiasm. "Hopefully a coma?"

I'm caught in relief over Colette and a swoony feeling

as I lose myself in Dylan's eyes. They're filled with an intensity that's directed at me.

Is it okay to make out with someone if you've got animal blood on your lips? According to box office numbers, teenage girls and soccer moms alike seem to think so.

I piece my brain together. Why am I here?

"The treasure," I groan. "I missed it. I didn't get to it in time."

"You sure about that?" He doesn't take his eyes off me as he tilts his head to the right. I follow his gesture to the sprawling lawn, the overgrown rose bushes, the ancient gnarled oak, the orange fire swirling on the ground beneath it ... fire, what?

"There's a fire!" I shout, completely confused. Am I hallucinating? I pull myself to my feet.

Dylan holds my arm as I try to steady myself. Yelling seriously hurts. Come to think of it, any amount of speaking has been painful. My bones ache as Dylan and I race towards the flame. As we move closer, I see that it's not really a fire, just a bright funneling orange light that glows like an ember. It spews up from the earth like a fountain and then falls into a lava-like puddle, only to rise again.

"It was way bigger when I first got here," Dylan says. "I think it's dying down."

I'm about to throw myself on the heat and tunnel through the dirt with my hands, when I remember that someone else needs to be in on this.

"We gotta get Colette." I'm hypnotized by the tiny glowing tornado. Time to turn around. As I do, she's already stirring.

"Colette!" I shout, even though the effort slices into my vocal chords. "Look at this!"

Colette has turned to her side and is grinning sleepily at me, calm and confident, like we knew this was a guarantee all along. I have a sudden sickening thought.

"What happened to Cora? Where did she go?" I'm sweating, turning in a circle, looking for ghostly signs. I'm in no mood for more possession, murder, strangling, or nasty beverages.

"Here." Dylan has picked up my bag and is thrusting something into my hand. I look down to see a six-inch wooden coffin.

"Mama Pearline said you'd need this, too," he says.

Mama Pearline? But how did he . . . ?

"I'll explain later," he offers, smiling at my confusion. "She said you'd know what to do when you needed to know. Whatever that's worth. I hate that cryptic crap. Just tell me what to do, thanks. Specific directions to follow, like: Open jar. Hold breath to avoid puking from stench. Pry open girlfriend's mouth. Force-feed her nasty drink to get some freaky thing out of her and save her life." He rattles off the last part proudly. My heart does a little cheer at his use of the word girlfriend.

I'm distracted by a dark low-lying mist gliding nearby like a creepy cloud.

"What do you want to bet that's what's left of Cora?"

I turn to see that Colette has made her way beside us. Honestly, for a girl who's just spent her evening dancing at a ball, then getting choked by a ghost until she faints, she's looking pretty put together. Sure, a little dirt on her cheek, but mostly Colette looks like one of those girls in the action movies, the ones whose lip gloss stays in place all through the apocalyptic zombie attack.

"Incredible," I murmur, shaking my head at her. I make a mental note to ask her what brand of mascara she's wearing after we get this all sorted out. Now, where are we? Yes, creepy mist, tiny coffin, cute boy, buried treasure.

The mist begins a winding gesture around the gnarled roots of the oak. I open my miniature casket and softly croon an old funeral dirge I remember. It's as if the tune has been waiting to emerge from my torn throat. Years of the beautiful haunting processions pounding past our café left their melody in me. Now it's time to lead Miss Cora home.

"I am sorry for you, Miss Cora," I murmur between hums. "A tough break. I bet you weren't always the murdering kind."

I know this is true, and feel practically pious about my willingness to reach out and forgive the woman who just took over my insides and came very close to killing me. I have my peace, though, and she's got to have hers.

The mist pokes upward, like a finger pointing at its funeral bed.

"May you find your way in the Summerland." I smile

as the mist pours into the coffin. She's exhausted. "I forgive you, Cora."

"Me, too." Colette turns to toss this remark over her shoulder while she's using . . . a compact . . . to dig beneath the glowing funnel. Yes, she's directing the earth with the heel of one of her ivory pumps and scooping the dirt with the mirror of her pressed powder compact. Resourceful. Cora's spirit nestles into the box like she's tucking herself in for some much-needed rest.

"Blessed be." I whisper. I hold the small coffin reverently in my arms. I wonder where I should put it now?

"What? Oh my god, oh my god—holy mother of . . . "

I look up from my hands to see Colette's own tugging up the steel lid of a box to reveal sunlight. Well, it looks like the sun. The moon is bold and the beams of light shining down catch the glint of these gold and silver bars. All I can think is how we're going to get it out of here. How heavy is it?

"It's real," gasps Colette as tears stream down her face. "We're not insane."

The bars shine in the bright moonlight like some real-life pirate's treasure. I see her face being choppily reflected in them as I lean over to look at the loot. It's like a dream. No wonder she thought it might all be some delusion. Hell, half of this has been in our dreams.

Dylan stands now, staring at the haul, his jaw and eyelids pulled open about as far as they are built to be.

"Well." Colette scrapes the dirt off her heel turned

shovel and repositions it on her foot. Is she human? How in the hell is she still walking in those?

"Guess it's time we wake up Mrs. Courteau. Half of this is her family's, after all," she says.

"Wow." I shake my head. "Col, you are made of better stuff than me. Do we *have* to? She's so much nicer half dead and passed out." I wave my arm toward Lucille's limp body.

Colette smirks. "Yeah, I get that."

I stay in position, nervously holding the doll-sized pine box. I wonder if it would be bad mojo if I got one to store my makeup brushes in. Yes, probably. Disrespectful at least. I notice that the box seems to be getting warmer. Not hot, it's just that the mist was once so frigid it chilled the wood. Now, it's practically room temperature—like a tepid bath. Is this what a soul feels like when the venom's been poured out and all that's left is the pure essence? I feel sheepish about my reverie on the cool look of miniature coffins as I register the fact that I am literally holding a person's spirit—guarding Cora's soul.

A hacking sound jolts me out of this awe. Colette's been slapping Lucille into consciousness. It looks like she's almost enthusiastic about it. If it were me, punching the wench awake would be a viable option.

Dylan stands a few feet behind Col, acting as her bodyguard. Impressive. He doesn't do magic, and he's still brave enough to fight. Lucille seems like she's choking on something. She hacks and hacks. Black foam spills from her lips, like she's heaving Coca-Cola. We all just stare. Her eyes bulge from their sockets, circling around and darting from side to side as though loose in her skull. She leans forward. Colette's been holding her in a sitting position while she revives.

Lucille pushes her arms away weakly, and my friend is happy to oblige, stepping aside as the liquid coal heaves from the woman's mouth. I'm getting anxious. Whatever this lady's done, I don't think she's a murderer. She doesn't deserve to die like this.

Then I notice something. As the black bile empties itself from her throat, her eyes begin to focus. The moonlight shows her face turn from a pale green to her typical creamy complexion. The muddy stuff is thinning and she seems more in control. I remember what my mother said about resentment:

"Stella, it's like drinking poison and waiting for someone else to die."

I know Lucille's finally releasing her own venom, the hate that must have made her body so hospitable to a vengeful being like Cora.

Colette gently rubs her back, like she's comforting a sick friend. I exchange a look with Dylan, one that clearly says, I don't know if we need to go THAT far.

She did try to screw Colette over—majorly—and she did almost get her strangled to death. But Colette's forgiving nature has rubbed off on me. I find myself softly caressing the pine box like it's soothing the content inside.

"So." Colette drops the word out, brows raised as

Lucille's vomiting exorcism subsides. Colette cocks her head toward the upended fortune. "Saved you some."

Lucille turns to look. Her shock is beyond description. Shock at the gleaming gold and silver, perhaps? But I suspect even more shock at the fact that not only have we not killed her, we're actually letting her in on the cut.

"You get half of that. That was the deal struck between Jack's great-great grandfather Courteau- your distant grandfather-IN-LAW-and my distant BLOOD-related aunt."

The word "blood" threatens to recall the sickly liquid bubbling in my tummy. I take a deep breath. It's time to get out of this place.

"Ladies, shall we?" I gesture toward the bars in the lockbox like I'm a game show host showcasing a sports car.

LOST & FOUND

SPREAD

*M*rs. Courteau's eyes bulge almost like they did when she was vomiting up her anger.

"Is—is that it?" she asks.

I'm about to respond with a sarcastic remark when I realize that she's crying. Lucille has human emotions? Wait . . . she's sobbing. "I . . . don't deserve this."

Yup, you got that right. But I can feel myself softening a bit. There's no way I can deny the shift—it's practically created a chasm. This is not the woman who fed the dark underbelly of Voodoo to rob a teenage girl. This is a woman who's been pushed off her throne, terrified of losing the thing that holds her together—her money. And now she sees the hollowness. This is a woman who loves her son . . . and quite possibly her family. She hasn't left her current husband nor robbed him via lawyers and custody battles. She didn't take the last he had and try to marry another rich man. She could have very easily with her looks and manipulation skills.

Lucille follows Colette, rising and walking timidly toward the gold. The light dances so brilliantly off the bars that I'm momentarily blinded. My eyes sting as I glance down. I still hear Lucille, crying more quietly now.

"I don't deserve this," she keeps saying.

"No, you don't," Colette wisely agrees. "It's a good thing I'm so nice."

"And it's a good thing we don't always get what we deserve." My voice is just above a whisper, speaking with GG's same lilt. I can picture her smiling at me in her kimono bathrobe, clutching her crimson mug of crappy instant coffee. She wasn't the mother she wanted to be— maybe she didn't deserve my mom. I've misjudged my mama's spirit, her love, her understanding. Maybe I don't deserve her. Hell, I'm not sure I deserve a friend as true as Colette either. I don't deserve the adoring look that I'm getting from this guy whom I've been virtually lying to. My grandmother was right. It's a good thing we don't get what we deserve.

I find myself smiling at Lucille. She stares back and then nods. She heard me. In this moment we stand together. Crazy, confused, lost, and magical.

"I think I've earned a bit of this," I say.

"Agreed," Col replies.

"Dylan, too."

"Agreed." This time Dylan joins her chorus.

"So . . . " I ponder. "How do we lift these out of here?"

Carry them. Colette stands guard as we take the bars, in a few trips, to the back door of Lucille's house. When we're nearly finished I make a point to talk to Lucille.

"She should be with you," I say, holding out Cora's tiny coffin.

"Is she okay? Her hate, it was . . . consuming. Worse than mine." She stares nervously, her expression a combination of sympathy and fear, like sitting beside a dear friend with a highly contagious disease.

"Yes, I think she's okay. She's found her own peace." I know it's true. There's very soft warmth emanating from the box, something almost like . . . tenderness. I know she wants to be with Mrs. Courteau.

I give Lucille another nod and hold it out for her to take. She gently grasps it like she's holding precious jewels.

"I know where she'd like to be," she coos. The moment is both sweet and creepy. Such is my life these days.

"Jack . . . we should talk."

Poor Jack. Poor Colette. It can't be easy breaking the news to your recently drugged-by-his-own-mother boyfriend that the two of you are, in fact, invited to the same family reunion. He's still in shock from the bizarre explanation that Lucille gave him upon opening up the car door and finding her dazed boy waking up from his little pill nap.

We waited until he got a shower, fresh clothes, and some hot grits in his belly before Colette filled him in on this icky bit of information. The sweet guy tried to kiss her, but she turned to give him her cheek—a good opportunity to explain.

"I told you the Royal Family is distantly related. It's really not that weird. You could be like some aristocratic noble couple. The name Courteau would probably grant y'all some kind of immunity," I had half-teased, half-attempted to salvage Colette and Jack's relationship earlier, as we were carrying gold into the house.

It really is too bad. I don't think it should be an issue, but Colette can't get past it. Ah, well. They were an awfully cute couple.

Dylan can be relied on to whistle the theme from *Deliverance* while we start in on our bowlfuls of grits with butter, filling the awkward silence between Colette's nervous throat clearings.

Jack's face wears a strange forlorn expression as if to say, "Of course. Of course this is happening to me." He does perk up at the sight of his family's share of the fortune. Who wouldn't?

Now we are down to the last spoonfuls, pondering our futures.

"Not too bad, Lucille," I say, surprisingly impressed by her cooking skills.

She gives a quick nod, not at all taken aback by my use of her first name. It just feels natural. I listen to her chatting with her son, patting his back, trying to comfort him with plans.

"I just called your father to tell him that we're keeping the house and everything in it. Time to come home." She turns to the rest of us to explain. "Mr. Courteau left for Virginia to go golfing with a friend who was close to his father. He runs the bank our home was refinanced under." She says "refinanced" with a fair amount of difficulty. This has to be the first time she's been transparent. She's almost likable, the real Lucille.

The words swim around in my mind. The real Lucille. I check back in to hear the rest of her explanation.

"Even the closest of friends get tired of helping you out when it keeps stinging their pocketbook. With our debt, we weren't making any payments. My husband was making an attempt—a pretty futile attempt—to buy us a little more time."

"Buy more time? For what? Do you mean we were really going to lose the house?" asks Jack.

"We would have but not anymore," his mother clarifies. "In fact, I think we may want to acquire another kind of house."

Another house? Whatever rocks her world, I guess.

She must see the puzzled expression on our faces as we sit at the massive marble countertop of her kitchen in the stately mansion.

"The Garden House," she explains. "It's an enormous greenhouse and nursery just outside the city and it's for sale. I enjoyed gardening as a girl. I only began to recently do it here out of necessity—I wouldn't have before because, well, I didn't think it would look good for someone like me to be that involved in dirt. Tending a few flowers is one thing, but . . . When I started cleaning up the rosebushes and my sweet olive after I let the gardener go, that's when I realized how much I enjoyed it."

I feel a bit of pity for her being a member of the Courteau family. What a restricting way to live. Of course, it was her own fault. She could have done as she pleased. Who would have cared if she kept her own garden? She must have been really insecure about her background and upbringing to be so obsessed with playing the part of the wealthy Lady Courteau.

Colette sips her orange juice, nodding a little as if in agreement with what I'm thinking. Are we reading each other's minds now? This could get really weird.

Too late. As if to answer my question, Colette poses one herself.

"Stella, don't you use botanical stuff in some of your lip balms? What about that hibiscus mask you make?"

I haven't had the chance to tell her, but as I've been sipping coffee and clearing the crazy from my own mind, I've been enjoying my own little dream.

"Yes, I do," I reply, raising one eyebrow in suspicion.

We finish up breakfast. Lucille lets us know about a

few contacts that deal in gold, as well as the information of some reputable accountants. Bizarre to think that I may need an accountant. My daddy usually handles the books for our café; maybe he could help with my project.

Colette and Jack exchange a stiff hug goodbye. Perhaps they can be good friends . . . eventually. There wasn't any hostility in their breakup, after all.

We reach for our belongings in the coat closet by the door. I grab Dylan's tuxedo jacket and realize that he hasn't told me anything about what happened to him the night before.

"Okay." I narrow my eyes, holding onto the garment like it's a reward for information. "How did you know . . . everything?"

"Give me SOME credit!" Dylan exclaims. "You think I didn't notice your lame excuses? You think I didn't see you and Colette on different occasions lurking by Mama Pearline's? I deliver right near that shop. I got worried . . . and nosy. That crazy woman wouldn't say much of anything when I asked her, but on her way out of town yesterday, she stopped by the roaster. Handed me that creepy doll coffin with a note taped to it."

He tugs the coat from my grasp and fishes a folded piece of notebook paper from the pocket. With one quick motion he unfurls it and clears his throat.

"*Coffee Boy,*" he begins in a halfway decent impression of an elderly Louisiana woman's slow drawl, "*am leaving town indefinitely. Too much funny business. Don't want no part. That girl you're after—Evie's grandbaby*

—is going to get herself in a heap of trouble. Try looking for her where the Courteaus bury some of their dead. Give this to her if you need to. Make her drink all of it. Bring the coffin. You'll know if she needs it. Good luck, Pearline."

"Wow," I breathe.

He continues speaking as if I've said nothing. "I risked my life roaming through several of New Orleans oldest cemeteries to find where the Courteaus were buried. I found Ash Grove where most of them were and figured I'd follow you there later. So, after I tucked Jack into the backseat of his mom's car, then slashed her tire based on a little gut feeling, I headed there to wait for you. No show. Then I drove around the back gate of the house, spotted a couple of crazy WITCHES." He grins widely at the word, proud of his bust. "You were shaking pretty violently and fell to the ground just as I was running in. Luckily, the gate was open. Those spikes would have hurt to climb." His smile has grown so wide it's practically wrapping to the back of his head.

What else is there to do? I throw my arms around his neck and kiss him the way I've been wanting to. He pulls me in closer, consuming me right back. So much braver than I even knew. So much cooler than I gave him credit for. The secrets have spilled out, leaving room for this warm feeling to grow. There's no other place to be right now. No other place.

"Nice."

The word pierces the moment. My lips still locked on

Dylan's, I glance to the side to see Colette, arms folded, an unabashed audience.

"Nice is right." Dylan doesn't miss a beat, holding me close and showing no sign of embarrassment. Suddenly, I'm the one who feels embarrassed—a little shy. I need some time for the two of us to be together alone.

"I don't even mind the chicken blood." He smacks his lips together. Now I want to trade spots with Beatrice. That coffin seems like a good place to hide.

Dylan laughs and kisses me again, making me forget my setback in oral hygiene.

"Let's get together later. Just us. No work. We can talk and be silly and—"

"Have coffee?" Dylan offers.

"Yes, chicory coffee," I reply, certain that this is the greatest idea anyone has ever had.

Suddenly, the strain from last night catches up to my body. I want to climb into my bed and sleep forever. Colette's gaping yawn supports this.

Dylan helps me put on my cloak and assists Colette with her capelet, then opens the front door for us. I hold my heels in my hand and insist on going barefoot as we head to his truck. He and Jack lift the gold in sections to the passenger seat. Colette and I hop into the pickup bed. We huddle together to keep warm. Dylan gets into the driver's seat and slides open the back window.

"I feel bad. I'm sorry I don't have a blanket for you girls."

"It's cool. Just leave that window open and crank up the radio," Colette replies.

"You got it," he answers, turning the key in the ignition.

We can hear Dylan messing with the dials on his half-busted tuner, stopping on a fuzzy AM station. He revs the engine once and starts down the street. Colette and I lean our heads against each other, broken with fatigue. It's a bright morning. The sunlight and the wind from the open drive sting my eyes.

Through the gusts and the static, a lilting fiddle comes through. A soft voice crooning behind it as we head toward home.

> *"We loved each other then, Lorena,*
> *Far more than we ever dared to tell,*
> *And what we might have been, Lorena,*
> *Had but our loving prospered well."*

EPILOGUE

When Dylan brought us home, he first stopped at my place. It was Sunday morning, so the restaurant should have been packed. Right about this time my mother would have been running around, preparing what she could before she headed to noon mass and Dena took over for her.

My mom. Oh God. I reached into my cloak, feeling for my phone in one of the pockets. I had turned it off when setting out for the night.

Thirty missed calls from guess who.

A closed sign hung over the front door. Colette patted me supportively, and she and Dylan followed close behind as I walked to the front door. It opened before I touched the handle. My mom, Colette's mom, my dad, and Dylan's mom all stood there, crammed at the entrance.

How do you explain? Thankfully, Lucille had phoned

my parents while we were eating. Well, as I later found out, once my dad knew I was safe, he asked my mom to take them off the speakerphone.

He didn't want the details.

As my mom told me later, "Stella, most dads worry about their daughter not being treated right by a boyfriend. They don't have to worry about them not being treated right by a ghost." We laughed for a while over that. My mom was more hurt than angry—well, she was plenty of both.

"Mama, you wouldn't have let me mess with any of this if I had told you how dangerous it was."

"Perhaps. But remember, Stella, just because I don't practice magic doesn't mean I don't know a few things. GG was my MOTHER."

We've kept growing closer, me and my mom.

It's been six months since we cashed in our fortunes. Colette and her mother bought a beautiful row house a few blocks down. Dena went into a partnership with my parents, and is about to open the second Evie's. She is going to train a few new cooks for both cafés. And now Col has some time to get into what she's really in love with—being an extra-credit, extra-curricular maniac.

Colette and Dena and my mom and I are planning a trip to France this fall. Maybe Colette will meet some hot Parisian boy. I'll make her a mojo bag for good measure.

My mom only has to oversee the café now, but she still likes to step in to cook. Sometimes we hit up mass without her having to ask me, but we ride in my car. And in her newfound free time, she's helped me with one of my dreams.

We bought a little shop that had been vacant for some time. Lucille gave me a deal on some of the botanical ingredients I needed (deal being she hooks me up for free—we both agreed that was fair—you know, after her trying to kill me). Now I sell my cinnamon and beet root lip balms and crushed mineral eye shadows. I get paid to play with pigments. I get paid to be the Magician card. I've hired on a couple girls from school to help—handcrafting face masks and makeup is time consuming when you work them with phases of the moon. I imbue them all with positive energy, and every shade has its own special magic. It's why we named my company Hex. Okay, none of my cosmetics hold curses, but I just thought the name sounded cool. My makeup is full of mojo. I add mint to this for quick cash, a dash of cayenne to that for fast-working spells, ginger for clarity, sage for protection, rose petals for love. The shop is conveniently located next to my favorite roaster. We share a cup of chicory most mornings, and I park my car and let him drive me home from school most afternoons. The brick-and-mortar shop is only open on weekends, acting as a lab when I want it during the week. I do most of my business through my website, which ships everywhere. My shop lab is a tiny kitchen with a desk in the corner. It's graced with one photo: GG holding my mother in her lap.

Jack hangs out with us sometimes. He's going out

with a new girl. She's nice, almost obnoxiously so, like he is, so that's . . . nice. He helps his family with the nursery. I visit Lucille—sometimes to pick up an order, sometimes to deliver body lotion (she buys cases of Calm, my lavender "mellowing" cream), and sometimes I just pop in to make sure that she hasn't gone completely nuts again. She'll fix tea and we'll talk a bit. When I feel uneasy, I gently rub the clear charm dangling at my throat. It was GG's. She used to keep some of her heavy perfume in it.

My mom cleaned it out and filled it with holy water.

"To keep you safe," she explained, as she fastened it around my neck.

"Holy water for protection? Sounds pretty witchy."

"I'm Catholic, Stella. WE started that."

I pretended as if I hadn't heard her. "Mrs. Fortunat, the Voodoo Queen of New Orleans." I laughed, and she rolled her eyes.

But every time she sees me leave, I watch her eyes flit to my necklace, making sure it's still there.

Because whatever you believe, a little protection is never a bad idea in this town.

That's how things are in the Crescent City. Magic takes you places—doesn't matter if you wanted to go or not. The city transforms you. Coffee roaster, trophy wife, mother, daughter—everyone's a card in her deck.

And this is how we like it.

ABOUT THE AUTHOR

Mary Jane Capps spent a good portion of her childhood chatting with the moon, pen-in-hand. After spending her adolescent years in a dark place writing the kind of bad, depressing poetry she wasn't cut out for, she spent her early adulthood as a busy counselor writing whenever inspiration struck. She has since published a variety of poems and essays. Mary Jane has planted herself in the peninsula of Tega Cay, South Carolina, where she lives in a grown-up tree house with her magical daughter and freakishly understanding husband. It's just the right place for conversations with the moon.

Find out more about Mary Jane on her website at
MaryJaneCapps.com

www.facebook.com/storytellingspark

www.instagram.com/maryjanecapps

ACKNOWLEDGMENTS

I've been blessed with a crowd of loving, generous people, but I'm going to keep to those most involved in the creation of CRESCENT.

I am so grateful to my husband, Jake, for being my biggest fan and refusing to take my fears at face value. To my daughter Bronwyn, for being a constant reminder that it's supposed to be fun.

To Melissa Kline and Mishelle Crutchfield for their hard work. To Kimberley Marsot for her stunning cover design, and to Katherine Trail for the formatting. To Nicole Ayers, my extraordinary editor. To my dad, for being convinced I can do anything, and to my mom, for being the kind of woman every woman might want to be.

Thanks due to Ashley Sanchez for being the first person who didn't marry me and didn't give birth to me to read the manuscript, and for the nice things she had to say. Big thanks to Wendy Stonebraker, for being a huge boost of support and encouraging me to cool on the f-bomb. To Valerie Azevedo, for being there. Thanks to Deborah McCullough for blueberry pancakes and reliable cheerleading.

Finally, thanks to Cafe Du Monde and Morning Call, for beignets, cafe au lait, and dreams being realized.

PLAYLIST

My Heart by The Ettes
Since You're Gone by The Pretty Reckless
Bloodletting by Concrete Blonde
Everybody Knows by Concrete Blonde
Pictures Of You by The Cure
Tomorrow, Wendy by Concrete Blonde
Upstroke by Bojibian
The Truth Is In The Dirt by Karen Elson
Dreams by The Cranberries
...I listened to an obscene amount of Concrete Blonde
writing this one.